Iris & Lily
Book Two

Angela & Julie Scipioni

ACKNOWLEDGMENTS

Cover art by Pietro Spica
Used with permission
www.pietrospica.it

Lyrics from
"Lift Me Up," "The Path," and "Halfway Round the Moon"
© Rick McKown
Used with permission
www.RickMcKown.com

Iris & Lily: Book Two is the second in a three-volume series.

To women everywhere.
May you find strength for the journey.

Book Two

From: Iris Capotosti <iris.capotosti@gmail.com>
To: Lily Capotosti <lilycapotosti@gmail.com>
Sent: Fri, September 10, 2010 at 10:10 AM
Subject: Moving on with our girls

Dear Lily,

It's been barely a week since we left Iris and Lily at the altar. During that time, I've been thinking. You know, no one actually forced our girls to get married back then, just like no one forced us to start writing about them now. But in both cases, once the idea was hatched, it was as if we had no choice but to run with it, even though we didn't know – couldn't possibly have known – what we were getting into.

There was no way the Iris we grew up with could have resisted the opportunity to act out the fairytale romance she had been dreaming of. Even now, I still feel that overwhelming urge to escape to another dimension. But ever since we started writing, instead of fantasizing about the future, I've become addicted to reminiscing about the past. There Is something magical about the way one thought trickles into another, then the thoughts flow into a stream of words that come gushing out in this river of pages. They have nowhere else to go, I guess, and I have no choice but to follow them.

I'm anxious to move on now, curious to see where they'll take me, where they'll take us.

Love,
Iris

Dear Iris:

Maybe it was a week since those young women stood at the altar. But maybe it was a lifetime – or just as likely, an instant. It makes me think about this matter of choices. We all walk around as though we have free will, but I find myself asking, "Free will to do what?" I mean, we can't possibly know the ramifications of any of our "choices." Yet we are held accountable for them, and are forced to make them. Like blindfolded children trying to cross the highway.

Makes me want to just close my eyes and run.

Love,
Lily

1. IRIS

Iris was thankful that the apartment in Santa Ida wasn't too big; in fact it was just the right size for a recently wed couple, with a tad of space to spare for a little one, whose arrival both Iris and Gregorio were impatiently awaiting, now that they had already been married for several months. It was the equivalent of what a real estate agent back in Rochester would call a "starter home," only this was an apartment, and a rented one at that. Iris didn't need much room, anyway, as she had brought very few belongings from America, mostly because she didn't own anything worth shipping, except for some clothes and books, and a few cooking utensils she feared she might not find in Italy, such as the measuring cups she used when whipping up her favorite Betty Crocker recipes, and a baster for roasting her Thanksgiving turkey, without knowing whether she would even be able to find one in a country where the holiday was not celebrated, or who would be around to help eat it. As for Gregorio, he had only brought what he needed from his mother's place, and left the rest behind. Isabella did not seem to be in any hurry to empty out his old bedroom, nor to have any pressing desire to find another use for the space in which her son had grown from boy, to adolescent, to man.

After her stint managing the household at Chestnut Crest, Iris felt a bit like a little girl playing house when she cleaned the compact apartment. During their honeymoon, she had discovered that Gregorio was remarkably neat and, like Iris, who had very little experience sleeping in hotels, always pulled up the bedclothes and hung his used towels neatly on the racks before they left their suite, and this behavior was replicated at home. With no one making a mess, her job was shamefully easy, and the dust rag encountered very little resistance as she passed it over the few items Gregorio had bought to furnish the place. Iris wasn't quite sure whether the furniture suited her taste or needs, not really knowing what alternatives were available, or ever having set up a place of her own. She thought it very sweet of Gregorio to have gone out with his mother and purchased everything before the wedding so the house wouldn't be empty when they returned from their honeymoon, though she secretly wished he would have waited for her so they could have shopped for their very first pieces of furniture for their very first home together, even if it meant sitting on folding chairs for a while. No sense fretting about it now; she was sure there would be another opportunity in the not too distant future, when their growing family would justify the move to a larger home.

Apart from dusting and sweeping the floors, her other daily chores included cleaning the bathroom, mopping, and occasionally waxing the old floor tiles (this was the most strenuous job, requiring her to get down on her hands and knees, though the fact that Gregorio always noticed and complimented her on the shine made it worthwhile), and doing the laundry, which took more time than she would have imagined. Gregorio used a new towel for every shower, and insisted the sheets be changed twice a week, on Mondays and Fridays, so both the week and the weekend would start out with fresh linens. Iris was happy to comply, as she herself enjoyed climbing into bed between crisp, fragrant sheets, something she hadn't known enough to miss as a child until her first overnight at Auntie Rosa's.

In addition to the linens, there was, of course, the matter of

Gregorio's clothes. Being a doctor, he certainly had to be provided with a clean white shirt to wear to the hospital every morning, even though he changed into operating room garb when he got there. In order to run the washing machine, which took two full hours to complete its cycle, Iris had to hook up one hose to the faucet in the bathtub, and place another hose in the tub for drainage. She had been surprised to find that dryers were not common in Italy, not that she minded; she adapted quite happily to hanging the clothes on the line. She found that the chore relaxed her, and she loved resting her cheek against a pillowcase that smelled of sunshine and sea breeze. Of course, line drying took much longer, sometimes an entire day, depending on the weather. It also meant that everything had to be ironed, including Gregorio's underwear. She had tried hand-pressing those at least, but Gregorio had mentioned, in a tactful way of course, that he was used to a neat crease in his boxer shorts. It was no bother, really, when there was already a pile of ironing; besides, putting her talents and experience to use looking after her husband and their home was her job now.

Iris had already flitted through the bedroom and living room, and was humming contentedly when she reached the dining alcove, where dusting always provided her with a welcome excuse to indulge in reminiscing as she ran her cloth over a small collection of photographs she had framed and hung on the wall. There was one of her and Lily on the farm, two scrawny girls being glared at by a hulk of a cow; another one of the two of them, now shapely teenagers in grass skirts and leis performing at a luau with Uncle Alfred; one of her mother taken in front of a Christmas tree, laughing and surrounded by a dozen Capotostis of various ages and stages of awkwardness; one of Iris in her wedding gown standing between her somber-looking father and a beaming Auntie Rosa; and the most recent, one of Iris and Gregorio standing on a sandy beach in Sardinia's Costa Smeralda, where they had spent their honeymoon.

Almost anyone hearing the sigh which escaped Iris as she gazed at the newlyweds would have likely classified it as a sigh of contentment. What memories she must have from her honeymoon on a Mediterranean island! An island where she had finally lived out her lifelong dream of swimming in water so clear it was like floating in a precious sea of liquid emerald, sapphire, and turquoise. She could thank her lucky stars, as Auntie Rosa would say, and of course Gregorio himself, who had chosen such a lovely resort, which she soon learned was a favorite among scuba divers precisely because of those limpid waters. It was then that she also discovered her new husband's passion for diving; how surprised she had been! How much fun they would have now that they would be spending all of their time together, learning all the other details about one another which couldn't fit into an airmail envelope! It became obvious, for example, that she had married a man who possessed an admirable dose of courage, a man who would dive to a depth of twenty meters (sixty-five feet!) or more. The mere thought terrified Iris, but when Gregorio said he had signed her up for a beginner's course so that one day they might dive together, she forced a nervous smile and said it was a fantastic idea. She didn't want to give him the impression that he had married a scared little girl terrified of broadening her horizons; besides, everyone knew the happiest married couples were those who shared the same interests. But the idea of strapping on all those weights, then sinking herself to the bottom of the sea, where she would depend on a tank for each breath, seemed like flirting with death. She did take the trial lesson, though, but rather than dispelling her fears, it had only served to reinforce her instinctive aversion to the activity.

She had been sorry for disappointing Gregorio, and told him she saw no reason why he should not take advantage of the diving anyway. It was only when Iris had insisted, saying that since he was already an expert, he should go ahead and join the other divers, that he agreed. He was kind enough to want to include Iris anyway, and suggested that she accompany the group on the excursions, even if she didn't dive. The first morning they set out on the rubber dinghy, she had enjoyed bouncing over the waves with the group of divers, the wind in her hair, the sea spraying her face and arms and legs, as she admired the spectacular views, giddy with the sense of adventure. But once the anchor had been dropped, and Gregorio and the other divers had disappeared under water, her giddiness turned to nausea, and her exhilaration to anxiety, as she bobbed about in the boat, her eyes trained on the little streams of bubbles floating from her husband's mouthpiece to the surface, until they disappeared from view.

After the humiliation of puking all over the instructor's gear bag, Iris had begged to be excused from further excursions. She explained to Gregorio that perhaps she just needed more time to adapt to the sea, and would prefer to do so from the beach, if it was all right with him, of course, and by no means did she expect him to give up diving on her account. He had said that was very considerate of her, and understood her preferring to remain closer to shore for the time being, and even bought her a mask and snorkel to help her get used to swimming in the sea.

As the dust cloth glided over the picture frame, she felt lucky to have all those heavenly swims to think back upon. With no one telling her what to do, she had found herself strangely at ease in the clear, shallow water, and her self-confidence had grown steadily, until she was spending hours each day kicking the restlessness out of muscles unaccustomed to a life of leisure. She thought of the secluded little beach she had come upon, where she had even dared to sunbathe topless for the first time. She hadn't felt comfortable baring her breasts, however unremarkable they might be, at the hotel beach, in front of people she saw at dinner every evening, and had remained one of the few women who got her money's worth out of both pieces of her bikini. She had such vivid memories of lying in the warm white sand of her secret beach; she could still feel how each fine hair on her skin tingled as the salt water was dried by the sun and wind; how all those delicious sensations caressing her body had made her yearn to be touched.

She recalled the hottest hours of those lazy afternoons, when the Sardinian sun would have scorched her skin, had she not

7

repaired to the shade of the beach umbrella as she waited for Gregorio to return, while devouring one novel after another. She had never envisioned her honeymoon as a time to catch up on her reading, so had come unprepared, with only two paperbacks in her suitcase, but had discovered a bookstore in town which catered to tourists, and carried an assortment of foreign editions. She had been lucky enough to find a copy of *The Thorn Birds*, and immediately became engrossed in the plight of the lovely Meggie growing up with all those brothers, and found herself hoping that the handsome Father Ralph would leave the priesthood (even though she knew it was not right) and they would at last be reunited, never again to part.

One of her favorite times of day had been when the sun released its hold, and she showered away the sand and salt from her tanned body, and dressed for dinner. She had always adored eating at restaurants, though most of her experiences had been at diners, or at places not much fancier than the Sizzling Skillet or the Luau. The waiters at the hotel restaurant wore black jackets and bow ties and spoke several languages, though often no words were needed. After the first evening, for example, all Gregorio had to do was raise an index finger, and one would come right over with another of the many bottles of mineral water they would share during their stay. And when Gregorio waved a dismissive hand at the candle, it was promptly removed, never to reappear. When Iris questioned him about the candle, he explained that in addition to distorting his view of her lovely face, the flame would burn up what little oxygen there was in the crowded dining room. Iris, who had never thought of candles in such threatening terms, and in fact found them rather romantic, smiled and said she didn't mind. She had no doubt he would feel differently about the candlelight dinners she would prepare for them in the comfort of their own home, where they would have access to all the oxygen they could possibly desire.

Candles or no candles, what counted most in any restaurant was the food. Iris would have been hard-pressed to choose her three courses each evening from among all the tantalizing dishes described by the waiter, had Gregorio not been such a connoisseur when it came to picking out the freshest fish, crustaceans and mollusks, and ordering for them both, while waving away the wine list. Iris had thought it so thoughtful of him to want the very best for her, that she had been too embarrassed to admit she hadn't yet developed a taste for the seafood he ordered. It wasn't until the fourth evening, when the waiter had placed in front of them yet another immense platter of tentacled creatures, and caught her staring longingly at a passing dish of pasta, which he identified for her as gnocchetti, a Sardinian specialty, and which he proceeded to describe in such irresistibly appealing terms, that she had felt bold enough to request a dish for herself, nodding enthusiastically at his winked recommendation to accompany it with a glass of local Vermentino.

Iris had begun enjoying her dinners more once the kind waiter had started slipping her suggestions; not that she had come on her honeymoon to eat, of course. She may not have had much experience, but she did know that the greatest pleasures of the perfect honeymoon were to be enjoyed in the bedroom, not at the table. Iris recalled how she had gasped in delight when Gregorio had led her through the luxurious sea view suite and out onto the balcony, where she had immediately pictured herself each morning, wrapped in her new silk robe, glowing and ravenous from a night of lovemaking, sipping cappuccinos and munching on flaky croissants while admiring the colorful rock formations of the windswept coast, the flowering oleanders of the lush gardens, the sparkling spectrum of blues and greens of the cove below. The fantasy had lasted a few hours shy of a day, when she had discovered while stretching out in the king size bed after their first real night together, that Gregorio's habit of showering, shaving and dressing before breakfast was as immovable as his disdain of room service.

Walking out onto the balcony of her apartment to shake out her dust cloth, Iris replayed in her mind images of the splendid view from that suite, breathtakingly beautiful by day, heartbreakingly romantic by night. She recalled lying in bed in the moonlight, watching the silver beams dance upon the gently rippling water, listening to the waves softly lap the beach, feeling the sweet breeze caress her skin, while she waited for her husband to emerge from the bathroom. On their third night together (the second having been spent flying across the ocean), he had confessed that he simply couldn't relax until his teeth were properly brushed and flossed. Iris could relate to that, being a faithful flosser herself, but she thought that perhaps he could have switched his main flossing session (which for some undisclosed reason took close to a quarter of an hour) to the morning, at least for the duration of their honeymoon, though she hadn't said so to his face. She also hadn't said anything about his insistence on closing the shutters and windows before joining her in bed, thus locking out the sound of the waves, the glow of the moonlight, and the perfume of the myrtle scented air, together with the mosquitoes he claimed to have heard, which would undoubtedly put their repose at risk.

If on their wedding night Iris had been impressed by Gregorio's knowledge of female anatomy, during their honeymoon she had come to realize that it was far superior to her own. Even in the dark, he knew exactly where and how to touch her to achieve arousal. Despite the lack of such silly frills as candlelight and champagne, which some people probably needed to set the mood, each time they had relations, Gregorio's pinging and probing brought Iris to a state of sexual fulfillment in a matter of minutes. Though she had never made inquiries into her husband's sentimental history, she was inclined to believe his expertise had been acquired through his medical schooling, rather than through previous girlfriends. And as Gregorio taught Iris what to do to return the favor, she had been thankful to have such a knowledgeable and patient partner.

When there was not another particle of dust to be found in the apartment, Iris decided to spend some time out on her own small balcony tending to her plants and admiring the view which would never be a feature of any starter home in Rochester. It took only a fleeting thought of Rochester to lead her to thoughts of Lily who, in a matter of hours, would be married and off to enjoy a honeymoon of her own. Iris wondered whether she and Joe had already had sex, whether he would be as gentle and considerate a partner as Gregorio. Wrapping her arms around herself, she stood there looking off into the distance, thinking, waiting for the late spring sun to chase away a sudden shiver, but its rays reflecting off the surface of the sea were far too bright, far too invasive, far too optimistic for her mood. Forced to look away, she blamed the intensity of the Italian sun for the drops dampening her lashes, trickling down her cheeks.

After trading in her dust cloth for a pair of pruning scissors, she knelt on the worn terrazzo tiles, tucked the hem of her sundress under her knees for padding, and turned her attention to the lineup of geraniums in terracotta pots along the perimeter of the balcony. Pausing to sniff the earthy scent of the wilted flowers she clipped from their stems to make way for the buds ready to bloom into plump clumps of coral, images of Auntie Rosa meticulously dusting the dozens of artificial geraniums bought on sale at SaveMart to beautify the basement guitar studio flashed through her mind. She was struck by the thought that those lifeless, scentless flowers were the last Dolores had seen before falling asleep in that basement forever, then blamed that thought for the fresh tears springing to her eyes.

Iris was feeling dizzy; it must be the sun. Shifting her weight from the balls of her feet to her heels, she placed her hands on the balustrade and pulled herself to a standing position. She dragged a hand over her damp brow and moist eyes, commingling perspiration with tears. She was home alone, as she often was, and there was no reason why she couldn't admit to feeling sad, no reason why she couldn't indulge in a little private cry. No reason whatsoever, except that she was afraid it wouldn't be so easy to stop once she got started. With one hand on the small of her back, the other on the balustrade, she stood still until she regained her balance, and the black veil clouding her vision lifted. Blocking the sun with a hand, she took her eyes for a tour of the craggy Ligurian coastline, allowed them to explore the indigo sea of the

Golfo Paradiso, coaxed them into patiently following the course of a dinghy as it tacked east toward the promontory of Portofino. Iris exhaled with a puff reminiscent of her mother's sighs, then breathed in deep, through her nostrils. The air coaxed up the hillside by the gentle breeze was sweet, laden with iodine and the aromas of sage and rosemary and jasmine it picked up along the way.

Squinting her eyes against the combined brilliance of sun and sea to the west, she could make out the shape of the *lanterna*, the lighthouse that marked the entrance to the port of Genoa. It made her think of the bent little fellow with the ruddy cheeks and blunt nose crisscrossed by a network of spidery purple capillaries, whom she had met in the old town center of Santa Ida the first morning she had walked down on her own to shop for groceries. She had set off full of enthusiasm, appreciating the privilege of actually being able to go somewhere without a car, not that she had any choice in the matter for the time being. Gregorio needed his car to go to work, and was reluctant to buy one for Iris, until he was confident she had mastered driving a vehicle with manual transmission on the hilly coastal roads. Once inside the shop recommended by Isabella, Iris had found herself the object of scrutiny of the local housewives and old ladies who spoke a language of suspicious glances and incomprehensible dialect as they systematically cut in front of her. Resigned to the fact that she would get bumped to the end of the line until they all finished, Iris stood timidly to the side, listening to the questions and answers being exchanged, going over her notes as if she were cramming for a quiz. The little man was the only person remaining by the time she could utter *"Buongiorno"* to the shopkeeper, limbering up her tongue to pronounce the items on the list she had compiled with the help of an English-Italian dictionary and a calculator to figure out how many grams were in a quarter of a pound.

"Good morning, miss!" the grinning man blurted out when he heard her voice, casting his words into the silence left by the shopkeeper, a tight-faced woman who ignored Iris, apparently deeming the task of wiping the blade of a long and undoubtedly very sharp knife on her spotted white apron more worthy of her attention. The smile was a welcome sight to Iris, who was having difficulty adjusting to the Ligurians' aversion to parting their lips for any reason that was not strictly necessary.

"You American, miss? I live in Brooklyn for fourteen years!" he said. "But now I come back. This brings me back," he continued, pointing out the door to the sea. Iris returned the smile, which was instantly snatched from her lips by the shopkeeper, who suddenly wanted to get down to business. Iris stammered through their negotiations, caught unprepared for the barrage of questions shot back at her in response to her request for one hectogram of prosciutto. *"Cotto o crudo? San Daniele o Parma?"*

A stream of perspiration was trickling down her back and making her armpits sticky by the time Iris had managed to secure a packet of *crudo* (she had to say *"basta!"* to the lady three times before she would stop slicing); a sliver of Asiago cheese (she had to keep saying *"più"* or *"meno,"* whose meanings she kept mixing up, and gesture with her hands, to direct the angle of the woman's knife on the cheese wheel in hopes of obtaining a wedge of the desired size); a tub of goat milk ricotta (at least she thought she guessed the right animal when the lady asked, *"Vacca, pecora o capra?"*); a chunk of Parmigiano (Reggiano, that was easy); some canned tomatoes (*pelati, polpa o passato?*); a half-kilo packet of penne, one of spaghettini, and two liters of milk *(intero o scremato? fresco o a lunga conservazione?)*; and, at last, counted out the right number of thousands of lira in multicolored banknotes of various dimensions.

The little man, who had witnessed the transaction in silence, amusement upturning the corners of his white moustache, stooped to pick up one of her bags and accompanied Iris out the door, without purchasing anything himself. *"E dove vai, Americano?"* the shopkeeper called after him.

Instead of replying, the little man said to Iris, in a secretive tone, "That's what they call me here, *l'Americano*. Now you here, so there's an *Americana*, too!"

"I'm Iris. *Piacere*," she said, tilting her head in lieu of extending her hand, which was occupied by a shopping bag.

"*Piacere,* Miss Iris," he replied, touching the brim of his cap. "In New York, we have the Statue of Liberty. Here, we have the *lanterna*. You see?" he said. Her eyes followed the crooked index finger pointing toward Genoa, then returned to his face when he spoke. "Is different. But beautiful. Both, they tell you to come home. When you have two homes, you have none. You feel nostalgia always." The flicker of faraway memories swam through the man's eyes, now two rheumy pools of sentiment. He handed her the grocery bag.

Iris tried to imagine herself here, in this little seaside town, a wobbly old lady tossing leftover scraps of pasta to the stray cats, the townsfolk still calling her "*l'Americana,*" entire decades later. Her throat tightened uncomfortably. "*Grazie,*" she said to *l'Americano,* who reminded her a bit of her Grandpa Capotosti. Impulsively, she planted a kiss on each of his scratchy cheeks; he blushed, and tipped his cap to her again as she turned to start her walk back up the hill, the handles of the plastic bags cutting off the circulation in her fingers.

Whenever she walked down the hill to town, she found *l'Americano* strolling along the banks of the dry riverbed that in the rainy season delivered runoff from the mountains behind the town to the sea. He walked leisurely, but not aimlessly, his hands clasped behind his bent back, his round little paunch leading the way. She never spotted him lounging on benches, or playing cards at the café with the other men. Each time he saw her, he stopped and tipped his hat.

"Good morning, Miss!" he would greet her in English.

"*Buongiorno, Signor Americano!*" Iris would reply in Italian, and they would smile at each other and walk on.

Each time she gazed at the *lanterna* from her balcony, she recalled the words of *l'Americano*. Months later, she had come to understand what he meant about two homes being like no home. She thought of the folk song she used to strum on the guitar, back when she had one, about being five hundred miles away from home. It had seemed like a staggering distance for anyone to wander. Now she found herself ten times that distance from her birthplace; from her parents, or rather from her mother and father (referring to them as a single entity united by anything but endless litigation no longer sounded right); from Auntie Rosa and Uncle Alfred; from friends like Rita Esposito and Frances Jejune who could tease her about her past, and recite the names of everyone in her family in their proper order. And then there was Lily. How did she end up so far away from her Lily of the Valley? She should be with her today; she would go right now, if she could. But even if she had money of her own to buy a ticket, even if Gregorio had noticed how much it meant for her to be with Lily on her wedding day and insisted she go, even if she dropped what she was doing, grabbed her passport, and went straight to the airport just as she was, in her sweaty sundress, she would get there too late to tell Lily that there really was such a thing as fairytales. All you had to do was believe in them.

Iris gazed beyond the *lanterna*, to the west, covered her face to shut out the sun, the sea, the beauty, and sobbed into the scent of dead flowers clinging to her sticky fingers.

2. LILY

"I thought we'd get more money," said Lily. She tore open an envelope, pulled out a fifty dollar bill and placed it with the pile of cash on the back seat of Joe's car. "I didn't realize that the food bill was going to be so much. I was hoping our credit card would come this week."

"At least we'll have enough for a nice long weekend in Toronto," said Joe. "I've heard it's the cleanest city in the world. And our hotel is only thirty miles from Woodbine Racetrack - it's supposed to be one of the nicest tracks in the country."

Lily liked the idea of having her honeymoon across the border. Canada wasn't as far Italy but at least it was a foreign country. At least it felt sort of exotic.

"We have tickets to see *Camelot* tomorrow night, don't forget."

"I didn't forget." Joe kissed Lily and without making note of the signature on the card in his hand, he pulled a check for one hundred dollars out of an envelope and placed into the check pile.

"And I've heard there's really good shopping on Yonge Street. I'd like to walk around there, too."

"We'll do all of that," said Joe. "We're gonna have a fantastic time. I say we hit that track, make a killing, and come home with a bundle of money. Then we'll take a trip to the mall and spend the day buying whatever you need for the house."

"Sounds like a great plan!" She handed Joe a stack of cash.

"Here you go - the band is inside waiting for this. And when you get back," said Lily. "I will be in the front seat waiting for you, ready to start our new life together."

"Absolutely," said Joe. "Fasten your seat belt!"

They'd made plans to stay in town for their wedding night and then leave for Toronto the next morning. By the time they pulled into the *porte cochère* of their hotel half an hour later, Lily's feet were throbbing, and she was exhausted. Joe placed their bags onto a luggage cart, removed his tuxedo jacket, and laid it on top. The bellman whisked the cart away, tucking his two-dollar tip into his vest pocket. As they approached the front entrance, Joe swept Lily up into his arms. She let out a yelp as he carried her in through the set of brass revolving doors.

Lily squealed and Joe laughed as he positioned them into one of the compartments and spun them round and round. After several revolutions, the door came to a sudden halt, as the train of Lily's dress became lodged in the floor bearing. The door jammed, trapping them inside.

"Oh, my God!" cried Lily. "My dress is stuck - we're trapped!"

Joe laughed. "I have to put you down for a second so I can untangle you."

"Ow!" Lily cried, as Joe attempted to set her feet on the floor.

"What's the matter?"

"The dress is choking me - it's pulled too tight - I need a little slack."

Joe tugged at the train of the dress. "Boy, it's really jammed in there. There isn't enough give to set you down!"

"You have GOT to be kidding me!"

They stared at each other momentarily and then burst out laughing.

"Now you're stuck with me," said Joe, laughing at his joke.

"Hey," said Lily. "I'm just glad you stopped giving me the run-around."

"Good one!" Joe laughed.

"This could be a really bad sign," said Lily.

"It's a great sign!" said Joe. "If we can find our way out of this, we can do anything."

The concierge walked toward them. "May I offer assistance?"

"We're trapped!" said Lily, laughing so hard that she could barely get the words out. "My dress is stuck in the door."

"You're getting really heavy," said Joe.

"Sir," said the concierge, "I suggest you set your wife down and then attempt to loosen the dress from the mechanism."

"He can't," said Lily, wiping the tears from her face. "There's not enough give in the dress and when he sets me down it chokes me and the dress is going to tear. It's borrowed - I can't give it back all ripped."

"Can you remove it?" said the concierge.

"Remove what?" asked Lily. "The dress? I'm not going to take my wedding dress off in this revolving door!"

"Uh... Lil," said Joe. "Seriously, you're getting really heavy. I can't hold you up much longer. I can reach your buttons in the back. Maybe if I just undid a few of them, the dress would loosen up a little and I could set you down."

"OK," said Lily. "If you can get to them, just unbutton a few."

Joe contorted his body to bring his left hand behind Lily's head while holding her body up with his right, bolstered by his left knee. With a grimace, he unfastened the first ten buttons.

"It's not really helping," he said.

"Maybe if you loosen a few more," said the concierge. "Then your wife could pull her arms out of the dress and slide it down a bit."

A man and a woman passed through the set of doors directly next to Lily and Joe. "Congratulations!" they called, waving.

"Thank you!" said Lily, waving back.

"How's married life so far?" said the man. The couple laughed and passed into the lobby.

Lily looked at the concierge. "I am not going to take my arms out of this dress with people walking in and out of here."

Joe grunted. A stream of sweat ran down the side of his face and he hoisted Lily back up in his arms.

"I have an idea," said the concierge. He disappeared and

returned a few minutes later with a bellman and a tablecloth. "We'll hold this up in front of you so no one can see, and then once you get the dress off, your husband can work it free from the door." The concierge and the bellman opened the tablecloth and held it up over the door.

"No peeking," said Joe. Pointing his finger at the concierge and the bellman he added, "And I mean it."

"Of course not, sir," said the concierge.

A few minutes later, Lily cheered, and as the door moved, she left her dress in Joe's hands and deposited herself into the folds of the tablecloth, pulling it around her like a robe.

As Joe and Lily emerged from the door, the reservations clerks clapped and cheered. Joe and Lily looked at each other, then faced the front desk and took a bow.

"Well, that's one way to get a free night in fancy hotel," said Joe, shutting the door of their room and locking it.

"I hope the cleaners can get the grease out of Nancy's dress; she's going to have a fit!" Lily sat on the bed, still wrapped up in the tablecloth. She let out a deep sigh. "I can't believe it's only been one day since I got up this morning. Feels like a hundred years."

"I hope you're not too tired," said Joe, unclipping his bow tie and tossing it on the dresser. "Because the best is yet to come."

"Well," said Lily, "I certainly hope it won't get any worse!"

Joe laughed. He clasped one hand on each of Lily's shoulders and brought her to a standing position, facing him. "I know I can't promise you much," he said. "But I can promise you that life with me will never be boring. Now," he said, unwrapping the tablecloth from around Lily's shoulders, "Let's see what's for dinner."

Lily stood, clad in her slip and bra as Joe surveyed her.

"You're trembling," he said, taking her into his arms. "Are you cold?"

"A little," said Lily. It wasn't exactly a lie. She didn't want to tell him how nervous she was. As far as Lily was concerned, the one time they'd had sex, it didn't count because she wasn't prepared. It had often occurred to Lily that if Joe had just believed her when she said she was a virgin, then at least she would still be one tonight. But none of that mattered now. This was her wedding night, Joe would still be her first, her one and only, and there would never be another night like tonight. Now both the time and the place were right.

"I love you," he said.

"I love you too."

Joe removed his cummerbund and tossed it on the bed.

"Take a look at this," he said. He reached his hand into his pants pocket and pulled out a wad of cash. "Don't you just love the way that looks?" Joe placed the money on the night stand, and then took off his shirt and pants, then his socks and shoes, leaving them in a heap on the floor. Naked, he climbed into the bed.

"C'mere," he said, pulling Lily down into the bed and sidling up alongside her. He hiked her slip up around her waist and removed her underwear.

It was all suddenly going too quickly and Lily didn't feel ready, was still reeling from the stress and activity of the day, still worried about what she was supposed to do, and suddenly perplexed about why her mother had never told her what to expect tonight. Or Violet. Or even Lucy or Nancy. Of course she couldn't have heard about it from Iris. She hardly heard anything from Iris anymore.

"Can we get under the covers?" said Lily. "And maybe turn off the lights?"

Joe obliged and then returned to bed. He kissed her, and fondled her breast without removing her bra.

A sense of unease came over Lily, snaking itself around her budding desire. Her instinct was to recoil, to push Joe away. But this wasn't some uninvited lecher, preying on her innocence. This was Joe, her companion, her protector. Joe, with whom she'd exchanged vows this morning, danced and dined this afternoon, laughed just minutes ago. This was her husband. *Relax, Lily*, she told herself. *It's Joe.*

He climbed on top of her, and used his foot to spread her legs apart, before lowering himself against her. Lily trained all of her self-control to keep from reacting by pushing him away.

She closed her eyes, and took a deep breath, but was unable to extricate her desire from her belligerent mind. Arousal appeared and then disappeared again, like a mischievous child playing hide-and-go-seek. Once inside her, Joe moved his body to a quick rhythm. Lily opened her eyes just enough to take a peek at him. He had his own eyes closed and his face turned upward. The headboard rapped against the wall for about a minute, and then Joe collapsed with a groan.

Is that it? Lily thought. *It's over?* What happened to the ecstasy, the revelations of womanhood that she had expected as a sweet reward for her best attempts at purity and virtue? Even if she couldn't have fireworks, she'd hoped for more. What would she say to Joe when he expressed his disappointment?

"That was amazing," Joe said. "Did you have fun?"

It wasn't a question Lily expected him to ask at that moment, nor had she ever thought of "fun" as a word one would use to describe sex.

"Uh - yeah, sure," said Lily. "It was great." Maybe that's all there was to it, after all.

Joe got up from the bed, took a shower, brushed his teeth and pulled on his boxer shorts.

"Guess we better get some sleep," he said climbing back under the covers. "We have to return my tux before breakfast at my mother's. Then, we're off for Toronto!" He leaned over and kissed Lily. "Goodnight, Mrs. Joseph Diotallevi."

Lily smiled. "Goodnight." She was probably just too tired to enjoy sex tonight, and the skittishness she felt about it now was surely the result of a very long, very emotional day.

The next afternoon, they drove to Toronto, found their way to their hotel and settled in. Joe extracted the wad of wedding cash from his pocket and slid it in between the mattress and box springs.

"Now let's see what it's like to make love on top of all that money." Joe grabbed Lily and pulled her down onto the

21

bedspread. Their lovemaking followed a pattern similar to the night before, with Joe starting vigorously and finishing quickly, leaving him happily flushed, leaving Lily half-dressed, half-satisfied, and battling feelings of uneasiness. *It'll get better*, she told herself. *I have to give it some time.*

"I just took a look at the city guide here," Joe told her as they lounged in bed afterward. "It looks like Woodbine is running tonight and then they are dark the next two days - dammit!"

"Is there another track we can go to instead?"

"No - the tracks at home are closer than anything else. Shit." He sat up in bed and turned to Lily. "Do you think it would be possible to go see that musical thing another night?"

"I could check," said Lily. She was disappointed, but it was his honeymoon, too. They could see a musical almost anywhere. "Sure," she added. "I'm sure we can find something."

"You're a peach." Joe kissed her.

"Wow," said Joe as they entered the racetrack. He slowly took a three-hundred-and-sixty-degree survey of the room with the delight of a child on Christmas morning. People scurried about, machines spat out tickets, the air was abuzz with the sounds of laughter and excited conversation, and the clanking of silverware spilling over from the lounge.

"Would you look at this place?" said Joe.

"Cool," said Lily, though she didn't see how it was much different from Batavia Downs, or Finger Lakes Race Track, or Hamburg, or Vernon Downs - or any of the tracks she'd been to over the past couple of years. She likely just didn't know enough to be impressed the way Joe was. But it was enough that he was excited.

"Shit," said Joe, looking up at the tote board. "I didn't think it would take us that long to get here - I only have five minutes to play a daily double."

"Why rush it?" said Lily. "Let's go find a seat in the lounge, maybe order a cup of coffee. Don't bet this race - you can take your time and bet on the second race."

"The double is a huge opportunity to get us off to a good start. It sets up the whole day. I can still make it. If we hit this, I'll buy you the biggest hamburger they've got, and then tomorrow we can spend the day spoiling you." Joe brusquely placed a kiss on her lips. "You go into the lounge and find a seat - I'll meet you in there in a few minutes."

Lily poured a packet of sugar into her coffee as the first race played on the TV overhead. Joe hadn't returned yet, so she didn't even know which horse to root for. Shortly after the race, Joe sat down, beaming at her.

"I told you I had a good feeling about this track."

"Did you win?"

"We're halfway there," he said. "I didn't play that race straight, but if Morning's Glory wins the second race, we'll be in good shape. I put a nice bet on the double, too. Should be a great payout."

Joe leaned over and kissed Lily, "I'm having so much fun. After this race, let's order a nice lunch and enjoy the afternoon, OK?"

"I'm in!" said Lily.

"In fact," said Joe. "Let's buy ourselves a little insurance."

"What do you mean?"

"I think Morning's Glory is a sleeper in this race - his odds are really good. I'll collect on the double, but I'm going to go play him to win, too."

"But you already have money on him," said Lily. "Why don't you wait and see? Then if he loses, you'll have more money for the next race."

"What are you trying to do, Lil - jinx me?"

"No, I'm just saying that if Morning's Glory loses - "

"There you go again - do you want to put a curse on me? Jesus..."

"Sorry," said Lily. "I didn't know it was bad luck."

"Listen, just let me take care of the betting, OK? Your job is to sit here and squeeze for my horse to win. I'm going to go put a little extra on him."

Joe disappeared and Lily watched on the TV as Morning's Glory and Shenanigans crossed the finish line together. Joe came rushing into the lounge, flustered.

"Who won? Who won? What did it look like in here?"

"It looked like a tie," said Lily.

"It's called a dead heat," he snapped. "Damn it! They're calling for a print."

"What's a print?"

Joe remained silent, his eyes glued to the TV screen.

"What's a print, Joe?" Lily repeated.

"Jesus, Lil - it's when the race is so close they have to blow up the finish line photo. Just keep your eyes on that tote board, and pray that they put a three up there."

They sat for what seemed like an hour, during which time the hustle and bustle around them deflated to a murmur. Finally the number seven flashed up on the board, accompanied by a wave of cheers and boos from the crowd.

"Fuck!" screamed Joe. He kicked the chair and sent it toppling over onto its side. "Fuck!"

Noticing that other people in the lounge were watching them, Lily bent over and set the chair upright. She reached out for Joe's hand.

"Come sit," she said.

Joe slapped her hand away, still staring at the print on the screen that depicted Shenanigans crossing the finish line first by half a nose.

"He lost by a bob of the head," said Joe, slamming his form down on the table. "By a fucking bob of the head."

Lily took a napkin from the dispenser and dabbed at her eyes.

"Oh, Jesus," said Joe, sitting down and noticing the stares around them. "Jesus, Lily, I'm so sorry. Jesus." He slid his chair next to hers and placed his arm around her shoulder. "I shouldn't have yelled like that. You didn't do nothin' wrong."

"That's OK," said Lily. "You just scared me."

"I know, I know." Joe looked up at the print, and then back down at the stack of worthless tickets in his hand. "I thought we

24

were really going to hit it big on that one." After a moment, he added, "Shit!"

"Do you want to get something to eat now?" Lily asked.

"Better not," said Joe. "I have some damage control to do first. I'll be back in a little while."

He disappeared for twenty minutes, returning to the lounge as the bugle sounded the Call to Post. "Squeeze for number six," said Joe, placing a rushed kiss on Lily's lips. "This is our race, baby - I can feel it!" He rushed off excitedly.

Number six came in third. It was ten minutes before Lily saw Joe again. He sat next to her at the table, quietly staring down at the pile of tickets in his hand.

"How about a nice sandwich?" Lily asked.

"No. Thanks."

Lily's stomach growled. "Do you know who you're going to bet in the next race? I like number five."

"Lily," Joe said. "I don't even know how to tell you this, but - Jesus," Joe placed his elbows on the table and set his head in his hands.

"What is it?"

"We're out of money."

"What do you mean?"

"I mean we're out of money. It's gone."

"You bet it all? All of it?"

"Yes, Lil," he snapped. "I bet all of it."

Fear and anger shot through Lily's body. She couldn't decide if she should scream or cry, settling on neither one as a helpful way to respond.

"At least we only brought three hundred dollars in with us," said Lily. "I'm glad we had the good sense to leave the rest of it back in the hotel room."

Joe looked at Lily, and then back up at the results board.

"You have ten minutes until post time," said the announcer over the loudspeaker. "Ten minutes until post time."

"You did leave the rest of the money back at the hotel, right?"

Joe looked down at the floor.

"I wish I had," he said. "I wish to God I had."

"Are you telling me that you lost all of our money? Everything we had?"

"Not everything," said Joe.

Cool relief flushed through Lily's body.

"I left a hundred bucks in the safe."

"A hundred dollars?! That's all we have left? We had six hundred dollars when we got here, Joe. It's only the fourth race!"

Joe didn't look up at her. "I know."

"But Joe - one hundred dollars is hardly enough for gas and tolls and stuff for the way home."

"I know. Let's just get out of here." He tossed his tickets up into the air and they fell like confetti around them.

After a brief stop at their hotel to gather their things and their last one hundred dollars, Lily and Joe silently crawled through traffic on the QEW as they headed home. When they hit I-90, Joe maintained a steady speed of eighty miles per hour. Lily wanted to tell him to slow down, but she had the sense if she did, he would only go faster. She fumed and fought off tears of rage until they pulled into the driveway. What good would it do to scream and cry? It would only make matters worse.

They opened the door to their apartment at LaMont Manor. Joe walked in, dropped his suitcase on the floor, and plopped himself down at the dinette table. Lily abandoned her fantasy of being carried over the threshold, leaving it in the hallway.

"I feel like such an idiot," said Joe. "I ruined our honeymoon. You deserve better."

"You didn't ruin our honeymoon," said Lily, sitting next to him and taking his hand. He had in fact ruined the honeymoon, but clearly he felt bad about it - and she would get over it. Why rub salt in his wounds? For better or for worse, for richer or for poorer. This was a chance to show him what a good wife she was going to be.

"I'm glad we're back," she said. "I can't wait to get settled into our new home anyway. Who needs a fancy hotel?"

"You're a good girl, Lily." Joe kissed her hand. "They don't make 'em like you anymore."

It was a painful lesson, but if it was one they had to have, then Lily was glad they got it out of the way early in their marriage. Now they could put it behind them.

"Let's just make sure that never happens again, OK?"

"Absolutely," said Joe. "You have my word. I am so freakin' sorry."

Joe sat slumped in the chair, looking down at his folded hands in his lap. Lily could see his remorse, could feel his need for her comfort and forgiveness. He seemed so broken, so forlorn. All she wanted to do was make him feel better, let him know that it was OK, that she could rise above this. She wanted him to know that nothing was more important to her than he was. It was just money, and she didn't need money to be happy.

The physical desire that had so eluded Lily for the first two days of her marriage now swelled within her. She leaned forward and kissed him. She stood up and unbuttoned her blouse, letting it fall to the floor. She unzipped her jeans and peeled them from her legs, as her body awakened with arousal. Joe stood and led her to their bedroom, and they began making love for the first time in their new apartment on their new bed, as husband and wife.

Lily was thrilled at the way her own body was directing her as her fingers adeptly moved from being entangled in Joe's hair, then traveled down the muscular line of his spine, resting on his buttocks. She clenched his body against hers, her desire growing more autonomous with each beat of his rhythm. She wanted him more now than she ever had, and he seemed different, too, sharper somehow. He was as enthusiastic as he had been the past couple days, but there was an edge to the way he moved. She couldn't identify the quality exactly, except to say that he seemed rougher, more distant, and that when she peeked at him, she found a grimace on his face. No matter, whatever they were doing, it was working, and Lily felt fully engaged in their lovemaking for the first time. Her breath quickened as she prepared to surrender herself completely to the haze under which she was growing increasingly powerless. As her body dangled on the precipice of climax, Joe cried out, and then collapsed.

They lay side by side, panting, sweating. She waited for him to catch his breath, to turn to her, to touch her, to satisfy the craving that had been awakened by his remorse, and fueled by his need for her absolution.

Joe sat up and reached to the floor for his underwear. "I'm going to go put on the ball game, OK?"

Was he forgetting about her? Or maybe he thought she had already finished. "Sure - yeah, OK," said Lily, confused and fighting back tears of disappointment.

She heard him open and close the refrigerator door. Soda fizzled, ice cubes clinked, cellophane ripped open, the television buzzed to life.

"Wow! What a play!" said the baseball commentator.

Lily waited for her desire to subside, but her body continued to pulsate with it, as though Joe were still there, moving against her, urging it to life. Longing to resolve the passion that begged for just a little more, just one more moment, she inched her hands down to where Joe had been, wondering if she should get up and go into the bathroom first, yet knowing he would not get up from the couch at least until the next commercial.

"Hey, Lil!" Joe called from the living room. "Can you make me a grilled tuna sandwich? I love the way you do it."

Lily jumped up from the bed.

"Sure, baby," she said. "I'll be right there." She tiptoed into the dining area and retrieved her clothes from the floor. It was just as well. She would rather wait for Joe so she could share the thrill with him; it would be worth it.

3. IRIS

"*Piccolina!* Paolo has a confession to make," Gregorio called to Iris from the balcony, where he was pouring their guests a drink from a bottle of chilled Pigato d'Albenga. Iris had chosen the wine for the evening, as she did whenever they had company.

"Just a second, *Amore!* I'm coming!" Iris said, garnishing with sprigs of parsley the platter of *vitello tonnato*, a summer dish she had recently learned to make from her sister-in-law Cinzia: a round of veal simmered to tenderness in equal parts of white wine and water with carrots and celery and herbs, then left to cool in its own broth. The thinly sliced meat was arranged on a platter, and topped with a generous layer of homemade mayonnaise whipped up from the freshly laid eggs she bought at the local poultry shop (an improvement on Cinzia's store-bought mayonnaise), then blended with tuna, a couple of anchovies, and a some finely chopped capers.

Iris wiped her hands on a dishtowel, smoothed the hair which simply did not want to stay straight, and joined the others on the balcony. She took a sip from her glass of Pigato: smooth and velvety, yet persistent, with a mind of its own. Delicious.

"As I was saying," Gregorio said, "Paolo's a bit embarrassed. This is the first time we've had him over for dinner, and what with you being American and all..."

"Yes?" asked Iris, smiling, curious.

Paolo and Enrico, two surgeons who worked with Gregorio at the Policlinico in Genoa leaned against the balustrade. Marina, an anesthesiology intern, stood with her back resting against the chest of Enrico, whose arms were wrapped tightly around her. Off to the side stood Deirdre, a pretty, pleasingly plump girl from Cork whose hair was as black as her skin was white. Iris had met Deirdre one day on the beach, where they had been lying on towels just a few yards from each other, when they simultaneously pulled out their paperbacks. As soon as Iris noticed they were both reading *Hotel New Hampshire* she had started giggling and introduced herself, then offered to apply sunscreen to Deirdre's back, which was already glowing a dangerous shade of pink.

Iris was instinctively drawn to Deirdre's open smile and clear blue eyes that twinkled under a veil of impossibly long lashes, and the girls had instantly struck up a friendship, something they had both discovered did not happen easily with the twenty-year-old locals with whom they had virtually nothing on common. Hoping to introduce into their circle of friends someone who wasn't an anesthesiologist or surgeon, and possibly not even connected with the medical profession, Iris had convinced Gregorio to allow her to invite Deirdre to dinner. Besides, she was hoping Deirdre might fancy Paolo, who was attractive in that sterile sort of way typical of Gregorio's operating room colleagues, still single at thirty-five, and, according to Gregorio, in the market for a serious relationship.

"Well, what Paolo wanted to tell you," Gregorio began, for the third time, "is that he ate before he came."

"Is that true, Paolo?" Iris placed her hands on her hips, trying to look offended. Which she was, at least a little bit.

"Well, Iris," he said, pronouncing her name *Ee-rees*, the Italian way. "I arrived home from the hospital after eight hours in the operating room. My mother opened the door for me, and said, '*Poverino!*' She always calls me that, her 'poor little boy.'"

"Is your mother visiting, Paolo?" Iris asked.

"No, I live with her," Paolo replied. "I'm single."

"Yes, I knew you were single," Iris said, glancing at Deirdre, then back at Paolo. His pinstriped cotton shirt had been pressed with care, and was tucked into a pair of spotless white jeans; neat creases starting at his thighs followed his legs down to the tassels of his soft leather moccasins. A powder blue sweater, rolled up sausage-style, was tied around his waist. When Iris had asked Gregorio why so many Italian men wore their sweaters like that, he told her that it was dangerous to expose the stomach to the cold, especially during digestion; it could lead to an attack of *congestione*, a condition known to cause severe stomach cramps, sometimes even death. She soon learned of a number of other life-threatening pitfalls about which Italian mothers warned their children, like being caught in a current of fresh air, or swimming after eating, or drinking beverages with ice cubes in them, or marrying people from other regions.

"There was such an aroma when I walked in the door!" Paolo's eyes rolled as he relived what must have been an irresistible temptation. "My mother told me she baked a pan of *lasagne al pesto*. You know, she makes the noodles herself, and for the pesto she only uses the best *basilico*, from Prà."

"Didn't you tell her you were going out to dinner?" Iris asked, glancing at the others over the rim of her wineglass.

"Yes, I told her this morning, when she brought me my *caffelatte*, that I was coming here," Paolo answered. "And she said, 'But you told me Gregorio married an American girl, no?' and I said, 'Yes, Mamma, a nice girl from New York, Gregorio told you all about her, when he came over for dinner one night, the week before he went to America for the wedding.' And she said, 'Yes, I remember I made *ravioli al tocco*, and Gregorio said they were better than his mother's because she buys her ravioli from the *rosticceria*, and I make mine from scratch.' And then I asked her what that had to do with Iris, and she said she remembered Gregorio showing her a picture of Iris, by the Christmas tree, with a big smile on her face. She said she could tell she was American by her big, white teeth. '*Ma cosa ne sanno, quelle, della cucina?*' she asked me. She said nice smiles may be good for catching husbands, but not for keeping them. That's why so many Americans get divorced, she said. Because the women don't know how to cook."

"It just so happens, I grew up learning how to smile and cook at the same time," Iris said.

Paolo laughed. "What can I say? She figured I should have something to eat at home just in case. And I couldn't resist that dish of *lasagne*...""

"Of course!" Iris said, flashing her incriminating smile, then shrugging and throwing up her hands. Frustrated by her inability to communicate during her first months in Italy, she had become well-versed in gesticulation, and was finding it a hard habit to break. She nodded her head at Deirdre, indicating for her to follow her to the kitchen. Iris handed her friend a platter of *prosciutto crudo*.

"I don't know, Deirdre," she whispered, shaking her head. She picked up another platter where crescents of cantaloupe skated on their own juice. "My *mammone* alarm is ringing loud and clear."

"Mine, too. One hundred percent Mamma's Boy," Deirdre said. "What is it with these Italian men, anyway?"

"It's their mothers that are the problem. Their sons are the receptacle for all their dreams and anxieties and fantasies and phobias, and their insatiable need to be needed. They are their only hope for happiness, once they realize how disappointing their husbands are."

"What about Gregorio?"

"He's so considerate and sweet. I think he's always been a perfect son, without being a *mammone*. His father was a bit of a philanderer, from what I gather, but the subject is taboo. Gregorio sort of stepped in, to defend and protect his mother from suffering, I think. Isabella positively adores him. Cinzia could go there ten times a day, but if she doesn't see Gregorio at least once, she feels abandoned."

"Doesn't it give you the creeps that she is so clinging?" Deirdre asked.

"I picked up on it gradually, you know? It's not like all these details were written on his passport. And then I got to thinking, I sort of did the same thing with my father. I felt sorry for him when my mom left, so I turned myself into some kind of substitute wife and mother for him and my little brothers. And of course, after my cousin Dolores died, my Auntie Rosa latched onto me, too. I can sympathize with him, because I know what it's like."

"OK, but then you stopped clucking and moved away. You did the natural thing."

"But I still feel guilty sometimes."

"That's a prerogative of us Roman Catholics. So go to confession. Or get smashed. You'll get over it."

"Anyway, getting back to *Dottore* Paolo. I've only seen him a few times, but I thought he was different. What a letdown," Iris said. "Funny, how sometimes one gesture, or one comment can tell you all you need to know about a person."

"To be sure. It takes all of five minutes, like when we met. Paolo's too scrawny for me, anyway. I'd flatten him on the very first date!" Deirdre smiled. "At least I can relax and enjoy the dinner now. I'm much better at eating than I am at flirting."

"*E' pronto! Venite!*" Iris said, beckoning her guests to the table. Her Italian was close to flawless by now, though her accent remained. She always paid close attention to the speech of Isabella, Gregorio, and Cinzia, a schoolteacher whose three pregnancies had earned her the right to uninterrupted maternity leave at full pay for the past five years (Iris had mentioned the law in a letter to her mother, just for the record). The Leales all spoke perfect textbook Italian, and were eager to correct Iris when she made a mistake, the same way they corrected Cinzia's husband, Franco, even though he wasn't a foreigner, just an officer in the *guardia di finanza,* and more concerned with the Italian tax laws than Italian lexicon. To Iris, it seemed as though the women were always ready to pounce on her, and since she was mortified by her blunders, she often preferred to remain a silent spectator during conversations. Iris thought it nice that the family all lived in the vicinity: Isabella in Genoa, not far from the Policlinico, which made it convenient for Gregorio to look in on her before and after work; Cinzia and her family in Recco; Iris and Gregorio in between. Family had always been important to Iris, and she looked forward to Sundays, when everyone gathered for the midday meal at Isabella's. After Mass, Iris, who had quickly learned the words to all the prayers (including the priest's part), was escorted on Gregorio's arm to the pastry shop crowded with other churchgoers, where they ordered an assortment of *cavolini* and *cannoncini*, delightful cream-filled pastries that were placed with great care on little cardboard trays, wrapped up and tied with a ribbon for transportation to the Sunday dinner table.

Whenever they were together, Iris observed the prim and well-versed Isabella for examples of how she should speak, dress, and behave. She was determined to obliterate the unrefined ways of her haphazard upbringing, and assimilate the rules that would enable her to face a new series of circumstances and situations for which she had not been prepared. Her mother-in-law was the epitome of a *signora perbene*, and that's what Iris was determined to become: a respectable lady.

Dinners with Gregorio's colleagues afforded an ideal testing ground for her blossoming talents as hostess and conversationalist, while experimenting with ways to combine her consolidated culinary skills with new inspiration and ingredients from her adoptive environment. When the doctors sitting around her table eventually stopped discussing the patients and politics of the hospital, they always turned to Iris for entertainment, barraging her with questions about growing up in America in such a large family. Iris had grown adept at titillating their appetite for the bizarre with anecdotes extracted from the more humorous episodes of her childhood, sufficiently spiced up for their enjoyment. Gregorio beamed with pride at Iris's social success, and told her that their dinners had become something to speculate about beforehand and commentate afterwards in the sterile environment of the Policlinico operating room.

"Now don't forget, *Piccolina*," Gregorio said, kissing the top of

Iris's head. "You'll need to catch the four-thirty *rapido* back. Otherwise, you'll have to change trains in Ventimiglia and you won't make it in time for dinner at eight. It was very kind of Mamma to invite us, and you know how she values punctuality."

"I know. And don't worry, I wrote all the information down," Iris said, tapping the little notebook which was never far from her. She had studied the timetable beforehand, and was determined to make this last day of her father's visit extra special. So far, he said he was having the time of his life.

"Good girl. Here's some money," he said, slipping some bills into Iris's pocket.

"That's OK. I have money," Iris said. She still had not gotten used to spending money some one else had earned, even if that someone was her husband. She felt better now that she had picked up some of Deirdre's English students, who were eager to practice conversation with an authentic American.

"What you make with those little English lessons is your pocket money, *Piccolina.* It's not enough to show your father a good time in Monte Carlo."

"Don't worry about us, Gregorio!" her father said from the table, where he was seated within reach of the two items that made him feel at home anywhere: a coffee cup, and an ashtray. "I have money, too." He shook his pockets and chuckled at the sound of coins jingling. "We're not exactly what you'd call high rollers!"

"Well, you just go live it up for the day. I have to run – I have a complicated procedure this morning. I'll see you tonight."

"Ciao, Gregorio!" her father called as Gregorio waved and headed for the door.

"Have a good day, *Amore,*" Iris said, seeing him out, and pecking him on the cheek.

"He's one helluva guy you got there, Iris," her father said, lighting up his second cigarette of the morning. "Got any more of that expresso left there?"

"Sure, Dad." Iris thought of correcting him, but changed her mind as she poured the coffee. "But don't overdo it. Remember,

35

it's stronger than that stuff you drink back home."

"Sure, sure. You know, honey, I confess I was a little worried when you moved over here. Last time I was in It-ly was my Navy days, before the war. We docked at the port of Bari for two weeks. It was filthy, nothing like this. People were friendly, especially if you had cigarettes. But poor. Dirt poor."

"Well, that was over forty years ago, Dad. Why do people in America think things only change over there? That the rest of the world is stuck in some time warp? You know Auntie Rosa wouldn't have encouraged me to marry Gregorio if she didn't think I could have a good life here," Iris said, pouring a dose of dense, black liquid from a multifaceted espresso pot into the demitasse. Her mother hadn't been the only one worried about Iris going to live in a backward country; a number of people back home continued to ask whether she had a television, or running water, or electricity in her house.

"That's for darn sure. Nothing was ever good enough for her Iris. Up until Gregorio came along." Her father downed the espresso in one gulp, and stared at the empty cup, looking perplexed. "Darn stuff doesn't go very far, does it?" He drew on his cigarette and said, "That picture hanging over there, with that beautiful beach. That's where you went on your honeymoon, right?"

"Yep. That was in Sardinia," Iris said, following his eyes to the framed photograph hanging on the wall, thankful that she had thought of taking down the picture of her mother before his arrival. Iris had never heard her parents mention a honeymoon, nor had they ever gone on a vacation together, as far as she knew. The thought made her sad; she didn't know whether to downplay the beauty of the resort, or share it with him, but she thought her father would be happy for her if he knew how well Gregorio was treating her.

"Imagine, Dad," she continued, "the water really was all those incredible shades of green and blue. And the beaches were amazing, just look at that fine white sand! I never would have dreamed that I would actually swim in such a beautiful place one day."

"That's you in your bathing suit, so that obviously must be Gregorio standing next to you, holding that thing, with all those tentacles. It looks like some kind of octopus."

"Yes, that's Gregorio, and that's the octopus he caught." Iris laughed, recalling how reluctant she had been to touch it.

"Hard to recognize him with all that gear he has on."

"Oh, his wet suit is like his second skin. They had a fantastic scuba diving center in the resort where we stayed. First thing in the morning, he would get his air tank filled, and his gauges checked, then get suited up. He couldn't wait to speed off on the boat to a different point of immersion each day."

"Son of a gun! Did you go, too?"

"Well, I went out on the boat with him once, but I got seasick."

"That's a cryin' shame."

"No, I had a great time, anyway. I learned how to snorkel, and I went for some beautiful swims. I got lots of exercise, and a great tan."

"Yes, you sure did have a great tan. I can see that from the picture!"

"How was the food?" her father asked.

"Exquisite! They served all kinds of seafood I had never eaten before."

"Sounds pretty sophisticated. And I bet it was a real treat to stay in a fancy hotel. How was your room?"

"Absolutely stunning. Gregorio booked us a luxurious suite with a balcony overlooking the cove."

"Sounds like a fairy tale honeymoon, honey," her father said, grinding his cigarette butt in the ashtray.

"It was." She wondered how Lily's honeymoon in Toronto had gone; she had written to ask, but Lily had never replied to her letter, and it was no use asking her father. Everyone said there was lots to do in the city, like in New York. As far as Canada was concerned, Iris herself had never made it past Niagara Falls. "But that's enough chit-chat, Dad. We'd better get going. Monte Carlo awaits us."

"Mademoiselle!" The uniformed guard at the entrance to the Casinò de Monte-Carlo held up a hand to halt Iris. *"Quel âge avez-vous?"*

"I'm twenty-one. *J'ai* uh ... *j'ai vingt ... vingt et un ans."*

"Passeport, s'il vous plaît!"

Men in uniform always made Iris nervous, and her unease was heightened by her language handicap. She wished she had enrolled in that language school in Genoa like she had planned on doing, until Gregorio suggested she wait, saying that she would certainly have other more important things to worry about soon. Hoping her high school French would see her through, she fumbled around in her purse and produced her United States passport. The guard flipped it open, looked at her again, nodded, and pointed his chin at her father.

"Et monsieur?"

"C'est mon père!" Iris said. She looked at her father, with his salt-and-pepper hair ruffled by the breeze of the Côte d'Azur, his olive skin infused with a bronze glow after a week of espresso sipping in Portofino and Santa Margherita, Rapallo and Camogli and any café in between that afforded a view of the sea and the passersby. Tufts of chest hair peeked over the emerald green polo shirt he wore under his all-occasion sport jacket. Iris imagined seeing him for the first time, and was shocked to realize that as long as her father was not forced to reveal the contents of wallet, he could easily pass for an international playboy, or even a movie star.

The guard waved them in, and Iris took her father's arm, giggling. "He didn't believe you were my daddy – he thought you were my sugar daddy!" Her father roared with laughter as they entered the shiny marble foyer, paid their admission, and waltzed into the gaming room, arms linked. Neither of them had ever been to Las Vegas, or even Atlantic City. And here they were, frolicking around like the rich and famous, in Monte Carlo!

"It's not exactly like poker night with the guys from Sacred Family," her father said, transfixed by the piles of chips being swept away by the croupier at the roulette table. "How much do you figure that was, Iris?"

"Shhh," she said, suppressing a giggle, as heads spun around, and eyes shot them dirty looks. "I don't know," she whispered behind her hand. "But it sure looked like a lot. Let's lose these stiffs and see if we can find something more fun."

An hour later they reemerged into the sunlight of a fine June day in Monaco, content to be relieved of the twenty thousand liras they had decided to blow on the slot machines. Freed of their burden, they strolled along the promenade to admire the yachts, and gape at the sparkling shop windows displaying precious watches and gems and gold, her father pointing and balking and speculating about prices that were too high for those who had to ask. Before Iris could stop him, he buzzed the bell of the Bulgari boutique, where he insisted Iris try on a diamond and emerald collier. After making her model the necklace, he told the proprietor he didn't like it because it made his young girlfriend look too old. They were doubled over with laughter and still a few hundred yards from the station when Iris checked the Swiss watch Gregorio had given her for Christmas to replace her old Timex. She gasped when she realized their train was due to part in a just a matter of minutes, and announced that they had better make a dash for it.

"Jeepers Cripes!" her father said, as they settled in their seats. Struggling to catch his breath, he mopped his forehead with a handkerchief.

"Are you OK?" Iris asked. "I'm sorry I made you run!"

"Just a little winded," her father said between coughs. "Damn cigarettes," he muttered, reaching for the pack in his breast pocket. "Heck, that was fun!"

"Yes, it was. Thank you, Dad."

"No, thank you."

As the *rapido* sped east along the coast back to Genoa, Iris watched her father's gaze focus and refocus, focus and refocus on the stunning views that flashed past them, and wondered what he was thinking. His eyes bulged slightly from their sockets; the skin on his throat was more slack than she remembered from her visit home the previous Christmas. She was concerned to see the veins in his neck pulsating from the exertion, yet was relieved that they did not throb with the fury that had been compressed in them for as long as Iris could remember. For the second time that day, she imagined she were seeing him for the first time, and was struck by her impressions. She saw a mature but still handsome man sitting across from her, a man whose animated expressions revealed a curious mind, a fun-loving nature, a boyish spirit, and an unaffected sort of sex appeal. Iris could easily see how her mother had fallen in love with him, a man so obviously her opposite, all those years ago. There must have been a great deal of passion fueling their relationship, until it had derailed and exploded.

She wondered when things had started to go wrong, after how many kids and why. Now that she herself was a married woman, she struggled to gain a clearer understanding of her parents' mistakes, and a deeper compassion for their respective situations. She sometimes spoke to her father and Auntie Rosa on Sundays, when Gregorio offered her the possibility of phoning, but her efforts to keep in touch with her mother were erratic. Never having been in the habit of sharing confidences with her mother, Iris's timid attempts at establishing a deeper dialogue from a safe distance were either too vague to elicit a response, or were simply ignored, as was the existence of their last painful conversation. As expected, Betty Capotosti's sporadic replies were devoid of a mother's sentimental drivel for a daughter living overseas, which might have encouraged Iris to open new channels of communication; but neither did they contain criticism of Iris's choices, which may have closed them definitively. After dispensing a few words of generic affection, her mother always slipped into the more neutral territory of the legal reforms she was battling to achieve with her NOW sisters, often including newspaper clippings with highlighted paragraphs and notes in the margins. Iris read them with interest, discovering that her pride in her mother's activities seemed to have grown in proportion with the distance that separated them.

Thank God she and Gregorio would never end up like her parents. For one thing, they certainly wouldn't be having so many kids to contend with, maybe just two, or three at the most. Three would be perfect. But first they had to start with one. It was just taking a little longer than Iris had expected.

"You are *quite* the comedian, Carlo," Isabella said, after he recounted the episode at Bulgari's over dinner.

"Laughs aren't so easy to come by these days," he replied. "God has been good, giving me the opportunity to come over here, but He sure has been testing me."

"Things have a way of resolving themselves with time, Carlo," Isabella said. "Hopefully you can go back home rested and ready to start a new life."

"There's no new life for me, Isabella. Iris's mother and I were married in the Church, and in the eyes of God, she will always will be my wife, even if she does have bats in her belfry."

"I feel the same way, Carlo," Isabella said. "No one could take the place of Gregorio's father. No one." She made the sign of the cross.

"But you were widowed, Mamma. It's different," Gregorio said. "And *Babbo* didn't deserve you."

"Gregorio, you know I will not tolerate such talk. He was a good father."

"It's easy to be a good father when you are always on the road. All you have to do is remember to call every night and bring a present every time you come home."

"May I remind you that your father's job at the pharmaceutical company is what got you interested in medicine, Gregorio? Don't you remember?"

"Yes, I remember well. Especially the skiing vacations in Cortina, where he invited all those doctors and their families on the company tab, but we got left behind."

"That was his job, Gregorio. That was the way it was done. Did you feel you were missing out on anything, staying at home with your Mamma?"

"Could you please pass the champagne, Gregorio?" Iris said, wishing they would change the subject. She confessed to feeling a bit of a thrill when she walked into the wine shop in Monte Carlo and purchased a bottle of French champagne with the money Gregorio had given her. He never tired of reiterating his view that champagne was a waste of good grapes, so the investment had seemed oddly appropriate, especially since this was their last dinner with her father, and there was never anything to drink in Isabella's house, a form of prohibition Gregorio had told her went back to the days when his father was still alive, and overindulged in more than one vice.

Gregorio handed her the sweaty bottle, and Iris cringed slightly as she refilled her father's water glass with lukewarm liquid, thinking how absurd it was that the credenza of such a refined woman as Isabella did not contain an ice bucket or champagne glasses. Stealing a surreptitious glance at Gregorio, Iris filled her own glass, thanking the bubbles for the tiny explosions of joy they brought to both table and tongue. *"Non esagerare,"* Gregorio mouthed, taking the bottle from Iris's hands. No, of course one mustn't exaggerate, Iris thought, taking a long sip from her glass, savoring the way the bubbles tickled her nose and caressed her lips and teased her tongue, hundreds of tiny exclamation marks punctuating the pleasure of a perfect day, then vanishing.

The *lanterna* was clearly visible off to the west, the day her father left. She imagined him boarding his plane in Milan, as she stared off into the horizon, while rummaging through the balled-up tissues stuffed in the pockets of her denim skirt until she found one dry enough on which to blow her nose. Iris had wanted to drive her father to Malpensa, now that she had mastered her gear-shifting, but Gregorio said he didn't think it wise for her to drive three hours each way on the highway, when the bus service from Genoa was perfectly convenient. Her father had agreed, but convenient didn't stop her from crying all the way home after dropping him off.

Before her fantasies about moving to Italy had become a

reality, she had naively imagined the cadenced stanzas of her life strung together by a series of poetic reunions and goodbyes. The poetry had quickly lost its hold on her emotions, though, leaving them swinging between bouts of longing and nostalgia. She had cried for days after Jasmine and Violet and Marguerite had departed, following their seven-day five-city tour to Italy shortly after she had moved over (knowing Lily had a wedding to save for, they hadn't even told her about the trip so she wouldn't feel left out). Now, each arrival or departure was a reminder of the passing time. She hadn't factored that part into the equation, just like she hadn't considered the fact that her father would one day grow old. Seeing him with fresh eyes had made her realize that he may soon need her even more than he had in the past. The Little Boys were teenagers now, and would soon be leaving home. Counting on Lily for help was out of the question, since she had crossed enemy lines to side with her mother. Iris had hoped to broach the subject of Lily with him, to encourage him to take the first step toward reconciliation now that she was married, but her fear of spoiling the unique opportunity to enjoy her father's company, and see him enjoy himself, had made her postpone the conversation until it was too late. The older boys would certainly prove to be useless in time of need; of the older girls, only Jasmine seemed to have any patience at all with their father, but she was so taken with rescuing mistreated and abandoned animals and running her shelter, she had time for little else. Auntie Rosa was the one who had always been there for her father, whom she still referred to as her "poor baby brother." She and Iris corresponded often, and she frequently mentioned meeting him after dinner at the local diner, where the coffee poured out by the waitresses was not nearly as bitter, nor the pots as bottomless, as the grief he poured out to her. As for Uncle Alfred, he continued to prefer guitars to people, and would doubtless age in oblivion, wrapped in a cocoon spun by millions of notes, protected from all things evil by a force field of melodious Hawaiian music.

But today was a day of celebration, so she had better recover from her negative spin and get herself in a festive mood. She had cleared her schedule of English lessons for the entire duration of her father's stay, including today. She would have time to take a nice soak in the tub, give herself a pedicure and a manicure, then walk down to town and get her hair done. She had let it air dry that morning, which had left her with a head of unruly curls, already streaked with blond by her first swims in the sea. The summer they had married, exactly one year ago, Gregorio had said her uncombed hair made her look like a little orphan girl, which caused his heart to swell with tenderness. But with the approach of autumn, he had suggested a tamer look would be more suitable, and had come home one evening with a powerful blow-dryer and a set of styling brushes. The equipment tired her patience as much as her arms, and always left her with hair looking like a puffy helmet. She would let the hairdresser deal with it today. Gregorio had booked a table at their special occasion restaurant in Portofino to celebrate their anniversary; if straight hair was what he wanted, the least she could do was see to it that he got it, today of all days.

Although Iris couldn't quite relate to the image reflected in the mirror as she dressed that evening, going to the hairdresser always "boosted up her morale," to borrow one of Auntie Rosa's favorite expressions. As she applied a touch of eye shadow and mascara, she envisioned her spirits being unchained from the sadness of the day, freed to be lifted by the prospect of spending a perfect summer evening dining *al fresco*. By the time a smiling waiter seated them at one of the best people-watching tables in the world-famous *piazzetta*, Iris was feeling ashamed for indulging in such self-pity; she was darn lucky to be here, and darn lucky her father had been able to visit. When the waiter returned with two welcome flutes of champagne, a little dish of caviar, and one of black olive paté, she felt the joy for her good fortune once again bubbling to the surface.

"I have something very special for you tonight, Iris," Gregorio said. She recalled how shocked she had been, when he had surprised her on her twenty-first birthday with the eighteen-carat gold choker she wore this evening. It had taken her awhile to get used to the way it felt, so snug around her neck, but she had to admit, it did look stunning against her tanned skin, especially with the low-cut black dress she was wearing. She wondered what he had in store. It must be something that fit in his pocket, which was certainly a good sign.

"Can we have a toast first?" Iris said. She craved a sip of champagne, and wished to savor the anticipation for as long as possible.

"Certainly, *Piccolina*," Gregorio said. "*Alla nostra.*" He raised his flute to hers.

"To us," Iris said. She relished the sound of clinking crystal that announced the arrival of bubbly on her tongue. She smiled with pleasure at the taste, and giggled at Gregorio's grimace when he took a perfunctory sip and set the glass back down on the table with a definitive thud.

She studied her husband from across the table, and liked what she saw. His blond hair, moustache and goatee were impeccably clipped, and the clarity of his pale blue eyes was accentuated by a face which was perennially bronze from his year-round scuba diving expeditions. She had often tried to persuade him to spend a little time on the beach with her after a dive, or to go for an occasional swim without his wetsuit in the summer so that the rest of his body would tan, but he was adamant about going straight home and rinsing his equipment with fresh water and hanging it out to dry. Its non-Italian pallor was the only thing about Gregorio's physique that did not appeal to Iris, but unless she saw him naked, she never even thought about it.

Gregorio reached into the pocket of his double-breasted blazer and extracted an envelope.

"This gift to you is long overdue, Iris."

This was a real surprise, then. The possible presents she had been thinking of came in little velvet boxes, not in envelopes. She wondered what it could possibly contain. Could it be the title to a little used car of her own? Her heart raced at the thought of being able to take a drive down the coast all by herself, of not having to ask Gregorio to accompany her anywhere she couldn't get to on foot or by bus or train.

"Well, aren't you going to open it?" Gregorio stroked his goatee and smiled; he didn't even scold Iris for downing the rest of her champagne.

What else could come in an envelope, she wondered. It couldn't possibly be a ticket for a trip home, could it? Gregorio was no fool; he had certainly noticed how distraught Iris had been about not attending Lily's wedding, and again seen how sad she was at her father's departure. He was so sensitive, so incredibly thoughtful. That was probably what it was. She would much rather go home to see Lily and her family, than have a new ring, or even a car. Her eyes welled with tears as she looked expectantly at Gregorio.

"Not very many men would do this for their wives," he said, sliding the envelope across the table to Iris.

A little laugh escaped her lips; her stomach fluttered. How she adored surprises! She took a sip of champagne from Gregorio's flute, then reached for the envelope. She opened it, and was puzzled when her fingers encountered what felt like a normal sheet of paper inside the envelope. It didn't feel like an airline ticket at all. It seemed more like a letter, or a document of some sort. Maybe it was a car, after all. A little used jalopy would be fine, something easy to drive, and good on gas, which was so expensive in Italy; a liter here cost more than a gallon back home.

She glanced up at Gregorio. He toyed with his moustache, his eyes fixed on hers. She took another sip of champagne, set the glass down, and unfolded the sheet of paper.

"What is this?" she said, scrutinizing the paper in her hand. "It looks like a computer printout."

"Go ahead, Iris. You know enough Italian to read it for yourself."

"Leale Gregorio. That's your name, of course, then there are a bunch of numbers ... let's see. *Volume* four ml, *Conteggio* thirty million per ml, *Mobilità eccellente* ... followed by three little plus signs ... Gregorio, what is this? It looks like some kind of laboratory analysis or something."

46

"That's exactly what it is, *Piccolina*," Gregorio said.

"Is something wrong with you?" The panic rising in her chest was held at bay by the smile on Gregorio's face, by his promise of a special surprise.

"No, that's just the point, *Piccolina*. There is nothing at all wrong with me."

"Are you sure? What's this all about?" The sheet fluttered in her trembling hands as her eyes darted from the computer printout, to Gregorio's face, and back again. "*Seminogramma*, it says."

"Yes, Iris. That report is good news. It tells us that all my sperm levels are well above normal."

"Your sperm levels?" Iris asked.

"Lots of men refuse to be tested, they think their virility is being questioned. Fortunately, I am not one of them."

"You had your sperm tested?" Iris cried. Her face flushed as she noticed a pair of tourists from a neighboring table staring at her.

"Well, *Piccolina*, it has been a whole year now, hasn't it?"

"But you didn't even tell me you were going."

"I didn't really care to disclose the details of the procedure," Gregorio said. "I mean, it's not like I needed you to give me a hand or anything." He raised his eyebrows and smiled at his own attempt at humor.

Iris's hands trembled as she picked up his flute and gulped down the rest of the champagne, but the bubbles made her cough. She should be ashamed of being so materialistic. What had she turned into, dreaming of expensive jewelry, and cars and airline trips? She cleared her throat, and said, "Congratulations, or whatever you say in situations like this. I guess it's good news, right?"

"Very good news. Generally speaking, infertility problems residing with the female are easier to treat effectively."

"Infertility?" It sounded like a disease.

"Yes, Iris. When a healthy, young couple has regular intercourse without adopting any contraceptive measures and the woman fails to conceive, it's referred to as infertility."

"Infertility," she repeated.

"We love each other, *Piccolina*. And we both want children very badly, don't we?" Gregorio said, waving away the waiter, who had come to pour another glass of champagne.

"Of course we do. I'm sure they'll come, when the time is right. Maybe we just need to be patient."

"Time passes quickly, and we both know we want more than one child, so I think it is safe to say our patience has run out."

"It has?"

"Yes. But don't you worry. I'll handle everything for you at the Policlinico. Let's not worry about that tonight, though." He extracted a small rectangular packet from the inside pocket of his jacket and handed it to Iris. "For now, you should have this."

The packet was light, and she felt something move when she rattled it. She was disturbed by the discovery that she was infertile. Gregorio must have known how the news would affect her, and wanted to cheer her up with a real gift. She wished the waiter would come back with the champagne. She rattled the box again, and decided it must be a bracelet, maybe one to match the choker around her neck.

She tore away a corner of the paper and pulled out what appeared to be a thermometer in a box. "A thermometer?" she said, realizing that was precisely what it was.

"Yes! It's for taking your basal body temperature. First thing in the morning, before you even get out of bed. Then you mark it on this little chart here." He took a printed sheet from his breast pocket, and spread it on the table, anchoring the corners down with the little bowls of caviar and olive paté, as he indicated an example of a temperature graph. "It tells us when you're ovulating. When we know it's time, we have to move fast, so I can send my team in to get the job done." Gregorio winked.

"Oh. How clever," Iris said, staring at the empty flutes. She wondered whether this was a good time to give him the leather wallet she had bought for him with her lesson money, but she didn't feel like it.

"Maybe we should order," she said, squeezing her voice past the tightness in her throat. She tugged at her gold choker, then looked at her Swiss watch. Her father would be landing at JFK just about now. Was it only that morning that they had said goodbye?

4. LILY

Lily spent her days working in a little room in the back of the SaveMart. She didn't have interaction with any customers, which was one of the things Joe liked about the job. After all, you never did know who to trust these days. "You are just too gullible," Joe would tell her. He was right. She was willing to be friendly with just about anyone.

Her only real companions at SaveMart were the pliers, flathead screwdrivers, and mallets that were the standard tools of her work. On the floor under her work table was a box filled with the written instructions for every TV stand, tricycle, and lawn mower she had ever assembled. She found the documentation practically useless as it always made the process so much more difficult than it needed to be. As far as Lily was concerned, all you had to do was scan the instructions once, look at the picture on the box, and use common sense. If she ever got stuck, she would simply walk out onto the floor and look at the display model. There wasn't a question you couldn't answer for yourself by seeing the way something was supposed to look when it was right.

When Lily wasn't at work, she enjoyed setting up house. Her SaveMart discount made it possible for her to buy inexpensive wall hangings and other decorative items. She resolved not to spend a lot on the apartment since it was temporary and she wanted them to save as much money as they could toward a starter house; what little they had never seemed to go far.

Joe had curbed his gambling for the first few months, but it gradually increased again over time. At first, they just went to Batavia Downs with the family every Saturday. After all, they didn't go bowling or go out to eat every weekend like many couples did. Going to the track was their entertainment. And after all, as Joe said, they had to have some fun, didn't they? They couldn't just work all the time without an outlet. The rides home after the outings to the track were spent in animated conversation when Joe collected on a bet, but more often they were marked by the sullen silence of bad luck. Before going to sleep, Joe would come to her without fail, and either in celebration or in consolation, release his pent up emotion on her.

After about six months, Joe added a midweek trip to the track, to let off steam after work. With the advent of televised racing, and the proliferation of OTB parlors, stopping "for a race or two" on the way home from the store became a part of his regular routine.

Yet even given the limited funds, Lily did her best to create a warm and welcoming home. She knew she was no Betty Crocker, but there weren't many twenty-year-olds who could say that they had the competency to run a household. She was glad to be able to put her skills to work for her own benefit for a change, after spending years taking care of others.

"Geez, Lil," said Joe one night at dinner. "There's enough casserole here to feed an army!"

"Sorry," said Lily. "I guess I have to get the knack of cooking for two. Either that, or start inviting friends over."

Joe laughed. "Or," he said, with a glint in his eye. "We could start to fill the table up with some babies."

Joe and Lily spent most evenings eating dinner at home and then holding hands on the couch, watching TV, chatting about their days. Lily loved telling Joe stories of her customers - like the visually impaired man who bought a new curio stand for his wife, or the single mother who needed help assembling her daughter's first tricycle. And Lily hung on Joe's every word as he shared gossip from the shipping dock at La Casa Bella where Alfonso and the others would come to smoke or to listen to a game on the radio and hang out. Their routine was simple and easy, and Lily was grateful to finally have a home and a life of her own. Even their love life became predictably comfortable. Joe approached Lily for sex daily, sometimes twice in a day; his appetite for her never waned, and Lily grew adept at discerning the patterns of his desire, doing her best to be prepared and ready so that she would at least have a chance at participating before he finished and went on to the next activity. Sometimes he remembered to take care to please her, and sometimes he did not. Sometimes he unwittingly satisfied her, while at other times she was left to satisfy herself.

She also learned to detect Joe's mood by the way he behaved in bed. While he was always energetic and eager, if things were going bad at work, or if he and Lily were having trouble making rent, he was rougher, more hurried. Lily found the unpredictability of his moods titillating, like reaching inside a box of Crackerjack, hoping for a good prize. It was the potential that she most appreciated, the idea of arousing him that excited her, his craving for satisfaction that kept her anxious to please him.

Just before their first anniversary, Lily missed her period. She scheduled an appointment with the doctor, and gave Joe the official news.

"I'm going to have a son?" he shouted. "I'm going to have a son?!"

"Or a daughter," said Lily. "It might be a girl, you know!"

"I have a good feeling about this," said Joe. "It's a boy."

"I'm so excited," said Lily. "And scared. I can't wait to tell everyone - but I do feel kinda bad about telling Iris."

"Why?"

"Well, she told me when they got married that they wanted to start a family right away. She and Gregorio have been married longer than we have and she hasn't gotten pregnant yet. I suppose I'll have to tell her when she comes, but I don't want to make her feel bad."

"She's got it made," said Joe. "You think she feels bad because you don't have as much as she does?"

"I guess not," Lily replied.

"Let's face it, Lil," said Joe. "There are some things that money just can't buy. I guess she never planned on that." Joe grabbed his car keys and headed for the door. "You do what you want with Iris. I'm running over to tell Ma in person."

The following Sunday at family dinner, Joe stood up and said, "Everyone - I have an announcement to make."

"Jesus Christ," said Lucy. "Last time you said that, it was a baby. What the hell did you do now?"

"I went to talk to Uncle Frankie this morning. I told him that since I am having a son, I am going to need to make more money."

"Did you ask for a raise?" said Lily. They sure could use more money right about now. "What did he say?"

"I didn't ask for a raise," said Joe. "I did one better. I told him I wanted to move up from the shipping docks and work on the sales floor, with Alfonso and Anthony."

"Madon' " said Alfonso. "I hope he said 'no'. You don't have what it takes for that job. I know 'cuz I been doing it for five years."

"And you're making money hand-over-fist. Afraid of a little competition?"

"Yeah, that's it," said Alfonso sarcastically. "I'm afraid of you." He turned to Anthony, and with a sidelong nod toward Joe, he said, "Do you believe this guy?"

"He won't last a week," said Anthony. "You should just stay where you are, working on the docks with the *medigans*. You are too much of a hot head for sales."

Lily noticed Joe pursing his lips, the way he always did when he lost a bet.

"What did Uncle Frankie say?" she said, hoping to distract him from his anger.

"He said the same things these as these *stugots*. He doesn't think I have what it takes to make it up there with those guys. So I told him, I said, 'Uncle Frankie, I tell you what: you give me a month and if I don't produce you can send me back down to the docks, no questions asked.'"

"And...?"

"And I start next Monday," said Joe.

"No shit?" said Lily.

"No shit!"

"How much does it pay?"

"It's based on commission. You get a cut of the profits for each piece you sell, and you also get bonuses for selling financing packages at the bank, and whenever you meet your quota."

"What if you don't sell anything?"

"No sales, no pay," said Alfonso. "You're gonna starve."

"We're not gonna starve, Lily - don't you even give that a second thought. I don't care if I have to work morning, noon, and night. I am going make enough money so you can quit your job when Joe Jr. comes, so he can have a full-time mother."

"We don't know if it's a boy," said Lily. "Anyway, even if it is a boy, we haven't decided if we're going to name it Joe."

"You have to name a baby after his father!" shouted Lucy.

"Why?" said Lily, "It's a nice tradition and everything, but it's confusing. I don't want my son growing up being known as 'little Joe.' I'd like him to have his own identity."

"His identity comes from his family," said Lucy. She turned to Joe. "Whatsa matter with you? You can't have a boy and not name it Joe. Whatya doin' to me?"

"I'm not doing anything," Joe said.

"I still have a long way to go, yet," said Lily. "We'll cross that bridge when we come to it." Everyone at the table looked at Lily, probably just as shocked as she was that she would presume to put an end to a discussion that had such potential for shame and discord as what to name the next Diotallevi heir. Either they didn't get the analogy and were still trying to figure out what bridges had to do with anything, or the pregnancy had endowed Lily with a sort of authority that she was only just beginning to recognize.

That evening, Joe's mother called on the phone.

"Ma, take it easy," Lily heard him say. "She don't mean nothin' by that... What are you getting so worked up for?... I know, but - Ma, Jesus Christ... OK, OK. Yeah, OK."

Joe hung up the phone. "Lunatic," he muttered.

"What was that all about?" asked Lily.

"My mother is really pissed that you said we might not name the baby Joe."

"What did you say to her?"

"I told her I would talk to you about it."

"It's not really her business," said Lily.

"I know," said Joe. "But I just don't wanna hafta hear her bitchin' about it all the time."

"Just tell her that it's not up to her," said Lily. "We get to name our baby whatever we want."

"Well, she does have a point, though, Lil - it *is* her grandchild."

"But it's my baby," said Lily. "Doesn't that matter more?"

"Jesus, Lil, what is the big deal anyway?" Joe shouted. "Can't you just let her have her way? She is never gonna stop raggin' on me about this and I just don't want to hear it."

Lily's throat burned as tears sprang to her eyes. "It's *my* baby."

"Aw, don't go cryin' now," said Joe as he sat down beside her. "Listen, I know we can name the baby whatever we want, but my mother, well, she's not smart like you, Lil - she never finished high school, she never had a job - her family is all she has. This shit means everything to her."

"But she got to name her own babies," said Lily.

"Not really," said Joe. "My grandmother was a pain the in ass and my mother had to listen to her shit all the time about how to raise her family."

"So you would think that your mother would understand how I feel then."

"No. She figures she had to put up with someone else calling the shots in her life, and now it's her turn."

"That's crazy, Joe," said Lily.

"I know it is. But if you can't do it for her, at least do it for me, so she won't keep naggin' me about it."

"But then she'll think that all she has to do is call and yell at you on the phone and you'll talk to me, and then she'll get her way."

"Jesus, Lil - so what? It's not like she's asking you for that much, is she? Would it be so bad to name the baby Joe?"

"That's not the point."

"The point is that between the two of you, I have a pounding headache, that's the point. I gotta get some air. I'm going to OTB for a couple races. I'll be back in an hour."

"Joe - wait!" called Lily as Joe slammed the door behind him.

Two hours later, after Lily had gone to bed, Joe returned home. He climbed in next to her, pulled her nightie up and made love to her without speaking a word. Afterwards, he turned his back to her and pulled the covers up over his shoulder.

"I didn't mean to yell before," he said. "You know I put you first, don't you?"

"Sure," said Lily, unconvinced. She only had seven-and-a-half more months until she would be the mother. Things would be different then. Then, she would be the one in charge.

During the first trimester of her pregnancy, Lily took full advantage of Joe's repeated admonitions to stay off her feet and rest. She appreciated the perfect excuse to stay home from the track on Saturdays. She was still mad at her mother-in-law and her hormones were making it more difficult for her to control herself from speaking her mind. It was better to stay home and keep the peace.

"You don't belong there in your condition, anyway," said Joe. Lily suspected that he was glad to place his bets and have his fits without her around. And it was a relief to Lily to stay home alone with her paycheck and watch a movie on HBO. Sometimes Joe came home with money left in his pocket, and sometimes he did not, despite his promise to Lily on their honeymoon. Still, it did her no good to ride the roller coaster of emotion with him every Saturday night. The bills always got paid somehow, and she wanted to remain as calm and peaceful as possible, for the baby's sake. It was bad enough that her parents were still at each other's throats, unendingly dragging her into the middle of their latest battle.

One afternoon in July, Lily received a call from her father, whom she had only seen a handful of times since her wedding.

"You'd better come over here and get your mother, before I call the cops."

"What's going on, Dad?"

"She can tell you all about it when you get here."

Lily found her mother planted in the driveway at Chestnut Crest, arms folded across her chest. Ricci stood in the living room window, and her father stood guard at the back door.

"Mom," said Lily, getting out of the car. "What's going on?"

"Ricci and I have an appointment for counseling, and your father won't let him come out. Your father is telling me I have to leave; he says I'm trespassing."

"How can he say you're trespassing?" Lily asked. "Your divorce isn't final yet. It's your house, too."

"Not technically," said her mother. She used her hand to push back the auburn curls now streaked with gray that were plastered to her face by sweat. "When we bought this place, you kids were all small. Ricci was still in diapers - I didn't have anyone to watch you, so I wasn't able to accompany your father to the bank to sign the deed and the mortgage paperwork. As far as the law is concerned, this isn't my house; I was only a guest here. Now I am a trespasser."

Two police cruisers pulled into the driveway.

"Dad - you called the cops? Seriously?" Lily turned to her mother. "Mom, please, just get in your car and leave. We'll sort this out later."

"I will not," her mother replied. "The way New York State treats women in these cases is criminal, and if they want me out of here, they will have to arrest me and take me to jail."

Lily gently rubbed her belly. Even though it would be at least another two months before she would start to show, she wanted

57

to let her baby know that she would do her best to protect it from this family into which it would soon be born, a family that had become capable of such hostility.

"Dad - please... don't do this," Lily choked on the plea.

"I'm not doing anything," said Lily's father, crushing his cigarette out on the asphalt. "I've got the law on my side. Talk to your mother if you want to put a stop to this."

Lily's head swooned in the July heat, and she made her way to a chaise under the apple tree, as her parents continued their stand-off. She watched, helpless, as the fuzzy scene played out. She blinked, hoping to gain focus, as if she might make sense out of it and thereby concoct a solution. Her mother, her father, and the two policemen argued in the driveway. Her father shouted, but Lily couldn't hear what he said, couldn't make out the words; all she heard was the grind of hate. Her mother shoved him with both hands, causing him to lose his footing. Lily wanted to scream as the taller policeman put her mother in handcuffs, but she couldn't find her breath. Sweat poured down her face, and she gripped the arm rests of the chaise to keep from falling out of it. The policeman used his hand to keep Lily's mother's head from banging on the door frame as he guided her into the back seat of the squad car, just as they did with apprehended criminals on TV.

Everyone seemed to forget that Lily was even there, a horrified, helpless spectator. She closed her eyes and cried as the squad car pulled out of the driveway and drove down the street. She hoped that unborn babies had no memories and vowed to herself that once she had the strength to get up and leave she would never again visit her father at Chestnut Crest, both as a show of solidarity for her mother and in general protest of people fucking each other over in the name of the law.

The next morning, Lily awoke to cramps that twisted and gnawed at her insides. She groaned and rolled onto her back and when she did, she felt a gush of warm fluid trickle from between her legs. She bolted up in bed.

"Oh, no!" she cried. "No, no, no, no, no!"

"What's wrong?" said Joe groggily. "What the fuck is going

on?"

Lily ran into the bathroom, as the blood ran down her leg. She sat on the toilet just in time to catch a clot of blood as it slipped from her body and hit the water with a small splash.

"No!" she cried. "Joe! Call the doctor - something is wrong! Something's wrong with the baby!"

Lily cleaned herself, slipped a sanitary napkin into her underpants and then sat on the lid of the toilet seat.

"Yes, doc," said Joe. "She's right here." Joe handed Lily the phone.

"Hello? Dr. O'Connell?" Lily paused. "Yes, eight weeks, that's right... Uh-huh... yes... just now, about five minutes ago... Yes, I'm having cramps."

Lily plucked two tissues from the dispenser on the back of the toilet and covered her face with them as she rocked and tried to cry as quietly as she could. Joe stood dumbfounded in the doorway.

"But isn't there something else I can do?" Lily looked up at Joe and shook her head from side to side. "OK, OK, then I'll see you first thing Monday. Thank you, Doctor."

Lily handed the phone back to Joe.

"What did he say? What's going on?"

"He said that 'the pregnancy is likely terminating.'"

"What? What do you mean?"

"I'm having a miscarriage, Joe." Lily burst into tears.

"Let's get to you to the hospital then," said Joe. "I'll go get your slippers, you stay right there."

"Joe -" said Lily. "No. There's no need to go to the hospital. There's nothing they can do for me there."

"Then what do you need? Did he call in a prescription or something?"

"All I can do is rest and wait," said Lily. "He wants me to come in on Monday to get checked, but he said it sounds like the pregnancy is failing."

"Failing?"

"Yes," said Lily. "He said it's really common in the first

trimester, and that I shouldn't be too worried about it, that it's not like a baby yet or anything."

"He said that?!" Joe screamed. "I'm calling him back right now, what an asshole!"

"Please, Joe," said Lily. "Just help me get back to bed."

Lily stayed in bed all that weekend and then on Monday Joe drove her to the doctor where her blood test and an internal examination confirmed that Lily was no longer pregnant.

"This should progress like an ordinary period," said Dr. O'Connell. He placed his hand on Lily's shoulders.

"What caused this?" Joe asked. "What did she do?"

"Mr. Diotallevi, your wife didn't do anything to bring this about. Believe me - I've seen women throw themselves down the stairs in an attempt to provoke a miscarriage - without success." He turned to Lily. "Honestly, if you hadn't had a test done so soon, you wouldn't even have known you were pregnant. Next time, maybe wait until you've missed two periods before confirming."

It was better to not know what you were missing, even in this.

As they drove home from the doctor's office, Lily lowered the visor to keep the sun from stinging her eyes, which were already raw from sorrow.

"I blame your parents," Joe blurted. "No matter what that doctor said, I know it wasn't good that you were over there watching your mother get arrested, watching them fight like that. I don't care what the doctor said. I don't want you to go over there anymore, you hear me?"

"Whatever," said Lily. Whatever would get Joe to stop talking and let her grieve in peace. All she wanted to do was cry - for the son she wouldn't give him; for the baby she couldn't hold; for the anger she never unleashed upon her mother-in-law for tainting this experience for her; for the frustration of poverty that was making its mark on her marriage; for Joe's splintered loyalties and his ambivalence to her sexual needs; and for her mother in jail and her father's prison of rage. Every sadness for which she'd ever denied tears came looking for its due, and Lily just wanted to oblige.

Two months had passed since the miscarriage, but Lily still didn't feel normal. Her enthusiasm for keeping house had dwindled and she resented that her life seemed rife with responsibilities: balance the checkbook, go to work, clean the house, do the shopping. Joe was working in the evenings now and Lily sought pleasure in eating in front of the TV and was already starting to notice that her jeans were getting snug. Joe still approached her for sex almost every day, but Lily cared mostly about getting it over with now; it was just one more in a long list of chores.

She had forgotten that Iris and Gregorio had arrived the night before, and was at first surprised when Iris called to arrange a visit.

"I'm not really feeling myself yet," Lily told Iris over the phone. "I haven't been going out much."

"Of course, we were thinking of driving over to your place," said Iris. "Gregorio knows what an ordeal this can be for a woman."

"Sure - that'd be great, Iris - I can't wait to see you." She hoped she sounded sincere. Lily looked around the apartment, noticing what a mess it was; she had barely touched it since before rushing off to that awful scene between her parents. Her apartment looked much as her life felt these days. Confused. Sad. Neglected. The last thing she felt like doing was cleaning. She forced herself to retrieve the trash can from under the kitchen sink and then went from room to room, sweeping food wrappers, junk mail, the contents of overflowing ashtrays and used paper towels into it. She shoved the can back under the sink and dragged herself around the place a second time, collecting a stack of dirty dishes, which she dropped into the sink. She quickly spritzed the kitchen and bathroom faucets with Windex, wiped them down with a paper towel, and then sprayed a blast of air freshener into the middle of the living room. The buzzer rang before she had a chance to look at her hair or makeup.

"Lily! Lily of the Valley!" Iris shrieked when Lily opened the door.

"Iris!" Lily gave her sister an embrace, hoping she wouldn't notice that she hadn't showered. "C'mon in!" Lily stepped aside and held the door open, making way for Gregorio.

"*Ciao, Bella!*" chimed Gregorio, placing a kiss first on Lily's right cheek and then her left. Lily usually loved the scent of Gregorio's pipe tobacco, which reminded her of the incense they burned in Church at Easter, but she noticed that it was laced with the scent of Estee Lauder Youth Dew - the inevitable result of staying at Auntie Rosa's house - the way the cloud of dust followed Pig Pen around in the Charlie Brown cartoons.

"*Bella della Mamma!*" shouted Auntie Rosa, toddling into the apartment behind Gregorio.

"Oh! Hi, Auntie Rosa," said Lily. "I didn't know you were coming." Lily had seen very little of Auntie Rosa and Uncle Alfred since the wedding. They were on different sides of the Capotosti family conflict, so they couldn't talk about current events without butting heads and arousing tempers, and there wasn't much else to talk about. Iris was a popular topic of conversation, but whenever Auntie Rosa talked about Iris, she lamented about how much she missed her, and how sad it was that God wasn't producing a baby - especially for someone so loving and sweet as Iris. Auntie Rosa was also happy to reminisce about days gone by, but her constant interjection of "You know, Lily - I loved you both the same," was just proof that she didn't, and that she knew everyone was aware of it. It would have been easier if she'd just admitted it.

"After all," said Auntie Rosa, "I certainly want to see you - I haven't seen you since the wedding, and then of course your mother wouldn't allow me to do much."

Lily took their coats and laid them on her bed. When she returned to the living room, she found Auntie Rosa sitting in the rocking chair that Joe had bought her for her birthday, in anticipation of the new baby. She wanted to ask Auntie Rosa to get up. "That chair's not for you," she wanted to say.

"How do you feel, Lily?" Iris was perched on the edge of the couch, clutching a red leather bag in her folded hands. Her long, slender, manicured fingers sparkled with gold and diamonds. She wore a knee-length blue linen dress, cinched at the waist with a red belt, and red ballerina shoes. Her long neck was adorned with a double strand of pearls, and matching earrings peeked out from behind her perfectly coiffed hair.

"I'm pretty good," said Lily, smoothing out her hair and straightening her sweatshirt. "Tired. I must look a mess."

Although she hadn't planned to, she recounted recent events, pausing to gain her composure as she told them of the miscarriage, the agonizing weekend spent wondering whether she was still carrying a baby or not, the cold, factual visit to the doctor.

Auntie Rosa just shook her head, and clicked her tongue, the way she used to during the evening news.

"Your doctor is right, Lily," said Gregorio. "At such an early stage of pregnancy, there is little more than a cluster of cells that simply fail to thrive and so purge themselves." He took a toke on his pipe. "It certainly was a life, but could hardly be called a baby, even though it may have been so in your imagination. And this, of course, is where your grief and suffering is coming from. Do remember, Lily, that God knows what is best for us in these situations. If your feelings of despair don't subside in a reasonable amount of time, you may want to consider asking your G-Y-N about a pharmacological solution for depression."

Cluster of cells. Not a baby. Imagination? Didn't he get it at all?

Lily felt her eyes welling with tears. Iris blinked and a single droplet escaped from her right eye. At least now, Lily and Iris had one thing in common.

5. IRIS

"Hop right up there, *Signora*. This won't take long at all."

Iris placed a bare foot on the steel step-stool and pivoted around to rest her buttocks on the paper sheet. She was uncomfortable in her nudity, shivering with chill and agitation. A hospital gown might have helped, but by now she knew such amenities were not always provided by the public health care system, even if you were the wife of *Dottor* Gregorio Leale. Perched on the edge of the examining table, legs dangling, she wished she had the nerve to grab her clothes and run away.

"You just lie back now, and put your legs through there," the doctor or intern or technician said. He wore no name tag, but his white coat identified him as a man of authority; his baldness and bifocals vouched for experience.

The only thing to do was comply, and get this whole thing over with as soon as possible. She scooted back and lowered herself to a supine position, spread her thighs, and rested her legs in the stirrups, wincing as the cold steel made contact with the backs of her knees. She hated exposing herself in this way, although she knew the professionals in the gynecology ward must be forced to look at all kinds of disgusting sights every day. Not wanting to make their jobs any more unpleasant, she had given herself a pedicure and waxed her legs the day before. She would be mortified if word got around that *Dottor* Leale's wife were a slovenly American with hairy legs and overgrown toenails, in addition to being unable to bear him a child.

Isterosalpingografia. It had taken her some effort to remember, let alone pronounce, the term. Hysterosalpingograph wasn't much easier. With a wave of the hand and a puff of the pipe, Gregorio had dismissed her concerns about undergoing the exam, telling her not to worry, the name was more intimidating than the procedure. The doctor or intern or technician said exactly the same thing as he inserted the speculum, his perfunctory warning that the instrument might feel cold reaching her ears seconds after the impact reached her vagina, but that part she was already used to. In fact, though she always felt embarrassed, she had grown accustomed to the discomfort caused by all the probing and poking to which she had been submitted over the past several months; it was the psychological strain that was harder to deal with each time.

Women all over the world got pregnant, even when they were trying not to. It didn't matter whether you were rich or poor, smart or stupid, loved or neglected, having babies was the most natural process in God's creation. Maybe He had decided that someone had to pay for the fact that her mother had brought more than her share of babies into the world. She had not expected this, nor obviously had Gregorio. She recalled his first letters, how he had told her that she would make a wonderful mother, even before he had asked her to marry him. Now, as a woman and wife, she was turning out to be a total failure. To make matters worse, none of the specialists Gregorio consulted seemed able to diagnose the problem or prescribe a cure. They all reiterated that she was young and healthy and must learn to be patient, but they weren't the ones who had to listen to Gregorio's sermons each time he found a fresh box of Tampax in the bathroom cabinet. Month after month of temperature tracking, needle pricking, and pill popping had only produced one result: the transformation of marital relations into a job on a time clock. Sex had become the means to an end, and that end was the wail of a newborn, not the moan of a woman reaching orgasm. As her desire dwindled, taking down with it her self-esteem, and vice versa, Gregorio remained a stalwart inseminator, pouring his inexhaustible supply of semen into her at regular intervals, reminding her that she must rest, rest, rest, and stop running, sunning, drinking, thinking.

For a while, the days immediately following the ovulation-copulation frenzy had been Iris's favorite time of the month. Her pharmaceutically stimulated ovaries had hatched all the eggs they could, and Gregorio's sperm had been unleashed in staggering numbers. She forced herself to follow her husband's advice, staying in bed a bit longer, taking leisurely walks instead of jogging, reading in the shade instead of going to the beach, focusing on dreaming and hoping and praying instead of worrying. She had even gotten into the habit of going to morning Mass at the little church in town, and lighting a candle to the statue of the Blessed Virgin Mary. By the fourth week of her cycle, anxiety always got the better of her, as she obsessively monitored her temperature, the tenderness in her breasts, and any other signs that this might be her lucky month. She had bought a do-it-yourself pregnancy test, and hid it in her underwear drawer. She had already read the instructions, and would perform the test as soon as she was a day late. She planned to prepare a special dinner for Gregorio, and present him with the positive test strip, just as he had surprised her with his semen analysis on their wedding anniversary.

But despite her hopes and dreams and prayers, despite her obedience of Gregorio's rules, that dreaded day always came. No matter how long she would lie in bed with that thermometer in her mouth, the mercury refused to budge beyond the thirty-six degrees centigrade mark; no matter how convinced she was that the uncomfortable feeling in her tummy was caused by something she had eaten, the cramping continue to worsen. When she finally went to the bathroom, the hopes and dreams and prayers fell into the toilet with a splash, and were flushed away with the blood that gushed from her barren womb.

She prayed that those hopes and dreams might be rekindled

through this exam Gregorio had arranged, after a laparoscopy had led him and his colleagues to suspect there was something more amiss than a retroverted uterus. Iris was lying still, trying to obey the white-coated man's order to relax, recalling how excluded she had felt when Gregorio had conferred with the specialist to whom he had entrusted her case, when the door to the examining room was thrown open, admitting a blast of cold air and half a dozen chatting, white-coated doctors or interns or technicians on the heels of an older white-coated man. Iris shivered, folded her arms across her naked breasts, and stared at the ceiling, chewing her bottom lip.

"The procedure about to be performed on the patient is called an *isterosalpingografia*," the older white-coated man said to the group of younger white-coated men. Iris cocked her head toward the doctor or intern or technician standing between her splayed legs.

"*Mi scusi*," she whispered. "Who are those men?"

"Just relax, *Signora*," the doctor or intern or technician said. "These gentlemen won't bother you a bit."

How would he know what would or wouldn't bother her? How would he like to be lying there flat on his back, his testicles and penis swinging in the air for a bunch of white-coated women to see? Anger bubbled up inside her, but was deflated by a sharp pain jabbing at a place deep inside her. Her muscles contracted, her knees jumped out of the stirrups.

"It's nothing, *Signora*. You must lie back and relax," the doctor or intern or technician said, thrusting another instrument into her vagina.

Pens scribbled on notepads as the group of young white-coated men marked down what the older white-coated man was saying. She wished the anger would come back, but knew it wouldn't. It was never strong enough or lasted long enough to make her react. It only made her want to cry, like now. She struggled to control her voice as she raised her head again and addressed the bald pate between her legs. "What are all those men doing here?"

"Please lean back, *Signora*. Don't mind them, they are just medical students." The skull glistened, just inches above her pelvis.

"But do they really have to watch?"

The head finally looked up at her, the light reflecting off the lenses of the glasses, eclipsing the eyes. "This is a teaching hospital, *Signora*. Allowing students to observe firsthand is customary, and vital to their preparation for the medical profession. In your case, we did of course check with *Dottor* Leale as a personal courtesy, and he said he had no objection. Now, you really must lie back, so I can inject the contrast liquid into your uterine cavity. It is imperative that you relax, for us to get a good view." The head was lowered, as the doctor or intern or technician turned back to his business between her legs.

Doing as she was told, Iris lay back, holding in the tears.

"*Buongiorno*, Iris!" the saleswoman said, waddling across the shop to greet her, nylon stockings whispering of a conspiracy between her plump thighs.

The clothing store in Recco had been serving the Leale family for years. The shopkeepers were wont to inquire as to the family's health and well-being, registering news of illnesses, careers, marriages, births and deaths as racks were being browsed, clothes tried on, hems pinned. When the woman's greeting was accompanied by the question "*Novità?*" Iris knew exactly what kind of news she was hoping to hear.

Everyone she came across these days was either having babies or asking why she wasn't. Even Lily, who was a year younger and had married a year later than Iris, had managed to get pregnant before she did. Iris still cringed whenever she recalled Gregorio's chillingly clinical assessment of Lily's loss when they had visited after her miscarriage. Gregorio was certainly an expert when it came to medical knowledge, but what would he know about the emptiness a woman felt when the baby (or cluster of cells, as he put it) growing inside her failed to thrive, and was simply expelled, along with her dreams? The frustration Iris felt each month was torture enough; she could hardly imagine the suffering Lily must have endured. But at least Lily had had the chance to rejoice at the news that she was carrying a baby, wonder whether it would be a boy or a girl, try out possible names on her tongue to see how they sounded. She wished there had been some time for them to talk about their experiences more, sister-to-sister, but it had hardly seemed like a suitable moment, with Gregorio and Auntie Rosa listening and commenting on everything that was said. Iris might have even shared some useful advice with Lily, but felt uncomfortable, after noticing the way she was looking at her, her eyes zooming in on her clothes and jewelry with that mixture of smoldering envy and irritation that she had begun to display more frequently since high school - to be precise, ever since Dolores had died, and James Gentile had gone away to college. As if Iris were somehow to blame for Dolores's suicide, or for the fact that James couldn't love Lily the way she wanted him to, or that they had both disappeared from Lily's life right around the same time Iris herself had gone off to Buffalo. Still, thinking back on the dirty ashtrays and the stale air and the Coke cans sitting on the kitchen counter, she knew she should have told Lily what Gregorio always told her: a healthy lifestyle was indispensable for a healthy pregnancy.

But she probably would have mistaken her concern for meddling, and resented the interference. The last thing Iris wanted to do was give Lily another reason to not write to her. She had always been careful to downplay descriptions of her life in Italy in her letters to avoid stirring old resentments, but it was no use. Lily obviously thought Iris was the lucky one; the one who had more, the one who had it easy, the one whose privileges were served up on a silver platter with her morning cappuccino.

Lily would never understand that Iris had her problems, too, and that she would rather buy her clothes off the racks of SaveMart than from a boutique where she would be forced to make small talk and try on things she didn't need. It was sweet of Gregorio to want to buy her something to cheer her up following that awful procedure at the hospital the previous day, even though he had continued to insist all evening as she hugged her hot water bottle that the exam was painless and non-invasive. She could hardly think of anything more invasive that having foreign objects shoved into her uterus, but by now it was a moot point. The fact was, he was being thoughtful, and she didn't want to disappoint him by appearing uninterested.

"*Buongiorno, Signora Luisa,*" Iris replied, smiling courteously. "I'm fine, thanks. Nothing new."

Luisa clasped Iris's hand between both of hers, a doleful look in her eyes. "You're still so young. Enjoy yourselves a bit longer. Look at Cinzia, with three little ones. I don't know how she manages!"

"Iris needs a coat, *Signora* Luisa," Gregorio interjected, walking in the door. He had let Iris off before going to park the white Fiat station wagon he had recently purchased as a second car, in anticipation of their future needs. Iris was grateful for Gregorio's timely appearance, and for his diligence in shielding her at least from this sort of indiscreet probing. Iris still didn't think she needed a new coat, though; the one she had bought during her last winter in Rochester was still in perfectly good condition.

Iris had never been very interested in shopping, even as a teenager, when the first suburban mall had opened, probably because she had always lacked the three basic elements required to make it enjoyable: free time, spending money and girlfriends. Fashionable boutiques could be found in every town along the coast where she now lived, and until a baby came along, she had plenty of free time, though her main provider of money and friendship was Gregorio. She did have another girlfriend besides Deirdre, now that she had met Liz, a sculptress from California married to a ship captain from Torre del Greco, at the Foreign Women's Club in Genoa. But Iris knew that Gregorio would feel bad if she were to choose their company over his. He seemed to truly enjoy choosing her clothes for her, and watching her model them, and she had to admit that seeing the glint of approval in his blue eyes when she emerged from the dressing room in an outfit he had selected made her feel pretty special.

Each shopping expedition provided an opportunity for the

wide-hipped Luisa and her sparrow-like sister-in-law Mina to infuse the youngest woman in the Leale family with the impeccable style and classic elegance that had always distinguished *Signora* Isabella in the courtroom, and *Signora* Cinzia in the classroom. Iris didn't preside over anything or anyone, but once sequestered in the fitting room, she was relieved of her jeans and blouse, and coaxed into pleated skirts, twin sweater sets, tailored jackets and cuffed trousers. Luisa and Mina buttoned and zippered her into tweeds and twills in somber colors and sensible cuts, until the lack of oxygen in the close quarters made Iris reel. Sweaty and dizzy, she became disoriented to the point where she was rendered incapable of indicating any preference at all, and succumbed to the consensus of whatever pleased Gregorio and the ladies.

"How about a nice loden, Iris?" Gregorio asked, holding up a dark green woolen overcoat with leather buttons.

"A loden?" Iris asked. She recalled seeing dozens of coats identical to the one Gregorio showed her, during a stop they had made in Innsbruck while returning from a ski vacation in Tyrol.

"Why not?" Gregorio replied. "Of course, you have your fur coat for special occasions, but lodens are so practical. Mamma has one just like this, and she loves it." Iris only wore the silver fox Gregorio had surprised her with when it could not be avoided. The coat made her sweat, partly out of guilt for being an accomplice to the pointless slaughter of innocent animals, partly because the coat was far too warm for the mild Ligurian climate.

"*Venga, Signora Iris. Si accomodi,*" Luisa said, slipping the loden from the hanger and sliding Iris's arms into the sleeves. At least lodens all looked alike, she thought; it couldn't take long to pick one out.

"Oh my, green certainly does suit you. Doesn't it suit her, *Dottor* Gregorio?"

"Absolutely!" said Gregorio, his eyes twinkling. "And lodens last forever!"

Iris stared at her reflection in the mirror: boiled eyes, boiled wool, boiled nerves. "I'm all for things that last forever," she said, coaxing the corners of her mouth into a smile as she shrugged the coat from her shoulders.

"I need a drink," Iris said. "And I don't mean a cup of Earl Grey."

"To be sure," Deirdre said.

"I'll order. Gin and tonics all around?" Liz said, signaling to the waiter.

The three sat at a table at the rear of the café which hosted the weekly meetings of the Foreign Women's Club, where a consolidated core of stoically non-integrated British expats and bored Genoese Anglophiles imparted survival tips to fresh arrivals, such as where essentials like baked beans and Marmite could be purchased, or where one might find an English-speaking veterinarian. The sensible suits hanging in Iris's armoire and the prim sweater sets with mother-of-pearl buttons that crammed her dresser drawers would have been perfect attire for the afternoon teas, but Liz, whose Californian penchant for doing as she pleased without a care for what others thought, such as using the bidet in her seafront villa as a planter for her philodendron, always wore jeans to the gatherings. If Liz, at forty, said they could wear jeans, Iris and Deirdre, still in their twenties, were happy to oblige.

The room was abuzz with a British version of excitement as the president announced the program of the Queen's upcoming visit to Genoa, then introduced the guest speaker, who began by assuring the ladies of the immense pleasure they would reap through participation in the origami course scheduled (only she pronounced the word "sheduled") to commence in one week's time. Liz leaned close to Iris and Deirdre and raised her glass. "To the privilege of not being born British," she said. Deirdre giggled and clinked her glass against the others; Iris managed a half-smile, then took a long sip from her drink.

"So what's the craic, Iris?" Deirdre said.

"What do you mean?" Iris said.

"Yeah, what's going on, Iris?" Liz said. "You're looking a bit down in the dumps today."

"I am?"

"Yes, you are. Is Doc Greg putting in too many hours and neglecting you?" Liz said.

"No, it's not that. It's just ..." Iris took another sip of her drink, then touched the knuckles of her index fingers to the corners of her eyes, hoping to block the tears forming there before they could smear her mascara.

"What the bejesus is wrong with you?" Deirdre said, placing a hand on Iris's arm.

"What's wrong with me is that I'm not pregnant." Iris sniffed, and rummaged through her purse for a hanky.

"Neither are we!" Liz said. "And you don't see us crying. Seriously, Iris, what's the problem?"

"The problem is, it doesn't look like it's ever going to happen. Not unless I have surgery," Iris said. There was nothing like the sympathy of girlfriends to trigger a cry, but this was neither the time nor the place.

"Surgery? Why?" Deirdre said.

"We got back the results from the hysterosalpingograph."

"The what?" Deirdre said.

"It doesn't matter. The fact is, my fallopian tubes are almost completely blocked. The chances of me getting pregnant are practically nil. Gregorio says there is a very good microsurgery team at the Policlinico. He's going to set it up."

"And how do you feel about that, Iris?" Liz asked.

"I want to get it over with as soon as possible."

"You know, there's no law against not having children," Liz said.

"But I want children. Gregorio wants children. Everyone wants to have children. It's only natural."

"Is it? Look at Salvatore and me. We never had children. He's away on those container ships for months at a stretch, and every time he comes back, it's like another honeymoon, only better."

"Really?" It sounded romantic, but, quite honestly, one honeymoon had been enough for Iris. She wanted to get down to the business of real life.

"Really. Of course back in the beginning, each time he would disembark, we would get all those romantic notions about having a little baby to love and raise, but each time we decided to hold off till the next time. We still had so much to discover about each other, so much of the world to see. Before I knew it, I was forty, and then it was too late, but I wouldn't change a thing. It's been a great life, a satisfying marriage, and it keeps improving with time. Everything would have been different with kids. I'm not saying better or worse, I'm saying different."

"But don't people give you a hard time?"

"Oh, yeah. Especially back home. But not so much anymore. It's astonishing how people think they have a right to pass judgment on such a personal choice. Friends, family, even casual acquaintances seem to think they have a moral duty to protect you from a life they consider selfish and shallow. Oh, the looks on their faces! Accusatory. Contemptuous. Distrustful. As if I were less of a woman for following any instincts that were not of a maternal nature. As if they were somehow personally threatened by our honesty to ourselves and each other, and our desire to live our lives with the spontaneity the responsibility of children inevitably takes from you."

Provided that you had any spontaneity to work with, Iris thought. Lately, she had begun to wonder what had happened to the spontaneity Gregorio had demonstrated when they first met. He had been the one to surprise Iris by kissing her on that day on the boat on Lago Maggiore. He had been the one to astonish her by flying across the ocean to ask for her hand in marriage when they hardly knew each other. If that wasn't spontaneity, or maybe even recklessness, what was? Now she couldn't get him to stroll a few steps on the seafront promenade in Nervi after Sunday dinner unless they planned it at least a day in advance, or hop in the car and drive to a pizzeria on a weeknight to satisfy a sudden craving, instead of eating dinner in front of the evening news. Had she imagined that spontaneity at the beginning, or had it simply vanished? Unless it hadn't been like that at all. Unless his actions had been dictated by some premeditated strategy. He had been

74

well over thirty, and launched in a career with a promising future at the Policlinico. The only thing lacking was a wife and children. Perhaps Iris had just crossed his path at the right time? She wondered if he ever regretted his choice, considering the outcome. Or whether Liz and her husband regretted theirs.

"Do you ever regret it?" she asked her.

"To tell the truth, no. Especially when I take a closer look at my inquisitors when they ask me about my life, and I see their haggard faces, with the wistful looks and the bags under their eyes. They act as though they didn't have the same choices as me."

"But it's natural I should want a baby. I grew up in a big family."

"And was that so idyllic?"

"Most of the time," Iris said. She thought of the dime-store presents piled under the Christmas tree, and of the charred hot dogs on the Fourth of July, and of fourteen people gathered around one big table, fourteen sets of elbows rubbing as fourteen forks fed fourteen mouths that talked and chewed and laughed and screamed and fought and cried. "But maybe there were just too many of us," she added.

"Or maybe you only remember what you want to remember. It's easy to do that, from over here on this side of the ocean."

"But it would be different with us. We only want two or three kids, and I think I would be a good mother. And it would make Gregorio so happy."

"I am sure, Iris. Just remember to be true to yourself. And remember to have a Plan B."

"What do you mean?"

"You need a life, with or without kids. Why don't you get a job? It'll take your mind off the whole thing. Sometimes that's all it takes, and at least you'd be getting experience in the meantime."

"I can try and get you some more students," Deirdre offered.

"Thanks, Deirdre. No offense, but I wouldn't mind doing something more challenging than speaking English. I never looked for anything because I thought I'd just have to quit if I got pregnant. Plus, I didn't think Gregorio would approve."

"Iris, you can't live your life based on 'what ifs' and 'I didn't thinks'. Let me talk to Salvatore. He has lots of contacts in the shipping business. They always need bilingual people in the office, and it's hard to find anyone with really good English. Just take my advice, and don't mention anything to Gregorio until the time comes."

"Do you think it's a good idea? I don't want to hide anything from him."

"I think it's a great idea," Liz said.

"Me too," Deirdre said.

"Maybe you're right. Just ask, though." Iris said. "As for Gregorio, I guess we'll cross that bridge when we come to it."

"I also think we should order another drink," Liz said, signaling to the waiter as the speaker concluded her presentation to a round of polite applause.

Whether it was due to the release of tension from having shared her concerns with her friends, or having drafted a Plan B, or the hilarious way Liz had of imitating the ladies at the club, or the two gin and tonics on an empty stomach, Iris couldn't stop laughing as she drove the trio home, up and down the slopes and bends of the Via Aurelia, in her practical white station wagon. They had just passed the town of Nervi, when she rounded a curve too quickly, and was waved down by the *carabinieri* at a road blockade.

"*Merda!*" Iris said, as she pulled the car over. Swear words sounded nicer to Iris in Italian, though she used them infrequently, and only when Gregorio and his family were out of earshot. "What am I gonna tell Gregorio if I get fined for drunken driving? He's already cut off my glass of wine at dinner!"

"No one's going to fine you, Iris. They're looking for terrorists at these blockades. Just pretend you don't speak Italian," Liz instructed her. "That's what I do when I get stopped. It's quicker, not to mention more fun."

"I'll never be able to fake it," Iris said as one of the officers approached the car, one hand on the Beretta slung over his shoulder. Her usual agitation at being confronted by authorities must have been quelled slightly by the cocktails; instead of feeling intimidated by the officer's uniform, she found herself admiring the black jacket with silver buttons, the white bandoleer hanging diagonally from his left shoulder, the red stripes running down the outside seam of black trousers.

"It's child's play," Liz said. "You'll see."

"We'll back you up," Deirdre said.

"*Buongiorno,*" said the officer, touching the rim of his hat as he nodded his head and peered in the window, scrutinizing the occupants of the car.

"*Buongiorno,*" Iris replied, imitating the worst of the accents she could recall hearing that afternoon at the Foreign Women's Club.

"*Documenti, per favore,*" the man said.

"*No capisco,*" Iris said, flashing him a smile. "I don't understand."

"Documents. *Patente. Passaporto.*"

"Oh, yes!" Iris said. "Sure. Just a minute. *Momento.*" She reached for the purse Deirdre passed to her from the back seat. She fumbled with the zippers, then took her time fishing for her wallet as she reviewed her options. She did not want to show him her Italian driver's license, and did not have the habit of carrying her passport around with her. She glanced at the photograph of her smiling father at an outdoor café in Portofino, which she always carried in her wallet, and noticed the corner of a blue card sticking out from behind it, hoping it was what she thought it was. She tugged at the card, and was happy to discover she had never removed her New York State driver's license from her wallet after her last trip home. She handed it to her interrogator.

"Iris Capotosti?" the *carabiniere* inquired. "This is you?"

"Yes, sir," Iris replied.

"*Ma il nome è italiano.* The name is Italian."

"Yes, my grandfather. *Mio nonno.* Capotosti. He came from L'Aquila. Abruzzese," Iris said, dropping her eyes to his firearm, which was eye-level with her, fortunately pointed to the ground.

Liz placed a hand over her mouth. "Lay off the Italian!" she said, wrapping the words in a fake cough.

"New York?" the *carabiniere* asked, as he perused both sides of the document.

Iris was not sure what the question was. She answered, "Yes, New York. Rochester, New York."

"*Mio zio sta a Yonkers.* You know Yonkers? My uncle stays there."

"Sure, Yonkers! Fantastic place. You should visit!" Iris said, as she continued smiling up at the man. He was probably around her age, possibly younger. Her eyes were drawn again to his firearm; the sight of a loaded weapon so close up both fascinated and frightened her.

"*Signorina* Capotosti," the paramilitary policeman said, reverting to his formal stance. "This is not Monza. No Gran Premio." He wagged his index finger in Iris's face.

"No," Iris said, shaking her head in agreement, like a child sensing she would get away with a scolding instead of a spanking if she acted as though she had learned her lesson.

"*Vada, vada.* You go. But remember. *Prudenza.* This road is *pericoloso*, Italian drivers are *pericolosi.* Very dangerous! You know?"

"Yes! I know," Iris said, smiling up at him and batting her eyes. "Like Italian men are *pericolosi!*"

The *carabiniere* handed Iris back her driver's license, touched the brim of his hat and made a circular motion with his forearm, indicating that she was free to go.

"Jesus, Mary, Joseph and all the Holy Martyrs! Who would've guessed our angelic little Iris was such a fine fibber?" Deirdre said with a laugh, as they drove away.

"Funny," Iris said. "It was easier than I thought."

She hoped the nice young *carabiniere* would never have to fire that dreadful gun. Or that he wouldn't be too disappointed if he ever made it to Yonkers.

If Iris did not deem the Foreign Women's Club worthy of her wardrobe, the Genoa branch of Transoceanica was even less deserving of such ladylike finery. When the part-time job opportunity presented itself with surprising rapidity through Liz's husband, Gregorio had been adamant that Iris politely decline. They did not need the money, he said, and she must avoid getting run down. But Iris had found the nerve to insist that it would be good for her to get out of the house more, that working half days would leave her plenty of time to take care of him and the house and still get her proper rest, and that having something else to think about besides babies would help her shake off the depression she had been experiencing. In the end, Gregorio surrendered to her Irish-Abruzzese stubbornness and consented, as long as she promised to quit the moment she became pregnant, which would no doubt happen soon after her operation.

When Iris was interviewed for the job, she found the title of "foreign correspondent" intriguing; it conjured up images of a quick-paced environment akin to that of an international newsroom. Though the telex room did add a touch of "breaking news" urgency to the ambiance when the machine spontaneously came to life and spewed out notices of general averages and total losses, Iris's job consisted of translating the technical correspondence that bounced back and forth between marine insurance claims adjusters in London, New York, New Delhi, Stockholm and hosts of other cities around the world, and the consignees, shippers, and forwarding agents on the Italian end. She performed her duties in a dreary shaft of a room, where she sat at a massive walnut desk for four hours each day. On the left corner of the desk sat a grey telephone with a rotary dial, which rang twice a day: once just minutes after she arrived, when Gregorio called before scrubbing up to check that she had made it to the office and wish her a good day; the second time a few hours later, when Gregorio slipped away from the operating room between surgeries, to call and tell her to make sure not to miss her train, so she could spend a restful afternoon at home. One day soon, she promised herself, she would stay in the city for lunch (she saw no real need to tell Gregorio), so she could go to the music store when it reopened for afternoon business. Iris always stopped to admire the guitars in the window, though the shop was still closed when she arrived in the morning and already closed for lunch when she left. She had been eyeing one acoustic guitar in particular, an Italian-made Eko, which was reasonably priced. She toyed with the idea of buying it at the end of the month, when she received her first paycheck. Ever since playing a few tunes with Uncle Alfred during her last visit home, she had been thinking of taking the instrument up again. Uncle Alfred had been patient, as usual, but as she struggled to remember the most basic chords, she was embarrassed at having forgotten so much of what he had taught her.

On the right hand corner of the desk stood a stack of technical dictionaries with yellowed pages and fractured spines. Between the volumes and the phone were two towers of color-coded folders containing the sheaves of documents that Iris must sift through in search of substantiation that a claim should be settled. Her daily goal was to make the pile of new files on the right diminish, by consequence of which the pile on the left would rise. Though the job could not be defined as exciting, Iris felt a surge of satisfaction each time she uncovered a determining piece of evidence: a surveyor's expert opinion, a remark scribbled on a bill of lading, a mistranslated clause, a photograph of the insufficient lashing of cargo or the broken seal on a container door. Each completed translation, each settled claim, each transfer of a folder from the right pile to the left, filled Iris with a sense of order and sometimes even pride.

The dozen other young women employed by Transoceanica shared an open space where they assembled the documentation that became the files that ended up on Iris's desk, as they gossiped in Genoese dialect, to the amusement of their boss, Elio Bacigalupo. Italians had a fetish for formal titles, and anyone with a university degree was called a doctor: *il dottore* for men, *la dottoressa* for women. *Il Dottore*, as Bacigalupo was referred to by the girls (Iris, by virtue of the fact that they spoke English together, was given the privilege of calling him Elio), sat at a cluttered desk at the rear of the room, where he was close enough to keep an eye on the girls and, more importantly, eavesdrop on their conversations as they stapled and typed and filed. A polyglot and pedagogue by passion, provocative and observant by nature, Elio had the habit of writing down on a chalkboard that hung behind his desk the juiciest morsels of gossip he overheard each day, accompanied by a comment in Latin, or Swedish, or Mandarin Chinese, which he translated for Iris. He had taken a special liking to her, and had insisted that she be segregated from her co-workers so she could concentrate better on her translations. Iris agreed that it would be difficult to hear herself think in the chatty common room, but suspected the real reason the boss gave her a private office was that he wanted to keep her to himself. He visited her office several times a day, having decided that she must learn a selection of expressions in Genoese, which he repeated to her and made her repeat to him, until she got the pronunciation just right. He sat in front of Iris for endless stretches, his logorrheic tongue keeping pace with his wandering mind as it skipped from one topic to another, while Iris fidgeted with her pen and glanced repeatedly at the pile of files awaiting her attention.

His soliloquy sailed through explanations of the ideograms he was currently studying, to the theories of Noam Chomsky, to random conjectures about Iris, her family and her private life, interspersed with accounts of his experiences abroad and unsolicited confidences about his past and present love affairs. Though some of the information he shared was interesting or humorous, Iris grew increasingly irritated by his visits and bored by the anecdotes which he, like all those who loved the sound of their own voices, repeated *ad nauseum*.

Each morning between eight and a quarter past, the Transoceanica girls arrived in their smart street clothes, disappeared into the cloak room, and reemerged a few moments later dressed in their uniforms of a white cotton blouse and a grey linen skirt, both of which were always wrinkled from use. Fashionable footwear was also abandoned in the cloak room, in favor of open-toed house shoes with rubber soles that whined their way up and down the tiled corridor outside Iris's office. Iris worked with her door open, and at first, she always looked up from her paperwork and smiled when she heard someone approach; those passing always took a peek at the foreign bird in a cage but never stopped to say hello. Eventually, she learned to tune out the squeaky announcements of possible visitors and keep her head buried behind the stacks of dictionaries and files.

One morning, the cloakroom door had been left open a crack, and as she walked by, she overheard the girls giggling and mimicking her accent, referring to her as the *Regina americana*, "the American queen." She slipped into her office, embarrassed and hurt that the girls would talk about her behind her back, but a part of her wondered whether it was her fault; whether she should try harder to make friends with them, maybe bake them a batch of brownies or something, while another part of her wondered why she should care. The truth was, she did care, but not enough to wear one of those dreadful grey skirts and shuffle around the office in slippers.

"Why don't you have some more spinach, Iris?" Isabella asked. "It's rich in iron, you know. Good for a woman's blood."

"Thank you, Isabella," Iris said, taking the serving dish from her; it was hard to ruin steamed spinach. Iris marveled at the lack of creativity her mother-in-law put into the food she prepared, and figured her insistence on preparing a meal for the family every Sunday must stem from a sense of duty connected with her role as an Italian mother, rather than from the joy of preparing and sharing a meal with those she loved.

Filial duty rather than a craving for his mother's cooking was certainly what bound Gregorio to this tradition; he and Iris never missed Sunday dinner, unless there was an emergency at the hospital. When the conditions were good for scuba diving, he went out early and managed to be back before noon, in time to pay his respects to God at the last Mass, then to his mother, who would be upset if she were to find out he had been diving. She had always objected to the sport, and tried to convince Iris to join forces in discouraging him from going, but Iris remained neutral. As far as she was concerned, Gregorio could dive all he wanted, as long as he didn't try to make her take lessons again.

"Speaking of spinach, you need to finish yours, Antonio!" Cinzia said to her eldest son, named after her deceased father. At least someone would bear the man's first name, if Iris could not do the family the honor of providing an heir to his surname.

The collective consumption of spinach was interrupted by the jangling of the phone. "*Santa pazienza*! Who could be so rude as to call at one o'clock on a Sunday?" Isabella said.

"Shall I get it, Mamma?" Gregorio asked, already half-standing.

"No, I make the rules here, and I'll enforce them." Once a judge, always a judge, Iris thought, as Isabella dabbed the corners of her mouth with her napkin, rose, and shuffled off to the telephone in the hallway on rectangles of felt, polishing the marble as she went.

"*Pron-to?*" Not everyone could cram such a dose of irritation into two short syllables. The table fell silent, all ears pricked for clues as to who the untimely caller might be. "Yes, this is Isabella." Pause. "Yes, Iris is here." Longer pause. "*O Madonna santa! O Dio santo!*" She raised her voice a notch and called, "Gregorio! Gregorio!"

"What is it, Mamma?" Gregorio said, pushing away from the table and scurrying off to his mother. Iris looked around the table at the raised eyebrows, turned heads, cold spinach, frozen forks; she wondered whether she had heard right, why Isabella had mentioned her name.

"Hello … oh … I see … when? … good God … I'm so sorry … of course … No, I'll take care of it … don't worry. We'll call later … I will … Goodbye." Iris had heard Gregorio speak in English many times, but had never before heard his voice falter. In fact, his calm, even voice had been one of the first qualities she had admired in him, that day he had met her and Auntie Rosa at the train station. Unlike the males in her family, he never spoke in an unnecessarily loud or emphatic tone, but always conveyed a sense of authority, and reassurance. She had often imagined that voice issuing orders in the operating room, while he monitored the vitals of the patients he kept suspended between life and death. The voice dropped to a murmur as Gregorio conferred with Isabella, then returned to the dining room, straightening his tie as he walked, his mother gliding in on his heels.

"Iris," Gregorio said, again in control, concise. "That was your sister Violet."

"Violet?" Iris could understand Isabella's intolerance for phone calls during meal time because her father had always enforced the same rule, but it angered her that she wouldn't make an exception for an overseas call from her sister. "Why didn't you let me talk to her?"

"It wasn't necessary."

"What do you mean, it wasn't necessary?" Anger flushed her face, tightened her throat. "If she called, it was because she wanted to talk to *me*, I'm sure."

"Violet told me what she needed to say," Gregorio said, pulling his chair next to hers and taking her hand. "Everything will be all right."

"What do you mean?" The very fact that he felt it necessary to say that meant that something was *not* all right. "What's wrong? Has something happened to Violet?"

"No, nothing has happened to Violet," Gregorio said.

"Well then, what *has* happened?" Violet did not get up at seven AM to make an overseas phone call to Gregorio's mother's house, just to tell Gregorio to tell Iris that nothing was wrong. Even if she was fine, there were three other sisters, seven brothers, a father, a mother, an aunt, an uncle and a dozen nieces and nephews to worry about on the other side of the Atlantic.

"It's your father." Gregorio cleared his throat. "Myocardial infarction."

"What?" Why couldn't he just talk like a normal person for once?

"*Piccolina,* your father has had a heart attack."

"A heart attack! Oh, my God! I have to go see him. Please, can I go, Gregorio?" Iris jumped to her feet, her eyes darting around the room. There must be an escape route, an emergency exit.

"It's too late, Iris," Gregorio said. "They did what they could."

"What do you mean, it's too late?"

"Your father is deceased."

"But he was fine! He wasn't sick a day in his life!"

"I'm sorry, *Piccolina*." Gregorio said. She hated that calm voice. She hated the way Isabella just stood there; she hated the way Franco just sat there, she hated the way Cinzia and the kids just stared at her. No one spoke, no one ran to her, no one threw their arms around her and hugged her tight. No one told her it was all right to cry, because no one wanted to see her cry, and no one knew her father well enough to want to cry with her.

"It can't be true!" Iris said, grabbing the edge of the table for support. There was too much life in him, too much emotion, too much anger, for him to be dead. A pain shot through her chest; she was sure she could feel her heart breaking, like her father's had. Shock and grief took control of her body, making it tremble and convulse in strange ways. The merry-go-round of faces with immobile expressions spun around her as she slid to the floor. The shiny marble was cold against her cheek; arms tugged at her, encircled her, but could not rescue her from the grip of grief. It pulled her down toward the blackness, away from the spinning faces and receding voices. Downward she spiraled, down, down, until the blackness swallowed her.

A scratchy woolen blanket smelled of Isabella. A hand with a wedding band and neat nails clasped her hand.

"Daddy," Iris whimpered.

"You need to rest, *Piccolina*," Gregorio said, pushing her hair back from her damp forehead. "You've had a terrible shock."

"I want to go to Daddy."

"There's nothing you can do for your father now."

"I want to go. Please, Gregorio." She tried to get up, but could barely lift her head from the pillow. She had never felt so weak.

"You just stay put, *Piccolina*. You're in no condition to go anywhere now."

"But I have to see Daddy. And poor Auntie Rosa. And poor Violet and Lily and everyone. And poor Mom. I need to be there, with them."

"I'm taking care of it. I'll look into available flights tomorrow when the agency opens."

"I want to go now!" Her chest heaved with emotion, tears stung her eyes.

"What you want and what's best for you are not always the same thing, *Piccolina*. You lost consciousness, and you need to recover from the shock before you we can even discuss the possibility of moving you from here. That's why I'm going to give you a little injection now. You must rest."

"But I don't want to rest. I want to go home."

"Shhh," Gregorio said. "Everything will be all right." The tone of his voice was calm and firm, the look in his blue eyes steady and reassuring. She hardly winced at the prick of the needle.

"Daddy," she moaned, as the blackness returned, enveloping her, releasing her.

"Welcome back, *dormigliona*." Iris blinked, as Gregorio smiled down at her. Why was she sleeping on Isabella's sofa? Could she have dozed off? The last thing she remembered was the phone ringing, and then Gregorio's voice speaking in English, and then …

"Gregorio. Please tell me it was a bad dream."

Gregorio stroked his goatee, shook his head. Iris trembled.

"I'm cold," she said. Gregorio tucked the blanket closely around her, but the prickly wool made her shiver more. She tried to get up, but Gregorio anchored the blanket in place with his hands.

"I have to go," she said.

"First you have to recover, *Piccolina*."

"There's no way I can recover. I just have to go. Please take me to the airport. I'll find a flight." Iris rubbed her eyes. They felt like they were filled with sand, or shards of glass. "What time is it?"

"It's Monday morning," Gregorio said.

"What do you mean, Monday morning?"

"You were in a terrible state, *Piccolina*," Gregorio said. "I had to keep you sedated all night."

"But I didn't want to sleep! I want to go home."

"And you will go home, very soon. You have reservations for tomorrow."

"Tomorrow? But I need to go now!"

"Look at you, you must realize you are in no condition to travel. There was no way you could make it on a flight this morning. If you feel up to it in a while, I'll take you home and we'll pack your bag. Then you can rest. Rest is what you need. And tomorrow I'll put you on that plane. I've already told Violet when to expect you."

"I wanted to talk to Violet. Why didn't you let me?" Waves of blackness washed over her, weighing her down, like a gull mired in an oil slick. A series of images pierced the numbness of her mind: images of a man smoking Parliaments and drinking coffee and handing out nickels on allowance day and mowing lawns and shoveling snow and fixing bicycles and slaughtering rabbits and medicating wounds and laughing and yelling and denying you what you wanted, but never leaving you alone. She tasted sweet tea sliding down her throat, watched a suitcase being packed with an old lady's sad suits and sweaters before the blackness came for her again.

Iris sat speechless and motionless, strapped into her seat next to Gregorio as he drove her to the airport, the pelts of dead animals lying across her lap. Puffs of yellow dangled from mimosa branches, a sharp winter wind rustled the fronds of barren date palms. She squeezed her eyes shut against the sun shining in a cloudless sky. She couldn't say where her father was now, but he must wait for her. She couldn't let him go until she saw him one last time, until she told him she understood.

6. LILY

Despite all the predictions of failure that had been made regarding Joe's sales career, he had led the La Casa Bella sales chart his first month, and for several consecutive months after, and earned the award for top salesman by the end of his first year. Joe had a sense for people; he had radar for their vulnerabilities and the skill to exploit their weaknesses. He oozed opiate Italian charm topped with old-fashioned courtesy. He was a natural. He sold furnishings and appliances with the same ease and determination with which he'd won Lily over and persuaded her to marry him.

By the time they celebrated their third anniversary, Lily and Joe had managed to purchase a starter home - a bungalow in the section known as Dutchtown, which they'd managed to buy with a government-funded mortgage whose greatest feature was that it didn't require any money down. On moving day, they lugged furniture and unpacked boxes until they both collapsed from exhaustion.

Just before midnight, the clamor of the phone startled Lily from a freshly fallen sleep. She sprinted across the carpet, stubbing her toe on the box marked "living room", which sat in the middle of the floor. She had to get to the phone before it rang again and woke Joe.

"Shit!" she called, finishing the trip to the phone hopping on one foot. "Hello?"

"Hello... Lily?"

"Yes," she whispered groggily. Lily didn't recognize the voice, although it conjured a familiar sense of dread. "Who is this?"

"It's Dr. Bob."

Doctor Bob. The Capotosti family friend with a prescription pad. He must have been a real doctor, although as far as Lily knew, no one had ever gone to see him in an office. Dr. Bob would willingly write you a script for painkillers or sleeping pills, no questions asked - just remember him at the holidays. Maybe if he hadn't been such a convenient pharmacist, someone would have noticed that Dolores was in trouble when there was still time to save her. But easy supplies of Vicodin and Valium have a way of blurring priorities. In addition to helping Dolores recover from her divorce from Julius "the creep" Corvo, Dr. Bob oversaw Lily's father's pharmaceutically managed state - which toggled from rage to stupor - during the very messy separation and long awaited divorce between Lily's parents. There were only a couple of reasons why Dr. Bob would call Lily, and only one reason to do so at eleven forty-seven on a Saturday night.

"I'm afraid I have some bad news," said Dr. Bob.

"What is it?" Lily's knees grew weak and her heart thumped.

"It's your Dad," said Dr. Bob. "He's had a massive coronary. He's passed."

He's passed. What the fuck was that supposed to mean? Lily did not attempt to mask her anger. "You mean he's dead?" she shouted.

"Yes," said Dr. Bob. "I'm afraid so." After a long pause, he added, "Are you there? Are you OK?"

"Yes, I'm here."

"The only local family members I haven't been able to get a hold of are Louis and your mother, Lily. Do you think you could pass the word on to them?"

"Yeah, sure." *Pass the word. The circus is coming to town. Star Market is having a special on ham. Dad died.*

Joe emerged from the bedroom. "What the hell is going on?"

"My father died." Lily let the receiver drop into its cradle. "My mother and Louis are not answering their phones. I have to go knock on their doors and tell them. Then I suppose I'll need to go over to Chestnut Crest." *So many things to do. And then I'll probably start feeling sad.* Lily wandered to the back door and pulled on her boots.

"Now? It's the middle of the night," said Joe.

"I don't know, Joe - my father just died. I've never done this before." Lily fished her car keys out of her purse. "Can I just call you later?"

"I don't see why you have to be the one to go around in the middle of the night waking everyone up. We're in the process of moving here."

"Yeah, well, Violet and Alexander both have little ones at home." Lily cringed. Watching her siblings have babies reminded Lily of her own failed attempts at staying pregnant, of the cousins her children would have had. If her first pregnancy hadn't ended in miscarriage, her baby would be more than two years old by now. Even if her second one had gone to term, she would have a toddler running around, getting into trouble. At least she'd done the right thing by keeping the second pregnancy a secret from everyone except Joe. Her sisters wouldn't know what it was like to fail at anything, and her mother sure couldn't relate - even if she took enough time away from her social crusades to try. Lily sure didn't need more questions to field. Joe's were bad enough, grilling her about what she'd done and where she'd been as if she had somehow caused the pregnancy to purge itself from her body. As if she didn't feel bad enough about it as it was. Having a baby was the one thing she was sure she could get right. Women all over the world did it all the time - sometimes even by accident. She didn't know what it was about her that wasn't put together right. How was she supposed to know why these things happen, especially since the doctors didn't even know? Everyone liked to call it the miracle of life. Miracles are God's to give. Or not.

"Plus, I'm closest. I don't mind. What would I do here anyway? It's not like I can just go back to sleep." She could, though. If she turned the lights off and climbed into bed, she was pretty sure she could fall right back to sleep, pretend none of this was happening.

After Lily had delivered the news to Louis - who just stood in his living room and stared as though he were trying to discern whether Lily was really standing there telling him that their father was dead or whether he was only having a bad dream, Lily drove to her mother's and banged on the door. A light flicked on in a second floor window, followed by the back porch light, followed by a finger pushing aside the curtains, followed by Lily's mother's face through the crack. ·

"Did he crash the car, or did he have a heart attack?" she asked Lily through a voice thick with sleep.

"Heart attack," said Lily.

As they pulled into the driveway at Chestnut Crest, Lily's mother let out a yelp. Lily realized it was the first time either one of them had been there since the day her father had her mother arrested. Lily suddenly doubted the wisdom of bringing her mother there, considering that the Order of Protection her father received stipulated that she wasn't allowed within a hundred feet of the place. But maybe the Order of Protection wasn't valid anymore, now that there was no one left to protect.

They stepped into the kitchen to find Auntie Rosa sitting at the table, rocking and weeping. Charles was on one side of her, William on the other, holding her hands. She looked up at Lily and her mother, her mouth agape, her eyes wide, and Lily braced herself for a display of loyalty-induced hysteria. She might kick them out. Or blame them. Or worse, she might look at them with those eyes of crucifixion she saved for serious suffering.

"Betty! Betty!" Auntie Rosa called out through her sobs. "He's gone! My baby brother is gone!"

"Yes, I know," said Lily's mother, raising her right hand, touching the knuckle of her index finger to the end of her nose, in a vain attempt to hold back ambivalent tears.

Lily had stood in this very same spot when she'd heard about Dolores. The same clock measured the moments as they dragged past, and the same strange sense of confusion surrounded her. Although now the kitchen was surprisingly tidy; clean dishes were stacked in the drainer, and a fresh hand towel hung over the door handle of the stove. Either her father had learned to care for himself, or he had found a woman. In any case, Lily wondered if he had arrived at the realization that he didn't need Lily as much as he'd thought he did. Yet if he had realized that, then surely he would have also realized that he had placed unreasonable expectations on her. She'd always known that day of awakening would come for him. So why hadn't he apologized? Why hadn't he called her and said, "Hey, Lily of the Valley, I'm putting on a pot of coffee. Why don't you bring over some sweet rolls from Dunkin' Donuts - we need to talk." That was how it would begin. It would end with him telling her how sorry he was, how unfair he had been to her. He would tell her he loved her, they would hug, and Lily would once again consider this place home. He couldn't have died yet. They weren't finished. They were still so mad at each other.

One by one, members of the family appeared. Henry, Alexander, Louis - all red-eyed and silent. Violet stepped into the living room, and upon seeing the empty chair where her father always sat, and the smoke stand that still held an ashtray full of Parliament butts, she fainted and fell to the floor.

"Violet!" shouted Lily's mother. The boys picked Violet up off the floor, carried her upstairs, and laid her in the room that Ricci used when he was on break from classes at NYU.

As the black sky turned gray, the room filled with Capotosti children, Jasmine and Charles being the last to file in.

"Where's Uncle Alfred?" Lily asked.

"He had to go to the hospital to fill out some paperwork," said Auntie Rosa. "I couldn't do it, I just couldn't do it again." She and Lily exchanged a glance that reflected a memory of Dolores. "He'll be back soon."

By six o'clock, every seat in the living room was occupied except for their father's beat-up, threadbare, spring-worn old chair. Auntie Rosa limped across the room, and sat down in it.

"I can't b'lieve it," she groaned, caressing the armrests, as if she could still feel him there. "I just can't b'lieve it. First Our Lord took my little sister Teresa, then Ma and Pa, then Dolores, and now this - my *bebi*... they're all gone."

Auntie Rosa took every death personally, as if God snatched specific people up from the earth deliberately to cause her pain - as if no one ever died whom she did not love, and as if no one who ever died left anyone behind but her.

Lily felt conspicuous as hers were the only set of dry eyes in the room. She wished she had fainted like Violet, then people would really think she was suffering, that she cared, but without all the expectations of performance. In hopes of escaping the scrutiny of her sobbing siblings, she retrieved the dirty ashtray from the smoke stand and took it into the kitchen to empty it. She pulled the iron skillet out from the cupboard, and a carton of eggs from the refrigerator. It had been years since she had prepared breakfast in this kitchen, but her hands remembered where everything was, and she moved among the appliances and utensils as if she were one of them. It felt more honest than sitting in the next room crying for all the wrong reasons, or not crying for all the right ones.

The aroma of freshly popped toast drew people into the kitchen, and Lily busily set plates and flatware at the table, pouring orange juice and setting a pot of coffee to brew.

Auntie Rosa sat at the table. "I'm not hungry, Lily," she said, picking up a half slice of toast and spreading orange marmalade on it.

The back door opened and Uncle Alfred entered, his eyes rimmed with sorrow, holding his gray wool fedora in one hand and a plastic bag, through which their father's personal effects could be viewed, in the other. Auntie Rosa spied the bag and let out a wail. Uncle Alfred froze in his spot, as if in shock at the sight of family members gathered around the table for a meal, his brother's presence defined only by his wallet, his watch, and a brown plastic prescription bottle.

Auntie Rosa reached her hand toward Uncle Alfred. "Lemme see, Al... lemme see." Uncle Alfred walked forward mechanically and placed the bag into her hand. "Oh, *bebi, bebi*... my little Carlo," said Auntie Rosa, opening the bag and reaching her hand inside. "Alfred!" she cried, her eyes widening. "Where are the other medications? There's only one here."

"They took them, Ro," said Uncle Alfred with a sob. "The paramedics took his medications and brought them to the hospital and the doctors kept them all except that one. They wanted to do an autopsy." Uncle Alfred's bottom lip trembled. "An autopsy, Ro." He gasped. "I told them we did not want that. 'No autopsy,' I said. Then they asked Dr. Bob all sorts of questions and asked him to sign some sort of paper before they would let me go."

"Jesus, Mary, and Joseph," said Auntie Rosa, crossing herself. "Thank God Dr. Bob was there, is all I have to say." She sat quietly for a moment with her eyes closed and then let out a deep sigh. "Sit down, Alfred, have some toast. You've got to keep up your strength, after all." She surveyed the mound of eggs and bacon on the table and said, "My goodness, Lily, I can't b'lieve you did all this. You remind me of Iris."

"Oh, yeah," said Lily, filling a row of cups with hot coffee. "We're just two peas in a pod, me and Iris."

By seven o'clock, Violet emerged from the stairway, holding an elastic band between her front teeth, her fingers entangled in her thick chestnut-brown hair, weaving it into a braid.

"Has anyone called Marguerite or Iris?" she asked softly.

"Iris!" Auntie Rosa wailed. "I couldn't do it, Violet... I can't do it... And today is Sunday; I'm quite sure they are all at Isabella's enjoying a nice family dinner... what a terrible shock it will be... Iris will be devastated."

"Don't worry about it, Auntie Rosa," said Violet, "I'll take care of it. I'll try her at home and if she's not there, I try Isabella's. I'll get a hold of her."

Violet grabbed her purse and went into the sunroom. Jasmine pulled the doors closed behind her, taking a place next to Auntie Rosa on the couch. After about ten minutes, muffled weeps began to periodically escape through the cracks of the door. Violet emerged, blowing her nose.

"I talked to Marguerite and Gregorio - he insisted on breaking the news to Iris; he wanted to make sure she was properly prepared. Marguerite was out of town; she'll be here this evening. Gregorio said he'd make arrangements for Iris. Since it's Sunday, it's complicated, but his friend owns a travel agency and he's going to get Iris on the first available flight. A flight tomorrow morning."

"Oh, thank the Lord," said Auntie Rosa. "Did you hear that, Lily? Iris is practically on her way."

"Yes, I heard. So is Marguerite."

"Poor Iris... over there all alone."

"She has Gregorio." Jasmine patted Auntie Rosa's hand. "He will take care of her until she gets home. Don't worry."

Funny, thought Lily. *I thought Iris was home.*

Violet swung her long braid over her shoulder, then bent and picked up her purse, retrieving a small note pad and a pen from inside. "We'll have to make the arrangements. And write an obituary."

"I've got that handled," said Henry. "I'm gonna run upstairs and take a shower, so I can be at the funeral home when they open at nine o'clock."

Violet opened her mouth and drew in a breath, but Henry disappeared up the stairs before she could speak. She leaned over and whispered to Jasmine, who just shook her head "no."

Violet sat on the couch and let out a sigh. "Within twenty-four hours this place is going to be lousy with Capotostis. We'd better make sure there's food and everything. William, could you snoop around and see if you can find any cash we can use to feed people? Then each of us will have to keep track of whatever we spend out of pocket, and we'll make sure everyone gets reimbursed, OK?"

"I'm quite sure Iris is going to pay an arm and a leg to fly here on the spur of the moment like this," said Auntie Rosa.

"Well, Auntie Rosa," said Jasmine, "I'm not sure we can do anything about that, but I don't think we need to worry about Iris. She can manage just fine."

After Iris had moved to Italy, Auntie Rosa's favoritism of her had blossomed into a fixation, as though she could compensate for the distance between them by thinking and talking about Iris at every opportunity, perhaps creating the illusion of her presence. She saw the world through her own personal Iris lens. When she'd stopped over unexpectedly one Saturday while Lily and Joe were having their new furniture delivered (thanks to a hearty discount and installment payments from La Casa Bella), Auntie Rosa exclaimed, "Wait until Iris sees this!" When Auntie Rosa saw the letter to the editor that Lily had published in the local paper presenting her argument for a traffic light in front of SaveMart as a way to cut down on traffic congestion, she called Lily and said, "Did you send a copy to Iris?" And when Lily had announced that she was pregnant, Auntie Rosa cried out, "Oh, poor Iris!" Lily sometimes wondered if her aunt had been relieved about the miscarriage, just to save poor Iris from feeling bad.

Perhaps Auntie Rosa recognized Iris was living the life that she herself may have lived, had it not been for any one of a number of events that had transpired along the way. They were events over which she had no control, but that had irrevocably shaped her destiny: her parents' decision to emigrate to America, Teresa's drowning, the Depression, Irene Capotosti's crippling arthritis which did not afflict Auntie Rosa physically but which - by emotional association and because it left her mother dependent upon her for everything - rendered both of them invalid.

If things had worked out differently, perhaps Auntie Rosa would be the one living on the Ligurian seaside, married to a successful doctor, shouting, "*Ciao!*" and "*Buongiornò!*" from her terrace as townspeople passed on their way to work or to the market. If things had worked out differently, maybe Iris would be sitting here, offering her a baby to hold, and Lily would be the one Auntie Rosa would have to miss and wonder about. That would undoubtedly have been easier, but wouldn't have provided nearly the same degree of suffering, which was the one thing Auntie Rosa loved nearly as much as she loved Iris.

It was probably a good thing that Auntie Rosa had no children of her own, no one to whom she could pass along the legacy of guilt and punishment that had become marks of the Capotosti crest. Still, it didn't stop her from trying to make a daughter out of Iris. All those years of whisking Iris away on the weekends, of sneaking special presents to her, of holding her close in bed and stocking the cupboards with Iris' favorite treats, and still, Iris up and moved away. She left her, just as everyone she'd loved left her. As it turned out, it wasn't a bad deal for Iris, though. She enjoyed all the benefits of having a mother all to herself, and now - being far away - none of the responsibilities that came along with being an adult child in this family, whose string of needs never seemed to end.

So much depended on who stayed and who went away.

Still hoping to provoke her own grief, Lily returned to Chestnut Crest the next morning to see what tasks needed to be done. Perhaps going through her father's desk to look for necessary papers, or through his dresser to find something to bury him in would make her sad, would finally produce tears. At the very least, being around people who looked like her and shared her history could inspire her and serve as a model for how she should grieve.

"Marguerite! I was hoping I would you see you this morning. What time did you get in?"

"Hey, Lily of the Valley," said Marguerite. She ran red fingernails through her thick dark hair. It was one of the few times in recent years that Lily had seen Marguerite when she wasn't meticulously put together, with her nails matching her lips, matching her bag, matching her commanding presence.

"I got in late. I know I look a fright."

"You don't," said Lily. "You actually look pretty great."

"Thanks to Jane Fonda," said Marguerite, gliding her hands over her slender hips. "She is my new idol these days. Do you work out, Lily?"

"Work out? Like go running?"

"Yes - exercise, fitness... it's great for the skin and hair, too. Not that you can tell from looking at me right now."

"I'd hate to think what anyone could tell from looking at me," said Lily.

"Well," said Marguerite, taking stock of Lily's clothes and hair. "You get a free pass for now, but when all of this is over, you should check out Jane's videos, and give yourself a little health and fitness makeover. In fact, I'm going to leave you my copy - believe me, you'll thank me for it."

Lily immediately felt even more self-conscious and exposed. As an active member of the artist community and as someone who always wore the latest styles, Marguerite knew about such things, and if she thought Lily needed a makeover, then she must look even worse than she thought, even worse than she felt. She reached into her purse and fished out a tube of pink lipstick, squeezing it into the pocket of her jeans.

It was strange for Lily to be sitting in the room where she had spent so many hours of her youth surrounded by her sisters, none of whom she felt she really knew. Over the years, the gap had widened, their ages being the smallest of the wedges between them. By nature of Lily's position as baby girl of the family, she was the last one left at Chestnut Crest - left to fend for herself and eventually for their father, too. She knew they didn't agree with her decision to side with their mother during the separation. They didn't understand; they'd only heard their father's side of the story and they never bothered to ask any of the kids who were actually there. They never bothered to ask Lily to tell them her side. If just one of them had offered her some guidance, looked out for her, she wouldn't have had to choose a parent. She shouldn't have had to.

"I have a unique look," said Violet. "It's called toddlerhood. I can't get Olivia to take a nap to save my life. She always wants to be up and looking around, like something fantastic might happen that she'll miss. It's exhausting. She wants to be part of anything and everything that goes on."

"Sounds like someone I know," said Jasmine, playfully poking Violet in the side with her elbow.

"Are you kidding me?" said Violet. "I would love to take a nice nap in the afternoon, grab a cup of tea, drift off while watching *General Hospital*. Of course that would mean that someone else would have to take some responsibility for the practice for a change."

"Why don't you hire an assistant? Just because it's your practice, doesn't mean you have to do everything," said Jasmine.

"Assistants cost money," said Violet. "I'm a midwife, not a doctor. I can't afford that kind of expense."

"You'd better do something," said Jasmine. "You know that those babies are not going to stop being born."

Lily's eyes stung. She was glad her sisters didn't know about the second miscarriage. They never asked her questions about why she hadn't gotten pregnant again and she didn't offer any explanations. She had so little in common with them as it was; she couldn't afford to feel much more different.

"What you're doing is so important," Jasmine continued. "And not the delusional kind of importance that I have about my work." Jasmine twisted a lock of her long, wavy honey-brown hair with the fingers of her right hand.

Lily reached her own hand up and ran it through her wild mop of curls - the texture of which was too coarse to be worn in the bob cut that she had recently attempted. After years of growing it out, Lily's hair had finally grown back to the length she preferred, but Lucy had convinced her to try for a more modern look. "You should look like you *are* a mommy, not like you *need* a mommy," Lucy had told her. "Short hair is so much more chic." Lucy dug into her ear with her pinky finger. "I've always worn my hair short. All of the most sophisticated celebrities wore short hair - Marilyn Monroe, Lucille Ball... all of them."

It had taken a mere hour to cut off, but it would take years before Lily would again acquire the mane that had been a lifelong trademark of the Capotosti sisters. She wondered if she had the patience to wait. She wondered why, when she loved long hair so much, she had allowed herself to be talked into cutting hers. Again.

"Aren't things at the shelter going well?" Marguerite asked. "I thought since that bastard of a partner moved away, your adoption rate was improving."

"So much of what I do isn't even about the animals anymore," said Jasmine. "It's the business side of things - funding and regulations and community affairs. I really just want to help find homes for some of those little angels, but I spend way too much time on paperwork."

Lily was struck with the familiarity that her sisters had for the details of each other's lives: they were obviously in touch with each other, chatting on the phone, maybe even taking weekend trips to visit one another.

Lily was embarrassed that she didn't even know enough about Jasmine's life to offer a comforting word of reassurance. Then again, her sisters knew nothing about her life, either - not about their new home, certainly not about her life as a Diotallevi. She hoped they would not ask. As long as the details remained private, Lily could pretend that she and her sisters had more in common besides grief and death; she could pretend she was one of them.

"Iris is getting in at eleven, right?" said Jasmine.

"Didn't you hear?" said Violet. "Gregorio called earlier. There was no way for her to get out today. She has to wait until tomorrow."

"But I thought the wake was tomorrow," said Lily. "Are they changing it?" She and Joe had already gotten approved vacation time for Tuesday. Changing the wake was really going to mess things up.

"No can do," said Marguerite.

"You're kidding!?" said Jasmine. "Why don't they just push everything out a day?"

"It's all been booked," said Violet. "Obituary ran in this morning's paper."

"Shit," said Jasmine. "What does that mean?"

"Sounds like it means that by the time Iris gets here, the wake will be over," said Marguerite. " Damn... I feel so bad for her."

Lily did too. Even though their father would be dead, they would all get to see him one more time. And if Iris were there right now, she sure would not be having any trouble finding her tears. Their father deserved to be surrounded by weeping daughters. And Iris deserved to be here.

"Does Auntie Rosa know?" Lily asked.

"Please," said Marguerite. "We had to give her one of Dad's Valiums. Ricci drove her home."

"I still can't believe she couldn't get a flight out today," said Jasmine. "She probably went to that travel agent that tried to help us change our ticket home when we went there," said Marguerite.

"That was nuts," said Jasmine. "I half expected to get off the plane in Rochester, Minnesota."

The exchange might have gone unnoticed by Lily, except that Violet glared at Marguerite, who looked quizzically at Jasmine, who looked at Lily and then cast her gaze down at the bedspread. When had they all gone to visit Iris? Why hadn't she been invited to go? The four women sat in awkward silence until Lily excused herself to go to the bathroom.

As she closed the bedroom door behind her, Lily heard Violet say, "Nice going, Marguerite."

"What?" said Marguerite. "How was I supposed to know we weren't telling Lily?"

The next two days were a whirl of people and errands and emotion and empty beer bottles. By the time Lily arrived at the wake, she still had not shed a tear. She sat at the back of the room, ducking out every hour or so to have a cigarette. Sometimes she would stand alone, gazing out over the gray leafless cemetery across the street, and sometimes she would find Louis, or Violet's husband Todd there, also having escaped to catch a breath of fresh air.

"So," Todd would say. "This sucks."

"Yes, it does," Lily would reply, as they stood shivering in the February wind.

The line of people moved into the funeral parlor, and shuffled up to the casket to cross themselves and offer up a prayer for Carlo Capotosti's soul. Lily watched as family and friends of family cried and hugged and chatted. She struggled to remember the names of those whom Auntie Rosa, Marguerite, Violet, and Jasmine knew so well and seemed so happy to see. To anyone who bothered to notice, Lily may have looked disinterested, sitting against the wall next to her mother, when in truth she just didn't know what to do with herself. Sharing the company of a fellow outcast was better than sitting alone and unnoticed at your own father's wake.

Lily checked her Timex wristwatch. Joe would be getting out of work soon. She was glad that Jasmine and Violet and all the others would see him at her side, comforting her. She wanted them to realize that even if she didn't belong with them, at least she belonged with someone.

"Hey, you -" said Marguerite, holding her hand out to Lily. "Wanna come up with me and say good-bye?"

Even if you didn't know that Marguerite lived in Manhattan, you could tell by the way she looked that she wasn't from Gates. Her maroon brocade suit fit snugly to her curvaceous form, and her wavy hair pertly bounced with the cadence of her confident stride. Lily accepted her warm smile and her hand.

"I don't know if I've ever seen Dad just lying down that way," said Marguerite.

"Me neither, now that you mention it."

"I guess this is one way to get him to stay put and stop screaming so much."

"I guess." Lily's father looked somewhat as he had on her wedding day - which was one of the few times she'd seen him in a nice suit. His salt-and-pepper hair was combed and sprayed firmly into place. A white rosary was carefully braided through his folded hands.

"Hey - check this out, Lily," said Marguerite. She reached down and pulled up the cuff of her father's pant leg, revealing the famous shiny red socks printed with tiny green trees that John had given him one year for Christmas, and which he reserved especially for the holidays. "It must be Christmas," he would announce to the family, as he raised the legs of his pants, "I'm wearing my special socks!" Then he would scratch himself, and laugh until he provoked a coughing fit.

"Oh my God," said Lily with a giggle.

"John picked out his clothes and wanted him to wear those socks. What a wise guy."

The boys had been more involved in the arrangements than Lily - even mysterious Henry, whom no one understood and who simply disappeared and didn't talk to their father for months at a time - even he was crying.

"Lily," said Marguerite, placing her arm around Lily's shoulder. "Do you remember that tiny ceramic Dalmatian that Charles gave Mom one year - the one that used to sit up on the window ledge by the kitchen sink?"

"Wasn't it like dressed up like a fireman? With a red hat and a red coat?"

"Yeah - yeah... don't you remember that time we teased Dad with it, by having it follow him around the house?"

"I do remember that!" said Lily. "First we took it and put it on his smoke stand, just before he sat down to watch the news -"

"And then we put it in the medicine cabinet right next to his aftershave, when we knew he was going to go get ready for church." Marguerite started to gently laugh.

"He kept saying, 'What the hell?' and 'What is going on here?'" A wave of giggles rose up from Lily's belly.

"And then he sat down for a smoke before church, and we had placed the little dog next to his coffee cup."

"Oh, my God," said Lily, trying to squelch her laughter, "When we got into the car to go to church, and he found that little dog on the dashboard -"

"He screamed at the top of his lungs, 'Jeepers Cripes! Where the hell does this dog keep coming from!?"

Lily and Marguerite stood wrapped tightly in each other's arms, their bodies rocking with the force of their efforts to stay quiet. Lily was barraged with images from her childhood. She saw her father getting off the city bus and retrieving his leftover saltines from his suit coat pocket, saved just for her. She saw herself sitting on his lap as a child, trying with all her might to pry apart the fingers of his clenched fist to get the penny inside as he looked on, giggling at her efforts. She saw him at the head of the table on Easter, mumbling prayers she couldn't understand and sprinkling them all with Holy Water that he stole from the vestibule at church. The memories rose and spilled over her, gushing like the tears that now flowed freely down her cheeks. Lily and Marguerite clung to one another as their bodies convulsed with sobs. Lily wondered if she would ever be able to stop.

The firm touch of Joe's hand against Lily's back caused her to look up and find him there, wearing a black suit, a white shirt, and a silver satin necktie. His hair was combed straight back from his face, gelled in place, making his nose appear more prominent and lending him an air of authority. Lily could imagine him saying to his customers, "Buy this furniture. Sign here." They would do it without question, whether they wanted the furniture or not. Marguerite looked up and deposited Lily into Joe's open arms.

"Hey Joe," said Marguerite.

"Hey," said Joe. He leaned over and gave Marguerite a peck on the cheek. "So sorry for your loss."

"Thanks." Marguerite turned toward the casket, crossed herself, and then walked away.

"You doin' OK?" Joe asked Lily. He wrapped her in his arms and kissed her on the top of her head.

"Yes, I just hate this. I hate wakes. And I feel so out of place here."

"Let's go then," said Joe.

"I can't leave, Joe."

"Why not?"

"It's my father's wake - I have to stay for the whole thing." After a moment she added, "Don't I?"

"Let's just tell everyone you don't feel good - they can't make

104

you stay if you're sick. We'll go back to the house, unpack a few more boxes, order a pizza... just you and me... wouldn't that be nice?"

"Yes, but -"

"Look, Lil - do you really think anyone is even going to notice that you're gone? I know they sure as hell won't notice that I'm not here. Marguerite is the only one who even said hello to me, and that was because I went up to her. I'm sorry to say this, but they don't care. If you were Iris or Violet, they would notice, but you know how they are - you know you're not one of the chosen ones."

"I know you're right," said Lily. "But still, I can't just leave."

"Leave it to me," said Joe. He tightened the grip of his arm around Lily's shoulder. "Just stick with me and if anyone stops us, let me do the talking."

Lily looked back over her shoulder at her father's body as Joe turned and led her toward the door.

The following afternoon, the family was to meet at the funeral home and then form a motor procession to the church. Lily arrived before anyone else. She stood in the doorway of the viewing room. Her father's now closed casket sat at the opposite end of the room. Lily slowly marched toward it, accompanied by the pungency of eucalyptus and the melancholy of organ music that wafted down from the speakers in the ceiling.

Lily stood at the casket with her hands shoved into the pockets of her parka. This was the last time she would ever stand in her father's presence.

"I'm so sorry that you died, Dad. Especially so suddenly like that." She struggled to find something meaningful to say – if not for his ears, then at least for her own. "I remember once you took me with you on errands and we stopped at Howard Johnson's. I got a Coke and you got a piece of pecan pie and a cup of coffee, remember?" Lily's tears left streaks of black mascara trailing down the front of her face. "You probably don't. Anyway, I asked you about lockjaw, of all things - I must have heard about it on TV or something. You told me it was called 'The Grin of Death,' and I was horrified. I told you that I wanted to die in my sleep and you said, 'Not me. I want to know it's coming. I want to have time to make my peace with God.'" Lily blew her nose and deposited the used tissue into the pocket of her coat, oblivious that it had fallen straight through and landed on the floor at her feet.

"If I could only ask you one thing, if we could really have a conversation right now, I would ask you if you had a chance to make your peace." Lily broke down sobbing. People should at least be able to die the way they want to. Out of tissues, she wiped her face with the palm of her hand, dragging mascara and tears and snot across her cheek. "I really hope you did."

A door slammed and Lily spun to see Iris standing in the entrance. Her hair - now auburn - was perfectly styled around her heart-shaped face. A sifting of snowflakes - rivaled only by the diamond studs in her ear lobes - twinkled momentarily on her shoulders and then melted under the diffused lighting of the funeral parlor. As she walked toward Lily, she seemed to float, wrapped in her fur coat, her poise, and her beauty. Lily was reminded of the quote that used to hang over Iris' bed when they were in high school: *Beauty is silent eloquence.* Yes, that was Iris.

"Lily - oh, Lily!" Iris hugged Lily and she buried her face into Iris' collar, wishing to disappear into the softness as they sobbed together.

"I didn't get a chance to see him," said Iris. Tears rolled down her face. "I wanted to see him again, you know?"

"I know," said Lily. "I'm so sorry."

"But at least now this is how I will remember him," said Iris. She placed a photo of their father onto the lid of the casket.

Lily picked up the photo. Their father was seated at a table at an outdoor cafe by a shimmering blue body of water, which was dotted with yachts and sailboats. He was tanned and smiling, a cigarette in one hand and a tiny white ceramic cup in the other.

"Where did you get this photo?" Lily asked.

"It was taken in Portofino last summer when he came to visit me. Isn't it cool?"

"Oh - I didn't know he went to Italy." The photo must have been taken shortly after Lily's wedding. Which she paid for herself. Because her father didn't have any money.

"Lily, you should have seen him. He was in his element. We had to pay to sit at that table, and he stayed there nursing that espresso all afternoon. He said, 'I paid for this table, and I'll be damned if I'm going to get up until I'm good and ready.'" Iris took the photo from Lily and carefully set it back on top of the casket. "Yes, he was certainly a different man when he was there. Everyone thought he was my sugar daddy - like he was some sort of famous playboy with a young girlfriend!"

"I've never seen him so happy," said Lily. "I almost didn't recognize him."

In so many of Lily's recent memories of her father he was screaming, or crying, or cursing, or sick. She did not know this dapper man lolling in the sun by the sea. He only existed in a photograph. Maybe that's what happens when people get some distance from their troubles. Lily couldn't help but realize that she was part of what he ran from, and Iris the place to which he fled.

Iris dabbed at her tears with the white cotton handkerchief she'd pulled from her brown leather clutch.

"Let's remember him this way," she said. "Sitting in Portofino, without a care in the world."

"Wishing that he had been that way would make us feel better, but you know Iris, it's not true. It's so sad, but it just wasn't true."

"It was true that day, Lily. Can't you just let me remember the good times? And can't you do the same?"

Lily tried, but when she closed her eyes she only saw him angrily struggling for his life, desperate to make his peace with God.

"I guess I can't," she said.

The sisters stood, each with one hand on the casket, the touchstone to their common past.

Dear Lily,

The last time I saw Dad alive was the Christmas before he died. We
were saying goodbye to each other at the airport, in Rochester. He
hugged me in his usual melodramatic way, but for some reason, it didn't
seem overdone. It was as if all our unspoken feelings had to fit into that
one embrace, and I was afraid of leaving something out. I couldn't bring
myself to let go, until Gregorio dragged me away. I think it was then,
during that visit home, that the consequences of my choice to move so
far away really started to sink in. I realized all kinds of things, good or
bad, could happen to anyone in the family, at any moment, and I
wouldn't be there to share the joy or the sorrow. Just like I hadn't been
there for your wedding, or when our sisters' babies were born, or when
you lost yours. And now I know that you lost two, poor Lily.

There was such a deep look of exhaustion in Dad's eyes that day, I knew
no number of good nights' sleep would ever cure the weariness. Not the
kind of sleep you get on this earth, anyway. I can't say exactly what it
was, but something shifted inside me, and I broke down and cried in his
arms like I had never done before. I bawled all the way to New York, and
never stopped until we were over the Atlantic, when Gregorio finally
slipped me a Valium to shut me up.

But I'm grateful I have such happy memories of his trip to Italy. That was
the first and only time I saw Dad as just a man, on the first real vacation
of his life, toting a secondhand suitcase he had picked up at the flea
market. He said he couldn't really afford the trip because he was
concerned about being able to help the younger boys out with school
expenses. I guess when there were so many of us, the worry (like
everything else) was spread so thin, it didn't do anyone any good.

Maybe by the time he got down to the last three, there was enough of some things to go around. He also said he couldn't rest until he knew where I was living, and how Gregorio was treating me. I don't know if it was true, or whether it was just the argument he used to justify the trip to himself, but that's what finally convinced him to come.

Dad shouldn't have died like that, without any warning. He was my father, he was the one who was supposed to know what was best for me, and make me do it, even if I couldn't see why. As kids, we always had to figure things out for ourselves, and managed to survive just fine. We didn't have a choice then, but as I got older, I felt like I needed more help, instead of less. Like I was already tired of trying to cut it on my own.

As Auntie Rosa said, I could count my lucky stars I had Gregorio. But it wasn't the same. Nothing is the same when your father is gone.

Love,
Iris

From: Lily Capotosti <lilycapotosti@gmail.com>
To: Iris Capotosti <iris.capotosti@gmail.com>
Sent: Mon, September 27, 2010 at 2:10 PM
Subject: Re: The last time I saw Dad

Dear Iris:

If nothing is the same when your father is gone, then I guess things should have gotten better for me. But of course they didn't. It wasn't until after Dad died that I discovered how much he just couldn't stand me, how angry he must have been all that time. I mean, when he said he couldn't give me any money for my wedding (seemed like no one really wanted any part of it), I figured he was broke, not that he needed it to come see you in Italy - not to mention that he never even bothered to come by and see my new house, which was less than five miles away.

We had so much unfinished business, Dad and I. A few years after his death, I decided to go visit his grave - first time I'd been there since the burial. I thought I could finally have a talk with him, say the things I could never find a way to say to him when he was here. I even brought him a cup of coffee from McDonald's. I sat down on the grass, lit up a cigarette, and started to say my piece. I melted into a blob of sorrow as all those memories came flooding back, all just as painful as they'd been back then. I don't know what I thought I was going to accomplish. Did I expect him to reach out and comfort me from beyond the grave? Hug me and tell me he loved me?

He couldn't even do that when he was alive.

Love,
Lily
.

110

7. IRIS

Whoosh-whoosh. The sliding doors at the end of the hall slid open each time someone exited, then snapped shut again, separating the pool of stayers-and-waiters from the stream of comers-and-goers. Iris followed the stream, her rapid steps propelled by the excitement that had climbed as the plane descended, and now bubbled through her veins like fizzy water, washing away her exhaustion.

Each time the doors slid open, her eyes searched the slide-show of images on the other side for snatches of recognizable elements. She had no doubt she would find her sisters even more attractive and accomplished than the previous time she had seen them, and that their reunion would certainly be more cheerful, considering their last get-together had been for their father's funeral.

This was a magical time, when the Capotosti siblings were in their prime, confidently cutting a swath for themselves in the world, not a grey hair or wrinkle yet to be spotted on any of them. After an absence of over two years, Iris was looking forward to catching up with their lives, their families, their careers, their children. What worried Iris about the other side of the sliding doors was having to face the impact of the passing time on the older generation. Her father's death had made her painfully aware of the fact that everything did not stay the same for them, that there came a time when those people whose unchanged presence and unwavering affection had been a point of reference in her life would suddenly grow old, fall ill, die. There would be no hugs smelling of Hai Karate aftershave and Parliaments on the other side of those sliding doors; not today, not ever again.

Whoosh-whoosh, a tall woman with a thick veil of dark hair. *Whoosh-whoosh*, a furry hat with a pom-pom sitting atop a snowy head. *Whoosh-whoosh*, two little girls waving and jumping. *Whoosh-whoosh*, Iris broke into a run and was on the other side, too, the pom-pom ramming her solar plexus. Auntie Rosa might be slowing down, but she certainly wasn't losing her touch.

"Lover-dover!" she cried, pressing her head into Iris's belly, her cane dangling from her wrist. "I can't b'lieve you're here! I just can't b'lieve it!"

"Aunt Iris! Aunt Iris!" Violet's daughters chanted, Olivia instigating her younger sister Castanea to run circles around Iris and Auntie Rosa, their arms extended, pretending to be airplanes. The selection of the girls' names was just one example of Violet's sensitivity and originality. "Flowers are beautiful," she had written to Iris, back when she was expecting Olivia, referring to their parents' quirky tradition of naming the Capotosti girls after blooms. "But they're delicate, they get trampled, they wither. I told Todd that if we have a little girl, I'd like to name her after a tree, rather than a flower." Iris had never talked about baby names with Gregorio; no sense giving names to dreams you know won't come true.

"C'mon, old lady, don't be a hog!" Violet said to Auntie Rosa, placing an arm around Iris to pry her away from their aunt. The hat slid askew, the fake fur pom-pom slipping to one side like a scoop of melting ice cream atop a slice of hot apple pie.

"Violet!" Iris cried, as the sisters hugged, and she buried her nose in Violet's velvet hair, filling her nostrils with the familiar scent of what used to be her favorite herbal shampoo until she moved to Italy. Violet and Iris corresponded regularly, exchanging photographs and news of vacations, jobs, and family, but there were no words to encapsulate the scent of a sister's hair, the warmth of her hug, the look of understanding in her eyes.

Iris was the first to break their embrace; she held Violet at an arm's length to get a better look at her. Physically, she was a beauty: she stood tall and confident, her long dark hair cascading down her back, the multicolored flecks in her grey-green eyes twinkling with benevolence and intelligence, each well-coordinated movement quick and supple, denoting a well-exercised physique. She had little use for cosmetics, which would have detracted from her timeless, symmetric features, marred the rosy brushstroke of her lips, compromised the translucence of her skin, masqueraded the twin half-moons under her eyes that reminded Iris of the heroines in the nineteenth-century English novels she enjoyed reading.

"It's so good to see you! And the girls have grown so much!" Iris said. "Come here you two!" She squatted to embrace Olivia and Castanea.

"I was hoping Lily would be here, too?" she said, checking to see whether she may be standing off to the side somewhere, waiting her turn to be hugged. Maybe she was just a little late; incredibly enough, the plane had landed right on schedule.

"I called her earlier to give her your flight information, but she said she had a tummy ache or something," Violet answered, waving her hand in front of an annoyed expression, as if the excuse were a fly buzzing around her nose. "You look great, Iris! Let me see the new ring you told me about …. Oh my God! That is amazing. Gregorio sure knows how to treat a girl!" She held Iris's hand closer to observe the emerald-cut ruby surrounded by diamond chips, set in a band of eighteen carat gold. Auntie Rosa strained to get a look.

"I can't b'lieve it!" she said, wagging her fake fur pom-pom. "That Gregorio is a gem!"

"Yes, he sure is," Iris said, but her thoughts were elsewhere, skimming over memories of Lily's past stomachaches. She recalled her recurrent "I don't want to go to school if Iris is staying home sick" stomachache of their childhood, when Lily would moan until their mother finally took her temperature, too. As soon she left the room, Iris would sneak the thermometer out of Lily's mouth and put it in her own, then pass it back, complete with her fever, before she returned. Then there was her "feeding chickens and milking cows is not my idea of a summer vacation" stomachache, which had secured her early release from their cousins' farm, leaving Iris stranded there, saddled with both their responsibilities, and both their cows to show at the fair. Maybe this was her "I don't really want to see Iris" stomachache.

"Let's get out of here," Iris suggested to the three generations of females still clustered by the door. She was sick of airports: of the expediency they promised, which at any moment could turn into hardship or disaster; of the imposed intimacy with strangers caused by a coincidence of time and place; of the short-lived joy of reunions and the lingering sadness of separations which took place within their chaotic walls.

"Uncle Alfred can't wait to see you!" Violet said. She squeezed Iris's shoulder, as the two headed to the baggage claim area, while Auntie Rosa minded the girls. "Todd stayed with him so Auntie Rosa could come to the airport. She was so excited, she called me five times today. I promised her I would deliver you promptly and safely to her doorstep, but trying to get through to a Capotosti, especially an old one, is like trying to get through a brick wall!"

"Don't I know it!" Iris said. After a pause, she cleared her throat and asked, "How is Uncle Alfred doing?"

"Well, suffice it to say he doesn't really have the strength to play the guitar anymore." Violet sighed. "But he still gets up every day, washes and shaves and dresses himself. It takes him ages, but he doesn't want any help. You know how fastidious he is."

From the vantage point of another continent, Iris had become adept at freezing the past and its inhabitants in her favorite poses. Wishful thinking and happy memories were her greatest indulgence, but now she would have to swallow the meat and potatoes of reality. It presented her with a different version of Auntie Rosa, the old woman who hobbled along beside her, leaning on the worn cane that had belonged to Grandpa

Capotosti; of Uncle Alfred who couldn't even hold a guitar; of time and events flying past her, dispensing ageing and illness upon those she loved in her absence.

"Hello?" At the tenth ring, Iris was just about to hang up, when Lily's voice came over the other end, breathless and barely audible over the rhythmic music and bass line accompanying a singer, instantly recognizable as Michael Jackson. Iris wasn't exactly up on pop music culture, but "Billy Jean" had made it to the top of the charts in Italy, too.

"Hi, Lily," she shouted into the receiver. "It's me, Iris!"

"Oh, hi Iris," Lily said, wheezing. "Hold on a sec, would ya?" There was a thud as Lily set the receiver down; the music and Michael's hiccuping voice were silenced. "Now if I could only find my fucking lighter," she heard Lily mumble.

"Sorry about that, Iris," she said a few seconds later, sucking in her breath. Iris could picture Lily cradling the receiver between her shoulder and ear as she lit up a cigarette.

"Did I catch you at a bad time?" Iris said, wondering why she should feel apologetic. It wasn't as though she called a hundred times a day.

"That's OK, I was just scrubbing the bathtub. I can't seem to get the stains out. I'd rather just move," Lily said, and sucked in another breath. Iris could picture her squinting her eyes against the plumes of smoke rising in curlicues around her face.

"When did you get in?"

"Last night. Didn't Violet tell you?" Iris said.

"Yeah, I'm sorry I couldn't make it to the airport. I was feeling a little queasy."

"Queasy? Violet said you had a tummy ache, but she didn't mention the word 'queasy'." Maybe Iris had jumped to conclusions too quickly. "Is there something you aren't telling me?"

"It's not what you're thinking."

Iris had been hoping Lily would get pregnant again soon; she had been lighting candles to the statue of the Blessed Virgin

115

Mother for her, too, whenever she went to church. Each time she lit the two votive lights, always choosing two that were side by side, Iris prayed for a double miracle to bless them both. Iris fantasized the she and Lily would become mothers at the same time, like the Virgin Mary and her barren cousin Elizabeth. They would write letters to each other, at least once a week, to compare notes on how they were feeling, share tips on how to deal with nausea and their changing bodies, what their hopes and fears were. By the time their babies were born, each would have a diary of the other's pregnancy. Motherhood would be such an incredibly emotional experience for them to share as women, after all the little things they had shared as little girls. And Iris definitely wanted Lily to have a baby to love, whether or not Iris could; so why did she feel that twitch of relief when Lily dismissed her suspicion that she might be expecting? She pushed the thought aside, to get to the point of her call.

"Listen, I know it's short notice, but I wanted to know whether you and Joe would like to come over to Auntie Rosa's for dinner tonight." Thank God for food: talking about it, preparing it, cooking it, serving it, and eating it could take so much strain out of relationships. "I promised Uncle Alfred I'd make him some pasta. He hasn't been eating much, but his eyes lit up at the idea. He'd love to see you, you know. And so would I."

"Joe works nights. He never gets home before nine or ten," Lily said.

"But you're free, aren't you?"

"Apart from SaveMart and housework, my calendar is pretty wide open these days," Lily said.

"Please come then. Around five. The older they get the earlier they want to eat."

"Sure. OK. See you then."

"Sorry if I'm late," Lily said, standing at the threshold of Auntie Rosa's front door as if she were a guest, rather than one of the family.

"You're not late at all," Iris said. "Come on in and give me a hug!" As Iris gathered Lily in her arms, she was flooded with tenderness. She had forgotten how much smaller Lily was than she; the top of her head only came to her shoulder, and the bones in her arms and back seemed so fragile. Lily's hair smelled of coconut and pineapple and mango, like one of those tropical punches they served at the Luau; it was also laced with the smell of cigarette smoke, just like the air at the night club.

"I've missed you," she said.

"Me too," Lily said, pulling away. Iris only caught a fleeting glimpse of Lily's grey-green eyes, before they darted away. They were dry now, and attractively made-up, but they still looked like her funeral eyes of two years ago.

"Auntie Rosa's helping Uncle Alfred get ready for dinner. He looks so frail, Lily. When was the last time you saw him?"

Lily looked at the floor. "I don't really remember. I stopped over a few times after his operation, but Auntie Rosa always said he was resting. There's been a lot going on, too, between work and Joe and the house and all."

"Yeah, I know what you mean. I can't believe it took me so long to make it back." Gregorio had offered to bring her over for Christmas the previous year, but Iris had declined, and kept the information to herself. She would have loved to spend the holidays with her family, and of course with Gregorio, but being with both at the same time confused her.

"Anyway, I was really shocked when I saw him last night," Iris sighed. "It's just not fair. He always walked five miles a day, never drank booze or coffee, never smoked. How does someone like that end up with lung cancer?"

Lily shook her head and looked up at Iris, who didn't know what else to say.

"Why don't you come and give me a hand in the kitchen?"

"Sure. Lead the way," Lily said, as if she hadn't been in Auntie Rosa's kitchen hundreds of times.

"Oh, would you mind taking off your shoes first?" Iris said. "Auntie Rosa likes to keep the place as germ-free as possible."

Lily kicked off her sneakers, and followed as Iris led her past the table she and Auntie Rosa had set with the good china and linen napkins.

"You and me making dinner again, Lily. Just like the old days, except you can hardly move in these efficiency kitchens," Iris said, clearing a space on the counter, then taking a bottle from the refrigerator. "But there's an upside; now the cooks get to drink on the job!"

"I don't really drink," Lily said.

"Oh, come on, just a drop. Keep me company." Iris set out two glasses, "There isn't much of a selection at the liquor store over in the plaza, but this is a decent Verdicchio. I hope you like it." Wine and cooking were two things that always relaxed Iris, and she hoped they'd help dispel the vague sense of unease that had descended upon her the moment Lily walked in the door. If Lily would at least write once in a while between visits, they wouldn't have to waste precious time cracking the shell of unshared facts and feelings that had formed around each of them in the meantime. She uncorked the bottle, and poured two glasses.

"You're pretty good at that, Iris."

"As they say, practice makes perfect. Good wine doesn't come in screw-top bottles over in Italy. *Alla salute*," Iris raised her glass.

"*Salut*," Lily said, following suit.

Iris took a sip from her glass, then checked the pot on the stove. "Almost boiling."

"But you don't even have the sauce started yet," Lily said.

"This is quicker. And just as delicious, if not better. You'll see. Go ahead, break these eggs into the serving bowl, one for each person," Iris instructed.

"You're making me cook?"

"Don't you want to learn a new recipe? It will be fun," Iris said, passing Lily the eggs. "Here, beat them with this," she said, passing Lily a fork.

"So you're saying this is an authentic Italian dish, right Iris? With no tomatoes? No pork butt or meatballs or sausages? Are you sure?"

"Absolutely!" Iris said. "Look here," she showed Lily the

contents of a skillet, which she stirred with a wooden spoon. "Cubed bacon, thick-sliced if you can find it. I learned this recipe right in Rome, the very first time I went to Italy. I made it for Dad and the boys when I got back, and they loved it. What are those guys up to these days anyway? I never hear from them."

"I don't hear much either. I guess they're still tying to find their way, you know? William keeps switching girlfriends, Charles keep switching jobs, and Ricci keeps switching schools."

Iris wished she had time to organize a dinner or something, and invite all her siblings, but was daunted by the sheer number of lives and schedules and preferences to coordinate. Uncle Alfred would love seeing everyone all gathered together, like in the old days. It saddened her to think he might have to wait for his funeral for that to happen; she, for one, had decided not to wait. Her thoughts were interrupted by the growling of her stomach, which joined the symphony of sizzling and bubbling and beating in the kitchen. The sounds and smells apparently had a similar effect on Uncle Alfred. His eyes were as wide as those of a child in a candy shop as he shuffled in on the arm of Auntie Rosa, who smiled stoically as she used Grandpa Capotosti's cane to help them along. Uncle Alfred was looking dapper after his rest and grooming, his movements slow but well-controlled as he lowered himself to his place at the table.

"Aloha, Uncle Alfred," Lily said, going over to give him a quick hug, then returning. She took a sip of wine and lowered her voice before speaking again. "Wow, I didn't realize he had gone so downhill, Iris."

"You can imagine how shocked I was when I saw him last night," Iris said, in a whisper.

"Is it almost ready, Iris?" Uncle Alfred called from his seat at the table. "I'm dying of starvation," he said, chuckling.

"You stop that talk, Alfred!" Auntie Rosa said.

"It'll only be a minute, Uncle Alfred! We won't tolerate anyone dying at our table!"

"And I'm not dying until I eat your spaghetti, that's for sure!"

"Then maybe I'll just make you wait a few more years!" Iris

said, stirring the spaghetti in the pot, before turning her attention back to Lily.

"Now just add some grated pecorino to those eggs, would you?" Iris said to Lily. "Oh, and some of this." She handed her a pepper mill.

"Sure. Geez, I can't wait to spring this recipe on Lucy. She'll have a friggin' cow," Lily said. "She thinks if spaghetti's not swimming in tomato sauce and meat, it's not worthy of the name. Her and her goddamn secret sauce."

Iris lifted a strand from the pot with a cooking fork and tasted it; since moving to Italy, she would not allow anyone to interfere with her ruling as to when the point of *al dente* was reached. "Everyone come to the table!" she called, draining the spaghetti in the colander. "Ready, Lily?" she asked, dumping the steaming pasta into the egg mixture. "Quick now, toss it so the steam cooks the eggs."

Though Iris always derived satisfaction from setting food on the table, she let Lily present the steaming bowl of *spaghetti alla carbonara*. Auntie Rosa grasped Uncle Alfred's hand as Iris and Lily sat down.

"We're the only ones left," she said. "God took them all. Pa, Ma, my little sister Teresa, my baby brother Carlo, then last year, my little brother Bartolomeo." She paused to make the sign of the cross. "The good Lord only knows why he went to live down south in that trailer park instead of spending his last years here with me and Al."

"Let's not start with that again, Rosa," Uncle Alfred said. "You're going to ruin our appetites." Iris had forgotten how much like a married couple they acted.

"Uncle Alfred's right. Let's give thanks instead." Iris bowed her head. "In the words of our father, and your brother Carlo, before every meal: 'Grace before meals bless us our Lord and these Thy gifts which we are about to receive from Thy bounty through Christ our Lord amen.'"

"Amen," they all repeated, crossing themselves. As Iris began serving, she paused to look at those gathered around the table.

Distilled joy twinkled in the eyes of her aunt and uncle as they watched her: the Capotosti fiber was resilient, the spirit strong and capable of savoring the gifts of the present, of rising temporarily above the indelible pain of the past and postponing the inevitable suffering of the future, at least long enough to enjoy a heaping plate of spaghetti in the company of family. She looked at Lily, and wondered what her present was like; whether her life with Joe made up for her disappointments of the past, and provided a solid foundation for her future happiness. From what she heard, Joe was a good provider, and Lily had only taken the job at SaveMart until she became a mother, just like Iris had taken hers at Transoceanica. They were both biding their time.

"You girls playing any guitar these days?" Uncle Alfred asked, winding spaghetti around his fork, and delivering the slippery bundle to his mouth on a tremulous hand.

"I'm working on it, Uncle Alfred," Iris said. "Look!" She held up her left hand to display the callouses on the pads of her first three fingers; she still had trouble using her pinky. "I got myself a guitar a while back."

"Maybe you'd play me something after dinner?" he said. "I don't have much of a grip anymore but I can still slide on the steel, or strum that old ukulele."

"It would be so much fun to play with somebody for once, especially with you, Uncle Alfred! I only play when I'm home alone. We could do something from our Hawaiian repertoire," Iris suggested. "Lily will sing, won't you, Lily?"

"I'm so out of practice," Lily said, poking at the spaghetti in her plate.

"We could do 'Beyond the Reef,'" Iris suggested. "That's easy."

"Oh, girls! Why don't you do that 'No Kau a Kau' song? I used to get goosebumps every time Lily sang that one."

"Why not, Lily? It'll be fun, like old times," Iris said.

"Fun? Like old times?" Lily shook her head.

Iris reached under the table, and squeezed her sister's hand.

"I'll see what I can do," Lily said.

"That would be great," Iris said.

When the last strands of spaghetti had been wound around the forks, and the last scraps of bacon and egg mopped up from the plates with thick slices of crusty Italian bread, Auntie Rosa gripped her cane in one hand, and placed the other on the table, grimacing as she pulled herself to her feet. "Now, you girls go visit," she said. "I'm sure you have a lot of catching up to do. You just carry the things to the sink for me, and I'll do the washing up."

"Of course we'll carry the dishes to the sink, Auntie Rosa. But you sit yourself back down for a few minutes. We made a promise to Uncle Alfred. The dishes can wait."

Auntie Rosa could be a pretty darn stubborn Abruzzese at times, but if there was one person who could have her way with her, it was Iris. Having only made it halfway to her feet anyway, she obeyed without resistance, and dropped back into her seat.

"Would you mind clearing, Lily, while I get us set up?" Iris asked.

"Sure," Lily said, as Iris walked away.

Entering Uncle Alfred's bedroom, she spotted the instruments lined up around his bed like a cluster of old friends come to pay their respects. They had never strayed far from his side for as long as Iris could remember, and it moved her to think they would be there to see him through to the end. From the instruments, her eyes roamed to the bed, neatly made and puffed up with extra pillows by Auntie Rosa, who knew all about how to cushion the suffering of the ill; then to the closet, where she imagined Uncle Alfred's crushed velvet jackets and tuxedos, cummerbunds and bow ties, moth-balled and zippered up in garment bags; then to the night table with its tray of little brown bottles that looked as out of place by the bed of a man who had never taken so much as an aspirin, as Kentucky bourbon in a holy water font. Iris sighed, and picked up Uncle Alfred's Harmony Consolectric. Like her aunt and uncle, the old Hawaiian guitar seemed to have grown lighter and more frail with age. Uncle Alfred was air-washing his hands when she returned to the dining room and set the instrument in front of him on wobbly legs. The glint in his eyes and the smile on his face sent a rush of tenderness flowing through Iris; gone was the sick, aging man, back was the bandleader of Alfred's Hawaiian Trio.

"I got this back before you were born, Iris," he said, running his hands affectionately over the tweed-lined table top, along the strings, up the neck to the headstock. "I've had all kinds of guitars, but I never could part with this one. This is the one that got me hooked on Hawaiian music."

"Is the height OK for you, Uncle Alfred?" Iris asked, seeing him wince as he struggled to pull himself tall in his chair.

"It's fine, now that I can hardly stand long enough to tune up. You know, I never did think much of those fellows who play sitting down. Grown men looking for something to hold in their laps should get a cat."

"He plays too darn much," Auntie Rosa said. "I tell him to save his strength, but he pretends not to hear, even though I know he's wearing his hearing aid!"

"I'm sure I'll have plenty of time to rest when I'm dead, Rosa, but I have no guarantee that I'll have a guitar to play."

"Stop talking like that!" Auntie Rosa cried, scrunching her brow so hard that the puff of gray hair sitting atop her head shifted visibly, while Uncle Alfred chuckled.

When Iris returned from the bedroom a second time with the slide, the finger picks and the old Kamaka pineapple ukulele which, like Uncle Alfred and his Harmony, looked a little worse for the wear, Lily had finished clearing the table, and was standing off to the side, looking out the window.

"I just hope I remember something!" Iris said.

"Do you remember my first rule, to start with?"

"Yes, that I remember. Tune up." Though Iris didn't quite recall which strings corresponded to which notes on the ukulele, Uncle Alfred walked her through it in no time.

"Ready, Lily?" she said.

Lily walked over to them, the faraway look in her eyes making Iris wonder what she had been staring at out the window, what she had been thinking of and why. She knew so little about what

123

her sister thought these days. Maybe playing a song or two together would help bridge the gap.

While she wondered, the first bended notes slid from the guitar and into the room, followed by a swell of balmy chords that gently washed over the underlying current of sadness, coating it with sweetness. Iris, following Uncle Alfred's lead and lips as he mouthed the chord changes, began strumming the uke. She looked at Lily and nodded, knowing there was no way she could have forgotten the words to their old finale, holding her breath in the hope that she'd come through for them and start singing. Only when Iris saw Lily's chest rise as she filled her lungs, did Iris release the air in hers.

"Across the sea, where the trade winds blow
You came to me, so long ago
Now my love is lost, but I'll always know
You'll be here with me, when the trade winds blow.
Mine is the heart, that won't forget
The dreams we shared, without regret
We'll meet again, where love will be
No Kau, a Kau, for eternity."

As Lily sang, Iris looked at her dear old Uncle Alfred, his eyes half-closed, knowing he was right where he wanted to be at that moment, with a belly full of pasta, his fingers picking and sliding over the strings of his guitar, in the company of family. She looked at Auntie Rosa, always so hungry for togetherness, smiling and hugging herself as she gazed lovingly at one of them, then another, running her hands up and down her arms as if to chase away a chill. She looked at Lily, who sang with closed eyes. Iris waited for her lids to open, and reveal what was going on inside her. Instead, she fell silent.

"That's about all I remember," she mumbled, while Uncle Alfred and Iris played on. He and Auntie Rosa were still floating somewhere over Kona when Lily glanced at Iris, placed two fingers over her lips and jerked her head toward the door, indicating that she was going out for a smoke.

Dusk was just settling over the peaceful Valley Ranch cul-de-sac when Iris joined Lily on the porch.

"Thanks for singing, Lily," she said. "It made Uncle Alfred happy."

"Yeah, but it made me sad."

"Me, too," Iris said. "I'm starting to think they are inseparable."

"Auntie Rosa and Uncle Alfred?"

"No, happiness and sadness." Iris sighed. "Want some?" she said, holding up the bottle of Verdicchio she had brought outside with her, together with two glasses.

"Maybe just another drop," Lily said. "Want one of these?" she said to Iris, flicking her wrist to shake a cigarette from a pack of Merits.

"I haven't really smoked since high school," Iris said. "Anyway, aren't you smoking a bit too much?"

"Only occasionally. And aren't you drinking a bit too much?"

"Only occasionally," Iris said. She pointed her puckered lips at Lily, who placed a cigarette in them, and lit it. "Auntie Rosa would have a fit if she saw me. And so would Gregorio."

"You're a big girl now, Iris. Plus, who's telling?" Lily said, lighting her own cigarette. She threw back her head and exhaled, the waves of her thick hair brushing her narrow shoulders. Iris thought Lily looked fabulous with her hair this length, and that not even the best actresses could strike the poses that came naturally to her. It was a pity she seemed to have given up the idea of acting, and an even greater pity she didn't seem to be taking very good care of herself. Her pants were stretched too tight across her butt, and she was pale, as if she never got out in the fresh air.

"Speaking of Gregorio, how come he didn't come?" Lily asked.

"He wanted to, but he had too much going on," Iris said.

"Couldn't you have waited until he could get vacation, too?" Lily said.

"I suppose so. But the point is, I really wanted to come by

myself. It's hard to explain why. I guess I just feel like home is the one place that belongs to me. Even if now it's here at Auntie Rosa's, instead of at Chestnut Crest."

"And he just let you go on vacation without him? Without giving you a hard time?"

"It's not like I was going on a singles' cruise or anything, Lily. It's just home."

"I can't imagine Joe letting me go away all by myself," she said, blowing smoke into the evening air.

"I did have to do some finagling," Iris said.

"You mean you lied to him?"

"No, I didn't lie. It was just like we used to do with Mom and Dad when we were kids and had to ask for permission. It's all in how you ask for things. I knew Gregorio had signed up for this European anesthesiology conference in Amsterdam, and so I started dropping hints about how homesick I'd been lately, thinking about Dad being gone, and how Uncle Alfred probably wouldn't be around much longer, and how upset Auntie Rosa must be, and how frustrated and depressed I was about not getting pregnant. He basically suggested that a visit home might do me good. I made it look like it was his idea. The only thing left for me to do was agree and thank him for being so sensitive to my needs."

"Good thinking," Lily said.

"I think he was relieved, deep down. Gregorio works hard, and he needs his peace and quiet. I think he is a bit overwhelmed by our family."

"Well, it's not like you don't get to take vacations together or anything. I got that postcard you sent from that island last year. Where was it again? Sardinia?" Lily said.

"No, that's where we went on our honeymoon. Last year we went Corsica. It's just north of Sardinia, but it's actually part of France."

"Oh," Lily said, grinding out her cigarette with the toe of her sneaker. "Beautiful."

"Yeah, it was. Gregorio said the marine life was incredible. He was gone most of the day with his diving group. But I didn't mind. I went swimming, rested on the beach, read. The nature on that island is beautiful, still pretty wild, an amazing place for hiking and biking," Iris said. She took a drag on her cigarette. "But of course all those activities were off limits to me."

"What do you mean?"

"Too strenuous. Just in case. After my operation, they said I had a decent shot at getting pregnant, with one tube open. God forbid I should miscarry after all that work." She stubbed out her half-smoked cigarette on the ground, and set it on a fallen leaf, so she would remember to pick it up.

"Sorry about that, Iris. I know what you mean."

"I'm sorry about you, too, Lily." Iris poured herself some more wine. "I wanted to ask you something, while we're on the subject."

"What?"

"Well, you had your miscarriage a long time ago. Maybe there's another undiagnosed problem."

"What do you mean?" Lily asked, lighting up another cigarette.

"I've gone through a whole battery of exams, and Gregorio was tested too. It's actually a miracle anyone gets pregnant, when you realize how many factors can prevent it. You might want to consider investigating."

"I don't think we need any tests," Lily said, looking at the ground. "I got pregnant twice, and it'll happen again, when the time is right."

"Sure it will. It was just a suggestion."

Looking up at Iris, Lily said, "I can see Gregorio being in hurry and all, given his age, but it's different for me and Joe. We're both still young. We have time."

"Of course you do. But you know, it's really important to stay healthy in the meantime. Cigarettes might not be a great idea." Before Lily could criticize Iris for her wine-drinking, she added, "Do you get any exercise?"

"Not really, just the workouts I get housecleaning and lugging around stuff at work. I did have a free trial membership at the gym up at the plaza, but it was only good for two weeks. Anyway, Joe didn't like me going there because it was co-ed. Besides, those guys are crooks, making you sign a two-year contract. Anything can happen in two years."

"Yeah, I hate gyms, too. They're all so dinky and stinky where I live. I've always preferred to work out at home, at my own pace and to music I like. Queen is great, for example, and Freddie psyches me up. Mostly I just run now, though, since I started getting complaints about the music."

"Complaints? Who could that possibly bother?"

"Cinzia. You remember that picture I sent you last year, of our new house?"

Lily nodded her head.

"Well, the villa has three floors, and there's an apartment on each floor. Cinzia and her family got the ground floor, since they have three kids, and are always in and out of the house. Anyway, one day I was doing my biceps curls, or sit-ups or whatever, I don't remember, to 'Another One Bites the Dust,' and Cinzia came storming upstairs all hysterical, saying it was the kids' nap time, then went on to tell me how I wouldn't know, naturally, because I'm not a mother, but that children's needs take priority over all else. Blah, blah, blah."

"Sounds like a nice sister-in-law," Lily said. "Not that mine are much better."

"Cinzia's not bad, you just have to get used to her ways, like with all the Leales. After all, I have to remind myself, I'm the one who went to live in their country, and was accepted into their family, not the other way around. Plus, like Gregorio says, we should be grateful to have some little kids to liven the place up, since we don't have any of our own."

"So are you on the top floor?"

"No, we're on the middle floor, just above Cinzia. Isabella is on the top floor. There's a nice terrace there, where she likes to sit and read or sun herself in private, now that she's retired. There's a beautiful view of the olive groves from up there, too."

"Sounds nice."

"Yes. It's an ideal arrangement for everyone. Isabella's not getting any younger, and Gregorio's so much busier at the hospital since he got his promotion, he feels better knowing I'm right there if she needs anything."

It was ideal, no doubt about that. So ideal that Iris, ready to celebrate after they settled in, had thrown a nice little dinner party. In addition to Gregorio's usual diving buddies and Policlinico colleagues, she had invited her girlfriends Deirdre and Liz, who turned up with a bottle of Jack Daniels which they passed around for shots after dinner, a detail which was instrumental in convincing Iris to take out her guitar and play. It was only eleven o'clock when Gregorio started hushing their laughter and singing, for fear of disturbing his Mamma's sleep. He concluded the evening by brewing a pot of chamomile before sending the guests on their way. By midnight, the guitar had been returned to its corner behind the couch, and peace and order had been restored to the Leale villa.

"Speaking of mothers," Iris said. "I wanted to tell you something. I went to see Mom today. At least, I think it was her. There was another name on the doorbell at her apartment. But I did recognize the woman who opened the door and invited me in for a cup of coffee."

"I can't believe no one told you she changed her name," Lily said. Iris wondered who should have told her, if not Lily. She had always been the one who knew what their mother was up to; she could have written.

"But why Regina Masterly? Where did that come from?" Iris asked.

"She said she wanted a name that would sound both classy and bossy, you know? Like someone in control of things."

"Whatever works," Iris said. She reached for the bottle of Verdicchio, refilled her empty glass and topped off Lily's, from which only a few sips had been taken.

"She told me about her work with women's groups around the country. They're trying to devise some kind of a strategy to resuscitate support for the Equal Rights Amendment, even though the deadline for the ratification expired years ago. I don't really get much of this news in Italy. Do you know what's going on?"

"Of course, I've heard all about it," Lily said. "Many times."

"Interesting stuff," Iris said. "I'm kind of proud of her, actually. It would have been nice if she had asked how I was doing, though."

"You know her. She's always been more interested in the big picture."

They sat in silence for a moment. Through the screen door, Iris could hear the clinking of dishes. Auntie Rosa had insisted on washing them herself, shooing away the girls so they could have a little visit. Iris had gone along with her wishes, knowing she wouldn't be satisfied until she had sterilized everything in sight. A dog barked in the distance. The wail of an approaching freight train transported Iris back to the bedroom she had shared with Lily, to summer nights with the window thrown wide open, to the chirping of crickets commingling with their soft chatter, to hopes that a breeze would flutter in to relieve them of the heat, and that pleasant dreams would relieve them of reality.

"Remember ..." they said at the same time. A soft chuckle escaped them both; they looked at each other, then fell silent.

Lily lit another cigarette. Iris sipped her wine.

"Jasmine is coming for the weekend," Iris said. She'll be staying at Violet's. Marguerite's going to try and make it, too."

"I didn't know that. No one told me," Lily said, her voice wrapped tight around the words.

"I'm telling you now. I just convinced them today. I thought it would be fun if we could all do something together. Just us sisters."

"Sure it would," Lily said.

"I was thinking we could go horseback riding, then maybe grab a bite somewhere. I just got my period and my Italian stallion is not around to inseminate me, so I know I'm safe. I guess you are, too."

"Well, I'm not really sure," Lily said. "It's sort of that time of the month. And I don't even know how to ride."

"We'll just have a little trail ride, nothing strenuous. We'll have them saddle up a couple of old nags for the two of us. It's not often we get a chance to do something like this. Plus, the fresh air and exercise will do you good."

"Let's see what happens."

"Right, it's still four days away."

"I'd better get going. Joe will be home soon."

"Why don't you take some leftovers for dinner. There's plenty."

"That's OK. I don't think he's ever had spaghetti without red sauce. But I'll tell him about it, then maybe I'll try your recipe another night."

The sound of the freight train faded, the sisters said goodnight, and Lily walked away.

Iris held the reins loosely in her right hand, and rested her left on the horn; she loved how smooth and worn it felt, loved knowing it was there if she needed it. The saddle creaked and groaned between the seat of her jeans and the horse's wide back as they walked through the meadow. Iris breathed in the inebriating scent of open space, one of the things she missed most in overpopulated, overbuilt Italy. Growing up in a crowded household, she had developed an appreciation of space at an early age, and it was a luxury she would never take for granted. Rolling her pelvis with the gelding's slow gait, she patted his neck, sending clouds of dust into the sunlight, as she tightened her thighs around his muscular body.

She watched how Jasmine rode, a short distance in front of her, and pulled herself up tall in the saddle to imitate her, while drinking in the earthy spring air. It smelled of pine resin and bark and soggy grass and caking mud, blended with leather and horse. Iris thought of Gregorio and the sterile hospital smell he brought home with him; from here, they seemed part of another planet, rather than part of her daily life. In the beginning, she had thought it a pure, clean smell, and even liked the way it reminded her a little bit of hugging Auntie Rosa, back when she used to rush over straight from work in her nurse's uniform. Lately, Iris had found herself looking forward to the odor of Gregorio's evening smoke which would kill the sterile smell, and had gotten into the habit of handing him a filled pipe as soon as he got home. Now if she was busy doing something else when he walked in the door, he jokingly accused her of neglecting him. She wondered if there was a way of preventing little acts of kindness from turning into habits, then routines, then duties.

"Are you with us, Iris?" Jasmine called from the head of the formation, as they entered a copse. She was the most accomplished equestrian among them, having made great progress since the days of the pony she had kept behind the chicken coop at Chestnut Crest. She now had a real barn, and a real paint mare. Not to mention a second husband, two children, a goat, three dogs, and as many cats as it took to keep mice out of the hayloft.

"I'm coming!" Iris said, gently jabbing her horse in the ribs with the heels of the boots Violet had lent her. She had asked for a quiet horse, and had gotten her wish. Her mount had been just as content as his rider's mind to wander lazily behind the others.

Iris observed her three sisters in front of her, each with a long braid swaying to and fro against their backs, like a trio of pendulums. As they came to a clearing, the horses fanned out, and Iris stepped up her pace to bring herself alongside them. All her life, Jasmine and Violet and Marguerite had been clustered together, on the far side of Henry and Louis, while Iris had only had one sister by her side: Lily.

"I still can't believe she didn't come," she heard Marguerite say as she approached. "I mean, I came all the way from New York to do this together."

"Iris said she told her that maybe her period was late, so she didn't want to risk it, just in case." Violet said. "Of course, if that's the case, she certainly shouldn't be smoking like a fiend."

"Or doing manual labor, like hauling boxes and crates around, or loading people's cars, or whatever a discount store assembler does," Marguerite said.

"If you're talking about Lily, I can see her point. I know what it's like," Iris said, bringing her horse abreast. She was very disappointed that Lily didn't join them, and wondered whether funerals would be the only way for all five sisters to get together from now on. Though she spoke in Lily's defense, a part of her wanted to run over to her house, grab her by the shoulders, look her in the eye, and make her swear she wasn't just making up excuses. You didn't just lie about things like possible pregnancies and risking miscarriages.

"I'll bet Joe just didn't want her to come," Violet said. "He's always mister nice guy. A real charmer. Especially if you're in the market for a new bedroom set. But I don't think he really likes our family. Or at least he doesn't like her to spend time with us, for some reason. You guys don't live here, so you may not realize it. But whenever there's a holiday, she can only stay half an hour, tops, then she's whisked off to the Diotallevi family. Easter, Christmas, whatever. As if they were the goddamn Kennedy clan waiting for her at the freaking Compound or something."

Iris swallowed. She wished she knew whether Lily was hiding something. She wished she had the courage to ask her just that. But something always held her back, that same something that made her wonder whether she really had the right to just breeze back into town, expecting everyone to find time for her, feel close enough to spill out their guts to her, then just watch her disappear again for another year.

"Speaking of families," Marguerite said, "how are the Leales treating you these days, *Signora* Iris?"

"Oh, fine," Iris said. "They've all been very concerned and supportive, doing their best to help. I purposely didn't say anything to them when I went in for the GIFT procedure, but both Isabella and Cinzia showed up at the hospital. I didn't want to be stuck in a conversation with Gregorio's mother and sister where the topic was his sperm and my eggs. Apparently he had no qualms about explaining it all to them himself, though."

"I really wish you would have spoken to that fertility specialist

133

here in town, Iris," Violet said. "I'm quite certain he would have steered you toward *in vitro* rather than gamete intrafallopian transfer, especially with compromised tubes. I know of one hospital in Italy where they are already doing it."

"Yes, there's a center in Turin. But Gregorio is against *in vitro*."

"Why on earth is that? He's a medical man himself."

"Ask the Pope. The Catholic Church closes an eye on GIFT because fertilization still occurs inside the body, and not in a petri dish."

"How fucked up is that?" Marguerite said.

The horses walked four abreast through the meadow, swishing their tails, trying to lower their velvety lips to the tall, sweet grass. It seemed to Iris they were enjoying the saturated colors and smells of the mild spring morning as much as she. Iris said a silent prayer of gratitude for this day, for the sun above that warmed her back, for the sisters at her side that warmed her heart.

"I've done what I could," she said, more to herself than to anyone else. An awareness was budding inside her, as spontaneously as the wildflowers all around them. She cleared her throat. "I'm told I still might get pregnant one day," she said in a voice loud enough for all to hear. "But I'm through with all the fertility drugs, the laparoscopies, the probing and poking and consulting. All the years of trying and waiting and hoping. And now I find myself with no baby, no college degree, no career."

"But you still have a beautiful life," Violet said. "And you still have Gregorio."

"Yes, I still have Gregorio," Iris said. Nods of agreement and encouragement were exchanged all around. "Right."

She took a deep breath, loosened her hold on the reins, and said, "I think I feel confident enough for a run now." She jabbed her horse in the ribs with her heels, and he broke into a canter. Iris raced across the field with her big sisters, her loose hair flying, her heart pounding.

8. LILY

Three years after Lily's father's death, his estate finally passed out of probate and the house on Chestnut Crest was sold, with one-twelfth of the proceeds going to Lily. She immediately earmarked the funds for a new home.

"What's wrong with this house?" said Joe.

"It was a nice starter home," said Lily. "But this neighborhood is no place to raise children, Joe. Plus, none of our neighbors are ever home, and with you working so late, I just get so bored and lonely. Maybe it would help me to live in a neighborhood with children running around, with women my own age who I can hang out with. I've heard that when you're trying to get pregnant, being around little kids stimulates your hormones and everything." Maybe it would also stimulate whatever it took to stay pregnant. She would need all the help she could get.

"Still, there's no reason we can't spend some of that money," said Joe. "Let's take a thousand and go on a trip - have a little fun. Maybe even turn that thousand into three or four. Wouldn't that be somethin'?"

"Look," said Lily, surprised at her own sense of self-possession. "There is no way I am going to let you gamble any of that money." She girded herself for the trouble she knew her words would cause.

"Oh, you're not going to *let* me?" Joe looked up from his fried bologna sandwich, and stared at Lily with raised eyebrows. "Is that what you said - 'let' me?"

"Yes, that's what I said, Joe." Lily felt emboldened by the fact that it was legally her money, and how she chose to spend it was limited only by her ability to take ownership of it. She pulled on her rubber gloves and stepped up to the sink, with her back to Joe. She felt braver if she didn't have to look at him.

"After all, it is my money."

"Your money? Is that how we're playing it now?"

"That's how we've been playing it, Joe." Lily squirted a stream of dishwashing liquid into the flow of hot water. "Do you ever ask me before you blow your paycheck at the track?"

"I don't blow my paycheck at the track, don't exaggerate." Joe took a bite of his sandwich, and wiped his mouth with the back of his hand.

"Oh, that's right - you don't even have to go to the track to lose it all anymore. I forgot about last Saturday. I still can't believe you guys leave work in the middle of the day to go to OTB." Lily scrubbed at the flecks of Wheaties that had dried like cement onto the inside of a cereal bowl. The least he could do was rinse out his breakfast dishes, but then again if she could only win one battle today, she would rather not waste it on matters of housekeeping.

"You have no idea what it's been like during the market slowdown these past few months - standin' around all day, in an empty showroom. We just rot some days, staring at each other. It's enough to drive ya crazy. Of course, you wouldn't know anything about that, because you don't have to worry about paying the bills."

"I worry plenty," said Lily. "And I know people aren't spending money right now - don't I work at a store, too?

Joe rolled his eyes.

"When things are slow, why don't you read a book or something? Or make sales calls? If you're not going to use the time to make more money, at least don't use it to do more gambling." Under her breath, she added, "God knows you do enough of that already."

"Why do ya gotta bust my chops, Lil, huh?" Joe shook a pile of potato chips onto his plate. "I work really hard - and I make more money now than I ever have. "

"You're spending more, too, Joe - money leaves this house faster than it comes in. If you think I'm going to let my father's money get frittered away like that, you're crazy. Either we put the money into a new house, or you go on a budget."

"I am not going on a fuckin' budget," said Joe.

"Then I guess I have my answer," said Lily.

By the following Christmas, Lily and Joe had moved into their new three-bedroom split level, located precisely at 44 Trevi Way, in the heart of Gates. The schools had a great reputation, and almost every house on the street had a woman Lily's age with at least one child. Lily quickly became acquainted with her new next-door neighbors Steve and Donna, who had been transplanted to the area from Texas. Donna was a buxom blond with a two-year-old daughter, and the remnants of a drawl that reminded Lily of Grandma Whitacre.

Besides the neighborhood, Lily's favorite feature of the new house was the tree that gracefully danced outside the kitchen. She knew that if she took a twig to the garden store, they would be able to tell her what kind of a tree it was, but Lily preferred to think of it as "my tree." She sat beneath its branches to unwind at the end of the day, or to have coffee in the early morning. She hung a variety of bird feeders throughout its limbs and loved listening to the coos of the mourning doves, and watching the blue jays and cardinals streak their bold colors across the yard. Even in the middle of the night when she couldn't sleep, she would slip downstairs, quietly slide the patio doors open, and sit listening to the feathery twigs bobbing and swaying in the breeze, the way her hair used to do when it grazed her waist.

Joe's favorite feature of the house was the family room, which provided the perfect space for his recliner, a comfortable couch, and the biggest television set they carried at La Casa Bella. The advent of cable television sports was a gambler's dream, and Joe,

Alfonso, and Anthony spent frenetic Sunday afternoons crammed onto the couch like a three-headed, six-legged monster, monitoring their football bets and screaming at the TV.

"Son-of-a-bitchin'-bastard!" Joe shouted one Sunday, as the final score of the game flashed on the screen. He clicked off the TV and flung the remote control across the room, knocking a lamp off the end table.

"I knew I shouldna sat next to you," said Alfonso. "I ain't never seen such a jinx - I can't win when I watch a game with you."

"It's not me," shouted Joe. "It's those goddamn Vikings. I picked the right team, didn't I?"

Lily heart sank. The Vikings game was the last one on Joe's football parlay. She was hoping for a win; the mortgage was two weeks past due.

"I thought you bet on the Vikings," Lily said to Joe, confused.

"I did."

"They won, didn't they?"

"Yeah, but they didn't beat the spread. They only won by a touchdown, and I had them minus six, which means that bad kick for the extra point just cost me three thousand dollars."

"That's ridiculous," said Lily. "If they won, you should collect."

"OK, Lil – I'll go to my bookie and tell him you said so. Maybe he'll pay me the three thousand out of the goodness of his heart." Alfonso and Anthony laughed.

"We're gonna take off," said Anthony. "We're gonna watch the next game at Alfonso's house. Our only shot at winning is gettin' away from you - you're a Jonah."

"What's a Jonah?" asked Lily.

"It's from the Bible," said Alfonso. "There was this guy named Jonah and God had it in for him - he was on this boat full of people and God was going to sink the whole boat because of him, so they were forced to throw him into the ocean where he was eaten by a whale."

Anthony cupped his hands around his mouth. "Man overboard!"

"You goddamn guys are real funny, you know that?" said Joe. "Real goddamn funny."

"And don't call me until after the clock runs out on the next game, you hear me?" shouted Alfonso, as he pulled the front door closed behind him. "I don't even want to hear your voice at halftime."

"I ain't no Jonah," said Joe, not loud enough for anyone else to hear. He looked down at his parlay slip, ripped it up in pieces and threw them into the air. Picking up the receiver of the phone in the kitchen, he pounded out a series of numbers with such force that the wall seemed to shake.

"Yeah - this is number one-thirty-seven," he said. "What's the line on the late game?"

Joe muttered a string of numbers and cities and sports team names and hung up the phone.

"I have a good feeling about this next game, baby," he said, rubbing his palms together. "When do we eat?"

The first half of the late game passed in a blur of cussing and screaming, which Lily heard from the kitchen as she prepared Sunday dinner, using Lucy's "secret" recipe for sauce, which had become one more thing that most women seemed to be able to do without trying, but that Lily just couldn't seem to master. Even after six years of marriage, Joe would take his first mouthful of pasta, wipe his mouth, and proclaim, "You're getting there, baby!" Replicating Lucy's sauce was a rite of passage as a Diotallevi wife, and Lily would not give up until she got it right.

At halftime, Joe came into the kitchen, grabbed a beer, and paced in nervous circles around the table.

"How's it going?" Lily asked. She stood at the sink washing dishes, steeling herself for the answer she had come to expect.

"Those goddamn officials are crooked," said Joe. "Every last one of 'em has money on the Jets, I can just tell. I've got no shot, not a goddamn chance in hell. It's all been fixed."

Joe pulled a slice of Italian bread from the loaf that sat on the counter and dipped it into the pot of bubbling tomato sauce. He took a lusty bite, then grimaced and tossed the rest of the bread into the garbage can. He walked up behind Lily, cupped her left breast with his left hand, and with his right hand he reached down and clasped the flesh between her legs.

"If we hurry, I can get back down there before the third quarter starts."

Lily knew that if she didn't submit to him now, she would have to later, when she would be more tired and he would be more angry. Besides, according to the personal ovulation calendar she kept, it was day thirteen of her cycle, and getting her pregnant was something that Joe would not give up on until Lily got it right.

Three weeks later, Lily purchased a home pregnancy kit, paying cash so it wouldn't show up on their credit card statement. It was much easier to go through the process alone. That way, she only had to deal with her own anxiety, and console her own disappointment. The agony of the fifteen minutes she had to wait before that glorious pink line appeared on the detection strip was dwarfed by the days that inched her ever closer to the two-month mark. One more month to go before she would be in the clear and could triumphantly tell Joe - and the rest of the world - that she was finally going to have a baby.

On Saturday morning of the last week of her second month, Lily woke to cramping and a warm, sticky sensation between her legs. She lay in bed for half an hour, crying, unwilling and unable to get up and face the reality of her third miscarriage, berating herself for not taking her doctor's advice to try progesterone treatments. So what if there wasn't actually any proof that it would help? She had plenty of proof already that her body couldn't handle this on its own. Finally, she stumbled into the bathroom and took a shower. She slid a pad into a fresh pair of underwear. She washed the sheets, treating the blood spots with stain remover. She sent them through the machine three times before all traces of the incident were gone. She dried the sheets, put them back on the bed, and marked her calendar with a P, for period.

"It's landed! It's landed!" shouted Auntie Rosa. "Iris' plane is here!"

Auntie Rosa stood by the gate, an expression of pure glee tattooed across her face as her four-foot-ten-inch frame strained to see past the group of others who waited excitedly to welcome friends and family as they disembarked.

Welcoming Iris had become a Capotosti ritual that unfolded with disturbing - or comforting - predictability. It was a vestige of family tradition that would likely continue for a while; it didn't look like Iris was going to come back to stay any time soon. Lily had mixed feelings about Iris' arrival, but she hadn't gone to the airport last year and she could tell Iris had been upset; she would be hard-pressed to get away with it again. Besides, Iris had kept her promise not to wait so long before coming home again; Lily would have to find a way to travel the five miles to greet her.

As Iris' face appeared, a graceful head and shoulders above the approaching crowd of passengers, Auntie Rosa began jumping up and down in place, waving her arms and shouting, "Lover-dover! Lover-dover!" Though it was good to see Auntie Rosa excited about something for the first time since Uncle Alfred's death, each exclamation of joy at the mere glimpse of Iris was like ripping away a persistent, festering scab.

Iris and Lily had exchanged letters with greater regularity over the past year, but they never ventured into the churning waters of the past. They had never talked about what had happened the last time Iris came to visit, and when Lily received a letter from Iris shortly after she returned to Italy, it had taken her all day to muster up the courage to open it. She was sure it would be filled with criticism and blame that would spill out into the air around her once she tore the envelope open. There wasn't room for much more of that in her life. When she finally read the letter, she discovered that it was light and newsy. No mention of the horseback riding incident. That was Iris for you. Cheerfully dismissive.

She didn't know how she would have responded if Iris had pursued the matter. Lily had planned to take the horseback riding

141

trip they all went on the last time Iris was in town, but Joe had come home especially late from the track the night before. Lily knew that meant he was forced to take the back roads, because he didn't have any money to pay the highway toll. Their credit cards were consistently maxed out, and pay day was still several days away. The expense of going riding, plus going out to lunch, was more than Lily could manage. She felt bad about the lie she'd told her sisters about being late for her period and not wanting to risk it, and she hoped that this visit would be her chance to try and make it right, to show Iris and Violet that she was one of them. That at least she wanted to be.

Lily was just as content not to rehash the matter, but in the years since Iris had moved away, it seemed that the list of topics acceptable for conversation had become overgrown by those that were not. She couldn't write to Iris about the family, as their divergent relationships held too much potential for disagreement. And she certainly couldn't tell Iris what her life was like these days. That left the weather and the latest news on the few friends they'd shared. Iris went to as much trouble staying in touch with them as Lily did avoiding them. It was easier that way. Joe didn't like any of Lily's old friends, and they didn't really know Lily anymore, if they ever had. It hardly seemed worth the arguing she would inevitably have to endure in order to get Joe to agree to a girls' night out. Even if he wasn't home, he didn't like the idea of Lily hanging around a bar, where married women had no business being. She had enough to worry about right now without stirring up social engagements she couldn't accept.

"I can't b'lieve it!" Auntie Rosa cried. "I can't b'lieve you're here!" She encircled Iris with both arms, and gave her a full body hug, rocking Iris from side to side. Iris widened her eyes and stuck her tongue out and to the side in mock strangulation.

"Geez Louise, Auntie Rosa, give the rest of us a chance, will you?" said Violet. She playfully pried Auntie Rosa off of Iris, and gave her a hug and a peck on the cheek. Lily made no move toward Iris. Fighting for a position at the front of the crowd was only slightly more objectionable than standing still, waiting in line for her turn.

Iris finally tore herself away from the pack and walked over to Lily. The sisters stood face to face, and then silently embraced.

"How are you Lily?"

"I'm fine," said Lily. "Great." It was rather early to be lying, but way too late to start telling the truth.

Lily checked the skillet of goulash that was simmering on the stove. She turned the knob on the control panel, gently illuminating the kitchen with the light from the small range lamp. She poured herself a glass of Merlot, grabbed a pack of cigarettes and stepped out onto the patio. She picked up a green nylon folding lawn chair, and with one hand shook it open and placed it under her tree. She was glad to find that the leafy fronds were again long enough to tickle her shoulders, creating a small canopy under which Lily liked to rest - no thanks to Joe and his crazy clippers. Every month or two - usually the morning after a bad night at the track - Lily would find Joe in the backyard, wildly clipping away at the tree like a madman with no plan for when or where to stop, and with no understanding of what the tree would look like when he was done.

"It just looks so sloppy," he had told her one day. He compulsively snipped and clipped, boughs of wispy branches floating to form piles on the ground.

"It's not sloppy," Lily had protested. "It's supposed to look that way; it's free. It's expressing itself."

"Yeah, well, so am I expressing myself," he told her, as he continued clipping. After several bouts of uncontrolled pruning during which Joe completely ignored Lily's pleas for restraint, Lily learned to prune the branches to keep them out of Joe's way and then simply hide the clippers when she was done. Whatever frustrations he had hoped to unleash by pruning were spent on looking for his tool of destruction, and after a few short bouts of yelling, he gave up and went back inside.

Lily took a sip of the wine, and lit a cigarette, grateful that the smell of lawn chemicals had faded with the disappearing sun. She still could not understand why everyone in the neighborhood sprayed their lawns to kill dandelions - she thought dandelions were beautiful and took delight in a green lawn peppered with bright yellow tufts. She remembered she and Iris holding dandelions under each other's chin - a reflection of yellow against your skin indicating your love for butter. Lily wondered where they had learned that dandelion game. Where they had learned any of the nonsense posing as truth that they had picked up along the way.

A car door slammed in the driveway. Lily ground her cigarette into the grass with her shoe, and ran through the house to greet Joe at the front door.

"What's the matter with you?" Joe asked as he stepped into the foyer. "You look like you just lost your best friend."

"I'm just tired," said Lily. "It's after ten. Can't you get home a little earlier a couple nights a week?" Lily walked into the kitchen, and turned the flame off from under the skillet.

"Not if there's a customer in the store." Joe removed his suit coat and flung it over the railing of the stairs as he passed. He shuffled into the kitchen and sat at the place Lily had set for him. "Tonight I had this nerd who had a clipboard and a bunch of bogus low-ball quotes from the other stores on the strip. Jesus, nothing pisses me off like one of those guys who thinks he can beat the system."

"Did you close him?"

"He doesn't even know what hit him – he's going to wake up tomorrow with a sore ass, I'll tell you that. And he thinks I'm his best friend. Asshole."

"Nice commission?" Lily heaped a mound of goulash onto a plate.

"I buried him," said Joe.

"Good – the payments on the new loan start this week." Lily placed the steaming dish in front of Joe, and sat down across from him.

"I know, Lil, I know," said Joe, irritated. "Why do you have to bombard me with bills the minute I get in the door? I know we

144

have bills - I'm out there working my ass off every day. Believe me, I know we have bills." He shoveled a scoop of goulash into his mouth, followed by a gulp of grape soda. He picked up the salt shaker and furiously sprinkled his plate.

Lily finished the dishes and shook the last Merit from a pack she'd just started that morning. She always smoked more when Iris was in town. Emotions were more difficult to deal with as people who only saw each other when Iris visited were thrown together again, and directed by Iris' expectations to behave like loving brothers and sisters. Lily discovered she just wasn't that good of an actress - and now there was the added anxiety of trying to figure out how to participate in Iris' latest adventure - which was much more ambitious than horseback riding at Ellison Park. Lily waited until Joe had filled his belly and emptied his mind of the stories of his day. She followed him up the stairs, wondering how to begin, wondering if it even mattered.

"The Thousand Islands?!" Joe exclaimed. He removed his pants and tossed them onto the highboy that sat in the corner of the bedroom. Lily shook out the pants, folded them on the crease, and hung them over the rod.

"Why the hell are they going there?"

"For fun," said Lily. "They want to go to Alexandria Bay."

"Alex Bay isn't fun," said Joe. "It's a dive."

"I don't know," said Lily. "Violet said it's nice."

"What is Violet doing going away for the weekend, with two little kids to take care of?"

"Just because she has kids it doesn't mean she can't also have fun," said Lily. "Todd is taking care of the kids and the house. It's just one day, not really the whole weekend."

"Well, excuse me for having a job that requires actual work. If Todd was any kind of a man, he would be out in the world making his own money instead sponging off of his wife."

"He works."

"Big deal - what does he do, make Violet's appointments and do her billing? Might as well call him her secretary. Other than that, he doesn't do a goddamn thing. I'm sorry I'm not as good of a wife as Todd is."

"Why are we talking about Todd?" said Lily. "I was telling you that Violet and Iris want me to go with them for an overnight to Alex Bay, and you're over there talking about Todd."

"And you're defending him. Would you rather be married to someone like that?"

"What? No," said Lily. *Well, maybe.* "I'm not defending him, Joe - why are you attacking him?" Lily raised the bedroom window and pushed the curtains aside, hoping to clear the way should an evening breeze decide to arouse itself, wander in and ease the heat rising within her.

"I'm not attacking him." Joe's voice grew louder. "I just can't stand the way he lets your sister call the shots. He follows her around like a puppy dog, waiting for her command and drooling for a bone." Joe drew his necktie out from under his collar. "I don't like you being influenced by Violet. Hanging around with her will give you the wrong ideas."

"I'm not taking castration lessons from her," Lily said.

"Is that supposed to be some kind of a fucking joke?" Joe yelled.

"No! Joe, I'm just saying... we're just going to hang out," said Lily. "You know, have some girl talk."

"What do you guys talk about, anyway?" Joe asked.

"I dunno. Girl stuff."

"Do you talk about me?"

"They don't like to get too serious," said Lily, hoping to steer the conversation in a new direction. "Especially when Iris is here." Lily hoped that Iris' presence would cancel out Violet's since Joe had often commented favorably on Iris' quiet nature and her deference to Gregorio.

"That's another thing -" Joe let his white oxford shirt fall to the floor as he bent to remove one of his shoes. "The last time Iris was here, I seem to remember you ruined our entire Sunday crying because they went horseback riding without you. Did you forget about that?"

Lily burst into tears.

"Oh, Jesus Christ!" Joe pitched his shoe across the room. It hit the screen, popping it from its frame. The shoe sailed through the open window, and landed with a faint thud into the backyard.

"Let's just forget it," said Lily. She inched toward the door. "I didn't really want to go anyway. OK?" She slipped out into the hallway. "Let's just forget it."

Ten minutes later, Joe followed Lily down to the living room and sat beside her on the couch. He placed his head in his hands.

"I'm so sorry, Lil. I didn't mean to make you cry. But sometimes you just make me crazy." Joe forced a giggle and put his arm around her. "You make me a little nuts, you know? Last time, you were so upset that they went without you and now you're ready to jump at the chance to go with them, like a lost puppy."

"I just... I just wanted to be included. You don't know what it feels like to be left out by your own family, Joe."

"Oh, I don't?" Joe turned toward Lily and took her hands in his. "I never told you about Olympic Park? When I was little - like in the second grade, probably - my parents took us kids to Olympic Park. It was Report Card Day."

"I remember Report Card Day!" said Lily. "For every 'A' on your final report card, you got three free ride tickets."

"Right - and two tickets for every 'B' and one for every 'C'."

"Iris always had straight As and she used to ride all afternoon. I had mostly Cs and I ended up sitting around waiting for her for hours it seemed."

"Well, when my parents took us, Alfonso and Anthony were tall enough for the big kid rides, and I had to stay in Kiddie Land."

"By yourself?"

"Yeah, but I didn't really mind about that too much. The thing is, they told me to wait by the boat ride, and they would come back and get me when Alfonso and Anthony had used up all their tickets."

"I sat there by those boats all afternoon. I kept waitin' and waitin'. I started to notice that all of the other families were

147

leaving. I knew my brothers got better grades than me, but I knew they couldn't still be riding. I figured my parents forgot that they told me to wait by the boats so I started walking around looking for them." A look of bewilderment passed over Joe's face, as though he were trying to recount a dream in which nothing quite made sense. "I walked around for about an hour. Turns out, they all went home without me."

"You're kidding!"

"No, believe me, I am not kidding. They came back for me, though. Apparently I fell asleep on a bench by the Merry-Go-Round."

"They must have been so relieved to find you!"

"Not exactly." Joe looked at Lily and the bewilderment in his eyes shifted, darkened, replaced by a dark vacancy. "My father beat the crap out of me because I didn't stay by the boat ride like I was supposed to."

"Oh, Joe!" Lily threw her arms around his neck and began to cry. She wasn't sure for whom.

"I'm not telling you this story so you'll feel bad for me." Joe reached up and removed Lily's arms from around his neck. "I'm telling you so you'll know that I understand what it feels like to be left out by your family."

"I'm so sorry that happened to you," said Lily.

"And I'm sorry it happened to you, too," said Joe. "It would be really hard to find the money to send you to Alex Bay this week... but if it's that important to you, I guess I could borrow it from one of the guys at work. I just hate to see you begging your sisters like that. Maybe if you didn't go, they wouldn't keep taking you for granted the way they do."

"I guess."

"Does Violet even bother with you unless Iris is here?"

"Well, no."

"Then when Iris breezes into town, they expect you to jump. That's not how you get respect, Lily."

"I guess you're right," said Lily. The thought of turning her sisters down again created a sour taste in the back of Lily's throat, one that she could not push down, no matter how hard she swallowed - but what Joe said did make sense. He really understood her like no one else ever had. Maybe she was letting Iris and Violet take her for granted. And it wasn't like they would really miss her. "Plus, if we don't have the money..."

Joe took Lily into his arms. "We don't need anyone else, Lil. We have our home, and food in the fridge, and next time you get pregnant, maybe you won't lose it, and we'll finally have that baby. We don't need fancy trips and expensive jewelry and crap like that. Your sisters chase after those things because that's all they have. You and me - we have each other. We have a special bond, ya know?"

Joe slid his hand down over Lily's breast. The images of his face, so recently dripping with rage, and of his shoe bursting through the window screen were still fresh in her mind. She steeled herself against her inclination to flinch and push him away, torn between being repulsed by his cruelty and craving love and comfort, knowing that she would have to find a way to say "no" to Iris; the idea of it churned in her belly. Part of her wanted to gather Joe into her arms, to love the little boy who sat alone all afternoon by the boat ride, to show her gratitude to the man who insisted that she was too special to be ignored - and part of her wanted to scream at him, slap him, run from him. Yet what would she scream, where would she run to? What if it turned out that he was the only one who truly cared? Could she really afford to alienate him? Bound by the heavy chains of confusion, Lily's anger thrashed about inside her. Tamed by her fears, it finally acquiesced. Lily curled up inside herself, cuddling her rage like an exotic pet, unaware of its wild and dangerous nature, as Joe led her to their bed.

Lily pushed aside the sliding glass door that opened out onto the brick patio. "Hi, Donna!" she called, leaning out the door.

"Hey there!"

"You wanna have coffee?"

"Sure -come on over! In fact," added Donna, "It's almost noon -

why don't we have lunch - my sister just sent me some photos of her little girl's fifth birthday party. You have got to see how precious she is!"

"Great!" Lily replied, even though the sight of other people's children caused her to churn with envy. "I'll bring dessert - just give me a few minutes." Lily hadn't been able to finish her breakfast that morning. The first bite of white toast with butter seemed to scrape her insides all the way down, and she became immediately nauseated, a malady that was only exacerbated by the idea that Iris was sure to call today about Alex Bay. Lily still hadn't figured out what to say to her. It would be better to be gone when she called.

Lily reached up into the overhead cupboard and retrieved a plastic box which she kept stocked with Rice Krispies treats. Not only did the gooey-sweet squares literally cost pennies a piece (she'd done the math), but Donna assumed she chose to keep a supply of them because they were her daughter Nikki's favorite snack, and not because she couldn't afford more.

Donna sat down on the picnic bench, her hefty round body causing it to sway in the middle. She removed the plastic wrap from a platter of sandwiches - tuna for her and Lily, and peanut butter and jelly for Nikki - all in halves, perfectly sliced on the diagonal.

Growing up with a brood of live-in playmates, Lily never felt confident in her skills for establishing relationships with other women. She wondered if she and Donna would have been friends under any other circumstances; she was grateful for this accident of proximity.

Lily flipped through the photographs of a little blond-haired girl in a pink tiara and tutu. "I don't think I could ever move that far away from home like you did," she said. "We've moved twice since we got married and I would be happy to stay here for the rest of my life. Or at least until our children are grown."

"We go where the Lord leads us," replied Donna, smiling broadly. Lily wondered how one could be led to move to Rochester by God. She knew the stories about how St. Joseph and

St. Paul had dreams and visions where God spoke to them and told them what to do, but they were saints, and that was in the Bible, where God performed miracles all the time. Lily had to admit that the idea of getting instructions about how to deal with life directly from the Big Guy Himself sounded appealing right about now. She would ask Him how to help Joe get her pregnant. She heaved a deep sigh.

"Rough night?" Donna asked.

"Why do you ask?" Lily laughed nervously.

"No reason - you just look a little tired." Donna's gaze shifted, almost imperceptibly and for a split second, to a spot over Lily's head and to the right, before landing back on Lily with a warm smile. She tucked a tuft of bleach-blond hair behind her right ear. "Let's eat!" she said, with too much enthusiasm.

Confused and uneasy, Lily laid her napkin across her lap, took a sandwich triangle from the tray, and brought it to her mouth. Even if the bread came with lines scored on it, Lily wouldn't be able to cut them so perfectly. Since you were just going to chew it up and swallow it anyway, it seemed like a waste to put so much energy into it.

"What do we do before we eat, Nikki?" said Donna.

"We pray," said Nikki, in a tone that indicated that she was more irritated at the delay this would cause than she was delighted to have answered the question correctly.

Lily froze, her tuna sandwich half in her mouth, half out.

Donna bowed her head and placed her folded hands on her protruding belly. Lily placed the sandwich in her lap and bowed her head.

"Heavenly Father," Donna began. "We thank you for this food. May it nourish our bodies so that we may be energized to serve You, Lord. Let us remember those who have no food today. We pray that they would turn from their ignorance and give You all glory and honor so that their lives may be healed. We pray in the name of Your only Son Jesus, our beloved Lord and Savior. Amen."

"Amen," echoed Lily and Nikki.

"Oh, here - let Mama get that for you." Donna shoved a sandwich into her mouth, as Nikki struggled to use a small straw to punch through the perforated hole in her juice box.

Lily casually looked back over her shoulder in an attempt to discover where Donna's gaze had been drawn, and from where they sat, just over the top of Lily's tree, was her bedroom window, the screen still derailed. As she turned back around, she was met again with Donna's gaze and a flash of pity, or embarrassment; she couldn't tell which.

"I just don't understand why your tuna tastes so wonderful," said Lily, biting off the tip her sandwich. "I dress mine the exact same way, but it doesn't taste this good." A sense of panic rose in Lily, as she wondered how loud they had been the previous night. She made a mental note to close the window next time.

"Albacore," said Donna, picking up another one from the tray; she bit off half, and washed it down with several gulps of Coke. "Packed in water. Instead of the chunk light tuna. It costs a little more, but it's sweeter, and doesn't have as much of a fishy taste."

"Albacore?" said Lily, realizing that they were having a conversation that June Cleaver from "Leave it to Beaver" might have had. "Why didn't anyone tell me there was more than one kind of tuna?"

"Now that you know," said Donna, grabbing a handful of chips from a large glass bowl. "You can make it the same way. Sometimes all it takes is for someone to point you in the right direction." Donna placed several chips into her mouth and looked directly at Lily with raised eyebrows as she chomped down.

Donna took the last sandwich from the tray and ate it in two bites. She wiped her mouth, cleared her throat, drained her glass of Coke and took a Rice Krispies treat from the box, tearing it in half between long pink acrylic fingernails. "Lily, I hope you don't take this the wrong way, but the Lord has put it on my heart to talk to you about what happened at your house last night. I'm worried about you."

No sense denying it, or pretending she didn't know what Donna was referring to. Anyway, Donna was the closest thing

Lily had to a friend, and she was not the kind of person who would let a lie go by.

"It's no big deal, Donna, really, just a disagreement."

"Sugar, a disagreement is when you want to order a pizza and he wants Chinese take-out." Donna gestured toward Lily's bedroom window. "What was going on up there last night was way more than a disagreement. I was sittin' right here, and I saw a shoe come a-flying out that window. If it were the first time somethin' like that has happened, I might not be buttin' my nose in like this - but I know it's not the first. Or even the fourth or fifth. You'd be surprised how much I hear of what goes on over at your house, Lily."

The excuses and explanations Lily wanted to give scorched her throat, the heat rising into her face and finally releasing itself as tears that spilled down her cheeks.

Donna knit her brow and sidled over next to Lily. She put her arm around Lily's shoulder. "There, there, darlin'," she said. "Now you just go ahead and have yourself a little cry." She began rocking them both back and forth, as Lily wept. "Jesus knows your pain, Lily. He died so that you might have hope. He wants to help you." Donna chomped down on the Rice Krispies treat, and with a mouth full of rice cereal and marshmallow, she mumbled, "Won't you let Him into your heart?"

9. IRIS

"I found it!" Deirdre said, as soon as Iris picked up the phone.

"Found what?" Iris asked.

"The perfect job," Deirdre said.

"What new career have you got your feisty little Irish heart set on this time?" Iris darted back into the kitchen, the handset cradled between her ear and shoulder, to stir the béchamel before lumps could form. Cordless phones were a great invention.

"Don't be daft, you're the one always saying you're bored with a part-time job and no babies and a husband who works late, not me!"

"Besides perfect, what kind of job is it?" The butter and flour and milk mixture bubbled over the low flame, thickening to perfection as Iris stirred it in quick, circular motions with a wooden spoon. She stirred twelve times in a clockwise direction (once for each Capotosti sibling, her usual way of counting things), then counterclockwise, before inverting again.

"Listen to this: 'Luxury Riviera hotel seeks assistant manager. Applicants must have minimum three years experience in hospitality, strong background in sales and F&B, fluent English and second foreign language.'"

"So what exactly makes that perfect for me? The only qualification I have is fluent English. Me and about a billion other people."

"I thought you said you spoke some French."

"That was a zillion years ago, in high school."

"You speak Italian."

"Italian is not a foreign language when you live in Italy, Deirdre. Besides, I have no background in hospitality or sales, and I don't even know what F&B is."

"Food and beverage. I looked it up."

"Well, I can't see how I could have gotten that experience shuffling around musty files at Transoceanica."

"Think back on your life, Iris. It's all there!"

Iris turned off the flame and set the béchamel aside; she had already prepared the pesto, now she only had to boil the noodles. One of the things she appreciated most about Ligurian cuisine was the predominance of vegetables and herbs and the absence of heavy sauces, but adding a layer of white sauce to baked lasagna made the dish delicious. And it never failed to please the key players of the Policlinico hierarchy Iris had the honor of entertaining at the Leale table, whose level of simple elegance, creative fare and wine selection escalated in tandem with Gregorio's ascension to the upper echelons of the medical profession.

"Look at all those fancy dinner parties you host," Deirdre said. "And you could cook for a family of fourteen before you were as many years old. I call that solid food and beverage background."

"And I call that pure imagination."

"Everything qualifies as experience, Iris. It's just a question of presenting it the right way. Besides, you have worked other jobs."

"Yeah, at some of America's finest dining establishments. So they should hire me on the spot because I hold the record for selling the most Egg McMuffins in the summer of '75 and know what a monkey dish is?"

"How many beautiful, intelligent, English-speaking young women in the whole region of Liguria can say the same?"

"You Irish sure have a way with words."

"But Iris, just imagine all the jet-setters you'd meet! People from all over the world go to that hotel."

155

"Which hotel are we talking about, anyway?"

"I don't know exactly which one, the name wasn't in the ad. But it doesn't matter, it's in the area. And it has to be at least a four-star. Give it a try, come on!"

Iris did not have a clear vision of her future by any means, but she did know that she had learned all she cared to about the marine insurance business. She had dedicated far too much brain space to the storage of technical jargon; she was fed up with the sorry-looking clique of Transoceanica girls who snubbed her, and even her boss Elio Bacigalupo was really getting on her nerves lately whenever he opened his mouth to lecture her on his latest theory. Not only could she use a change, she would die if she didn't get out of that place soon.

"You know, maybe I will take a shot at it," Iris said. "What's the worst that can happen?"

Two weeks after sending in her application, Iris was pleasantly surprised, though not totally astonished (she had invested considerable effort in the preparation of a convincing résumé) when she was contacted by the Grand Hotel Stella di Levante for a preliminary interview. Though she held little hope of being hired, she was curious to get inside the hotel just to see it, and to learn more about the job, so she might consider it as a possible future career option. She was received by the general manager himself, Fausto Parodini, a pinch-faced Ligurian with a hook nose, referred to simply as *"il Direttore."* While they were reviewing her application in his office, a knock came on the door, which had been left slightly ajar.

"Scusate," a voice said, peeking in the room. "Am I interrupting something?" The man's voice exuded culture and class, and though its tone was one of cordial respect, Iris doubted it belonged to one of the *Direttore*'s underlings.

"No, *Dottore*, not at all! *Venga! Venga!* Come in, please, have a seat," the *Direttore* answered, motioning to an empty chair as he rose to shake his hand in greeting, fumbling with the papers strewn about on his desk as he hastily grouped them into a stack. Iris was amused to notice how the *Direttore*'s stance had subtly but swiftly shifted from one of supreme authority, to that of subordinate, leading her to presume that the man could be none other than Claudio Olona, the owner of the hotel, whose name appeared on the brochure she had studied in the lobby. The Olona family had owned the property for four generations, ever since it had been converted from a *belle époque* gambling casino to a proper hotel during the early years of the twentieth century.

"I didn't think you were arriving from Milan until this evening, *Dottore*. But since you're here, may I introduce you to Iris Capotosti? She is here to interview for the job as my assistant."

"*Buongiorno, Dottoressa* Iris Capotosti," the gentleman said, nodding his head in greeting. He enunciated each syllable deliberately, as if sampling the taste of her name on his tongue. He did not move to shake her hand or seat himself in the empty chair, but stood at the threshold, one hand still on the doorknob, the thumb of the other hooked over the edge of a finely-stitched pocket. Even from where she sat, Iris could tell that the fabric of his trousers was of the highest quality wool; she ventured to guess it might be Tasmanian, possibly even Loro Piana. Pockets like those were not tailored to host the calloused hands of common men, nor to jingle with their loose change.

"*Buongiorno, Dottore*," Iris replied, with a nod of her head and a polite smile. She hesitated briefly before adding, "Just Iris, please. Without the *Dottoressa*." She disliked the overuse of titles in Italy, but not because she could not claim one for herself. She might as well let him know from the start that a fancy degree was not one of the qualifications she could bring to the job.

"Would you like to see her curriculum vitae, *Dottore*?" The *Direttore* asked, holding up a neatly typewritten sheet.

"I don't think that will be necessary, *Direttore*. If you've summoned her for an interview, you must consider her credentials suitable for the job, correct?" the owner said, never taking his eyes off of Iris. "Tell me about your accent. North American? Australian?"

"American. Upstate New York. A place not many people have heard of, called Rochester, not far from the Canadian border.

Niagara Falls, that area. Between Buffalo and Syracuse." Why did she feel obliged to give this obviously worldly gentleman a geography lesson?

"Of course! I know it well. I studied for my masters in Ithaca, after obtaining my degree from Glion, in Switzerland. I enjoyed the Finger Lakes immensely, especially in the autumn. Some rather palatable wines are actually coming out of the area now. I think a lovely young lady from upstate New York is exactly what the Stella di Levante needs. A touch of international class. Don't you agree, *Signora* Iris?"

"Well, sure. If you think I can handle the job," Iris replied, wishing she could learn to choose her spoken words with the same studied precision as her written words, and project less surprise and more self-assurance into her voice. The man had caught her off guard, though; she hadn't expected the task of convincing the manager of her suitability to be miraculously and effortlessly lifted out of her hands; neither apparently had the nonplusssed *Direttore*, judging from the look of confused deference on his face.

"A touch of international class," Olona had said: she was thankful he could not see through her guise to the snot-nosed, scabby-kneed urchin who had to scrape bubble gum off the street if she wanted any at all. She was not yet sure whether she was more put off by the man's condescending attitude, or curious to find out whether he was as intelligent and cultivated as he thought himself. One thing she was sure of: if he was offering her this challenge, she would do everything in her power to rise to it. She might not know all she needed to know now, but she'd pick up what she was lacking along the way, as she always did. In the meantime, she was convinced that *Dottore* Claudio Olona and his hotel would benefit from her unique satchel of skills, which couldn't be summed up in one typewritten sheet.

"Then it's settled," he said, reaching to shake her hand. "Parodini will fill you in on the practical details. Welcome to the Grand Hotel Stella di Levante."

That evening at dinner, Iris cracked open a bottle of Berlucchi rosé, her favorite spumante, to celebrate the news of her job with Gregorio, figuring that the more elated she looked, the harder it would be for him to voice the objections he was certain to raise. He couldn't quite hide a grimace as he congratulated her on landing such a desirable position at one of the most prestigious hotels in the Riviera, and declined the flute she poured for him, preferring to stick with his favorite special occasion bubbly, San Pellegrino mineral water.

"Don't forget to tell them you can't work weekends. And that we've already booked our vacation to Ischia," Gregorio said. Since the year after their marriage, the couple had developed the habit of spending the last week of May in Ischia, where Iris visited the thermal baths, whose anti-inflammatory properties were purported to improve fertility, and Gregorio kicked off the summer diving season before the onslaught of tourists invaded the island.

"It's not like a regular job, Gregorio," she said, refilling her glass. "It's a hotel, open twenty-four hours a day, seven days a week. Try to think of it as a hospital for healthy people. But let's cross that bridge when we come to it. You don't walk into a job interview asking for time off. It all happened so fast! I can hardly believe it!"

"I'm very proud of you, *Piccolina*. But remember, you don't exactly *need* that job. You live in a beautiful house, drive a car that's large enough for a family of four, own a closetful of nice clothes you never wear. And you have a husband who happens to love the way you look in fine jewelry. God knows I work hard enough to provide you with all that. If you only had half an idea of the things I have to endure at the Policlinico. Take today. We had a patient with perforated diverticulitis and an onset of peritonitis. And do you know what that cretin Gardella said to me when he waltzed into the O.R.?"

The question did not require an answer. Iris knew Gregorio would proceed with his story without further prompting, and that it would lead to another one, and yet another, until the events of his day were unfolded and laid out before her. She had stopped trying to turn his soliloquy into conversation years earlier, when her comments were recurrently passed over, and his impatient or overly scientific answers to her questions left her feeling more ignorant than informed. It was just as well; she would be free to think about her new occupation. Gregorio may not think she needed that job, but she wanted it. She wanted to break out of that dusty office and swing from those four stars. She couldn't wait to write to Auntie Rosa and her sisters to tell them the news. She'd have to be extra tactful in her letter to Lily, and measure each word to make sure it didn't sound like she was bragging. Lily was so sensitive these days.

Iris tilted her empty flute, and poured herself another glass of spumante, letting it bubble over the edge just enough to irritate Gregorio, who looked at her disapprovingly, as he droned on.

Iris breathed a sigh of relief as the elevator door slid shut on the buzz of early evening activity, leaving her alone with her reflection. It had been a long day, and she looked tired. She should already be on her way home, but this was the time of day when her help was most needed to resolve those problems which were simply too complicated or delicate to be dealt with by the overworked front office staff who had their hands full with guests besieging them in all languages, asking for restaurant recommendations or driving directions, complaining about cocktail service or demanding to know why their laundry had not been delivered.

A circle of diamonds flashed as she rotated her wrist to glance at her Cartier Baignoire; she was even more dismayed by the sight of the late hour indicated by the watch's hands, than by the style of the timepiece itself (her thirtieth birthday present from Gregorio, though she had neither needed nor wanted another new watch). Gregorio would just have to wait for his supper, if he got home before she did. Looking in the mirror, she shook the frown from her face, and tilted her head to check her appearance, as the car whisked her up the six floors to the Terrazza del Cielo Roof Garden. Her hair was swept away from her face in a simple chignon, from which a few disobedient strands had strayed. At this hour, she couldn't blame them for wandering off on their own to curl up against her long neck, just below the ears where a pair of perfect pearls (her tenth anniversary gift from Gregorio) were centered on pink lobes. Her face, tanned from tagging along on her husband's scuba diving expeditions, required little make-up, just a touch of plum eye shadow and mascara to complement her eyes, and matching gloss to keep her lips shiny and moist. She extracted a tube from the pocket of her navy blue blazer and applied a fresh coat, rubbed her lips together to even out the color, then bared her teeth to make sure none had smeared. Whenever Isabella got lipstick on her teeth, Iris debated over whether to point it out or not, but in the end never did. If her mother-in-law was going to insist on wearing lipstick around the house, if she was going to keep marring the water glasses and staining the napkins Iris got stuck washing after the Sunday dinners someone at some point had decided should be hosted by Iris, she could just keep walking around with lipstick on her teeth.

Iris reached under the hem of her knee-length skirt, and adjusted the lacy stretch tops of her thigh-high stockings; like their wearer, they were starting to lose their grip and ready to call it a day. Iris couldn't wait to free herself of the garments and the role into which she had been constricted since morning. If she hadn't been summoned by the big boss, she might have hopped on the Vespa she had finally convinced Gregorio to let her buy, and made a detour to Paraggi before heading home. This was her favorite time of day to sneak in a swim, when the sun dropped behind the promontory, and most bathers packed up and migrated elsewhere. Plunging into the cool emerald water was an ideal way to cleanse herself of the stress accumulated by the end of a demanding day at the hotel. Though she never strayed far from shore, her swims made her feel as though she were leaving all earthly concerns behind, and entering another world. Floating on her back, she imagined her body as it would appear from the sky above or the sea below, rocking softly on the gentle waves, suspended between two dimensions. She could never stay long, but that didn't matter much, either; even a brief pause between her roles and responsibilities of hotel and home, a slice of time and space in which she could just be Iris, was a precious gift to herself, without making her feel too guilty.

The elevator jerked to a halt, just as she was smoothing her skirt over her hips and buttocks; a quick glance over her shoulder in the mirror assured her that the modest slit was centered perfectly between her legs. The door slid open, and the Assistant Manager of the Grand Hotel Stella di Levante clicked her high heels out of the elevator and into the Roof Garden restaurant. She was immediately drawn to the terrace, where she was captivated by the streaks of crimson and violet performing jetés and pirouettes against a backdrop of deep blue. The view was irresistible, and its beauty seemed to liberate her heart from the strings she had felt tightening around it of late. Here, it was free to dance with the clouds in the sky, fly across the gulf past Santa Margherita Ligure and over the promontory of Portofino, then soar out to the open Mediterranean.

"*Buonasera*, Iris." The voice came from behind her, startling her with its unexpected proximity. Once in a while, she still had difficulty deciphering the nuances that were a prerogative of the Italian language, such as the formal-friendly ambiguity created by the use of a polite greeting coupled with her first name. The person speaking to her now was both her senior and her superior, so it would be his call to invite her to address him by his first name, if he should so desire. Until he did so, she would keep referring to him as "*Dottore*" to his face, and "Olona" in her mind, the way she would refer to the American president as Reagan.

"*Buonasera Dottore*," Iris replied. Her composure in greeting the gentleman, achieved through practice, was belied by the blush infusing her cheeks.

"Not a bad view, is it?" he asked, standing next to her.

"It's simply breathtaking. I could stay here and stare for hours on end, and still never get tired of looking at it," Iris replied. "Not that I do," she hastened to add, fearing he might think that was how she wiled away her days. Olona was busy following the construction of a new hotel in Milan, and only came down to the Stella di Levante once or twice a month to meet with the *Direttore*, usually arriving in the evening, as Iris was leaving, and departing the following morning, as Iris reported for duty. Their brief conversations were limited to cordial inquiries about how the job was going, or amusing anecdotes about the owner's years at Cornell University, which he recounted in English.

"Of course you don't," Olona replied. "Or you wouldn't have obtained such impressive results on the job in your very first year with us." A smile visited his lips, then vanished as he turned to gaze at the panorama. The man's streamlined features, so perfectly trained in the exercise of conveying approval or criticism during the course of his constant quest for quality and efficiency relaxed; his expression turned pensive.

Iris was unprepared to respond to a compliment on her performance in the presence of such beauty, so remained silent. A full minute passed before he spoke again, his eyes still fixed on the view. "You're a sensitive woman. I think you'll agree that it can be unbearably painful to witness such loveliness." Odd he should say such a thing to her, even if she did consider herself sensitive; judging from his words, he must be, too. Regardless, she knew exactly what he meant about it being painful. An overabundance of natural beauty always stirred contrasting emotions within her: elation, despair; hope, despondency; anticipation, nostalgia.

"Suddenly, a splendid, apparently endless summer day begins slipping away from you," Olona continued. "Only as the day retreats, do you realize the full extent of its beauty. And just as the intensity reaches its climax, the end draws near. Soon, you are abandoned, left alone in the fading afterglow. Soon, the hopes and intentions and promises with which you started that day are swallowed up by the darkness. What is done, is done. What opportunities have been lost, cannot be brought back."

Olona spoke exceptionally good English, albeit in a rather contrived manner, perfected during the course of his privileged education abroad. His voice was soft when he addressed her, in contrast with the stiff, businesslike image that was projected by his tall, arrow-straight physique, perfectly poised beneath the fine fabric of his impeccably tailored suit.

"You wanted to show me something, *Dottore*?" Iris asked, detaching her eyes from the seascape to look at him. Olona pivoted to face her. His right cheek, awash with the fiery glow of the sky as it melted into the twilight, was tinged a deep shade of pink; his left was enshrouded in the shadows of the still deserted restaurant. The air held the promise of delightful dishes yet to be served, corks yet to be discreetly pulled and sniffed, wines yet to gurgle delicately from impressively labeled bottles, candlelit conversations yet to be engaged in. As she looked at the two faces of Olona, Iris tried to imagine how she might appear in that same light, to his eyes. Would her eyes and expression seem as spirited and contradictory as his?

"Yes, Iris," he said. "I did want to discuss something other than the view. As I was saying, I'm impressed with your progress. You've been doing a brilliant job filling in for the *Direttore* during his absence this week. I'd like your opinion on the new line of table linens I'm looking at. I told Parodini what I had in mind, but he sent me a sales rep with a suitcase full of rags so tacky I wouldn't serve my Saluki his dog chow on them. He's a Ligurian to the bone, always worried about saving money - as if it came out of his own pocket. Not that it's a negative trait, mind you, but it's not the only thing that counts. Do come with me." He turned and led the way to the far end of the restaurant, where two tables had been dressed with sample tablecloths. As he walked, she admired the way his suit jacket sat confidently upon his square shoulders, dropping to just the right length, following the fluidity of his movements.

Iris approached the first table, assessed its visual impact on her, lifted a corner of the tablecloth, let it glide between her thumb and forefinger. She turned to the second table and repeated the gesture.

"Egyptian cotton damask?" she said to Olona.

"Exactly," he answered.

"I definitely prefer the texture of this one, as well as its neutral shade," Iris continued, tapping her index finger on the second tablecloth, as her eyes surveyed the pink and green walls of the restaurant, the chaotic geometric decorations hanging from the ceiling like lopsided stalactites, the busy carpeting. "If I may say so ..." she started, but stopped in midsentence.

"You may," Olona gestured with a hand for her to continue. "Go on."

She didn't want to sound stupid, but knew that not completing her sentence would sound even stupider. "Well, it's just that I think the architect might have overdone it a bit when he designed these interiors. If I were a guest dining here, the only thing I'd want to look at - besides the man sitting across from me, of course - would be the sea and sky on the other side of those windows. Personally, I think too many colors are a distraction. Rather than complement the atmosphere, they disturb it. It's as if they were trying to compete with the view, but how can you beat the perfection of what's out there?"

"My thoughts exactly!" Claudio Olona raised his eyebrows and lowered his voice, as if he were about to share confidential information. "The architect was a family friend, you know how those things work. His father was a classmate of my father's in Milan, and during the last renovation he was given free rein to experiment. He's actually done quite a bit of interesting work in Italy and abroad."

"Hmmm." Iris did not wish to risk offending a family friend, and she knew virtually nothing about architecture. But she did understand enough about what tourists wanted to experience in a luxury Italian hotel overlooking the Mediterranean to know that the angular forms and loud tones surrounding her were not it.

"You don't seem impressed," Olona said.

"Well, it's not my place to say so, but I just don't feel that a hotel like this is the right stage for that type of experimentation. I think excessive visual stimulation disturbs the emotional experience." Olona cocked his head, looking her in the eye as she spoke. "In, um, my opinion, of course," she added. As if a man like him would care about her opinion regarding something she knew nothing about. As a rule, she preferred listening to talking, when people she considered her intellectual superiors dragged her into unfamiliar territory. Listening attentively, speaking only when she was sure of what she had to say, trusting her common sense to guide her, and answering questions with questions: these were the techniques she had developed to help her squeak by while adapting to her new country, striving to meet the standards of her new family, learning the ropes of new jobs, expanding her knowledge. Most of those intellectually superior people were more interested in hearing themselves talk, anyway, and were always in search of an audience.

"I prefer simplicity," Iris said. It would be difficult for anyone to find fault with such a statement, wouldn't it?

"Then it's settled. Simple. Elegant. That's the effect we want." Olona pointed to the table by the window. "It's the most expensive line, of course, but one mustn't skimp on quality, must one? Now the only thing left is to try it out. Would you care to join me for dinner?"

"Dinner? Tonight?" Now she was sure she sounded stupid. Her thoughts ran amok, wondering how she could possibly obtain Gregorio's permission to stay for dinner; whether she should even try; how she would look if she didn't. She had only remained after hours a handful of times, and had been fascinated by the transformation that came over the hotel at night. The guests she spotted in the late afternoon, exhausted from their day of sightseeing, reemerged from their rooms relaxed and refreshed, their duties as tourists absolved. The Italians could be singled out immediately, with their knack for looking stylish yet never overdressed in the casual atmosphere of a seaside location, while the foreigners were decked out in the elegant evening wear they had selected in perhaps months of planning what was for many a once-in-a-lifetime vacation. The Italians avoided aggregation, each couple or group talking and laughing among themselves, while the French and Germans and Swiss spoke in well-modulated tones as they sipped cocktails on the terrace. The Americans tended to strike up conversations with each other, exchanging experiences and insider tips with those who shared a common language, at times allowing some of the bolder British to join in. As the guests chatted and mingled, dusk fell and dots of light flickered to life, setting the coast of Portofino aglow. Iris had often imagined what she would do if she were the manager in charge of the hotel at that magical time of evening. She envisaged herself strolling among the tables, greeting the guests, inquiring whether they were enjoying their stay, now and then graciously offering a glass of Prosecco to repeat clients, or to those who had suffered any sort of negative experience, hoping her gesture might help make amends for any shortcomings of the hotel, of the Riviera, of Italy at large. She would signal silently to the barman when she saw tables that hadn't been cleared or ashtrays that hadn't been emptied, and he would send a waiter straight away. The staff wouldn't fear her, but rather respect her and want to please her, because she would treat them with kindness and fairness.

To be quite honest, she would be very happy to dine with Claudio Olona at his hotel tonight. After all, it was her job. After all, he was the owner. After all, didn't Gregorio work plenty of nights himself?

A half-smile appeared on the side of Olona's face streaked with ribbons of fading crimson. "Yes, of course. Tonight. It is almost dinner time, or hadn't you noticed? Please don't tell me you are one of those dreadful women who don't eat because they're always watching their figure. Yours is perfect."

"No. I mean, yes," Iris stammered, embarrassed by his reference to her shape. "To dinner. That would be nice. I just need to make a phone call."

"Of course, take your time," he said. "I have to run down to the office a moment. Shall we meet back up here in ten minutes?"

"Fine," Iris said, hoping hers were the only ears that picked up the crazy tam-tam of her heart.

The remaining half of Olona's mouth completed the smile, as he nodded, then turned and walked to the elevator, leaving Iris in the empty restaurant, suspended somewhere between sunset and darkness, duty and daring, curiosity and caution. She ducked into the restaurant's small office, and dialed her home number: no answer. She tried Cinzia's.

"*Pronto.*" Most people answered the phone with an interrogatory inflection, or at least a hint of curiosity, in their voices. Not Isabella; the sound of her voice was enough to inform the caller that he or she was disturbing, and had better make it quick.

"*Ciao,* Isabella. It's me, Iris."

"It's about time! Where are you, for heaven's sake?"

"I'm at work," Iris squinted her eyes and scrunched her shoulders, the way she used to wince as a child, right before she knew her father was going to start yelling.

"Still at the hotel? At this hour, *Cara*?"

Iris felt the hairs on her bare neck bristle. Over the years, she had come to despise being called "*Cara,*" even more than she had begun to dislike Gregorio's "*Piccolina.*" She had nothing against terms of endearment and knew it was possible that her aversion to people using them in place of her name stemmed from the fact that her father had always insisted that everyone be called by his or her full name, but she didn't think that was the reason. Maybe it was just that when Isabella called her "dear" it somehow sounded like she meant the opposite.

"Something unexpected came up," she said. "Is Gregorio there? I've tried calling home, but there was no answer."

Iris could hear the voices of children screeching in the background, and imagined the cozy scene of Franco and the kids in the living room engaging in horseplay, while Cinzia prepared dinner in the kitchen.

"Gregorio is on his way," Isabella said. "He just called ten minutes ago. He said he couldn't reach you, either. He sounded rather worried." Isabella said. "Understandably so."

"I was in a meeting with the owner," Iris said.

"But he called the hotel, and no one knew where you were!" In the beginning, Isabella had asked a few perfunctory questions about what exactly Iris's job entailed, but quickly lost interest; she had no idea how little time Iris actually spent seated at her desk.

"I don't sit in my office all the time. I move around, especially when I fill in for the manager," Iris said. No sense mentioning that she had left her pager in her office so as not to be disturbed. "Anyway, I called to say that I won't be home for dinner."

She squeezed her eyes shut, sunk her head deep into her jacket, waiting. After a moment of silence, she blinked, pulled herself up tall, took a deep breath. "Hello? Are you still there?" she asked.

"Yes, of course. Where else would I be? I was just trying to understand what exactly you meant by that," Isabella said.

"I meant that I have to work. I'll have a bite here," Iris said, again feeling as though she were a little girl, daring to tell her father that she had decided to stay home and pray instead of attending Sunday Mass with the rest of the family.

"What about Gregorio's dinner?" Isabella asked.

"There are leftovers in the fridge. Or perhaps he could join the rest of you at Cinzia's?" Iris suggested.

"Well, I don't know that he would be very pleased to do that. The little ones are particularly rambunctious this evening." Isabella lowered her voice and added, "I myself cannot wait to retire upstairs. And you know how Gregorio treasures his quiet time, after the long, stressful hours he puts in."

Iris looked up and waved at Paolo the Chef and Alberto the Maître d', who had just walked into the restaurant and flipped on the lights. Back from their dinner break, they would be going over the evening's reservations. Iris smiled, as Alberto placed a hand over his heart, then blew her a kiss. From the outset, she had perceived the importance of being on good terms with the pair, and now enjoyed the way they were able to joke with each other. She had been painfully aware of her lack of experience when she was hired, but instead of simply relaying the orders dictated by the *Direttore*, she found herself wanting to understand them, at times even questioning them, and had turned to the Chef and Maître for explanations and advice.

When her boss arrived late for scheduled appointments, leaving her to her own inadequate devices as she dealt with prospective brides and grooms and batteries of future in-laws, or meeting planners in charge of organizing corporate events at the hotel, she invited Paolo and Alberto to attend the meetings. When they were not available, she relied upon her innate resources and acquired skills, bluffing and biding her time as she waded her way through negotiations, taking notes of her clients' demands, surreptitiously marking the items that required clarification. Could the lemon sorbet between the fish and meat courses be replaced with green apple sorbet? Could a Rossese from Albenga be served with cuttlefish risotto? What was the maximum number of guests for which she could allow tagliatelle as a first course before ruling out noodles in favor of a short form of pasta, and were wild porcini mushrooms available in June? Paolo and Alberto could make life very difficult for her if they so desired, but she knew the door swung both ways. By fielding complaints from restaurant clients who demanded to speak with the manager, she was able to weed out and resolve minor issues, referring only the most grievous problems to his attention. Her aversion for conflict and abhorrence of backstabbing (a popular sport among hotel workers) did not go unnoticed. In time, her knack for diplomacy, her love of the business, and her honest desire to learn earned her their sincere respect and unwavering cooperation.

"Yes, Isabella. I know how much Gregorio needs his quiet evenings." Iris did not want to sound curt; all she wanted was to end the conversation before Gregorio walked in and forced her to start the discussion all over again. "Could you kindly just give him the message, and tell him to do as he pleases? To eat at home, or eat out, or eat with you, then just go on along to bed? I won't be late, but I don't want him waiting up if he is exhausted."

"Honestly, Iris. I really don't know what you are doing working in a hotel, anyway. Of all places!" Isabella replied.

"Thank you, Isabella. I really have to go now. I'll see you tomorrow." She replaced the receiver in its cradle and stared at the phone, as if it all those words had been uttered by the device, and not her mouth, as she stood by and listened. She could not swear to it, but Iris reckoned that was the first time she had ever hung up without waiting for the person at the other end of the line to end the conversation.

"*Buonasera*, Chef, *buonasera* Maître." Iris looked up and saw Olona approaching the pair, placing a hand on the shoulder of Alberto's black evening jacket.

"*Buonasera, Dottore*," they both replied as they shook hands with the owner. Iris admired the way he came across as genuinely friendly and unequivocally in control at the same time. "Your usual table, *Dottore*?" Alberto asked.

"Tonight I have the honor of dining with *Signora* Iris," he replied. "We would like to sit at that table in the corner, to see how we like the linens."

Iris walked over to the group; after a long, hot day of rushing around the hotel, her feet were slippery with sweat, and her face and hands felt clammy. She wished she had taken the time to freshen up in the ladies' room, instead of wasting it on a conversation with her mother-in-law.

"Wonderful," the Maître said. "I'll be right with you, so we can get you served before the crowds come in."

"Take your time, Alberto. We'll seat ourselves."

"We'll be serving some excellent *tagliata* of tuna this evening, if you're interested," the Chef said. "Accompanied by caramelized Tropea onions and balsamic vinegar reduction."

Much to her dismay, Iris's stomach spoke out of turn, growling its audible reply. She was famished, having skipped lunch to deal with an American family who had lost their passports at the beach in Monterosso, and seared tuna steak sounded absolutely divine. Her taste buds had been willing pupils over the years as she experimented with new foods, and her palate had evolved considerably since her arrival on the continent.

Olona stepped aside and gestured for Iris to precede him to the table, as he lagged a few steps behind. She felt self-conscious walking in front of him, recalling the fire the sun had thrown into his eyes as they had watched it sink behind the promontory. She imagined them roaming from the chignon pinned to the back of her head, down the nape of her neck to the ticklish spot between her shoulder blades, and descending her spine. She could sense their heat on her backside as his eyes dropped to the slit in her skirt. She could feel her stockings losing their grip again with each step she took, and worried he might notice their lacy tops peeking out, and perhaps even catch a glimpse of her bare thighs.

Olona held a chair out for her, guided it to the table as she sat, then seated himself. Was he being gallant with her, or were impeccable manners just part of his upbringing? Whatever the case may be, the deference and attention in his attitude made her feel as though she were on equal terms with him, as if she were a capable professional or an attractive woman worth spending the evening with. Or possibly both.

The Maître appeared at their table and lit the candle. Iris had repeatedly suggested that the candles at every table be lit, regardless of whether they were reserved, before the restaurant opened for dinner at seven forty-five, but the *Direttore* objected on the grounds that they might just as well hold ten thousand lira banknotes over a flame, if they were going to waste all that money on wax. Alberto proceeded to uncork a chilled bottle of Prosecco from Conegliano, which made a refreshing if unpretentious aperitif, poured out two glasses, placed the bottle in a silver ice bucket, then turned to hand the pair their dinner menus.

"Tell the Chef we trust him implicitly," Olona said to Alberto, waving away the menus. "The tuna *tagliata* sounds excellent," he continued, glancing at Iris, who nodded her approval, "and to start, I have to say, I happened to catch a glimpse of those scampi from Santa Margherita when they were delivered this morning. So fresh they were still twitching. I think they'll do for an antipasto."

Iris ran her fingers up and down the fine crystal stem of her glass, watching the bubbles float to the surface and burst. It had been an arduous day, and she was yearning to reward herself with a sip of the cold wine, but whenever she drank bubbly she felt it was bad luck not to raise her glass in a toast and look at the people she was sharing it with straight in the eye. Unless of course the other person was Gregorio, and the liquid in his glass was water. She couldn't imagine what she could possibly propose a toast to in this situation.

"To revelations," Olona said, as if he had read her mind, raising his glass before Iris could give the matter further thought.

Iris lifted her glass and smiled politely as the rims of the two flutes struck a delicate, high-pitched note. "To revelations," she repeated. She wondered to what he was referring exactly, and hoped to God it didn't have anything to do with her sagging stockings; she vowed to toss them in the rubbish as soon as she took them off. At the first sip from her glass, the bubbles tickling her tongue and the roof of her mouth distracted her from all other thoughts. Savoring the crisp flavor of the wine, she realized she was enjoying the moment immensely, and that it was the first time she would dine alone with a man since marrying Gregorio. Actually, if one were a stickler for exactitude, the truth was that it was the first time she would dine alone with any man other than Gregorio; with any man who did not abhor candles or turn up his nose at bubbly wines. She felt slightly disloyal thinking such thoughts, but it wasn't as though she was being unfairly critical; she was simply acknowledging opinions that Gregorio himself had openly expressed over and over (and over) to whomever would listen. Thinking of Gregorio reminded her that he would probably be home by now, and might try to call her on that mobile phone he had given her, which sat in her office. She just couldn't get used to carrying the thing with her; it was bulky, and she couldn't see the need, since the only places she ever went were home and work. She hoped he wouldn't be too irritated if she didn't answer. After all, she never called him when he was in the operating room, did she?

She glanced around the restaurant nervously, half expecting her husband to materialize right before her eyes, stomp over to her table, grab her by an arm, and drag her home. But the only people moving about were the dinner guests, who had begun to trickle in, suntanned and smiling, as Alberto greeted them, and a waiter seated them at their tables. The gentlemen smiled indulgently as the ladies gasped at the view of the satin sea and velvet sky, and the coast sprinkled with shimmering lights. She thought of the fish and chips and steak-and-kidney pies and wiener schnitzel and T-bone steaks they must eat at home, and felt proud to work in an establishment where the food was as divine as the view, and where she could play a role in making fairytale vacations become a reality.

"Iris," Olona said, as he lifted the dripping bottle from the ice bucket, serviette wrapped around its neck, and refreshed their drinks. He poured the Prosecco to just the right level, stopping precisely before the foam could overflow, with the practiced hand of a man who has filled many a flute. "You don't mind if I call you Iris, do you? Without the *Signora*?"

"No, not at all," Iris replied.

"Very well. As I was saying, Iris, don't think I haven't noticed."

"Noticed what, *Dottore*?" Iris asked, her voice catching on the nervousness that was darting around in her throat, blocking the way of her words as they tried to pass. What could he possibly be accusing her of?

"Please, Iris. Do call me Claudio," he said, smiling, their eyes locking. "Let's do it the American way."

"*Va bene, Dottore.*" Iris had never once heard Parodini call him Claudio, even when referring to him in his absence, and he was her boss. It was always, the *Dottore* wants this, what would the *Dottore* think of that. She didn't know whether to be honored or alarmed.

"As I was saying, don't think I haven't noticed what an excellent job you've been doing here at the Stella. You were an invaluable asset to us during the World Cup, dealing with those vulgar superstar soccer players and dreadful media delegations. And I also spoke recently to the owner of the *Eventi Eccetera* agency in Milan - he's a member of the club where I play racquetball. He had nothing but praise for the way you handled that car launch last February. He commended your organizational skills, and your creativity at adapting the leisure activities planned for the trade press to a solid week of pouring rain. Then there's my chiropractor, who was on the scientific committee of a

174

seminar back in March, and was astonished at how quickly you resolved the problems some of the foreign speakers who were having trouble projecting their presentations. He'll be coming back to see you, to make arrangements for his daughter's wedding."

"Thank you," Iris said, stopping herself before adding *"Dottore,"* yet unable to go a step further and pronounce his first name. "I like to make sure I'm around, just in case something goes awry at the last minute. I hate to risk a flop, after all the planning and investment people pour into an event."

"Yes, it's that pragmatic, hands-on, American attitude that I simply adore. I don't need a number-crunching *Direttore* managing my hotel. We have the *Ragioniere* for that. A necessary evil, but God knows one is more than enough."

The *Ragioniere* was a figure that both depressed and annoyed Iris. The title was awarded to those students devoid of any specific inclination or driving ambition, who opted to attend a vocational high school, from which they would emerge with sufficient accounting skills to land secure positions as bookkeepers or bank clerks. The *Ragioniere* at the Stella di Levante had been overseeing its administration for twenty years, and by virtue of diligence, devotion and non-delegation had attained a remarkable level of indispensability.

"Scampi di Santa Margherita," announced Alberto, who appeared at Iris's side to place a covered dish in front of her, and one in front of Claudio Olona. As he lifted the two silver domes simultaneously, the aroma of the grilled seafood banished all thoughts of the dreadful world of accountants from Iris's mind. "May I suggest another wine to accompany the scampi, *Dottore?"*

"No, thank you, Alberto. This is so pleasant. And don't be coming to check on us every five minutes. You've got a full house, and we can take care of ourselves." Alberto withdrew from the table with a smile and a little bow. Iris was impressed that the owner put his clients' need ahead of his own; that was the way it should be, that was true hospitality. *"Buon appetito,* Iris," he said.

"Buon appetito," Iris replied, pleased that he had said it first.

She recalled the time Isabella had invited the whole family to dinner at the Splendido in Portofino to celebrate her retirement, and berated Iris for wishing everyone a "good appetite" as their meal was served, on the grounds that it was not proper to recognize that one ate out of carnal pleasure. Iris had never thought of it that way, but added the expression to the list of things not to say in certain circles. Although it had become apparent over the years that Isabella could be a tad too stiff, Iris's consistent efforts to emulate her impeccable behavior had been worth the investment. Even now, for example, she was in a position to approach the crustaceans before her with the proper cutlery and manners. She pinned one down with the tines of her fork, adeptly peeling back its thin pink shell with her fish knife to reveal the plump morsel of white meat inside.

"You're an incredibly quick learner, Iris," Claudio Olona said, peeling his own prawn.

"It's not all that complicated, if you're patient enough," she said, half offended, half embarrassed that he could be so darn sure that the Capotostis had not been raised on scampi.

"I'm talking about the job, Iris," he said. Her cheeks burned, but she was relieved to detect no hints of condescension in his tone of voice or expression. If anything, his eyes conveyed appreciation, and a hint of amusement.

"You know, Iris, there is a difference between delegating, and slacking off. The *Direttore* has settled into a very comfortable routine since your arrival. You are the one the staff looks to for direction, you are the one the clients call when they need an urgent proposal. You have the brains to know what needs to be done, and the ability to get people to do it."

"The *Direttore* is busy with other things," Iris said, feeling slightly disloyal by even having this conversation while her boss was away, on the first real vacation he had taken since she had started working with him.

"Yes, like coming to the office just in time for lunch," Claudio said.

"But he does stay until late in the evening," Iris said.

"Iris, men who stay at work rather than going home to their wives and children at night are not martyrs. They're just not that interested in their families," he said. Iris sensed him sniffing around the boundaries of her comfort zone with his aristocratic nose. She wondered how many cozy evenings he spent at home with his own wife. Not many, judging from the comments she occasionally overheard. Trips to Rome, even Paris and London were frequently arranged for him by the concierge. Sometimes, when he wasn't even present in the hotel, she had seen instructions left by the switchboard for staff to advise all callers, including his wife, that the *Dottore* was in a meeting and must not be disturbed. In hotels, everyone's personal life was fodder for gossip, including the owner's, and probably even hers. She wondered how much Claudio Olona knew about her. He knew that Gregorio was a doctor, for example. He had mentioned it one evening when he ran into her, still in the office working on a list of contacts in the medical field that might be invited to the hotel for a site inspection of their conference facilities. She had quickly changed the subject, determined to avoid any overlapping of her personal life with her job. Here, she was making her way as Iris Capotosti, not the wife of *Dottore* Gregorio Leale. She had every intention of keeping it that way.

Nonetheless, the comment about men and their jobs stirred her thoughts. She recalled all the evenings she had rushed home to prepare a tasty dinner and set a pretty table, only for Gregorio to phone at the last minute saying an emergency had arisen at the hospital. On such evenings, she would set aside a plate for him, light a candle in the living room, where she would sit cross-legged on the sofa with her dinner tray and glass of wine and ate, passing scraps to Zenzero, the cat she had finally convinced Gregorio to let her adopt, while listening to old Beatles albums. To be honest, she didn't really mind those evenings at all, as long as Gregorio did not phone Isabella or Cinzia and ask them to keep her company, as he sometimes did. Solitude had been hard to come by in the Capotosti household, and for her it was a luxury to be enjoyed, not a hardship to be endured. She thought it unfair that the gift of an evening alone should be snatched from her, without her prior consent.

"Well, office work is one thing, but there are some jobs that just don't have regular hours," she said. "Anything can happen, any time of day or night in a hotel - or in a hospital." She was ready to defend Gregorio, if that's who his remark was aimed at. If there was a man who could be trusted, and looked forward to his quiet evenings at home, it was her husband.

Claudio Olona (she still couldn't refer to him as just Claudio, not even in her mind) suddenly seemed more preoccupied with dissecting his scampi than pursuing the subject of errant husbands. They ate for a moment in silence, chewing the tender tidbits, until all that was left on their plates were the empty pink shells and the decapitated heads, with their blank black eyes and wispy antennae. Iris looked at the soft, juicy pulp inside the head, which she had learned to savor once she had overcome her initial revulsion.

Claudio Olona wiped the corners of his mouth with his napkin. "Nice texture. Soft and smooth, easy on the lips."

"I beg your pardon?" Iris said, looking up from her plate.

"The napkin," he replied, "Or have you forgotten that we are here to try out the table linens?" He topped off their glasses with more Prosecco.

"No. Of course not," she lied, as she quickly dabbed at her own mouth. "I agree, a very pleasant texture." She took a sip of bubbly.

"And it is a pleasure to see such an elegant young woman with such an exquisitely shaped mouth use a product of such high quality," Claudio Olona said. "By the way," he added, looking her in the eye. "Feel free."

"I beg your pardon?" Iris said again, sipping again.

"The scampi. It's a pity to leave the best part. Feel free to suck."

She smiled, embarrassed at the suggestion, embarrassed that her embarrassment was again edging its way up her neck into her cheeks.

So this was how men did it. One minute, it was all business; the next, the professional praise mellowed out into compliments of a more personal nature, and generalizations were whittled into prods that were used to poke around in your private life. That was when they went in for the kill. She might not have much experience with men, but she was onto his game. She sniffed the scent of a challenge: perhaps it was time to prove to Claudio Olona that she was not a neglected little wife who spent too many evenings home alone; that even if she didn't grow up on scampi, she knew how to enjoy them; that yes, she was a fast learner, and could have fun at this game, too. What was the worst that could happen?

She picked up a prawn head. Holding it daintily between her index finger and thumb she sucked on it softly, coaxing the juice into her mouth. It was still warm, and tasted slightly salty as it slid over her tongue, and trickled down her throat. She forced herself to make eye contact with Claudio, certain he would be staring at her. His Adam's apple bobbed above the starched shirt collar and monogrammed tie that encircled his neck. He picked up a head from his plate and began sucking, his eyes never leaving hers.

She dropped her eyes to her plate, hoping the flush in her cheeks would subside. The dead black eyes of three more heads stared at her. She picked up the second one and looked at Claudio, who followed her example. They took turns sucking, slowly, deliberately, raising and dropping their eyes in silence, their expressions flickering in the candlelight, until they were finished.

Iris wiped her mouth, then dipped her fingers into the glass bowl of water with lemon slices and rose petals that Alberto had delivered together with the scampi. Claudio Olona also placed his fingers in the bowl, next to hers. As their fingertips touched in the water, a current passed through Iris's hand, shot up her arm. The surge warmed her to the core, causing the frustration frozen inside her to melt, and leak onto the swatch of silk between her thighs.

"Is everything fine?" Alberto asked, approaching the table. "Did you enjoy the scampi?"

Iris blushed. "Yes," she said. "Delicious."

"Exquisite," Olona said. "The best I've ever tasted."

Alberto lifted the bottle from the ice bucket to pour more Prosecco, and found it empty. "Shall I bring another of the same, *Dottore*?" he asked, as he cleared the dishes from the table.

"I'd like to stick to bubbly, though I think it's time to switch to something a bit more intense," Olona replied, stroking his chin. He had a strong, square jaw, without a trace of stubble, despite the hour. She wondered whether he had shaved again before dinner, like her father used to do on Saturdays. "Don't you agree, Iris?"

"Fine," Iris said, hoping he would not inquire as to her preferences.

"Why don't you bring us a bottle of that lovely Perrier-Jouët Belle Epoque, then?" Claudio Olona instructed.

"Very well, *Dottore*," Alberto replied with a nod of his head, then retreated. He returned a few moments later with the beautifully decorated bottle of champagne whose name Iris recognized from wine lists, but had never had the opportunity to taste. Alberto set down two fresh champagne glasses, uncorked the bottle, and sniffed. Claudio Olona tasted the champagne, nodded his head, and Alberto poured for both of them.

"To revelations," he said, lifting his glass in the same toast to which they had started drinking their first bottle. Iris touched her glass delicately to his, then took a sip of the champagne, delighting in its light, slightly nutty taste as the beads glided over her tongue. The Prosecco had been delightful, but this was sublime.

Alberto returned a few moments later with their tuna steaks. Iris's hunger had been both satiated and stimulated by the scampi. She would have been blissfully happy to sip champagne all night without eating anything else, but she did not want Claudio (the Olona faded away – at least in her mind - after the first sips of French champagne, whose powers of persuasion were admittedly superior to those of Prosecco) to think her one of those women who did not appreciate fine food. Their conversation meandered back to the hotel business, and as they ate and drank Iris expressed a desire to dedicate more time to sales and marketing endeavors, perhaps attend a few of the major trade fairs in Italy, maybe even in London and Berlin.

"You have my full endorsement, Iris," Claudio said. "Perhaps I'll accompany you when you go to London. I could introduce you to a number of acquaintances and colleagues. You can never know too many people in this business."

"That would be wonderful," Iris said, all worries of how she might get Gregorio to agree to her taking a trip to London with another man floating away on the optimistic bubbles of Perrier-Jouët. How she would love to travel more!

"Shall I draw up a proposal and draft a budget for the shows for your evaluation? There's the BIT and the BTC and the TTI in Italy," Iris counted them off on her fingers. "then there's the WTM and the EIBTM and the..."

"Iris?" Claudio said, holding up an index finger.

"Yes?"

"Let's enjoy our dinner now. We can discuss the details another time."

She blushed, again, or still; she couldn't be sure. "Yes, of course." She should learn not to speak of work and drink champagne at the same time. Not that she expected to ever have another opportunity to do so. As Claudio devoted his attention to pointing out certain remarkably unique traits of hers he had previously lacked the opportunity to notice or comment upon, Iris turned her attention to her tuna steak, so easy to eat in a ladylike manner, yet so difficult to swallow, bubbling as she was with compliments and champagne, both of which continued to flow freely.

Picking up her napkin from her lap and dabbing at her lips, she tilted her wrist to glance at her watch, and instantly thought of Gregorio, waiting for her at home. However vague and remote his presence in her life had become as the evening wore on, she was well aware that putting him out of her mind wasn't enough to make him vanish.

"Well, this has been lovely," she said.

"Yes," Claudio said, laying his silverware across his plate to indicate that he had finished. "Shall we succumb to temptation and indulge in one of Paolo's sinfully delicious desserts?"

Would Gregorio be sleeping? Waiting up? Furious?

"I'd love to," she said. "But it's been a long day. I really should be heading home now, if you don't mind."

"Of course, Iris. I hope I haven't kept you from anything."

"Not at all," she said. "I'll just stop by the office and gather my things."

"I'll come with you. I still have to make a call to Los Angeles, and this should be just the right time."

They rose from the table, passed by the kitchen where they peeked in to pay their compliments to the Chef, who was putting the final touches on one of his latest dessert creations, a baked cream custard with Bronte pistachios. On their way to the elevator, they nodded their thanks to the Maître, who was conversing discreetly with a couple of titled Austrians who had been staying in the fifth-floor suite for the past two weeks. Iris stepped into the elevator car she had ridden up in, two hours and two bottles of bubbly earlier. Nervous at finding herself alone in such close quarters with Claudio, she looked down at her puffy feet, and tried to concentrate on how good it would feel when she would finally be able to kick her shoes off.

As soon as the door closed, Claudio placed a thumb under Iris's chin, and tilted her head to his. The intimacy of his warm breath caressing her face, laced with the same pleasant flavors that lingered on her own tongue, made her inhale sharply. Claudio placed his mouth over hers, softly but firmly encouraging her to part her lips. His hand slid down her back, lightly tracing the curve of her bottom, and slipped under her skirt. His fingers wandered up her thigh, until they found the patch of soft, bare flesh between her stockings and panties. Iris felt her body being carried away by the riot of sensations stirred up by the magnificent sunset and flickering candlelight, by the exquisite food and inebriating drink, by the soft voices and stimulating conversation, by the unexpected kiss. She had indulged in each of the evening's pleasures willingly, and now that her hunger had been aroused, she was greedy for more.

The elevator jerked to a halt on the mezzanine level, where the offices were located. The cleaning crew had already passed, and a single light illuminated the landing. Iris pulled back, feeling lightheaded with confusion and champagne, freed from the ballast of practicality, rationality, Leale-ality. Claudio stared at her without speaking; the look in his eyes expressed more than she was ready to hear.

"I need to go," she said, in words she did not mean, in a voice that was not hers. The urge she had felt earlier to free herself of her clothes was overwhelming now. Everything felt so tight, so sticky, so unnecessary.

"Are you sure?" he asked. "There's plenty of room at the inn. And I do have connections with the boss."

"No. I mean, yes. I'm sure," Iris said. "Good night."

"Say it, Iris," Claudio said, tightening his grip on her elbow.

"Say what?"

"My name."

Iris hesitated. "All right. Claudio. Good night, Claudio."

"Good night, Iris," he replied, caressing her arm as he relaxed his hold. "I don't often have the opportunity to wine and dine a lovely woman who also enjoys talking about the hotel business. Thank you for your company."

"Thank you," she said, both relieved and disappointed that he was backing off so quickly. Maybe Claudio was a real gentleman, and not the womanizer she supposed him to be. For the first time since Iris had married, she wondered what it would be like to make love with another man. No, there was no sense lying to herself; she had wondered about that many times before, in a vague sort of way. But this was different. Now she was wondering what it would be like to have sex, right here and now, with this specific man, a real live man, whose lips she had kissed.

But that wasn't an option, and she knew it. If it were, would she be standing there like a frightened doe caught in the headlights of an oncoming vehicle? Would she force herself to walk away, hurry into her dark office to gather her belongings? Would she rush down the stairs to the garage and hop on her scooter and drive home through the night as fast as she dared? If she had a choice, would she steal through the front door of the slumbering villa like a cat burglar, taking off her shoes before she crept up the stairs and into her apartment? Would she be relieved when she heard Gregorio snoring, as she slipped into the bathroom to shower and brush her teeth? Would she eye her naked body in the bathroom mirror as she toweled herself dry, wondering whether Claudio would think her breasts too small or her hips too wide as she imagined the taste of his tongue again, and the feel his fingertips dancing up and down her thighs? If she had a choice, would she crawl into bed with a man who was such an expert at numbing the suffering of others, yet so oblivious to the pain festering inside her?

10. LILY

Sandwiches and sympathy became the foundation for Lily's relationship with Donna, although she had never taken Donna up on her invitation to invite Jesus into her heart, whatever that meant. With increasing frequency, Donna would greet Lily over the back fence with, "Did a shoe go through the window?" - the phrase that had become their private code that Joe had once again lost his temper and had taken hold of the closest object and launched it across the room. It wasn't always a shoe; sometimes it was a book, an ice cube - and once, even a bag of cotton balls, the description of which - with Joe enraged and furiously attempting to pitch the bag across the room only to have it float down and land limply at his feet - made them laugh so hard that they both had tears running down their cheeks.

"It's not funny," said Donna, trying to stop herself from laughing.

"It's kind of funny," said Lily, wiping her eyes.

"Seriously. Sugar," said Donna. "I've been your next door neighbor for how long now?"

"Two years," said Lily.

"Two years," repeated Donna. "And things have not gotten better between you and Joe. If anything, they've gotten worse."

"I know." Lily cast her glance down at the ground.

"Now I'm not sayin' this to make you feel bad, Lily, but you've got to do somethin' before the two of you destroy each other."

"Me? What did I do?" said Lily. "I didn't do anything."

"Exactly," said Donna. "You're as stuck as a wombat in a peat bog. Don't you think the time has come for action? Jesus' patience will last until the end of time. The question is, can you afford to wait that long?"

Lily was immediately struck with the level of chatter and laughter at Christ Covenant Church. Instead of the quiet prayer and somber ambience that preceded Catholic Mass, the vestibule at CCC was jammed with smiling, lively people who greeted one another with hugs and exclamations of joy.

"Donna!" A tall thin woman balancing a pile of teased honey brown hair on her head and wearing a thick layer of bright pink lip gloss raced toward Lily and Donna with outstretched arms. "Oh, it's so good to see you!" said the woman. She and Donna locked in embrace, laughing as they rocked back and forth. "So good to see you!"

"How are you?" Donna asked the woman. "I've had you on my heart, and I've been bringing you before the Lord every day in my prayers."

"Oh, thank you, thank you!" said the woman. "The Lord is faithful, the Lord is faithful. He has delivered me - the doctor said all is well. All is well."

"Praise God!" exclaimed Donna, releasing the embrace, and taking the woman's hands into hers.

"Donna," chimed the woman, holding Donna at arm's length and surveying her body. "How is that diet of yours going? I've been keeping you in my prayers."

Donna blushed, and looked down at the floor. "Not great, I'm afraid," she said sheepishly. "The spirit is willing, but the flesh is weak."

"Amen," said the woman. "Amen to that."

"Bethany," said Donna. "I'd like you to meet my next-door neighbor - and friend - Lily Diotallevi." Donna turned to Lily and said, "Lily, this is my dear friend and sister in the Lord, Bethany."

"Lily!" Bethany released Donna's hands and opened her arms, taking Lily into an embrace, rocking her back and forth. "It is so wonderful to have you here. So wonderful."

"It's nice to be here," said Lily, uncomfortable at being hugged so enthusiastically by someone she did not know, but touched by the exuberance of Bethany's welcome.

"Has the Lord blessed you with a husband?" Bethany asked.

"Do you mean am I married?" Lily asked.

"Why of course that's what I mean, of course that's what I mean." Bethany's slick bright smile froze in place, as a look of puzzlement passed over her face.

"Yes, I am." Lily replied. Worried that her request for clarification may have been misconstrued as mockery, Lily added, "Yes, the Lord has blessed me with a husband. We've been married almost ten years."

"Praise God!" shouted Bethany. "And how many little ones do you have?"

Donna nudged Bethany in the ribs with her elbow.

"None yet," said Lily, looking down at the floor. "But we're working on it."

Ten years? How did it get to be so late? What had she done with the time, besides wait? She waited for Joe to stop gambling, she waited to get successfully past three months of pregnancy, knowing that a baby would infuse new life into her marriage, and ease the nagging sense of failure that seemed to always be in her shadow, she waited to get happier enough to continue on and she waited to get miserable enough to leave. But no matter how long she waited, things always stayed the same; they remained just this side of bearable.

"Donna - you must bring Lily to the next PTW meeting. You simply must bring her!" Bethany's gaze shifted across the room. She shot her hands up into the air again, wriggled her fingers and shouted, "Phoebe! Phoebe!" Turning to Lily, but keeping her arms raised she said, "So blessed to meet you... so blessed. Donna - I'll talk to you during fellowship after service." Bethany flitted off, shouting, "The Lord is faithful, Phoebe, the Lord is faithful!"

"She is such a stitch," said Donna. "I wish I had her gift for pure joy."

"She sure is happy," said Lily. "Who's Petie W.?"

"It's a what, not a who - PTW - I was going to tell you about that but I didn't want to lay too much on you at once. Those of us who are married have a little get-together once a week for coffee and to chat. We call it the Proverbs Thirty-One Wives Club – PTW for short."

"Oh," said Lily. It must be obvious to Donna that she did not get the reference.

"Basically, it is our mission to strive to be like the wife outlined for us in Proverbs chapter thirty-one. But we also know how hard it is to be that kind of a wife in today's world. So we get together to offer each other support and encouragement."

"Cool," said Lily. She'd never given much thought to what kind of a wife she was. She took care of Joe, went to work, cleaned the house, did the shopping. What else was there to it, really?

A white-haired man dressed in a suit and tie entered the vestibule through the double doors that opened from the sanctuary. Piano music spilled out and extinguished the din of chatter as the crowd scrambled eagerly inside, clapping and singing.

Rise and shine and give God your glory, glory
Rise and shine and give God your glory, glory

"I'll tell you more about it later," said Donna. She took Lily by the hand and led her forward. "I want to get a good seat so you can really feel Pastor's passion and energy."

"Gee," said Lily, allowing herself to be dragged forward. "At Sacred Family people run to get the seats in the back so they can leave early without getting caught."

"Yeah?" said Donna with a smirk. "Well this ain't Sacred Family. You'll see."

Lily followed Donna down the aisle, accepting hugs and

handshakes from strangers who professed to Lily how wonderful it was that she had joined them and how happy they were to see her. She couldn't remember ever being received anywhere with such ardor. She and Donna settled into the front pew, and Lily realized that it was the first time she'd ever sat in front at church, having been taught that it was a place of honor that one should not assume for oneself.

Rise and shine and give God your glory, glory
Children of the Lord!

By the time the singing stopped, most of the members of the congregation were left standing with eyes closed, faces tilted toward the sunshine that streamed in through the skylight, their hands raised, palms to the ceiling. The piano whispered gently behind arrhythmic and spontaneous proclamations from the congregation.

"Thank you Jesus!" shouted one voice.

"Praise God!" called another.

"God is good and worthy of praise."

"Hallelujah!"

"Amen!"

Lily felt uneasy. Her inclination was to kneel and cross herself in silent prayer, but she looked down to discover that there were no kneelers. The room was bright and open, rather than dark and heavy as most churches she'd been in. There was no stained glass, no statues. Even the altar was stark and simple, bearing a vacant cross instead of a crucifix with the image of a dying Jesus hanging upon it. She surveyed the faces around her. They beamed in the morning light. Lily spotted Bethany's sparkling lips. As if aware of her gaze, Bethany opened her eyes and smiled at Lily with a warmth that melted her discomfort. Lily smiled back. Bethany again closed her eyes, and began moving her lips. Looking around, Lily noticed a small table at the back of the room. It was fitted with a desk lamp, the light of which shined on a man about her age, who was wearing headphones.

"What's that guy doing?" Lily asked Donna.

"Oh, he's the sound guy. He records the sermons on Sunday - and the entire service on special occasions."

"Why?"

"Sometimes people want to listen to Pastor's message during the week. Or maybe they can't get here because they're sick or whatever, but they don't want to miss out on the teachings."

"You're kidding." When Lily was a child, if you had the bad luck to get sick on the weekend the only consolation was that it got you out of going to Mass. "Really?"

"Yea," said Donna. "They sell copies of the tapes in the church bookstore."

Lily had to squelch a laugh. It was difficult to imagine people waiting in line to purchase a recording of Father Delaney preaching - especially since he seemed to talk about the same three subjects: the importance of tithing, abstaining from sex before marriage, and the evils of birth control. It seemed to Lily that if he wanted parishioners to be more generous when the collection basket came around, he might want to rethink his repertoire.

A man entered the sanctuary through a door behind the altar. Lily guessed that he was about forty-five years old. He wore a black suit with a gray shirt and a white tie, which accentuated the flecks of gray in his closely cropped black hair. Lily imagined that if she were close enough, she would be able to smell Ivory soap on his skin. Confidently, he approached the dais with a large Bible tucked under his arm. He placed the Bible on the platform, retrieved a piece of paper from his inside breast pocket, unfolded it and flattened it out in front of him. He looked up, and catching Lily's eye, he nodded and smiled. Embarrassed, Lily looked down, hoping he did not notice the blush in her cheeks, or that she was the only one in the room who was not rapt in worship.

"That's Pastor Halloway," Donna whispered to Lily. "He's a gifted preacher. Wait 'til you hear him."

"Good morning, my brothers and sisters!" Pastor Halloway cried.

"Good morning!" the people replied.

"Praise God for this amazing day and for the opportunity to gather here in love and worship."

The people replied with an assortment of "Thank you Jesus," "Praise God," and "Hallelujah!"

"I give special thanks for our guests this morning." Pastor Halloway looked at Lily and smiled a perfect white smile. This time she did not turn away. "If you are here visiting us this morning, please raise your hand so that one of our ushers may give you a welcome packet to take home with you today."

Donna jabbed Lily lightly with her elbow. "Raise your hand. They give you some really cool stuff."

Even though Lily felt conspicuous calling attention to herself in front of all those people, since the Pastor had already spotted her, failure to do so felt almost like a lie. She raised her hand to shoulder level, keeping her elbow bent. Donna grabbed Lily's wrist and hoisted her hand into the air. The white haired man appeared at the end of the pew and passed a gift bag to Lily. She glanced inside and then looked back up.

"Welcome," said the Pastor smiling. "We are so blessed by your presence."

Lily's eyes stung with tears. *Stop,* she thought. *What in the world are you crying about?*

Pastor Halloway took center stage. "My friends, are you in pain this morning? Do you feel forgotten, unloved, burdened by life's demands? It's OK to admit that, you know? You are in good company; some of the greatest figures from the Bible struggled and made a hot holy mess of their lives."

A tear escaped down Lily's cheek. She quickly wiped it away. *What are you crying about? Don't cry.*

The pastor looked directly at Lily. "I'm here to tell you that there is nothing you can do that will make you unlovable to God. Even if everyone else scorns you, even if they forget you, neglect you, take you for granted, blame you and shame you, you are innocent in God's eyes and He is here to soothe your soul."

Another tear tumbled down Lily's cheek. She turned to see

how far the door was from where she sat. Even if she could climb over the other people in the pew, she would have to walk the entire length of the room to get out to the vestibule. Now that everyone knew she was a visitor, they would all notice. It would be rude. She rummaged through her purse for a tissue, but the only one she found had a wad of bubble gum balled up inside. She closed her eyes. *Stop crying*, she demanded of herself. Surely she'd tamed wilder emotions than this. Yet the sadness that was bubbling up inside of her balked at her attempts to control it. She panicked. Donna pulled a tissue out of her pocket and surreptitiously handed it to Lily.

"Saul was a man who did everything he could to squelch the power of God in his life," continued the Pastor. "He was the original radical activist. Before his transformation, his cause was hate. But once God transformed him, his cause was love. Radical love."

"Amen!" shouted a man.

"Hallelujah!" cried a woman.

"In the beginning of chapter twelve of Paul's letter to the Romans, Paul invites us to present our lives to God, so that God might transform us. If we live this transformed life we will use our gifts, we will humble ourselves, we will love with pure love - offering that love to everyone, even to those who are unloving, who belittle us, who do us harm. When we are transformed, we will be empathic, zealous, prayerful, hopeful and humble."

It seemed that the Pastor's words were directed toward Lily, that he could read her thoughts, that he had somehow peered into her life and had seen the dramas that had been playing out. Joe's rage, the financial oppression they suffered, Lily's own anger and frustration, the sorrow over her miscarriages and the trouble she was having conceiving again, and her private but frantic search for an understanding of it all. Tears again came to Lily's eyes. She resigned herself to them, hoping that if she allowed them a little space, they would speak their piece, then leave her alone. She knew that sometimes if you just had a good cry, you could find clear enough of a path to go on.

Pastor continued. "The Bible, my friends, is God's love story. Even when we cannot imagine it, God goes on loving us. Even when our backs are turned to God, God goes on loving us. Even when we are apathetic, God goes on loving us. Even when we have failed miserably at this thing called life, God goes on loving us and pouring His blessings out upon us. There is nothing He cannot do for us, no gift He would not give to us if we would only surrender to His mighty will."

The remnants of Lily's composure crumbled at the idea of being loved so completely, of being treasured, of having her life transformed from one of confusion and strife to one of peace, at the prospect of being blessed with a baby. She wept.

"We gather here to remember that God loves us and that He is eager and able to perform miracles in your life. He stands at the ready, just waiting for you to say the word. He loves you so much, that He would never come into your life without your invitation. Won't you invite Him to heal your pain, to show you the way? Won't you let Him treasure and love you as His precious child?"

Lily buried her face in her hands, her body convulsing with each sob.

"Are you feeling the call of the Spirit this morning?" said Pastor Halloway. "Is God speaking to you? If so, I invite you to come forward and invite Jesus into your heart. Let the faithful lay their hands upon you, and usher you into the community of believers."

"Do you want to go up there, darlin'?" whispered Donna.

"I don't know," said Lily, gasping quietly.

Pastor Halloway stood at the front of the sanctuary, with his arms open wide. A young couple came forward, holding hands. They knelt on the floor, holding each other.

"Welcome, beloved children of God," said Pastor, as he laid his hands on their heads. "Thank you, Jesus, for your love for these, your lost sheep. In the words you gave us in Matthew, chapter eleven, verse twenty-eight, 'Come to me, all who labor and are heavy laden, and I will give you rest. Take my yoke upon you, and learn from me, for I am gentle and lowly in heart, and you will find rest for your souls. For my yoke is easy, and my burden is light.'"

The sadness within Lily rushed forth as she burst into wrenching, uncontrollable sobbing. *What is wrong with me? Please God, make me stop.*

"C'mon," said Donna, taking Lily's hand. "I'll go with you."

Lily and Donna sidled their way out of the pew and walked to the front of the room. Together they knelt with the few others who had gathered there.

Pastor laid his hands on Lily's head, sending a shock of energy through her body. She bolted in surprise, and her tears immediately ceased.

"Welcome home, child of God," Pastor said to Lily. "The Holy Spirit of our Lord Jesus be with you." He turned to the congregation. "My brothers and sisters, I invite you come up and pray with us."

Lily soon found herself surrounded by people. They reached out and placed their hands on her head, her shoulders, her back. With each touch, she felt waves of warmth and calm wash over her. She felt lifted from herself, as though she were dreaming and looking down upon her form, small and frail, encased by the caring embrace of these strangers who considered her one of them. A member of the family. The people around her prayed, some of them silently, some uttering strange words that Lily couldn't quite make out. But she didn't care what it looked like, or sounded like, or how bizarre it all seemed. All she cared about was this feeling that filled her so completely that for the moment she forgot the anger that had taken up residence inside her, and the fear she had learned to live with, and the stifling sense of lack that had become her constant companion.

"Pray along with me," said Pastor. "Jesus, I give you my life. Please transform me into an instrument of your love and peace. Bless my life and make it holy."

Jesus, I give you my life. Please transform me into an instrument of your love and peace. Bless my life and make it holy.

Oh, how I've missed you, said a voice. Lily was certain that the voice was of her own thought, and terrified at the prospect that it was not.

"You OK?" said Donna, as they drove home after service.

"I feel strange," said Lily. She sat in the passenger's seat of Donna's blue Dodge pickup truck, holding her welcome bag in her lap. The farther they drove from the church, the more she questioned what had happened. Not quite a dream, but unlike any other reality she had experienced - except perhaps that of getting stoned with Frances Jejune in high school - she was unsure of whether to file it under fantasy or fact.

"Bein' filled with the Spirit that way can be a little unsettling," said Donna. "Make sure you rest up today, hear? Take it easy. Give yourself a chance to get acclimated."

"I'm embarrassed," said Lily. "I can't believe I just fell apart like that."

"Now Lily, there's nothin' to be gettin' embarrassed about at all. God's got to break you open if he's gonna get inside," Donna took her right hand from the steering wheel, reached over and squeezed Lily's hand. "You should no more be embarrassed than an infant should be upon bein' born. It's natural." Donna pulled into her driveway and shut off the engine.

Lily checked her watch. "Man - it's forty-five minutes later than I told Joe I would be home. He's going to be pissed."

"The Lord will protect you," said Donna, patting Lily's hand.

Lily looked over at the front windows of her house, and with the recognition that Joe, his anger, his gambling, the bills, the empty nursery and all the challenges of her life were right there on the other side of the glass, the feelings of peace that had overtaken her only minutes ago began their hasty retreat.

"Donna," said Lily, turning toward her. "I loved the way I felt today, and I know I won't feel that way anymore once I go into that house." She began to cry again.

"God and the power of His Spirit are not confined by the walls of the church, Lily. Do not underestimate what Jesus can do for you." Donna pulled a tissue from the console and wiped Lily's tears. "Now dry your tears. This is a time for rejoicing - you've been born again in the Spirit."

"I don't know what to do."

"That's the beauty of it. You don't need to know what to do; it shall be revealed to you. You don't need to know where you're going. You only need to take the first step. Walk and pray."

"I don't know many prayers," said Lily. "Except the Our Father, and the Rosary, and the Act of Contrition."

"That's not prayin' " said Donna. "That's recitin'. You got to speak to God, tell Him what's in your heart."

"It's been so long since I've done that - if I ever have... maybe I did when I was little. I'm not sure where to start - I know I want a baby. I want peace in my house."

"Well now," said Donna. "What I can tell you is that all that your heart's desires are within God's power. What I can't tell you is how to pray - each person needs to work that one out on her own. All I know is that I feel closest to God when I am expressing myself in a free and creative way."

"That sounds like how I felt when I used to sing."

"There you go," said Donna. "The Lord God loves Him a good song, that's for sure."

"What kind of song?" asked Lily. "Like 'Amazing Grace' or something?"

"That's an oldie but a goodie, but there are so many beautiful songs of praise and worship, songs of gratitude and supplication." Donna closed her eyes, and hummed for a few seconds. "It don't matter how you talk to Him, Lily. You just got to get the conversation started."

The front door of Lily's house opened. "I better go. Thanks so much for taking me to church today, Donna."

"My pleasure. I'll call you about PTW, OK? It's less intense than worship service, and it's a chance to really talk things through. Plus," she added with a glint in her eye, "There's fresh baked goods!"

"That'd be great," said Lily as she jumped down out of the truck and used the weight of her body to slam the door closed.

As Lily stepped into the house, Joe's voice spilled out from the kitchen.

"I can't fuckin' believe it!" Joe shouted into the phone. "Did you see that goddamn guy? He was running like his asshole was on fire.... I know, I know... Jesus Christ, what a game, what a fuckin' game.... alright Ant - I'll talk to you tomorrow."

Lily stood in the doorway, wondering what to tell Joe about why she was so late returning from church. She flinched as he headed toward her, but he scooped her up, lifting her body right off the ground, spun her around in a circle and then set her back down onto the floor.

"What's going on?" Lily asked.

"I scored today, Lil. I scored big."

"You won? Really?"

"Why is everyone acting so surprised?" said Joe with a laugh. "I knew my losing streak was coming to an end. I knew it."

A losing streak? Is that what the past nine years had been?

"We're going to Palomino's tonight for dinner," said Joe. "But," he added, taking Lily by the hand and leading her toward the bedroom, "We're going to start off with dessert."

With groans and moans Joe devoured Lily enthusiastically, savoring her, taking his time in ways that increased her pleasure, as though he had suddenly discovered a set of instructions tucked under the mattress.

"That was amazing," said Joe.

"Unbelievable," said Lily.

The Proverbs 31 Wives Club met every Tuesday in the fellowship hall at Christ Covenant Church. The room was abuzz with chatter as Donna took Lily around, introducing her to the other women.

"You'll love our little group," said Phoebe, a slight woman whose ill-fitting clothes sadly reminded Lily of the hand-me-downs she grew up in.

"We're just like a huge family of sisters, mothers, and daughters," said Cora, an older woman with white hair and glasses whom the younger women all referred to as "Mom."

"Yeah," said Donna. "'Cept we're much more civilized than I was with my family."

"As long as you don't try to snatch up the last of Diane's lemon squares from Donna, you'll get along just fine," said Bethany with a wink.

"I don't deny it," said Donna, smacking her lips. "I do love those lemon squares. I know I shouldn't indulge, but I can't seem to help myself. At least I'm in good company, as Paul says in Romans chapter seven verse fifteen, "I do not understand what I do. For what I want to do, I do not do, but what I hate, I do.' Lord, help me!"

"Ladies! Ladies!" called Bethany. She gently rang a small crystal bell, holding the stem between the tips of her thumb and middle finger. "Tardiness is sloth in disguise! Let's take our seats! Let's take our seats!"

Lily followed the pack as they filed themselves into the arrangement of gray aluminum folding chairs - each of which was occupied by copies of *The Study Bible for Women,* and a book titled, *Learn to Be the Wife of a Satisfied Husband.* The chairs formed an unbroken circle, presumably intended to create a sense of common status among them.

"Is she the leader?" Lily asked Donna, gesturing toward Bethany as she took her seat.

"Technically, we don't have a leader," said Donna. "But Bethany is one of those people who just naturally takes charge. Plus, she's really well-known within the Christian community. Have you ever heard of *Christian Family News*?"

"No - what is it?"

"It's a local paper that all the churches distribute. Bethany writes a weekly homemaking column. She's a bit of a celebrity around here."

A petite woman with long straight black hair named Marie sat next to Bethany, produced a legal pad and pen from her canvas bag, and began taking notes. Bethany opened her Bible, and the circle grew quiet as the members of PTW folded their hands and bowed their heads.

"Dear Father, please bless our time together today, and lead the conversation in the way you would have it go. Thank you for bringing our sister Lily to our little group. Together with us may she come to understand what it truly means to be a Proverbs thirty-one wife. Amen."

"Amen," they all said.

"Since this is Lily's first time here, let's all open our Bibles to Proverbs thirty-one and follow along as I read."

"A wife of noble character who can find?" Bethany looked up, reciting the rest from memory. "She is worth far more than rubies. Her husband has full confidence in her and lacks nothing of value. She brings him good, not harm, all the days of her life."

When she reached the end of the passage, Bethany took a deep breath and then exhaled. "Does anyone have any thoughts to share about what that means to them? Anything jump out at you?"

"I don't think any of us here harms our husbands," said Phoebe. "I think we've at least got that part down."

"Oh really?" said Bethany. "So none of us argues with our husbands?"

"Sure, we argue sometimes, but -"

"You don't think that's harmful?"

"Everybody argues, though," said Diane.

"Not everyone," said Bethany. "I don't argue with my husband. I submit to him." She held up the Bible and vigorously tapped with the long pink nail of her index finger on the page from which she had been reading. "So does this wife - which is why the Bible says she is worth far more than rubies."

"I noticed something later on in the chapter," said a woman named Michelle. She looked to be around thirty years old, and wore a brace on her right knee. "At verse twenty-eight it says, 'Her children arise and call her blessed; her husband also, and he praises her: 'Many women do noble things, but you surpass them all.' I could be a better wife too," said Michelle, "if my husband and my kids respected me like that - praised me and called me noble. It's hard to keep giving and giving when you feel taken for granted."

"Michelle. Honey." Bethany closed her Bible and leaned in toward Michelle. "The Proverbs thirty-one wife is not that way in order to please her husband. She does all these wonderful things in order to please her God. She lives life as though she were married to our Savior Himself." Donna smiled broadly. "That's why her husband praises her. And that's why in verse twenty-three we read that, 'Her husband is respected at the city gate.' He succeeds in his endeavors because she serves him as she would serve the Lord - *not* because she feels respected. If our husbands are struggling, the first thing we should ask should not be, 'What more could he be doing?' but rather, 'What more can *I* be doing?'"

"Amen to that," said Cora, without looking up from her knitting.

"How long have you been married, Mom?" Bethany asked Cora.

"Forty-five years."

"Case in point," said Bethany.

Lily listened to the banter, thinking that the whole thing sounded ridiculous, but acutely aware of her recent fervent prayers for guidance, and of the way in which her own attempts at home were not getting her anywhere. It sounded off-the-wall, this idea of the perfect wife, or that any of them sitting in the circle had the capacity to approach that kind of perfection.

"Lily," said Bethany. "You look puzzled."

"I'm sorry," said Lily.

"No need to apologize, honey. How is God speaking to you through this Scripture?"

Lily squirmed in her chair. She would never presume that God would go to the trouble to speak directly to her, but her impressions were clear. "I think it's an ideal, you know? But I don't see how anyone can actually reach it."

"Thank you for your honesty, Lily," said Bethany. Her smile lingered upon Lily, but her eyes were filled with concern, the way a young mother looks at her newborn as it struggles to figure out how to release painful intestinal gas.

"Let's take a poll," said Bethany, raising her own bejeweled hands in demonstration, her silver bangles clanging against each other. "How many of you feel the same way Lily feels - that you don't think it's possible to reach this noble goal?"

Several women raised their hands.

"That's exactly what Satan wants you to think," said Bethany. "Because if you don't believe it's possible, you won't even try. And if you don't try, you can't experience that it *does* work, and you can't bring the glory and peace of Our Lord fully into your homes and marriages."

The women all lowered their hands. Lily grimaced at the idea that Satan was involved in all this. Wasn't he better occupied with wars, famine, and disease?

"But what about some of these references in this chapter?" said Lily. "All that talk about wool and flax, and merchant ships? Even if I wanted to try this, I don't know how to translate some of this so that it makes sense for me as a modern woman."

"And that, my dear Lily," said Bethany. "Is why we have this group, and why we have each other. Just don't expect to get support and encouragement from your secular friends - or even from your non-believing family members. They won't understand. They can't. They'll tell you it's a bunch of hogwash, and what about women's rights, blah, blah, blah." Bethany tugged on the tail of her sweater, smoothing it out over her bust and torso as she sat upright. "I mean, I'm all for equal pay and whatnot, but I'm a woman too, and I have a right to be happy without having all of those demands placed on me by the women's movement. If you ask me, women's rights has done more to make women miserable than it has to make them happy - the divorce rate is going up, kids are growing up without their fathers. It's a disaster." Bethany pushed the cuffs of her sleeves up toward her elbows and fanned her face with her hands. "Oh goodness! I've gone and gotten myself all worked up, haven't I?"

It was obvious that Bethany was passionate about the issue, and she did have a point. Lily thought about the break-up of her parents' marriage, and now the strife in her own.

"I don't think I'll be at the spindle until dawn," said Lily. "But what I'm doing sure isn't working."

Each week, PTW focused on a different topic, such as home management, parenting, and interpersonal relationships. Occasionally, they would bring in an expert such as the real estate agent who gave a talk on how to negotiate a deal, or the psychologist who spoke to them on how to defuse an argument and engage in active listening. Many of the topics were interesting and useful, and Lily methodically set out to put them to the test in her own life.

"I'm still not quite sure what to do about the whole gambling thing," she told Donna. "After all, the Proverbs thirty-one wife is supposed to be keen with finances, but I have no control over what he spends or how much he gambles. I never even see his paycheck. How can I be smart with it?"

"You can be smart with the money you make," said Donna. "But a woman does not have dominion over her husband - or his money. God has set it forth that the husband is the head of the household, just as Jesus is the head of the Church."

"But Joe isn't a Christian," said Lily. "He is not asking God to lead him as head of our home."

"First of all," said Donna. "You don't know what is goin' on in his heart or his soul. And in the second place, your obligation to submit to his authority is not dependent upon whether or not you think he's doin' the right thing. Leadin' Joe is God's job; followin' him is yours. Besides, even when he's gambling a lot I bet you haven't gone without food, have you? Doesn't the Lord provide?"

"I did take a few things from the food cupboard a couple times, like you suggested," said Lily. She didn't even get embarrassed about it anymore. "But no, we haven't gone without."

"Lily, the Word tells us, 'Do not muzzle an ox while it is treading out the grain.' Better that you take a box of elbow macaroni or two than to fall out of God's grace by screamin' at Joe and havin' that same fight for the hundredth time."

"Which fight is that?" Lily asked.

"It don't matter," said Donna. "They're all the same."

Lily pulled the calendar off of the refrigerator and flipped back a month. She counted out twenty-eight days. Then thirty-five, then forty-two, then fifty-six. It had been eight weeks since she'd had a period. She waited two more weeks. Nothing. She scheduled her doctor's appointment without telling Joe, and had so much trouble concentrating at work the day after her test that she assembled an entire shelving unit backwards, using an upside down photo as her guide. She took four breaks before lunch, slipping out to the pay phone to see if her results had come in yet.

"Yes, I know they're here," said the nurse. "I just saw them. Oh - here we go. Lily Diotallevi, right?"

"Yes!" said Lily. *Just read me the damned results already!*

"Positive," said the nurse. "The test came back positive - and your progesterone levels look really good. Would you like to schedule your next check up now?"

Lily hung up the phone and ran back to her station. Positive. Good progesterone levels. In just two more weeks she would be out of the woods. She was finally going to have a baby, a little one to hug and love, who would bring joy and peace to their home, whose presence would surely tame Joe's wild side and bring them all together as a family. A baby. *Thank you, Jesus.*

For the most part, telling people about the pregnancy was great fun; it was news that was met with hugs and questions and joyous laughter. But there were two people whom Lily dreaded telling - her mother, and Iris. She would have to tell Iris soon – before she heard about it from someone else. She decided to write it in her reply to Iris' latest letter, which for the last several weeks, had been stashed in the drawer where Lily kept the bills and the other neglected correspondence.

Dear Iris, She sat for ten minutes without writing a third word. She didn't want to just come right out and tell her without working up to it first. What could she talk about? She couldn't tell Iris about church or about PTW – the girls were right; Iris wouldn't understand. She had an important job at a posh resort hotel, had a wealthy husband who adored her and took her all over Europe just for fun. As Iris' world had expanded, Lily's shrank, until finally it was contained within the four walls of her house, along with her church, the grocery store, the cleaners, SaveMart, and the gas station, all of which were connected by approximately eight miles of generic suburban thoroughfare. Iris could never understand her world.

Lily scribbled a few notes about the new garden she was planning. She wrote about Jasmine's second divorce, and Violet's opening of her second birthing clinic. Chit chat brought her gratefully to bottom of the page where she penned, *Love, Lily. PS: I'm pregnant, with an expected delivery in the fall*. Detached. Factual. Hoping that would take some of the string out of it for Iris, but resentful that she didn't feel free to just be happy.

"Hi, Mom – It's Lily."

"Lily! Well hello! How are you?"

"Good – I'm actually surprised to catch you in. I've had more conversations with your answering machine lately than I have with you."

"Oh, that darned machine," said her mother. "That tape has been full for days."

"You could try listening to the messages."

"Who has the time?" Her mother's speech was garbled, no doubt due to the cookie that she was likely munching on while they talked. Probably Archway oatmeal raisin. Maybe with white icing. "But you didn't call me to talk about my schedule, now, did you?"

"No," said Lily. "I actually called because I have some news." Lily paused, but her mother didn't ask. "I'm having a baby. For real."

The line grew quiet. Finally, Lily's mother said, "Was it intentional?"

"Why would you ask me that, Mom?"

"I thought there were some issues with you... you told me just a few months ago that you and Joe had some issues to work out. Are you sure you still want a baby? You have choices about this, you know."

"I'm fine. Yes, I want the baby. Things with Joe are better now, Mom. They're fine."

"Things are fine now? How can that be? Things don't just get fine."

"Well they did." Lily knew to say any more, to tell her about Christ Covenant Church or PTW was to invite a debate that would begin with Adam in the Garden of Eden and take them to Pope John Paul II's doorstep.

"Well, I hope so," said her mother. "It's your best bet to work things out. I've worked with so many women like you who've gone through divorce in the past couple years – and let me tell you, it's a crime the way New York State treats women in divorce. It's legalized rape, I tell you."

"I just thought you'd want to know, Mom. About the baby."

"If that's what you want, then I'm happy for you."

Don't trip over yourself congratulating me, Lily thought. Lily wondered what she might have to do - short of getting raped by the New York State divorce laws - to get her mother's attention. At least that conversation was out of the way. It was enough for one day. Word would get out. She didn't care to invite the lukewarm congratulations from her sisters, and she definitely couldn't handle one more 'poor Iris!' from Auntie Rosa.

At six months, Joe insisted that Lily quit her job. On a chilly sunny day in November, Joseph Michael Diotallevi was delivered by Cesarean section, three weeks past his due date. He had the look of an old man when he was born, the result of a ten pound person crammed into tight moist quarters for too long. His skin was wrinkled, and his face had already developed beyond that of a newborn, complete with a decidedly Diotallevi nose.

As the nurse wheeled the bassinet into Lily's room for Joseph's first nursing, Joe stood with his hands shoved into his pockets, nervously jingling the piles of quarters he'd collected for the pay phone.

"A son," Joe said to Lily. "I can't believe I have a son!"

"Promise me we can call him Joseph?" Lily asked, looking down in awe at her newborn baby.

"I promise," said Joe.

At least "Joseph" was more classic and sophisticated than "Joe Jr." Anyway, it was clear to Lily in that moment, holding her son in the slanted sunlight of an autumn afternoon, that this was her child. No matter what Lucy called him, she could not call him her own.

"I have to go call everyone, Lil. I'll be back in a few minutes, OK?"

"Sure," said Lily, slipping her arm out of her hospital gown. She was glad to have some time alone with her new baby, and as the sound of Joe's quarters disappeared down the hall, she offered her breast to Joseph, and he attacked it with gusto. Lily was exhausted from the surgery, and her whole body throbbed in pain; thankfully, breastfeeding was mostly Joseph's job.

The afternoon sun streamed into the room, cut into slices by the mini-blinds before falling in stripes across Lily's bed. Lily drew in a breath and softly sang to her son, "Give thanks with a grateful heart, give thanks to the Holy One..."

Lily cupped Joseph's spongy scalp in her palm, and explored the curvature of his head.

"And now, let the weak say I am strong, let the poor say I am rich, because of what the Lord has done, for us..."

She traced the delicate shell of his ear with her index finger, in awe of this handiwork of God. She stroked his soft cheek as he sucked away.

"You really beat me up there, little man," she whispered.

Joseph stopped sucking, and a tiny stream of milk dribbled from his mouth. If Lily hadn't known better, she would have sworn he was smiling.

By the time she got settled back at home, Lily could not remember what life had been like before Joseph arrived.

Breastfeeding had become the greatest joy of her life, an intimacy that gave her pleasure at a level she'd never known. Nursing was a comfort to them both. No matter where they were or what was going on around them, they could simply and quickly retreat, no questions asked.

"I tried that once," said Lucy, scrunching up her nose and motioning her hand to her own breast. "When Alfonso was first born. It made me sick to my stomach."

"Why?" Lily asked.

"Oh, grabbing my own boob like that and stickin' it in his mouth so he could suck it the same way his father sucked on it... it just felt wrong." With a shudder she added, "How long do you plan on doin' it, anyway?"

"They say that breast milk is the best food for a newborn," said Lily. "At least six months - maybe longer."

"Six months? Jesus Christ - that means no one else can ever feed the kid for you - and think of all the time you're gonna spend at Sunday dinner up in the bedroom alone."

Kinda the point, thought Lily. Joe's parents and his brothers and his brothers' wives exemplified everything that troubled Lily about her relationship with Joe, even more so when they were all together at Sunday dinner. The inclusion they'd offered Lily in the early years had transmogrified into an expectation of her unwavering acceptance and unquestioning loyalty. Discussing "family business" with outsiders was strictly forbidden, and anyone who challenged the family morality challenged every member personally.

Since the family collectively agreed that nudity in any degree was unbearable (with the apparent exception of porno actresses), Lily happily escaped to a vacant bedroom or den anytime Joseph began to fuss, or anytime the dinner table became too volatile for him. Or for her.

The difficulty with which Joseph came into the world was reflected in his personality, as if he knew exactly when to sleep or eat, but considered such rules pointless and stupid.

Precocious in every way, Joseph rolled over at four months, took his first steps at ten, and had learned to peddle a Big Wheels tricycle by his first birthday. The more he grew, the stronger his will became. If Lily took him to the store, he cried to go home. If they stayed home, he cried to go out and play. By two years of age, Joseph had developed the vocabulary of a four-year-old, and Lily imagined that his difficult personality was the result of a frustrated old soul trapped in a baby's limited and powerless body. He demanded everything of Lily. Or at least all that was left.

Yet for all the struggles of his toddlerhood, Joseph possessed a capricious underlying sweetness. At unpredictable and unexpected times, he would present himself to Lily with outstretched arms. "Pick me up, Mommy," he would say, and Lily would take him into her arms, and he would hug her with his entire body, nestle his face into her neck and say, "I love you, Mommy."

"I love you too, my sweetness," Lily would reply, and then Joseph would wriggle himself free, and toddle off to some new adventure. Lily stood in awe of his sturdiness, amazed at his lack of appreciation for his status as a child. He seemed to have no awareness that he was a very small person who stood face-to-kneecap with the rest of the world. He would haul off and slap one of his cousins for refusing to relinquish a cookie or a toy, and would boldly announce, "Asshole!" if his father tried to put him into bed before he was ready. Lily knew he was destined to be something great - perhaps a lawyer or an entrepreneur - but she definitely would not have to worry about him surviving in the world. She wished she were a little more like him.

11. IRIS

The seeds of attraction planted during her first tête-à-tête with Claudio found fertile soil in Iris's imagination, where they were sprinkled generously with curiosity and desire, and quickly sprouted fantasies of future private encounters. In the same elegant style in which he had provided Iris with an excuse compelling enough to shirk her sense of conjugal duty for a few hours to partake in that first dinner with him, step by subtle step he initiated her into a world where business mixed with pleasure as naturally as champagne with caviar.

She was both thrilled and frightened as opportunities for such encounters arose during bona fide business engagements, first in Milan, then in Florence. On each occasion, Claudio's refined manners and chivalrous treatment persuaded her that no harm could come of two respectable professionals such as themselves indulging in a bit of pleasure while fulfilling their obligations. How ridiculously virtuous would she seem if she refused an invitation to dinner at the end of a conference to discuss a keynote speaker's comments, before driving back to Rapallo in Claudio's Mercedes SL500 convertible? How pathetically provincial would she look, really, if she were to ask Claudio to mind the manicured hand he placed gently on her knee during the drive home, when it wandered ever so slowly up her thigh, as she sank deeper and deeper into the soft black leather of the bucket seat? How hopelessly hypocritical would she feel if she pushed him away and hurried home without tasting the lips he made her crave, when he drew her close for a kiss before retiring to his suite, where, despite his entreaties, she could not find the courage to enter?

Such rationalizations scattered like fallen leaves in a brisk autumn wind when the opportunity for what was bound to happen sooner or later had jumped, unbeckoned, right into her lap. Weeks earlier, Iris had signed up to attend a two-day event in Rome, and the day before she was to leave, Claudio sent her thoughts into a tailspin and her conscience into a dither by announcing he would accompany her. The sigh of relief she heaved when he asked her to reserve a second room for him seemed soft as a baby's breath compared to the moans he expertly elicited from her the following evening at their hotel, as he treated her to his lover's menu of irresistible appetizers and sensuous desserts (with an interlude of champagne and smoked salmon delivered by room service), far more exquisite than anything she had ever tasted in all her years of marital sex. Replete with satisfaction but wallowing in unease when she awoke the following morning next to the only man she had ever slept with besides her husband, Iris reflected on how the value of impeccable manners increased in direct proportion to the awkwardness of the situation. As she crept out of bed to brush away her night breath before Claudio stirred and tried to kiss her, she was very grateful to him indeed for knowing how to make something so wrong feel so right, at least long enough for her to enjoy it.

Iris's rational side soon realized she was not cut out for the conniving entailed by an extramarital affair, however well-conducted, but was overruled by her renegade sensual side, no longer prepared to endure a slow and painful death by suffocation. Claudio intrigued and amused her, and she was exhilarated to be living out a tiny portion of her life in a secret place, where the pursuit of pleasure was not thwarted, but encouraged; where she was admired as an industrious young professional free from the demands of children who would steal time and energy from her job, rather than tolerated as an inept child-woman whose foreignness and lack of ability to reproduce made her a misfit for the life that had been so lovingly and meticulously laid out for her.

Although Iris was quick enough to sense that Claudio's savoir faire had not been achieved through his devotion to fidelity, he had never given her the impression she was one in a long string of casual relationships. Theirs was no sordid love affair; they weren't seeing each other for the sole purpose of engaging in sex, nor was she a mistress, expecting to be showered with expensive gifts or whisked away on exotic vacations. Their relationship was different, because they shared more than a passion for each other: they were both madly in love with the hotel business.

On the job, Claudio helped Iris accumulate valuable experience by involving her in management strategies with the *Direttore*, who was strongly encouraged to delegate more responsibility to her. Claudio openly praised her merits as she evolved professionally, but was implacable in his criticism of any crucial mistakes or errors in judgment she made along the way. She had been content with the modest bonus she received at the end of the season, even though she secretly felt her performance and commitment deserved more. But asking for more was not something Iris did, especially if it could give rise to the suspicion that she was reaping undeserved benefits by sleeping with the boss. Besides, as Gregorio said, they didn't need the money.

The evening prior to her scheduled business trip to London to attend an important travel fair, Claudio phoned her at her office, instructing her to leave for the day and sneak into the suite he kept at the hotel. Due to a series of pressing problems and conflicting schedules, she hadn't seen him for ten days, and their hunger was satiated in a matter of minutes. When they finished, she lay on her back, immobilized by the afterglow and by the thought of the evening that awaited her at home, where she should already be cooking dinner.

"*Ti voglio bene,*" she heard herself say. She had said the words to him in her mind many times before, but never out loud. Though they frequently conversed in English, she spoke the words in Italian, a language which offered two options for telling someone you loved them. Unlike "I love you" in English, the words "*ti amo*" were reserved exclusively for romantic love, whereas "*ti voglio bene*" had a wider range of applications. Literally, "I wish you well" was an expression that could be used to tell the person you were in love with that you cared deeply for him or her, but it could also be directed at a dear friend, a relative, a child. The words could be accompanied by a kiss on the lips, a peck on the cheek, a squeeze of the arm, a tousle of the hair.

The one thing Iris disliked about their relationship, apart from the deceit, was Claudio's habit of moaning and gasping with pleasure during sex, his exclamations a notch or two more passionate than when he indulged in an exceptional wine or gourmet delicacy, but never expressing any deeper sentiments. It reminded her of the way she used to feel back when her older brothers wiped their plates clean and burped after a meal she had prepared with loving care; sure, she could tell they liked it, but couldn't they think of something nice to say to her? If Claudio wanted to leave his emotions out of it, she would respect that, but today she was frustrated with the fact that she never felt free to express anything more than satisfaction or gratitude to him. She did care for him, otherwise she wouldn't have become involved with him in the first place. She decided that the expression "*ti voglio bene*" would not jeopardize the status quo in any way. It would not raise expectations, pose questions, or demand answers. Above all, it would not constitute a total betrayal of Gregorio, the only man to whom she had ever said the words, "*ti amo.*"

"You're quite a special woman," Claudio said.

It wasn't exactly the same thing, but it was a start. "Thank you," she said.

"You've done more for me than you can know," he said.

"I have?"

"Well, yes. You've made my visits to the hotel much more interesting and productive. And exciting." He flicked a finger at her nipple as if it were a fly on her breast. She giggled.

"And you've also worked wonders for my marriage."

"I have?" she said again. She scrunched a pillow under her arm and propped herself up on an elbow to look at him.

"Absolutely. Ask my wife!" he said with the peculiar half-smile smirk she sometimes found endearing, other times irritating. "On second thought, maybe you'd better not."

Each time Iris saw the framed family portrait of Claudio with his boys and wife prominently displayed upon his polished walnut desk, jealousy shot through her veins, poisoning her blood, making her gut roil with guilt. She had never asked him to remove the portrait, and he had never offered. She told herself she was superior to such requests; plus, the picture exerted some sort of morbid fascination on her. Occasionally, when Claudio wasn't there, she took the portrait in her hands to study it up close. His wife, Fernanda, heiress to one of Italy's top textile manufacturers, had at first struck her as pretty, in a snobby Northern Italian sort of way. Upon further scrutiny, Iris eventually decided that her features did not express particular beauty or intelligence. There was no sparkle in the dull, close-set eyes, no smile on the thin, tight lips. She was simply well-preserved. And why shouldn't she be? With all her family's money on top of Claudio's, she probably divided her time between the health club, the aesthetician's, the hairdresser's, and the designer boutiques of Via Monte Napoleone. Though Iris could not stop herself from succumbing to these occasional bouts of jealousy, she did not envy the woman's life one bit, nor did she envy her three impeccably dressed boys, with their washed-out Milanese complexions and the snotty looks on their doughy faces. Spoiled brats if she had ever seen one.

"I have more patience with my wife than I used to," Claudio said. "I've realized she's about as good as they come, as wives go."

"Really?"

"She runs a tight household, and organizes everything for the boys: school, sports, vacations."

They had never talked about his marriage before, except at the very beginning, when he chuckled away Iris's fears of being a home-wrecker by assuring her that one of the principal benefits of extramarital affairs was that they made it bearable for one to remain married. He sustained that by providing what the conjugal relationship was lacking, affairs were actually excellent therapy. Everyone in Italy had affairs; that was why marriages lasted so long.

Although Iris sometimes fantasized about leaving Gregorio for Claudio and moving into the suite at the hotel, she had never seriously considered it, and he had never so much as hinted such an option existed. She loved both men, in different ways, and for different things. Maybe there was some truth to Claudio's theory, after all. She, too, seemed to tolerate Gregorio's exasperating temperance better now that she had found someone with whom to indulge in the pursuit of pleasure. Still, she thought Claudio's comments rather cynical. Shouldn't he at least pretend that he would throw over his wife for Iris if she were free? Wouldn't that be the romantic thing to say?

"We spent last weekend up in Cortina," Claudio continued, implacable in his surprise mission to provide her with unwanted details. "It was Fernanda's birthday. The kids stayed with their grandparents, and we invited another couple of old friends up to the chalet with us. Just a quiet celebration, you know?"

"How nice," Iris said. She could hear the split logs crackling in the Alpine fireplace, as bright flames took the chill out of the evening air; she could hear the laughter of the foursome as they reminisced about previous weekends spent skiing together.

"We decided to just take it easy, and spend the day at the spa." She could see them wrapped in plush white robes; she could hear their groans of pleasure as the masseuse beat the kinks out of their backs, feel the jets of the Jacuzzi as they pummeled their aching joints and muscles. "Then we went to Fernanda's favorite restaurant for dinner." She could visualize him waving away the menus, conferring with the Maître, ordering just the right wine to accompany just the right dishes, leading the toast to his wife's continued health and happiness. "I was able to do that, and almost enjoy it. All thanks to you."

"Glad to be of help," Iris said, as Claudio stretched in the bed, with that half-smile smirk on his face. She imagined how he would spend the evening after she left. He would shower and dress, make a few phone calls, including one to his wife and kids, then go have a delicious dinner in his restaurant, from which he would admire the lovely view. Iris glanced at her watch and stood; she did not like the feeling of his sticky semen trickling down the insides of her thighs, but could not spare the time for a shower. She'd rinse off in the bidet, then hurry home to where she belonged, hoping none of the staff would see her slink away out the service entrance.

Five days later, Iris was again relieved to be back home. "I'm back!" she called out, as she entered the brightly lit hallway, her suitcase trailing behind her. She moved with the grace typical of women who had studied ballet as little girls; in one flowing action, she pushed the door closed with one foot, bent to lower her bag and briefcase to the floor, shrugged off her trench coat, and kicked off her high heels.

"*A-mo-re!*" If the singsong voice bouncing off the walls as Gregorio approached was any indication, her husband was in a particularly cheerful mood this evening. Iris's nerves were frazzled, and she was exhausted; she wished she had made it home before him, and had time to settle in, shower, unwind with a glass of wine.

"I was afraid I was going to have to eat all by myself," Gregorio said, extending his arms to embrace her. "Mamma and Cinzia insisted I dine with them earlier, but I knew you wouldn't disappoint me. Or Zenzero." The ginger cat had followed on the heels of Gregorio's slippers, its lively trot dicing its mewing into high-pitched staccato notes, reminding Iris of a long-ago sweltering summer afternoon spent singing into the blades of an oscillating fan with Lily. The cat pointed its quivering tail to the ceiling, shimmied and purred its welcome between the two sets of legs and ankles. The greeting she had received at the boutique hotels in Mayfair and St. Germain-des-Prés where she had spent the last few nights paled by comparison.

"It's good to be back home," Iris said, averting her face just in time to abort the kiss Gregorio attempted to deliver to her lips, which instead centered the dimple on her right cheek. He put his arms around her and she allowed her cheek to rest against his shoulder; her breath was quick and shallow. The strong, rhythmic beat of his heart against hers calmed her, steadying her erratic breath and slowing her racing pulse. It felt good to tell the truth: it *was* good to be back home. Like a repentant sinner steeping in the redeeming scent of incense in a church, Iris was uplifted as she inhaled the clean fragrance of Marseilles soap lingering on the surface of her husband's skin, and the indelible chemical nosegay of hospital smells that lay beneath.

"Your plane must have gotten in early," Gregorio said.

"My plane? Early?" Iris's thoughts ran in circles trying to remember what time she had told him she would be arriving.

"Yes. I was at the airport."

"When? Where? How come I didn't see you?"

"I was scheduled to oversee a complicated procedure, but I got out of it. Well, actually, the patient went into cardiac arrest before we even got our hands on him. So I thought I'd surprise you," Gregorio said. "I got to the airport just as the five-thirty-five British Airways from Gatwick landed, and I waited until the very last passenger came through the gate, but no Iris! I felt so foolish, like a stood-up fiancé, all alone with a bunch of roses."

"Roses? You came to the airport with roses?" Iris asked, her heart spinning out of control, her face flushing bright red with retroactive panic.

"Yes indeed, *Piccolina!* I'm in the mood to celebrate. The roses are in a vase on the table," Gregorio said. "Anyway, your phone was switched off, so I checked with the desk. They told me you might be on the next flight arriving at eight forty-five, but they wouldn't say for sure. At that point, I thought I'd organize something for dinner, rather than wait for three hours. Now, here it is only eight o'clock, and you're home already! How you managed that is beyond me."

"You shouldn't have bothered coming to the airport. I told you

I'd take a taxi like I always do," Iris replied, her struggle to remain calm sucking the color from her cheeks. Why had she let Claudio talk her into leaving London a day early and meeting him in Paris? He didn't seem to mind that it would mean rescheduling two important meetings at the World Travel Mart and taking a very risky gamble without the hedge of a prefabricated plan. However, refusal was never really an option with Claudio once he got an idea, and in fact, before even checking with her, he had already taken care of modifying her travel arrangements. This time his justification was an irrepressible craving for the oysters one could only find at his favorite *huîterie* in the sixth arrondissement. In the early days of their affair, Iris had relished the ironic sense of freedom she derived from not being offered the possibility to say no; the more decided he was, the less timorous and reluctant she felt. If Claudio insisted upon taking her to the Gritti Palace for the national hoteliers' conference being held in Venice, or to Rome for the tourist board workshop, where he would sleep in no other hotel than the Hassler, who was she to object? She was thoroughly impressed with the luxury hotels and Michelin-starred restaurants that were Claudio's milieu, and playing cicerone to her seemed to amuse him as much as it stimulated her.

London, Paris, and Claudio's doubt-free world were not here to bolster her confidence now, as she stood in the entrance of her home, wondering what was passing through her husband's mind. He had never once found the time to meet her at the airport in the past. Had he grown suspicious? And what were the flowers for? She imagined how the scene could have played out, she and Claudio arriving on the flight from Paris, and running into Gregorio and his bouquet of roses. She felt like throwing up, and it wasn't because of the oysters; which, by the way, she always found disgusting. Good thing there had been plenty of chilled champagne to chase the briny blobs of slime down her throat.

"Maybe you didn't come on British Airways after all? I saw an Alitalia flight on the arrivals board, too, but that was delayed an hour," Gregorio said, generously offering Iris an alibi. Could it be a trap? Maybe, but what else could she say?

"Thank God for that delay," she said in the most travel-weary voice she could summon to her aid, as her mind worked furiously to script a plausible scenario. Her face was still pressed against Gregorio's chest as she spoke; she could not trust herself to look him in the eye. "I was held up at the travel fair all morning, but I managed to catch the Gatwick Express in plenty of time. Of course, the darn train broke down and I missed my BA flight. Fortunately, I found a seat on Alitalia just as it was boarding. So here I am!" she concluded. "And that's the important thing, right?" She looked up at him, hoping to avoid further speculation on flights and schedules and airports and other minutiae that might consort with each other to trip up her already shaky footing, hoping he would not notice the twitch she felt tugging at the corners of her lips.

"Yes, *Piccolina*," Gregorio concurred as he released her. "That's the important thing. But you really have to learn to let me know when you have a change of plans. Otherwise we are going to have to seriously rethink this business of you working at a job that requires you to run off here and there like some sort of traveling salesman. Mamma and Cinzia and I had enough of that with my father."

"I know, I'm sorry," Iris said.

"Especially when there's no need for you to work. I understand a smart girl like you needs to keep her mind occupied, but what's wrong with working from home as a translator? You could keep your own hours, right here in the comfort of our own home. It's a pity neither one of us gets to spend much time here. Mamma was just saying yesterday that ... "

"I'm sorry, Gregorio," Iris said. "I wanted to call and let you know, it's just ..."

"I know, I know. If you have to choose between wasting time trying to get in touch and running to catch your flight, you go for the plane. And I'm glad you did."

"So am I!" Iris said. "All I really wanted was to get home as soon as possible. And here I am." She tried to keep the twitch out of her smile, as she was struck with the doubt that she may not have turned off the mobile phone Claudio had given her to use for their clandestine communications. All she needed now was for it to start ringing in her purse.

"Now, you go take a nice hot shower. What perfume are you wearing, anyway? It's not very feminine, if you don't mind my saying so. You have to stop letting those duty free saleswomen spray you with their dreadful samples every time you walk though an airport. I'll bet you can't wait to wash it off, can you?"

Without waiting for an answer he placed his hands on Iris's shoulders, spun her around, and sent her down the corridor, with an affectionate pat on her butt. "Now, be good and run along," he added. "You just leave everything right there. I'll deliver your suitcase to our room, just like they do at those hotels you can't seem to get enough of. Off you go, scoot! Like a good little girl!"

While Iris struggled to remember whether there was any compromising evidence that should make her worry about leaving her suitcase in Gregorio's hands, she had already been nudged halfway down the hall. In under two minutes she had checked the mobile phone (it was off) and hid it in her underwear drawer, removed her contact lenses, stripped, and was standing naked in the bathtub, trembling with exhaustion, worry and guilt. The ongoing lies were wearing her down, tautening her nerves to the point of snapping; sooner or later she would slip up, sooner or later, Gregorio would nail her. And then what? How could she face him? What would Isabella do? And Cinzia? What would she say to Auntie Rosa and her family, when she was disgraced and shipped back home? While her sisters and brothers were all busy with families of their own, having the integrity and courage to admit their mistakes and divorce when things did not work out, she was being despicably two-faced. How had she turned into a liar and a cheat? She longed for someone to talk to, but her only two friends had deserted her; Liz had moved to Miami after her husband was offered a job as captain for a cruise line, and Deirdre had gone back to Ireland to marry a widowed professor of Italian from Dublin, whom she had met in the Cinque Terre, where he was hiking the trails with his four sons. She could never write to Lily or her other sisters; she could never confess her sins in writing, and they would never understand.

She turned on the water full blast, as hot as she could stand it, hoping it would chase away the confusion and guilt and fear buzzing around her like horseflies around manure. Lately she had noticed that the more guilty she felt, the longer her showers lasted, and by the time she had massaged the third dollop of shampoo into her hair, her head and its concerns were swimming in an immense cloud of bubbly lather. She was just starting to calm down when a new wave of paralyzing panic shot through her. Knowing she had not a moment to waste, she forced her body to action, slipping as she hopped out of the tub, then slid across the hall to her bedroom, where she found her suitcase standing at the foot of the bed. The bold black letters *CDG GOA* clearly advertised that the suitcase, and consequently Iris, traveled on a flight from Paris. She clawed at the tag furiously, her wet fingers slipping as she tried to rip it off the handle. With a final yank, the elastic broke.

"What are you doing there?" Iris spun around, nude, hiding her hand behind her back, and the tag in the palm of her hand. Gregorio stood in the doorway, glaring at her. A mountain of lather slid from her head and floated to the floor, its bubbles disintegrating with a series of soft pops. She had no further alibis to invent, no further excuses to offer. She wished he'd say something, and get it over with.

"Look at the mess you're making!" Gregorio said. "You're dripping all over the new parquet!"

"I'm sorry ... I know ...," she stammered. "It's just that I ... um ... forgot something," Iris wiped ineffectually at the suds and water pooling at her feet, her rapid movements sending further fluffs of foam to the floor. "I'll mop it up right away!"

Gregorio sighed, shook his head. "No, just go finish your shower, I'll take care of it." Iris hurried from the room, her eyes downcast as she pattered passed him. Closing the door to the bathroom, which for safety reasons Gregorio had made her promise to never lock, she disposed of the tag in the toilet; she had to flush three times before the incriminating evidence stopped bobbing to the surface to haunt her.

"Everything all right in there?" Gregorio's voice called, minutes later, from the other side of the door. He had never once walked in on her; his respect of privacy was both appreciated and reciprocated. Memories of the promiscuous washing of faces and brushing of teeth with siblings before rushing off to school, and of brothers beating down the door while she tried to get the hang of using tampons were not easily erased from her mind.

"Fine!" Iris called over the running water. It still might be fine, right?

"Dinner's ready when you are!"

"Dinner? Really?" She wondered what he had managed to prepare, and why. Thoughts of her last meal with Claudio and of the raw bivalves still floating around in her stomach made her want to puke.

"I was going to try my hand at cooking something, but Cinzia made minestrone and gave me a potful," he yelled, as Iris tilted her face into the spray.

She could hear his words, though his voice sounded miles away, distanced by much more than the door separating them. As the water ran over her head, she thought of all the times she had lied, all the times she had sneaked around, all the times she had risked getting caught. For what? For a man who would skip his son's birthday to run off to Alba for the first white truffles of the season? She had a wonderful husband who took excellent care of her, and so did his family, really, if you knew how to interpret their actions. She should learn to take life more seriously, learn to appreciate what really counted, forget her superficial notions about "having fun" and "being happy." That was so childish. This was real life.

"After dinner we'll run up and say hi to Mamma. She's been on my back all week, questioning why I should put up with your trips," he called through the door. "But don't tell her I told you!"

"Of course I won't," Iris called to him. Instead of irritating her, his talk of Mamma was oddly reassuring, like Gregorio himself. He was older, wiser, and knew what was best for her. Why couldn't she just enjoy the love and security offered her by a man any woman in her right mind would give her eyeteeth to have as a husband?

"Don't you want to know why I came to meet you with the roses?" Gregorio called through the door.

"Of course I do." At least, she thought she did. She was so confused, it was hard to say. She lathered her scalp, her ears, her neck. One more time couldn't hurt.

"Remember that conference I told you about?" Gregorio said. "Next year? In Stockholm?"

"Of course," Iris lied. She had no idea what he was talking about. Every evening he rambled on about a different conference to be attended, a different colleague that had botched a procedure, a different scandal involving a different chief of department. There was no way she could remember it all. But at that moment, with her ears full of suds, she was more than happy to listen to anything that did not involve her directly.

"Well, guess who has been appointed to head the scientific committee?" Gregorio's hands beat a drumroll on the door. "Yours truly!"

A burst of cold water abruptly replaced the hot.

"*Heeeyy!*" Iris screamed. Cinzia must be using the goddamn dishwasher.

"I knew you'd be happy for me, *Piccolina*!" Gregorio cried. "I'll tell you more about it over dinner. Now dry off before you shrivel up like a prune!"

Trembling, she turned off the tap and reached for her towel. She felt misplaced, wasted, as if she had been carried out to sea by the current, and spent the past year rotting like a piece of driftwood. How had she strayed so far off course? She, who balked at breaking the rules; she, who always stopped at crosswalks, who would walk an extra mile rather than trespass on private property, who would not leave her car illegally parked for even two minutes, who spent twice as long as any Italian in any queue, because she waited her turn instead of cutting. She marveled that she could live with herself, that she could even look at herself, and not be disgusted.

Infidelity was wrong, no matter how you looked at it; she would be devastated if the tables were turned, and Gregorio should ever betray her. She wondered whether evil people actually knew they were evil, or if there were a pair of knobs inside their heads, like dials on a short-wave radio, one used to squelch the static interference of the conscience, the other to tune into a frequency that transmitted justifications for any imaginable transgression, twenty-four hours a day, seven days a week.

Her chin trembled, and tears stung her eyes as she dried herself, then wrapped her hair in the towel. She was thankful for the steam that fogged up the mirror as she opened the door to leave. Her eyes were the last thing she wanted to look at.

"Hey, *Piccolina!* That was some shower!" Gregorio said, walking into the bedroom. "Hurry up and get dressed before you catch cold. Then I'll tell you all about the conference."

"Just a second," Iris responded without looking up, pretending to fumble with a jammed latch on her suitcase as she struggled to regain her composure.

"Let me help you," Gregorio said, walking over to her. "You've worn yourself out so, you can hardly see straight. I honestly don't know about this job."

"Thanks," Iris said, eyes low.

Gregorio patted her on the head, then took her chin into his hand, and raised it toward him.

"*Piccolina*, your eyes are all red! You've been wearing your contact lenses for hours on end, haven't you? And you probably got shampoo in them, too, didn't you?"

"Yes, Gregorio. That must be it. Shampoo," Iris mumbled. She was still safe and loved, still in time to make everything all right again. Gregorio waited for her as she put on her glasses, slipped on a pair of white cotton undies, her favorite jeans and a sweatshirt.

"You're home now. You can relax. Let's go eat," Gregorio said, taking her by the hand and leading her out of the room.

"How was Paris?" Franco called out to her one morning the following week when they crossed paths outside the house.

"What?" Iris asked, stopping on the stairs that led to the parking area on the lower level of the terraced garden, where her red Vespa took up a small spot next to the fleet of practical white cars driven by the Leale family, and Franco's black Volkswagen Golf.

"Paris. You know, the capital of France," Franco replied. "Eiffel Tower. The Louvre. Baguettes and stinky cheese. Sound familiar?"

"I don't know what you're talking about," Iris said, averting her eyes as she sidled past her brother-in-law. Franco was dressed in his *guardia di finanza* uniform, either ready to go to work or just coming home. It was hard to tell, as his perennial five o'clock shadow always gave him a slightly disheveled look.

"Look, Iris. Don't deny the evidence." His words made her stumble; she grabbed onto the wrought iron railing and stood there, her back to him, her heart racing, her hands sweating. "I was on airport patrol monitoring the closed-circuit TV when you and Romeo passed through the other day. I recognized you right off the bat. You and that boyfriend of yours were waiting for your luggage. Which came off the Paris flight."

"What are you talking about?" Iris turned to face him. "I was on a business trip." If she could avoid telling lies, and reply to his accusations with more questions or an abridged version of the facts, she might be able to prevent herself from looking guilty.

"Funny, I seem to remember Cinzia telling me you were going to London. In fact, all I heard all week from her and Isabella was Iris in London this, Iris in London that. But whatever. London. Paris. It's all the same to me." Franco grinned at her from under the thick black moustache that made him look more like a Mexican bandito than an officer enlisted in Italy's war against financial crime and smuggling.

Iris replayed in her mind the scene at the luggage retrieval area of the small airport. It had been deserted, save for a handful of other passengers from their flight who were also waiting for their luggage. Claudio had placed a hand on her back as they waited, and gradually let it slide lower and lower, until it was resting on her rump.

"Claudio. Don't do that. Please," she had said.

Claudio had smirked, in the way that irked her. "No one here knows us, Iris. We've already checked." At Iris's insistence, whenever they traveled together, they had the habit of scrutinizing all the other passengers as they boarded the plane before them, to make sure there was no one they knew. Claudio never seemed to be overly concerned about being demonstrative in public, unlike Iris, who was terrified of being spotted. She often had to scold him, but he just laughed it off, seeming to derive pleasure from making her squirm with unease. She supposed it had to do with the fact that he was a man, and would actually not mind being seen with another woman, especially if she were well-dressed and reasonably attractive, a bit too tall to be Italian, and a good number of years his junior.

"I'm just saying," Franco continued, his bushy-browed eyes roaming over her features, observing her face from every angle, then straying down to take in the rest of her body, scanning her as if she herself were a piece of suspicious luggage. "No sweat. Your secret's safe with me. This family. These Leales. They're boring as hell, aren't they? But you shoulda told me. I woulda been happy to take up the slack for old Gregorio. Coulda kept it in the family."

What exactly did Franco want from her? Was he coming on to her? Or did he plan to blackmail her?

"Relax, I'm just kidding. Thing is, I won't be around much longer myself. You see, I met someone too. She works as a croupier on one of those Costa cruise ships. She passes through every fifteen days when she disembarks in Genoa. Remember when I went to Rome a coupla months ago? For that training course? It was all bullshit. She took me on a cruise with her. Mediterranean. That's her gig," Franco recounted, with more than a hint of pride in his voice.

"You must be joking!" Iris said, her low voice crackling with incredulity. She had always thought Franco and Cinzia were enjoying a life of cozy domesticity, comfortably installed in the downstairs apartment with their progeny, and Isabella descending from the third floor to lend a hand or word of advice. Wasn't anything the way it seemed?

"Nope, I'm dead serious. We got it all planned out. I even rented us a cute little apartment in Genoa," Franco said. "You keep it under your hat, you hear? I'll only be as good as you are at keeping my mouth shut. I'm gonna tell Cinzia any day now. Just waiting for the right time. You know how it is. There's always something."

"But Franco, you can't just leave! What about the kids?" Iris asked.

"Look Iris, I'll always love my kids," he replied through clenched teeth, straining to keep his voice low. He held his uniform cap in his right hand like a tambourine, and whacked it against his thigh for emphasis as he spoke. "But how will they ever respect me if I stay here with a wife who does nothing but complain about me? *(whack) Professoressa* Cinzia and our Fascist mother-in-law Judge-lady got it all figured out. *(whack)* They take turns cutting me down, humiliating me in front of my boys. *(whack)* They got all those rules to enforce, see? They got their Manzoni and their Leopardi to recite. *(whack)* They got their little Latin proverbs to quote. *(whack)* But one word neither of them ever learned the meaning of, in any language. And that's *(whack)* pleasure. *(whack) Voluptate. Piacere. Plaisir.* Someone musta deleted it from their vocabulary. *Capisci?*"

Iris stared at him in silence.

"No wonder the *vecchio* Leale got his goodies on the road," he said.

"What are you talking about?"

"Don't be so naïve, Iris!" Franco said. "With a lady like Isabella swimming in his tank, how can you blame her old man for engaging in a little offshore fishing?"

"Why can't you just talk straight? You mean her husband

cheated on her?"

"So you don't know all the dirty, dark secrets of the Leale dynasty? Isabella found out, and dropped enough hints to make damn sure the kids knew, too. Made them want to defend her, stick up for her. He was still going at it when I met Cinzia. Monday to Friday, that man was on the road. That's why they don't want to let you or me or anyone out of their sight. Which just kinda makes you wanna run more, don't it, Iris?"

Franco ran the fingers of his left hand through his thick, black hair. For the first time, Iris noticed a dusting of gray on his curls, and white bristles in his beard. In fact, it was probably the first time she had actually noticed him at all, as a man, and not merely as an appendage of Cinzia. She told herself he was doing something despicable, but as she looked at him, she could not find it in her heart to fault him. Instead, she sympathized with him, standing there with his soft little pasta paunch and his greying head full of plans.

Iris wondered what master of mismatching had thrown him and Cinzia in each other's paths. She tried to imagine them in the early days of their relationship, before she had ever met them. Perhaps they were neither enough alike nor different enough to be suited for each other. Perhaps the trick was to have everything in common, or nothing in common. To be mirrors or magnets.

"And what are you gonna do?" Franco said.

"About what?" Iris said.

"About lover-boy."

Iris was so shocked at Franco's stories that she had momentarily forgotten about her own predicament.

"It's over," she said. "Really. It was all a big mistake. I told him the very next day, after we came back from Paris. It was too risky. Suddenly, all I could think about was getting caught. I could actually see the look on everyone's faces. Gregorio's, Isabella's, Cinzia's, yours. And Auntie Rosa's, and my mom's, and all my sisters'." Her voice cracked with emotion; she wondered why on earth she was confiding in Franco, of all people. Perhaps it was because he was the only one there, the only one who asked, the only one who admitted to being as human and imperfect as she.

"Please, Franco. You have to promise you won't say anything. It would only hurt everyone. I told you, it's over."

"Don't worry, Iris. I have enough problems of my own right now," he answered. "But do you mind if I ask you a question?"

Iris trembled with relief. "Sure."

"You look all prim and proper when you dress in your business suits, but you've got this wild side, even a blind man could see it. You were just a kid when you met Gregorio. And he was already pretty boring, even then. Why did you marry him?"

Iris had the impulse to defend Gregorio, recite a list of his unsurpassable qualities, of his unique gifts, of his impeccable virtues. Instead, she answered, "Because he asked me to."

They stared at each other for a moment, then Iris asked him, "And you? What made you marry Cinzia?"

Franco shrugged, put his cap back on his head, and hitched up his trousers. "She said yes."

From: Lily Capotosti <lilycapotosti@gmail.com>
To: Iris Capotosti <iris.capotosti@gmail.com>
Sent: Friday, October 29, 2010 at 8:03 AM
Subject: Speechless

Dear Iris:

I'm speechless, really - shocked to read about your affair with Claudio.

The whole time we were growing up, you were the one who could do no wrong. Even when you did, you didn't. Do you remember that time we took Dad's car to the Club Car to go dancing and you backed out without waiting for the windows to defog and put a dent in his rear quarter panel? I agreed to tell Dad about it because you were too scared to do it, and he glared at me and said, "Who was driving the car?" and I said, "Iris," and he said, "Are you sure?" and I had to swear on the Bible that it was you, although I could tell he still didn't believe me, even after you confessed.

Even Dad - the king of blame and punishment - couldn't conceive of you doing any wrong. HIs reality was that you were perfect so I guess when trouble happened around you someone had to take the blame. And we know who was always standing nearby, don't we? I guess everyone likes to believe in a Virgin Mary, which then necessitates the existence of a Mary Magdalene. Can't have one without the other, after all.

I can see how stifling your life with Gregorio was, but what I wouldn't have given for that kind of peace and quiet and stability! (Not to mention financial security...) I would have given my left arm - and probably my right one, too - to have a husband like him.

Love,
Lily

Dear Lily,

I felt really embarrassed sharing the story about Claudio with you, especially now that I know so much more about what your marriage was like in those days. You turned to your new church for consolation, and you got your baby. I turned to a clandestine lover, and I got nothing, except a massive dose of guilt. Maybe I should have continued lighting those candles to the Blessed Virgin Mary, since you seem to think we are so much alike. Maybe she would have stepped in to keep me clean.

I know it was incredibly selfish of me, not to mention immoral, to get involved with Claudio. I never told anyone else about it and I still thank God that Gregorio never found out. He did everything in his power to make me happy, even though I was such a disappointment to him. What a prize I turned out to be, huh? A package deal, everything from infertility to infidelity. When I think back on the affair now, it's as if I'm looking back on another person's life, not mine. I feel so ashamed, just like I still feel ashamed about putting the dent in Dad's car (did you really have to bring that up?).

Like I said before, you weren't forced to marry Joe any more than I was forced to marry Gregorio. No one forced me to have an affair, and no one forced you to compound your mistakes by sticking with Joe and starting a family. I shared this with you because I wanted you to understand me, not judge me.

Love,
Iris

12. LILY

"Mommy, what the heck are you doing?" Joseph asked with a laugh, as Lily pulled packages of flour, sugar, baking powder, chocolate chips, and small jars of multicolored sugars, sprinkles, and food coloring from the cupboard, laying them all out on the counter.

"We're making cookies!"

"Yay! What kind of cookies are we making, Mommy?"

Lily surveyed the heap of bags and jars and bowls and spoons and cartons of eggs and sticks of butter, and replied, "Apparently, we're making every kind."

Lily rummaged through her rag-tag collection of favorite recipes, and then selected four varieties, based on the ingredients scattered in front of her.

"You want to help?" she asked Joseph.

"Yes – I want to!"

"Then go in the bathroom and wash your hands."

Joseph spun around and headed up the stairs.

"With soap!" Lily shouted after him. As Joseph grew into his pre-school years, he displayed a healthy curiosity for new activities, yet was more often than not thwarted by his own tendency to get easily frustrated. Lily was glad to see that he was in a happy mood. It was going to be a good day.

Lily and Joseph spent hours mixing and matching various

colors of frosting and decorations, designing cookies with special themes such as the polka-dot Santa, the zebra reindeer, and the puzzle cookie, which was one huge cookie comprised of the leftover dough from all of the recipes.

By dinnertime, every surface in the kitchen was covered either with a batch of dough, baked cookies cooling on racks, or partially filled leftover aluminum tins bearing holiday scenes – a couple nestling on a sleigh ride, children building a snowman, the star of Bethlehem shining high above a glowing manger.

The wonderful mess warmed Lily's heart: her pile of precisely cut and carefully painted roll-out cookies; the perfectly shaped peanut butter cookies with the signature criss-cross pattern across the surface; the rich and buttery Russian teacakes, and Snickerdoodles coated in a mixture of cinnamon and sugar.

And then there was Joseph's work: peanut butter cookies with a peppermint candy plunged into the center; Christmas tree cut-outs with every conceivable decoration on them; tea cakes bonded together as the melted chocolate he drizzled all over them cooled and hardened.

Joseph licked a glob of green frosting from his finger. "Mommy – I'm sick of making cookies. Can I go watch my Superman movie?"

"Sure," said Lily. "Thank you for being my helper - you did a great job."

"You did a great job, too, Mommy!"

Lily passed through the kitchen one last time, wiping down the counters, and turning on the dishwasher. She picked up a candy cane upon which a tea cake had been impaled, and with a mental note to fit in an extra workout that week, she pulled the cookie off into her mouth with her front teeth, and turned out the kitchen light.

Joseph was drowsily draped along the length of the love seat, purple frosting in his hair, his pants dusted with flour, his face glittering with red and green sugar.

"Hey, buddy," she said to him softly. "Got room for me?"

Joseph shimmied his small body toward the front edge of the

couch cushions, creating enough space for Lily to lie along behind him.

"Your cookies are just wonderful, my love," she whispered into his ear.

"Thanks," he murmured.

Lily kissed the top of his head. He smelled of cinnamon and sugar, cooled sweat and little boy. His breathing became quiet and his body still, and once Lily was sure he was asleep, she clicked the television off, wrapped him in her arms, and drifted blissfully off.

She awoke as Joe placed a kiss gently on her forehead. "Hi, sleepyhead."

"Oh, my God," said Lily. "What time is it?"

"It's almost ten," said Joe, stroking Joseph's head. He added, with a laugh. "You guys look like you've been attacked by the Keebler elves."

"Ten!" said Lily sitting up. "I have your dinner in the fridge; I just need to pop it in the microwave."

"Don't bother. I ate. I stopped by OTB for the late double. Good thing, too. I got the money for your overdue loan payment." He reached into his pocket and extended a small wad of cash to Lily. "There's four hundred dollars here."

Which meant he had another four hundred tucked in his other pocket, at least. Seed money for tomorrow.

"That's a relief," said Lily, taking the money. "Joe! What happened to your hand?" Lily asked. "Your fingernail is black!"

"Oh, nothin'. I was helping a customer load an ottoman into his car - a red Caravan - and I slammed my thumb in the sliding door, if you can believe that."

"Let me see," said Lily, grabbing his hand.

"Ow!" cried Joe, pulling his hand back. "Son of a bitch – Lil, didn't I just tell you that I slammed it in the door? Why are you poking at it?"

"Sorry..."

"Daddy!" Joseph softly cried, stretching his arms up toward his father.

"Hi, son," said Joe, lifting Joseph off the couch and taking him into his arms. "How would you like Daddy to build a fire?"

"Yes! Can I light the match, Daddy?"

"I don't know - were you a good boy today? Mommy," Joe said, looking at Lily, "Was he a good boy today?"

"Oh, yes, he was very good. He helped me make cookies all afternoon."

Joseph beamed. "Mommy, can Daddy have some of our cookies?"

"Absolutely," said Lily. "In fact, while you men are building the fire, I'll go make us all some hot chocolate. How does that sound?"

"With little marshmallows?" asked Joseph.

"Is there any other way to have hot chocolate?" Lily kissed him on the nose, kissed Joe on the lips, and went into the kitchen.

Lily placed three white ceramic mugs on a silver tray, along with a plate of assorted cookies, and brought them into the family room. She, Joseph and Joe sat on the rug in front of the hearth, dunking cookies, sipping hot chocolate, talking about who made which cookie, what Santa was going to bring, and how in the world he was going to fit down the narrow stove pipe. The fire raged in the wood stove, as an autumn storm sprayed the aluminum siding with the shrapnel of icy rain.

"Are you coming up?" Joe stood at the top of the stairway in his boxer shorts.

Lily walked to the bottom of the stairs. Putting her index finger to her lips, she said, "Shhh... I'll be up in a few minutes. I'm just cleaning up."

"Don't be long," said Joe, reaching down to adjust his erection.

Lily made her final rounds through the house, rinsing out dishes, picking up toys, stalling. She did want another baby, but sex at the end of a long day of housework and church work and chasing Joseph around was always a challenge; she would need to take a few minutes to get into the right frame of mind first.

Whenever Lily was tempted to try and avoid sex - which she

often was when she wasn't ovulating - she would hear Bethany quoting one of her favorite Bible verses: "'The wife's body does not belong to her alone but also to her husband.' Now ladies," Bethany would add, "God gave men powerful urges, and of course we do have our free will to refuse - as long as we're willing to take the chance that they may take their needs elsewhere."

Sometimes Lily fantasized that Joe would have an affair and that she would catch him - maybe she would discover a charge on the credit card statement for one of those motels where people were known to sneak off to meet their lovers. Infidelity was one of the few conditions under which marital separation was tolerated according to Pastor Halloway. Lily thought how about much easier life would be if all she had to worry about was taking care of herself and Joseph. She could get a job at one of the schools so she and Joseph would have the same schedule once he started school. Or maybe she could even go back to SaveMart part time. She and Joseph could get a little apartment, one that was easier to keep clean than the house, and on the weekends Joe could pick Joseph up and Lily could have an entire day to herself - sleep late, take long walks, maybe even go on a date, assuming anyone would be interested. But that would only happen if Joe cheated, and she was pretty sure he was splitting most of his time and money between the track and his bookie. He barely had enough for one woman, let alone two.

Even if Joe was unfaithful, and even if Lily did catch him, Pastor Halloway said that all attempts at reconciliation would have to be made. She'd eventually end up right back here, for sure. The only real way out would be if Joe died, like if he was speeding home from the track at eighty miles per hour, and hit a guardrail, and was thrown through the windshield, being killed instantly, or if all the stress of the gambling finally got to him and he had a heart attack at work, the ambulance failing to get him to the hospital in time. Then there would be no chance of reconciliation - and no one would be able to blame Lily. They would all run to her side in sympathy, bring her casseroles, give her money to help with expenses, and then after a year or so, they would introduce her to their attractive bachelor friends, and then maybe she could start over. Yes, it would be much better to be a widow than it would be to get cheated on. That would be the only real way out.

Lily raised her hands to cover her face and shook her head as if to banish the thoughts that seemed to visit her with increasing frequency, despite the self-recrimination that always dragged along behind them, and that would unfailingly launch her into a guilt-ridden act of servitude toward Joe, serving as admission of and penance for her shame before self and God.

Anyway, life was good these days. Thanks to the advice and support of the women at PTW, Lily had learned to avoid arguing, accept Joe for who he was, and work with their finances. It had been a relief to learn the value of true submission and to surrender the notion that she could change him. With a little creativity, she had been able to make it work. Instead of taking Joe's clothes to the cleaners, she laundered, ironed, and starched them all herself; it only took a couple hours a few times a week. She learned to mow, trim, edge, and fertilize the lawn so they could get rid of their landscaping service in the summer, and in the winter, shoveling snow from the driveway was great exercise. Why hire some guy to come by with his pick-up truck? They never came when you really needed them anyway. Also, homemade items such as bread were a fraction of the cost of store-bought, and since Lily was home all day most of the time, baking was no problem. Homemade tasted better, too, and Lily took comfort in the sweet warmth of cookies, breads, and pastries fresh from the oven. She still had time for church on Sundays, PTW on Tuesdays, and even the occasional coffee visit with Donna. On Saturdays - if she could get Joseph nice and tired out during the day and get him into bed early - she could have a few hours to herself to indulge in a quiet dish of fudge stripe ice cream with chocolate sauce and an uninterrupted movie on HBO while Joe was at the track. By the time he came home, she would be ready for him - ready to console him sexually if he lost and to satisfy him sexually if he won. It had taken years to figure it out, but Lily was proud to say that there was peace in her house. She could tolerate living this way for a long time.

As Lily pulled the living room curtains closed, she noticed the stillness of the neighborhood. Cars tucked away in garages, lamp posts lit, casting a yellow glow onto the puddles formed by the icy rain. There was no laughing, no children shouting, no music blaring, no mail trucks or school buses grinding and chugging along - all of the sights and sounds that gave this place life were suspended, as if the world were holding its breath. She found that she was holding hers at the thought.

"Hey Lil, are you coming up, or what?"

"On my way," said Lily, doing her best to inject a dose of enthusiasm into her voice. Fake it 'til you make it, that's what Bethany always says.

The following summer, Lily became pregnant with her second child.

"Pierce?" Joe repeated when Lily proposed the name. "Where the hell did you come up with that?"

"From the book of baby names," said Lily. "It means 'rock.' I want our baby to grow to be strong and solid."

"I thought you said you think it's a girl."

"I do. Pierce is unisex. Whether it's a girl or a boy, I want Pierce."

"It's weird. My family is going to make fun of it."

"Too bad," said Lily, becoming agitated at the prospect that he may argue the point further, and she would be forced to drop it. "You know, Joe, you got to name the first child. And we all have to live with 'Diotallevi,' which is also weird. I'd like to say my last name just once without having to spell it. It's weird, and it's a burden."

"OK, OK, calm down," Joe said with a chuckle. "Pierce it is. Might be kinda cool. Pierce Joseph Diotallevi."

"Really? Pierce Joseph?"

"Yeah - PJ for short."

Lily conceded, based mostly on her certainty that the child

inside was a girl. According to the old wives' tale, baby girls steal their mother's beauty, and Lily had felt drained of hers practically at the day of conception. Her hair immediately began to thin, and she developed acne and swelling of the feet. The baby would be Pierce Elizabeth, after her mother - a fine, dignified, and unique name.

At one-eleven on a stormy April afternoon, Pierce Joseph Diotallevi was born, his Aunt Violet in attendance in the delivery room, and his daddy and big brother Joseph in the waiting area. His coloring at birth was not unlike Joseph's – a promise of dark hair and an olive complexion, but with a hint of green in his eyes. From the moment of his birth, however, it was clear to see that he would carry something of Lily's as she bent over and placed a kiss on the tip of his finely chiseled Whitacre nose.

Lily's labor was short, and Pierce was a joy. He never cried unless he was in discomfort from being hungry or wet, and he started sleeping through the night by the time he was five weeks old.

As the spring passed, Lily did what she could to settle into a routine at home, although Joseph didn't make it easy. He would beg to hug his baby brother, and then would pinch him or pull his hair so that Pierce would cry and Lily would have to pry him out of Joseph's arms. He liked to sneak into Pierce's room when he was sleeping, get under the crib and jostle the mattress until Pierce woke up and then pop out and shout "Boo!" launching Pierce into a terrified fit of screaming.

One afternoon, Lily set Pierce in his infant carrier on the kitchen table so she could fold laundry and get dinner started. She turned her back to answer the phone and when she turned around again, she discovered Joseph sliding the carrier toward the edge of the table.

"Joseph!" cried Lily, snatching the carrier from the table. "That is very dangerous! You could seriously hurt your baby brother like that. Do you want him to go to the hospital?"

"Yes, I do," said Joseph, folding his arms across his chest.

"But why?" said Lily. She pulled Pierce up out of carrier. "He's such a nice baby brother." She turned Pierce around to face Joseph. "Just look at how cute he is," Lily said. "Why do you want him to go to the hospital?"

"I want you to take him back. He's stupid," said Joseph. "I wish he was a dog instead."

After telling Joe the story that night after dinner, Lily said, "We have to do something, Joe. In addition to the extra laundry, meal preparation, and keeping my eyes on him constantly, I am really struggling; I'm just exhausted."

"He'll be in school in a couple months," said Joe.

"I can't last that long," said Lily. "I might not make it to the end of this week. I need you to be around a little more. I need some help."

"Lil, you know I have to take all the hours I can get at the store now."

"But you're not even at the store half the time when I call, Joe. I called you two hours ago to ask you to bring home diapers and cigarettes and you were already gone. If you weren't at work, you should have been here so I could have a break."

"What would you be doing if you had three boys, like my mother? Or twelve kids like your mother did? Do you think they called their husbands at work crying because they couldn't handle being a housewife? Goddamn it, Lil - it's not rocket science." Joe wiped his mouth with a white paper napkin, balled it up and threw it down onto the plate. "And after working a twelve-hour day, I don't need to hear about how hard it is for you to stay home all day." Joe pushed his chair back, got up from the table, and went down into the family room.

The next afternoon, Joe came home unexpectedly from work. He poked his head in the front door, and said, "Anybody home? I've got a surprise!"

"Daddy, Daddy!" cried Joseph, running to greet his father at the door. Lily followed, with Pierce in her arms.

"Are you ready for a surprise?"

"Yes Daddy – I'm ready!"

"Here it is!" Joe stepped through the door, revealing a chestnut red puppy with a curly tail, which he held in his hands.

"A puppy!" squealed Joseph.

Joe set the puppy down on the ground. It ran in circles around the living room, with Joseph following, trying to catch up enough to grab it.

Pierce wriggled and bounced with delight at the sight.

"You bought a dog?" said Lily. "Without even checking with me?"

"I was thinking about what you said last night," said Joe. "And I figured if he had a puppy to distract him he wouldn't be after Pierce all the time. You said he wished for a dog."

"But Joe, dogs are a lot of work, and I will be the one who has to clean up after it. I can barely keep up with things as they are."

"Jesus, Lil - can't I do anything right? You asked me to help out, so I spend a fortune on this dog to help keep Joseph out of your hair," said Joe, "And you're still not happy. Anyway, with the hours I work, I'll feel better knowing there's a watchdog in the house. This guy at work has been trying to get rid of his dog's litter, so I figured it was meant to be. He said it was a purebred," said Joe. "A Basenji."

"That's a Basenji?" asked Lily. "Did this guy tell you anything about Basenjis?"

"Yeah," said Joe. "He said they were great family dogs and very gentle with the kids. Why?"

"Did he also happen to tell you that they don't bark?"

"It don't bark? You've gotta be shittin' me!" said Joe. "Then never mind, I'm taking it back and get a different kind."

"I don't think so," said Lily, gesturing toward Joseph. They both laughed in spite of themselves as they watched Joseph rolling around on the floor, the puppy jumping on him and lavishing his face with long wet kisses.

"Looks like he's our dog now," said Lily, with a sigh. Maybe Joe was right. Giving Joseph something else to do, something of his own to care for wasn't the worst idea in the world. Anyway, what was one more task for the list?

"Joseph, what do you want to name the puppy?"

Joseph sat up, the puppy still bounding all around him. "He's just like I wished," he said. "I want to call him 'Wishes.'"

"Wishes it is," said Lily, as the puppy pounced at Joseph, knocking him over with a flurry of giggles.

Having the puppy distracted Joseph for the first few weeks, but as the summer wore on, his behavior again became erratic, with Wishes sometimes becoming the object of his antics, as he pulled her tail, or dressed her up like Superman, or spanked her too harshly when she nipped at him in self-defense. Wishes in turn acted out by urinating on the carpet and chewing on furniture, shoes, and anything else she might be able to get her jaw around.

September couldn't come fast enough for Lily, but Joseph's first day of kindergarten was a traumatic event for everyone - for Lily, for Joseph, undoubtedly for the other students, and for Mrs. Cameron the teacher.

"Mommy, don't go! Mommy, come back! Don't leave me!" Joseph screamed when Lily dropped him off.

Lily walked out to the parking lot, fighting back tears, her own repressed screams urging her to go back, pick him up in her arms and take him home with her. She willed herself to drive away without looking in the rear view mirror.

Lily sobbed all the way home, partly from embarrassment, partly from the bittersweet sorrow of her firstborn beginning school. Even though she had been anxious to get him out of the house and desperately needed the break, her heart wrenched at the image of Joseph plastered up against the picture window, screaming and crying for his salvation. Reports from the teacher that first day included stories of biting, pushing, and throwing toys.

"Just give it some time," Donna told her. "Nikki did the same thing to me when she started school. In a month, he'll be completely acclimated."

The morning routine of dropping Joseph off at school continued to be marked with tears and angst. The week before

Thanksgiving, Mrs. Cameron sent a note home with Joseph, asking Lily to stop in and see her the next day.

Lily sat on the edge of the bed, attempting to wriggle out of her jeans, a process similar to that of wriggling into them, which she had engaged in that morning, except that taking them off meant that she could finally breathe again. She had delayed buying new jeans both because it was an expense she wanted to avoid and because she'd hoped to fit back into the ones she already owned. She'd been embarrassed to continue wearing her maternity pants, but free time was still at a premium; she still hadn't even had time to work a daily walk into her routine. She did finally make it back to PTW, determining that her spiritual health took priority over losing weight. She hoped it wasn't sacrilegious to pray for help in zipping up her fly.

"Joseph's teacher wants to see me tomorrow during her lunch hour."

"What about?" Joe pointed the remote control at the TV and clicked on a hockey game.

"Well, he got off to a rough start there at the beginning, but I thought he was doing better now." Lily pulled on her pink flannel pajama tops, and reached back to pull her hair out from under the collar. "Don't you remember? I told you how he was lashing out at the other kids."

"We can't help it if that teacher is bad at her job," said Joe. "What is she blaming you for?"

"It just makes me nervous," said Lily. "Like when the nuns used to ask us to stay after school. It was never for a talk about how wonderful we were."

The next day, Lily greeted Mrs. Cameron with a warm smile.

"Please, have a seat, Mrs. Diotallevi." Mrs. Cameron gestured toward a tiny table surrounded by tiny chairs. Lily balanced half of her derriere on one, saying a quick prayer that she would not lose her balance.

"As you have probably guessed, I have some concerns about Joseph," said Mrs. Cameron. "He is clearly confused about boundaries, and when we see that, it usually means ambiguous rules and a lack of accountability at home - a sign of domestic strife."

"I don't know what to tell you," said Lily. "I'm very sorry. I will work with him on that." Lily had no idea what that meant, or how she might accomplish it, but it sounded like the grownup thing to say. It seemed ridiculous even to her, as she sat with her knees scrunched to her chest.

"Mrs. Diotallevi," said Mrs. Cameron. Her tone made Lily shrink just enough to feel better suited to her chair. "We have a cooperative relationship with children's services through the school district." She handed Lily a card.

Lily glanced at the card: *Rachel Jacobi, Ph.D., School Psychologist.*

"A psychologist?" Lily's stomach lurched. "Isn't that a little drastic?"

"If there are issues that need attention," said Mrs. Cameron, "it's generally more efficacious to address them early. I've taken the liberty to make a preliminary phone call," she said, leading Lily to the door. "Dr. Jacobi was able to squeeze you in at four-thirty tomorrow afternoon." Mrs. Cameron looked at Lily over the top of her bifocals. "I do hope you can make it."

"I don't know what to tell Joe," Lily told the women at PTW during sharing time that afternoon. "He gets furious if the teacher blames us for anything - he says it's their job to teach the kids how to behave. I shudder to think how he'll react when I tell him that she wants me to talk to the psychologist."

"Now there's no sense in telling your sweet husband anything of the kind," said Bethany.

"But I can't lie to him." Lily may not have known as much about these things as Bethany, but she knew this one.

"You're not lying," said Bethany, with a snort. "It is your duty as a Godly wife to protect him from unnecessary exposure to worldly irritants, to provide him with an oasis; a fortress of peace. He's got enough on his mind, what with his job and everything. Go see the psychologist, and then if they decide there's an issue, just pray to the Lord and He will provide you with the perfect opportunity to bring it up. Lying and using discretion about what he needs to know and what he's better off not knowing are two different things. No sense in both of you worrying about it now, is there?"

"No, I guess not," said Lily. "When you put it like that."

The next day, Lily woke to a flat and unrelentingly gray sky. She strained to conjure up even a memory of the sun. She didn't feel like wrestling with her jeans, so she resigned to wearing her maternity pants, even though they were a bit long, for lack of a fully pregnant belly to take up the girth. Who cared what she looked like at the psychologist's anyway; all she cared about was getting it over with. She rummaged through the front closet for an umbrella. The one she finally found had three bent spines detached from the fabric. She couldn't imagine a scenario in which arriving for her appointment with such an umbrella over her head would be better than not having one at all. She tossed it back into the closet.

Rachel Jacobi was about Lily's age. Several inches taller than Lily, she displayed broad shoulders and wide hips, but in perfect proportion. She moved especially gracefully for her size and looked as if she were walking *en pointe.* She welcomed Lily into the office, set about offering her a drink, placing a box of tissues within reach, and finally taking a chair opposite the red leather one Lily had chosen.

"Thank you for coming in to see me, Mrs. Diotallevi," said Rachel. "I know this isn't a pleasant task." Her voice was smooth, sweet, and fragile - like ribbon candy. If she yelled, her words would surely shatter into a million pieces.

"Oh, sure," said Lily. "Please call me Lily - and I'm sorry I'm soaked - I couldn't find my umbrella." As she smoothed the fabric of her white blouse she noticed a dark splotch just over her right breast. By the time Lily had cleaned both the boys up and dropped them off at Donna's, her only concern had been getting to the appointment on time, and getting home again. Lily used her fingernail to scratch at the mysterious stain – was it Pierce's vomit or a splatter from the ice cream that Joseph had begged for, which she had given him just so he would stop crying and let her get out the door? Lily looked up to see Rachel smiling at her the way one might smile at a mentally challenged child who was trying to force a square block into a round hole.

"I know you are aware that I've spoken with Ida Cameron," said Rachel.

"Yes, she told me she called you, but I'm not really clear on why." Lily sat up, pulling up out of her torso, expanding it to its full length, as if the added stature could compensate for her sense of inadequacy.

Rachel made a note on a pad of paper.

"Sometimes we just like to check in with our parents, make sure everything is OK. As you know, Joseph has been acting out a bit. Sometimes it's just a matter of personality, or of having too much sugar, or too little sleep - but sometimes it can be a sign of other things."

"Oh."

"Why don't you tell me a little bit about what's going on at home?"

"I'm sure it's nothing out of the ordinary. My husband does work a lot, but he still sees the kids as much as possible. He just adores them."

"That's great," said Rachel. "And how about you?"

"Well, of course – they're my children."

Rachel smiled her special-child smile again. "No, I mean, how are things between you and your husband, if you don't mind my asking? Do you have a respectful relationship?"

"Oh, yes, of course," said Lily. That definitely falls into the "doesn't need to know" category.

Rachel asked a few more questions, and Lily provided whatever answers she expected would lead to a dismissal.

"Again," said Rachel, standing up and straightening out her dress. "I do appreciate your taking the time to come in this afternoon - now that we've gotten to know each other a bit, I'm hoping that you'll feel more comfortable reaching out to us if you ever feel the need. OK?"

"Yes, sure... I will do that." Lily was relieved to gather her things and head for the door.

"My goodness," said Rachel, looking out the window. "I can't believe it's getting dark out already - and it's still raining. Wait just a moment, and I'll walk out with you." Rachel lifted a beige trench coat from the rack and slipped her arms into the sleeves. She flipped off the lights to her office, closed the door behind them and turned the key. "My car is in the shop, so my husband is picking me up tonight - I'm so relieved." She cinched the belt of her coat around her waist. "I hate driving home in rush hour traffic, even when the weather is good."

A gold Dodge Intrepid sat along the curb just outside the entrance to the school. Before Rachel had the chance to step out into the rain, her husband jumped out of the car, opened an umbrella and ran to her side.

"Good night, Lily," said Rachel.

"Good night," said Lily.

"Lily?" said Rachel's husband. His face was partially obscured by the umbrella, and while she didn't immediately recognize his voice, the sound of it evoked a flourish of butterflies in her stomach. "Lily Capotosti? Is that you?"

Lily took a step toward the voice, and as she did, she landed her foot in a puddle, filling her shoe with cold water. The man tilted the umbrella slightly to the side and stepped into the glow of the flood light that hung over the door.

"James?" The concerned look on Rachel's face was the only thing that kept Lily from reacting by running to him, embracing him with laughter.

"What are you doing here?" he asked. Rachel cleared her throat.

"I had, um, an appointment with, um, your - wife?"

"I retained my maiden name - for professional reasons," said Rachel. She turned to James. "Lily and I were just having a chat." Rachel winked at Lily.

"I wasn't sure if that was you, but I heard Rachel say your name, and you're the only person named Lily I've ever known." James looked Lily up and down. "I don't know what's more bizarre - the fact that we're running into each other right now, or the fact that it hasn't happened before today."

"Wow," said Lily, staring at him. He was just as handsome as Lily had remembered. His smile was just as charming, his eyes were as brown and warm, the tiny crow's feet adding a delightful dimension of surprise to looking at him. "You live here in town?"

"Sure do." James put his arm around Rachel's shoulder and drew her close to his side. "We've been married six years."

"That's - wow, that's really amazing." Lily's chest radiated with heat as she realized that not only had James married, but he'd settled down in Rochester. "Wow." *His wife is a doctor*, Lily thought. *Stop saying "wow."*

Lily looked from James to Rachel, Rachel to James, huddled together under their perfectly unbroken umbrella, perfectly dry, looking like an ad for diamond rings. Both of Lily's shoes were soaked through. The rain beat down on her, plastering her hair to her head and face. Rivulets of water trickled down her neck and into her stained blouse. A shock of arousal shot down her spine.

"We really should be on our way," said Rachel. "The traffic is going to be horrendous in this downpour."

"It was great seeing you, Lily," said James. He turned and opened the car door for Rachel, and closed it again after helping her inside. He turned toward Lily one last time. "Here," he said, holding the umbrella out to her. "Take this - I have two more in the car."

Lily reluctantly took the umbrella from James, wondering how much of the past it was intended to make up for. Too late. She was already drenched.

"Take care of yourself, OK?"

James and Rachel drove away, leaving Lily standing in the teeming rain under the glow of the floodlight, the opened umbrella at her side.

That evening after dinner while Pierce was sleeping and Joseph was engrossed in watching a Teenage Mutant Ninja Turtle movie, Lily brewed a cup of tea, and grabbed her latest copy of *Christian Family News*. As she pulled the drapes closed over the living room window, she noticed a large black car parked in front of the house, the front seat illumined by the dome light. When the driver turned and noticed Lily in the window, the light flicked off and the car inched away down the street. Lily double-checked the window locks, the front door, and the sliding glass doors to the back patio before sitting down to read, but her mind was crowded out by memories of James, and of how thrilled he must be tonight. After seeing Lily, he was surely safe in the knowledge that he had made the right choice, and thrilled at having ended up with a successful, beautiful wife.

"Glad I could help," Lily said to herself.

"Anything exciting happen around here today?" Joe gave Lily a peck on the cheek and handed her his coat.

"Nope," said Lily, "not unless you count the mail coming early." Or seeing a psychologist. Or running into an old boyfriend. Or watching a strange black car out in front of the house – all of which fell into the category of protecting him from unnecessary exposure to worldly irritants.

"Daddy!" shouted Joseph, as he ran toward Joe and launched himself into his arms.

"Ow!" Joe grunted in mock pain.

"Be careful, you guys," said Lily.

"Did I hurt you, Daddy?" asked Joseph.

"You can't hurt me - I'm Superman!"

"Oh, yeah?" said Joseph. "Bet you can't catch me - I'm Donatello!"

Joseph squealed and ran away, with Joe in exaggerated pursuit as they headed for the family room.

They engaged in a battle to determine whether Superman could in fact beat Donatello in a fight, the result of which was one broken lamp and an extremely wound-up child. It was after eleven o'clock when Joseph was finally settled into bed.

Lily washed her face and then collapsed onto the bed next to Joe. "It's not healthy for him to go to bed so late, Joe. He needs his sleep." And Lily needed hers, even though the Proverbs 31 wife "gets up while it is still dark.... her lamp does not go out at night." Lily wondered what the Proverbs 31 husband was up to all that time. "And all that sugar doesn't help, either."

"I hardly think that Joseph is going to grow up to be a murderer because I let him stay up late and drink juice, Lil," said Joe.

"But maybe it really is a contributing factor to his behavior. He's really just so wild much of the time."

"He's all boy, that's all it is. He's like his Daddy."

"I'm just saying that maybe we could try to make sure he gets a little more sleep and a little less sugar late at night and see if it helps."

"And listen to him moan and cry while I'm wishing I could spend time with him? I am not going to come home to that every night."

"Can't you please work with me on this?" Lily had to be sure Rachel Jacobi never asked to see her again.

"I have a job already, Lil." Joe flicked on the TV. "I can't do your job too."

Accepting that the conversation was over, Lily rolled onto her side. She hoped Joe was also so worn out from his play that he would just go to sleep tonight. She listened as his breathing slowed, becoming deeper, finally decorated with the rattle of a snore that meant she was alone at last. The nagging feeling in her gut was closely followed by memories of the day. The embarrassment of talking to Dr. Jacobi, the humiliation of running into James, and the way he looked at her. She remembered getting lost in his eyes, once upon a time. She savored the image of him smiling at her, his delight at seeing her. Her body grew warmer and her breath quickened. The worries of the day were obscured by the fantasies that filled her mind, as she comforted herself in the way that she had always hoped James would one day.

The next morning Lily found herself staring out the window

studying the branches of her tree as they bobbed and swayed in the wind, flipping feathery leaves over, showing first their silvery underbellies, then their shiny green top coats. Silver, green. Silver, green. Silver, green. Like a thousand tiny hands waving hello, perhaps saying "thank you" for all the times Lily had saved them from the wrath of Joe's clippers.

The morning sun hid behind stubborn black clouds. Gusts of wind intermittently roused the branches of the tree, inciting them to animate their dance, to double their cadence, to take their part in the storm that seemed to be brewing just beyond the horizon.

Again Lily thought of them, of James and Rachel, an attractive, clean-cut, polite couple who probably chatted about their day while stuck in traffic on the 490 expressway. Of them. Of Rachel and Lily. Rachel with her tailored dress, her gentle voice, not an errant hair on her head; Lily with her scraggly hair, stained blouse, and baggy maternity pants sagging in soggy folds around her puddle-soaked shoes. She and Rachel had nothing in common. Except for the experience of loving James. Of them. Of Lily and James. Seeing James made Lily wonder what she could have done, how she might have been able to cause things to turn out differently so they might have ended up together. James was surely thanking his lucky stars that things had turned out exactly as they had.

Lily used to imagine having a chance meeting with James, but in her fantasies, she was visiting Rochester from New York City or Los Angeles, where she would be working as singer or an actress. She would look fabulous, and he wouldn't be able to take his eyes off her. She may not be able to do anything about her status as housewife, but she could try at least to lose her baby weight and get into shape. She wondered if she still had that exercise tape that Marguerite had given her. It was probably still in a box in the crawl space. After all, she just might run into James again one day - at school, or even at Tops Market. He must go to the grocery store every now and again. Next time she saw him, regret would register in his eyes instead of relief.

Bethany always said that having social relationships with men was a dangerous proposition. Maybe this was the sort of thing she was talking about. An idea about a man gets into your head and before you know it, he's living there, following you around - to the grocery store, the school, out to the mailbox, even up to bed with your husband by your side. "Venture out into the world when you must," Bethany would say. "But remember that is where temptation lays in wait for you." Lily wondered what Bethany's fantasies were like - since she always said she acted like she was married to Jesus, maybe she dreamed about making love with Him too.

Over the next several months, Lily added two additional Jane Fonda tapes to the one Marguerite had given her, which she rotated through daily during Pierce's nap time. By Pierce's second birthday, she had sweated and grunted her way to her pre-pregnancy weight, and found that she enjoyed her new muscle tone and stamina. Sweet treats were saved for special occasions and she was looking forward to a small slice of the yellow cake with chocolate frosting that she had made from scratch for their family birthday celebration. Joe had promised to try and get out of work early so they could all sing "Happy Birthday" together. As evening fell, Joseph, Pierce, and Wishes happily occupied themselves by playing fort under the kitchen table. Lily draped a red plaid blanket over the tabletop, and anchored it down around the edges with the legs of the chairs.

The front door bell rang, which was a rare occurrence at any time, but especially at eight-thirty at night. It wasn't Halloween, and it wasn't Girl Scout cookie season.

Lily peered through the peephole to see a heavy set man in a navy blue pea coat and dark woolen hat standing on the doorstep. His image was distorted through the lens of the peep hole, making his nose appear comically disproportionate, leaping out from his face. A long black car was parked in the street.

Wishes faithfully rushed to Lily's side, wagging her tail. She looked up at Lily. "I appreciate the effort, girl," Lily whispered to the dog, "but a nice bark would really come in handy right about now."

"Can I help you?" Lily said through the door.

"Yea - I'm a friend of Joe Diotallevi's," said the voice. "I need to have a word with him - do I have the right house?"

The man said "Diotallevi" correctly on the first try, but it seemed odd that a friend would use Joe's last name at all. Besides, any of Joe's friends would know that he was at work at this time of the day. Lily's first inclination was to tell the man that he did not have the right house, but then she feared he would go knocking on Donna's door, and she was bound to tell him that he had it right the first time. He didn't look like the sort of man that liked being lied to. Besides, he gave her the creeps. Lily considered telling him that Joe couldn't come to the door right then, so he wouldn't know that she was home alone with the children. But if she told him that Joe was there but not available, he might ask to wait.

"I'm sorry," Lily said finally. "He's at work." The man's countenance was unnerving. Her heart pounded. All she cared about was getting him off her doorstep and away from her house.

"He's at work, huh?" The man swiped his nose with the back of his hand.

"Yes, that's right," said Lily. "My brother is here with me," she added. "Is there anything he can do for you?" She was stronger now, but she wasn't strong enough to handle this guy. She was pretty sure God would forgive the lie.

"No, that's OK," said the man. He took a step back and leaned toward the living room window, cocking his head first to the left and then to the right. Lily was glad she'd started pulling the curtains closed after dinner. The man finally turned, walked across the lawn, and got into the car through the passenger door. Lily stood watching the distorted image of the car in the street, looking like it was miles away, yet feeling like it was parked on her chest. *Please leave, please leave, please leave.*

After several minutes, the car pulled away and disappeared down the street. Lily grabbed a cigarette, matches, and an ashtray from the kitchen and returned to her post at the front door, watching in case the car returned, trying to devise a plan for what she would do if it did. She smoked three cigarettes, lighting each one off the butt of the previous one, before her heart slowed down and she felt that it was safe to stop watching.

"Mommy - " Joseph poked his head out from under the table. "What time is daddy coming home?"

"Oh, my God," Lily was struck with the realization that she had never called to tell Joe about the man. To warn him?

"He'll be here soon, my love," said Lily. "Would you like a fruit roll-up?"

"Yay - fruit roll up!" cheered Joseph.

Lily pulled a foil wrapped treat from a box in the cupboard over the sink and handed it to Joseph. "Help your brother open his, OK? Now go on back into the fort and don't come out until Daddy gets here, OK? You can surprise him."

Lily picked up the phone and frantically pounded out the number to the La Casa Bella.

"Good evening, thank you for calling La Casa Bella, where your beautiful home is our business!"

"Hi, Monica, it's Lily. Is Joe around?"

"Hi, Lily - let me check."

An instrumental version of "Feelings" played over the phone line.

"Lily? I know he was here a few minutes ago, but now I can't find him."

"Can you page him?"

"Sure. Hold on." She didn't return until the second verse finished. "He didn't answer, Lily. Can I have him call you?"

A wave of nausea roiled Lily's fear. She shouldn't have waited to call him. Why hadn't she called him?

"That's OK, Monica. It's fine. He's probably already on his way home."

Lily returned to her spot by the front door, this time waiting for her husband's car to pull safely into the driveway. When it finally did, Lily heaved a sigh that was mostly of relief, yet was tinged with a trace of something else. Something that resembled disappointment. She busied herself at the stove, warming up the lentil soup for Joe's dinner.

When Joe entered the kitchen, Joseph leapt out at him from under the blanket.

"Daddy!" cried Joseph. "Oh, no - Daddy! What happened to your face?"

Lily spun around to find Joe standing in the middle of the kitchen, directly under the lamp of the ceiling fan. His bottom lip was split and marked with congealed blood. His left eye was red and swollen shut. The pocket of his suit coat was ripped. Except for a gasp that escaped, Lily remained silent, not wanting to frighten the children.

"What are they still doing up?" Joe shouted at Lily.

"Did you get a boo-boo, Daddy?"

"Yes, Daddy got a boo-boo," said Joe. "Now take down your fort and go to bed.

"How did you get your boo-boo Daddy?"

"At work. Take down the fort and go to bed," Joe yelled.

"But we're having birthday cake, Daddy," cried Joseph. "We're going to have a party!"

Joe grabbed Joseph by the wrist and slapped the back of his leg with such force that his feet lifted off the ground. Joseph wailed.

"Joe!" cried Lily, scooping Pierce up into her arms and pulling Joseph to her side.

"I said take down the fuckin' fort and go to bed!" He grabbed the blanket and pulled it from the table in one motion, then he picked up a kitchen chair and threw it across the room. When it hit the wall, it knocked a mug off the shelf, which shattered as it hit the floor. Wishes jumped out from under the table and with a growl she nipped at the cuff of Joe's pants. "Get outta here, you goddamn mutt!" shouted Joe. He shook his foot loose, kicking Wishes in the head, sending her running from the room with her tail tucked between her legs, and sending Joseph and Pierce into a joint fit of hysteria.

"Joe – stop! You're scaring us!" Joseph encircled Lily's waist with his arms and buried his wails in her belly. "C'mon sweetie, let's get you up to bed. It's OK – Daddy just needs a little alone time."

After settling the kids to sleep, Lily found Joe lying on their bed, still dressed in his suit.

"They're finally quiet," she said. "I had to read 'Mother, Mother, I Want Another' five times before they settled down."

Joe did not respond.

"You want to tell me what's going on?"

"I need you to come down to work to sign some papers tomorrow." Joe was staring at the ceiling.

"What for?"

"I need to get a new loan."

"Another one? Joe, we can barely make the payments on the ones we have."

Joe covered his face with his hands and began to sob. Lily sat on the bed next to him. He reached out and pulled her down to himself, hugging her head and shoulders against his chest as he sobbed. Lily wanted to tell him about the man who came to the door, about how she could have called him, but how she became so scared she didn't think of it until it was too late. She wondered if that also fell under the category of protecting him from unnecessary exposure to worldly irritants.

Joe loosened his belt buckle and unbuttoned his pants with his right hand. Lily heard him lower his zipper as he used his left hand to push her head down toward his crotch.

"What are you doing, Joe?"

Joe reached into his boxer shorts and took his erect penis into his hand. He urged Lily's face toward it.

"Joe – Joe – no, not now... let's talk. I want to talk to you. We need to talk."

"Just do it," he said, clenching the back of her neck in the grip of his left hand, and separating her lips with the tip of his penis. "I need you to."

Tears came to Lily's eyes as he thrust himself against the back of her throat, pushing her guilt and fear and shame back down inside.

13. IRIS

Whenever she thought back on it, Iris marveled at how little her status at the Grand Hotel Stella di Levante was affected by the termination of her affair with Claudio Olona. Any worries that his bruised male ego might lash out at her in the form of unwarranted criticism or restrictions of her role had proven totally unfounded. He continued to authorize her business trips, and still insisted she stay at the very best hotels in order to remain abreast of the latest trends and stay aware of the level of luxury he - and their guests - expected of the Stella di Levante.

Any illusions that Claudio would suffer inordinately on a sentimental level had evaporated as quickly as the tears of anxiety that dampened Iris's cheeks the day she summoned her courage and blurted out that she could no longer risk jeopardizing her marriage and must end their relationship. Claudio had taken note of her decision with the aplomb possessed only by those who do not bog themselves down with weighty emotions; he simply squeezed her arm reassuringly and said not to fret: he understood completely. The frequency and duration of his visits to the hotel dwindled with time, leading Iris to suspect he had found a suitable replacement in whom to vest the dubious honor of keeping his marriage afloat by providing him with the things that *Signora* Olona did not.

Although Iris had not expected a man as refined and self-possessed as Claudio to try and sway her with menacing threats or pathetic supplication, she had not anticipated such impassivity. The wave of relief that swept over her when the affair was pronounced over was followed by one of bewilderment, then one of anger. It incensed her to think that by not suffering, he was, in effect, making her suffer, even though she was the one who had left him.

Gregorio's predictability and steadfastness were instrumental in redirecting his secretly wayward wife's haywire emotions into their predefined channels. Though unaware of the beneficial effect he exerted on Iris at that stage of their marriage, Gregorio reaped its rewards. Iris still kept long hours at the hotel (she would throw herself from the Terrazzo del Cielo rather than give Claudio cause to reprimand her) but rushed home with renewed zeal each evening to fulfill her wifely duties. She prepared the bland meals her husband preferred, and actually felt a surge of pride when he interrupted his viewing of the evening news, or his recapitulation of his day at the hospital to compliment her on the boiled rice or poached fish. Routine consoled her, and there was no better place to find it than right at home. Each evening after brushing her teeth and flossing, she climbed into bed and closed her eyes in silent prayer, thanking God for the serenity Gregorio provided, and for his blissful ignorance of her past folly. It was enough that God knew, and it was to Him that she asked for forgiveness. It wasn't a bad marriage, even if it was a little boring, she often commented to herself as she propped her weary back against her fluffy pillows and opened to the bookmarked page of her latest novel. And with so many books to read, there was no reason she couldn't make it last forever. After all, wasn't that what she had vowed to do at the altar?

Things improved at work, also; Iris soon realized that without Claudio constantly distracting her, she was more focused on her objectives, and less likely to overlook any of the numerous details involved with the day-to-day operations of the hotel. The duties and intensity of her work load varied, as low seasons blossomed into high seasons, and all seasons faded into years, while Iris soaked up experience and knowledge, gaining confidence and credibility. As time passed, she remained committed to proving her valor as second-in-command, but found that the more she put into the job, the less *Direttore* Parodini needed to. Claudio continued complaining about him, in the same half-tolerant, half-affectionate way she had heard him complain about his wife, but that didn't mean he really wanted to eliminate either from his life, which in turn meant that Iris would never make the leap from Assistant Manager until the *Direttore* retired, and that would not happen for at least another ten years.

Iris felt a strong sense of allegiance toward the Grand Hotel Stella di Levante, even toward Claudio and *Direttore* Parodini, just as she had toward her previous employers. It wasn't only a matter of their significance in her life or the importance of her role; loyalty and duty had been part of her upbringing and were traits of her character (despite the occasional slip-up). Nonetheless, she sometimes longed for a new challenge, in a new place. One little voice inside her (the one planted there by Gregorio), urged her to stay put and relax in the comfort of a secure job and familiar environment from which, save for emergencies, she was guaranteed Sundays off, while another little voice argued that she had learned all she could and advanced as far as possible at the hotel, that the predictability of the her days at work was starting to bore her, and that boredom was one thing she could find without even leaving the house. Comparable positions at the other prestigious hotels on the coast were held by the same stale generation of men cut from the same rusty mold as Parodini, who had no intention of budging their butts from their nicely padded swivel chairs, and for Iris seeking employment at a hotel in another part of Italy was obviously out of the question. Iris listened to both voices, made her evaluations, and decided nothing.

One Sunday afternoon following family dinner, an emergency summoned Gregorio to the Policlinico. Iris was trying to decide how to spend this windfall of free time, but the familiar twitching in her restless muscles told her that her legs had plans of their own; she washed the dishes, changed, and snuck out the door. Her favorite jogging path led her up the hill to the Via Aurelia and along the high road to San Rocco, where she ran in the shade of umbrella pines while enjoying the spectacular view of the Golfo Paradiso, from Camogli all the way to Genoa and Savona and beyond. She jogged for a full hour, but fantasized herself as some female Forrest Gump in Italy, running on and on and never stopping until she had toured the length of the west coast all the way down to Calabria, circled the toe of the boot, run up the heel, and back north along the Adriatic coast. She would like to run until she had nowhere else to go, and nothing else from which to flee. Instead, she circled back down the path home, where she found the gate locked, and no answer to the bell. She vaguely remembered that at some point during the dinner table conversation, a comment had filtered through to her constantly wandering mind regarding a plan to take the boys to Recco for an ice cream; since only five could ride in the car, Isabella and Cinzia had probably thought themselves clever, and snuck out with the three boys, not knowing she was gone.

"Shit, shit and double shit," Iris muttered as she rattled the locked gate, swearing in English and sweating in Italian.

"Trouble?" someone asked from behind her. Iris turned around to face a slender, smiling woman in a silky, powder blue warm-up suit.

"Looks like I got locked out," Iris said, still panting. She wondered who the woman was and where she had come from. Not too many people just happened to walk by the Leale villa, stuck way up there on top of the hill.

"Sometimes these things happen for a reason," the woman said. Who was this friendly philosopher, and where had she come from? Iris was curious. "My name's Beatrix" the woman said, as if reading her mind. "Would you like to call someone, or drink a glass of water? I live right next door."

"Next door? I'm sorry, I've never seen you around," Iris said, wiping the back of a hand across her dripping brow.

259

"Yes, right behind that twelve-foot wall of laurel hedge that surrounds your property. What are you people hiding from, anyway? Doesn't that make you claustrophobic? But there I go again, transferring my phobias to other people, instead of minding my own damn business." Beatrix rolled her perfectly made-up eyes and waved a hand in front of her tanned face. "Getting back to why you've never seen me: I just rented this place. I spend most of my time in Milan." Accustomed to the reticence of the Ligurians, Iris was amused by the bits of unsolicited information being tossed in the air like corn popping in an uncovered pot. She caught each one, and gathered more of her own: the expensive brand name embossed on the breast of the woman's jacket, the matching sweatpants, the spiffy sneakers sporting the designer logo of two interlocked C's. She really knew how to dress for a walk, Iris thought, feeling like a slob in her grey gym shorts, faded T-shirt and beat-up running shoes, but she had never seen the point in squandering money on clothes she was only going to sweat in.

"Walking in the fresh air is supposed to work wonders for me, so they say, but nothing's happened so far. Except of course meeting you. That is, if you plan on telling me your name."

"Yes, I'm sorry, it's Iris."

"Well, are you coming, Iris?" the woman said, starting to walk away, obviously grateful for the excuse to interrupt her walk.

"Sure, thanks," Iris said, falling into step next to her. "I'm sorry, I'm not sure I got your name right. Did you say Beatrix or Beatrice?"

"You say that an awful lot."

"Say what?"

"That you're sorry. I couldn't help but notice. Anyway, it's Beatrix, as in Beatrix Potter. My mother was English, from the Lake District, and she grew up on Potter's stories. My first doll was Peter Rabbit. The first cup I drank from had Peter Rabbit on it. I went to sleep in a room decorated with Peter Rabbit wallpaper. And now my shrink wants to know why I can't relate to men. Maybe it's because I've never found one with a fluffy tail beneath his coat."

"I love Peter Rabbit! Oh, and how about Flopsy, Mospy and Cottontail? My mother used to read us all those stories when we were small." Iris's memory hopped up onto that old sofa of her childhood and snuggled up close to the warm, soft mother she shared with Lily and a couple of little brothers who squirmed and wriggled on her lap, as they settled in for a cozy read, amid the sucking of thumbs and the calming cadence of their mother's voice.

In her new neighbor's kitchen, Iris gratefully accepted a glass of cold water, while Beatrix lit up a cigarette, and immediately launched into conversation, as if with an old friend she hadn't seen for years. Beatrix revealed that she worked as a freelance headhunter, and that her therapist had suggested she temper her multiple Milanese neuroses with ample doses of the sunny Ligurian climate and countryside, from where she planned to work a few days a week.

Beatrix was as intrigued by the transplanted American dwelling on the hilltop, as Iris was by a woman who traded yuppies like baseball cards. When Iris asked for a second glass of water, Beatrix blew away her request with a puff of the lips and uncorked a bottle of chilled white wine. After all, she said, it was still the weekend, and getting close to dinner time. By the time Cinzia and Isabella returned, Iris's head was spinning with her share of the bottle and dozens of details regarding important people she had never met, who worked at companies she had never heard of, all compliments of Beatrix, who, by then, quite possibly knew more about Iris than anyone else in Italy, Gregorio included. From then on, whenever Beatrix was in the neighborhood, and Iris managed to slip out of the house, the two women would get together for a chat, sometimes over a cup of tea, but more often over a glass of wine or a shot or two of the single malt whiskey Beatrix insisted was a better remedy for whatever ailed a body than a liter of the chamomile tea Mrs. Rabbit forced down Peter's gullet after he overdosed on stolen veggies.

Some weeks later, Iris was contacted by the owner of the soon-to-open twenty-four suite boutique hotel, the Dimora Baia dell'Incanto, in Paraggi, just a stone's throw from Portofino. The caller, who identified herself as Mariella Mangiagallo, said that Iris had been highly recommended by a mutual acquaintance, a certain Beatrix Bonacorsa of Milan, and wished to know, in the event Iris might possibly be interested in the position of General Manager, whether she would be available to meet as soon as possible to discuss the matter. Interested, she was; available, she was; hired, she was.

The first six months of working in a makeshift office amid the noise and dust of the building crew hurrying to complete the job by the contracted completion date were frazzling, but Iris used that time to interview prospective staff and develop sales and marketing strategies to launch the new property. A promotional event slated to take place in New York City provided a welcome and long overdue opportunity for her to sneak in a quick visit home to see her family. She could ill afford the time, but if she didn't go now, who could say when she would have another chance? If she managed her time well, in the precious few days available she would be able to see Auntie Rosa, her mother, her sisters, and whatever nieces, nephews and brothers turned up at the traditional spaghetti dinner she cooked for everyone at Violet's place each time she visited.

When Iris called to say she was in town, her mother invited her to the annual Susan B. Anthony luncheon at which she had been asked to say a few words. Betty Capotosti (that was the name on her mother's badge, meaning she had apparently relinquished her *nom de guerre* and returned to her former identity, if not to her former self) was seated next to Iris at a round banquet table. Iris admired her mother's natural elegance and poise, and noticed how smooth and fresh her fair-skinned face still appeared, framed by the soft waves of her naturally auburn hair. Iris thought it ironic that despite twelve pregnancies, her mother's hair was still thick and only slightly streaked with grey, while Iris had been coloring hers for a few years already. The other women were deferential toward her mother, and poised to listen to anything she had to say, making Iris conclude that by now her mother must be regarded as some sort of leader on the local women's rights scene.

"I have to admit, some of your stories about Italy surprise me, Iris," she said, ice cubes clinking as she took a sip from her water glass. "For example, when you first moved over there, and answered a letter I sent to you, addressed to Iris Leale, you were quick to inform me that in Italy, when a woman marries, she acquires the right to use her husband's surname, but still officially goes by the name she was born with."

"I thought you'd find it interesting to hear that Italy is not as backward as you always seemed to believe. Imagine, one of my old friends from college even addressed a letter to me as 'Mrs. Gregorio Leale.' How antiquated is that? Even Gregorio thought it was odd," Iris said. She hardly got any letters anymore, though, except from Auntie Rosa; everyone else was using email. Iris disliked using a computer at home, too, but enjoyed the simplicity and immediacy of communication.

"And now, I'm hearing about this glamorous career of yours," her mother continued. "The only female hotel manager in the area, you say? Interesting. What special challenges does that present you with?"

Iris opened her mouth to reply, but before she could answer, her mother turned to remark on a discussion between two other women at their table convened to honor the suffragette activist who had fought and died in Rochester.

Auntie Rosa, whom Iris invited to dinner at Il Giardino, her aunt's favorite Italian restaurant, had reacted to the news of her career advancement as Iris might have expected. Though she was well into her eighties, she celebrated by devouring the heaping dish of spaghetti bolognese that sat in front of her with cheer and greed, interrupted by sporadic exclamations of, "I can't b'lieve it!" and "I guess I must have been hungry!" Only when she had mopped up her plate with a chunk of crusty bread, did she devote her full attention to Iris.

"Well, aren't you a clever little Lover-dover!" she said, as she wiped tomato sauce from the corners of her mouth, using her napkin to muffle the burp that escaped her. "Of course those people want you to run their hotel, honey. Who wouldn't? They can count their lucky stars to have you, let me tell you. I'll bet Gregorio is so darn proud of you!"

"He never comes right out and says so to me, but he always mentions my job when he introduces me to people from the hospital. You'd think I built the hotel with my own hands, the way he goes on about it sometimes," Iris said.

"Of course he boasts! Let him! What man in his right mind wouldn't be proud of you? Whatever a woman does, reflects on her husband and family, you know!" Auntie Rosa lowered her voice and raised her index finger. "Remember, though," she continued, leaning close, "you always have to use a little bit of psychology with men. Let your husband do the talking. If you start bragging about your job with those other doctors, not that you would ever brag, not my Iris!, he might feel upstaged. Men don't like that. Especially not doctors. I've worked with enough of them to know. For fifty-five years I worked with them! If anyone knew how many diagnoses I made before they did, just by talking to my patients!" Auntie Rosa shook her head slowly, and crossed herself. "For fifty-five years!"

"I never talk about my job at home. Gregorio always has so much to say about the hospital and everything he has to deal with, the politics of his department chief, his two-faced colleagues, his conferences. All I can do is listen."

"*Brava!* That's what men love. A wife who listens. Now tell me what it's like there at that Dimora place."

On sisters' night out, each of the girls shared her reaction over their second bottle of Chardonnay; all except Lily, who, with the excuse of not being able to find a babysitter, had opted not to join them.

"That's amazing, Iris!" Jasmine said. "It sounds divine. To think I went to college all those years, and now most of my conversations are with caged animals, while you're over there hobnobbing with the rich and famous."

"As soon as I can organize some time off from the Center, I'll be over to visit!" Violet said. "You'll at least invite me to lunch at your fancy hotel, won't you? And I'm coming solo, unless any of you ladies want to join me. I just have to leave everything organized for Todd so he doesn't flush the business down the toilet while I'm gone."

"Someone was *just* talking to me about Portofino the other day!" Marguerite said. "I was on the phone with this artist from Milan I'm trying to line up for a show - he had *just* been there to see one of his wealthy clients. Give me your card, and I'll hook you up with him."

The following night, Iris surprised Lily by knocking at her door with a foot, juggling in her arms a pizza and a bottle of domestic Merlot she assumed was Lily's favorite, since it was the only brand Iris had ever seen in her house.

"Iris! It's you!" Lily said through the screen door, her eyes darting past Iris to the street. "I was wondering who could be pulling into the driveway at this hour. It's a little early for Joe."

"Yes, as you can see, it's only me!" Iris said. "I'm sorry I didn't call. Is this a bad time?"

"No, I'm glad you came. But I'm sorry you can't see the kids, they're already in bed." Lily said, opening the door. "Two miracles in one night. Let's open that wine."

The first sip of Merlot made Iris grimace; she suspected Lily bought this brand because she couldn't afford better, or didn't know better. Iris had debated over buying something more palatable, but worried Lily might think she was putting on airs if she presented her with a fancy label. Intentions and interpretations did not always coincide, especially where Lily was concerned.

When Iris slipped into the conversation the news about her job change, Lily said, "You're so lucky, Iris. I wouldn't mind going back to work, once Pierce is a little older. I don't know what exactly I'd do, but there's got to be something better than SaveMart around here."

"You already have the best job in the world, taking care of two kids. Between them, and the house, and Joe, you must have your hands full. How's Joe's business going, by the way?"

Lily lit a cigarette, sipped her wine. "Oh, he's a great salesman, that's for sure." She still hadn't touched the pizza.

"Well, I think you're lucky you get to stay home with the kids and enjoy them while they're small. It's such a luxury these days," Iris said, tilting her head to catch the mozzarella topping as it slipped from the slice of pizza in her hand. Lily didn't have it so bad, in this nice big house all on her own, with her two beautiful boys, and no in-laws walking in and out as they pleased.

"Yeah, that's what the ladies at my church group say." Lily's eyes scanned her sister's face, as if to test her reaction.

"So you're still going to that same church, I take it? What was it called again?"

Lily nodded. "Christ Covenant Church."

"You've been involved with them for a long time now. Don't you ever miss the Catholic church?"

"Not really. At CCC there's more of a community spirit, you know? The women get together once a week to talk about how to deal with problems; it's kind of like a support group for wives and mothers. The kids all know each other, too."

"Do they have a choir? Maybe you should consider joining, if they do."

"Like you said, I have a full-time job here. It doesn't leave much time or energy for anything else. Besides, I haven't sung in ages."

"But you have a gift, Lily. You should find ways to cultivate that talent in any circumstances, even now, and then when the time comes, you'll be ready to get up on that stage again. You'll see." Iris knew it would happen, sooner or later. She took a sip of her wine, thinking she would like to belong to a church group, too, though she wouldn't know where to find one. Things worked differently in Italy. "I haven't been so good about going to Mass lately, with the new job and all," she said. It had been even longer since she had been to Confession, and certainly didn't plan on going now; she would be too embarrassed to tell the whole truth, and she was too old to cheat.

"You'd think churches in Italy would be the best in the world, right there in the cradle of Catholicism, in the shadow of the Holy Father himself," she continued. "But most churches I've been to are either tourist attractions, or mausoleums. They're beautiful buildings, not congregations. Catholics have the monopoly, and I guess that's what happens when you have no competition." Iris realized she was rambling. She poured more Merlot for both of them; maybe it would help her shut up, and help Lily open up.

"You didn't come all this way to tell me about churches," Lily said. "Why don't you tell me about the new hotel."

Iris opened her mouth to do just that, there was plenty to say about the place, starting with the clear, emerald waters lapping the beach of Paraggi below; the spectacular views of the secluded cove; the brimming blueness of the infinity pool which blended into the aquamarine horizon; the exquisite feeling of privilege that infused her when she strolled the terrace, imagining the international clientele and celebrities she would soon be greeting at the Riviera's most talked about new boutique hotel.

"Can I bum one of those?" she asked, when Lily shook another Merit from the pack. Lily passed her one. The cigarette trembled in her mouth as Lily held the lighter for her, squinting through the smoke. Iris took a drag on her cigarette, looked at the ceiling. Lily wouldn't really want to hear all those beautiful descriptions, would she? They would only confirm her belief that Iris was on a perennial vacation, and Iris didn't feel she should have to justify working in a pretty place by citing all the hassles and long hours and problems she could already see coming with Gregorio before the hotel had even opened.

"Really, it's just a job," she said, her elbows on her knees. "I don't even know why they hired me, I don't have any real qualifications, just my hands-on experience from the other hotel I worked at, and a friend's recommendation. And of course being American helps over there - as if that were a some sort of credential."

It was better to leave it at that; as it was, she still came across sounding pretty lucky, without filling in the fancy background. Besides, Iris could see that Lily was already far away, just like she could see the veil of sadness trapped under the glassy look in her grey-green eyes. It was strange how when she thought of Lily she always pictured her eyes twinkling with the vivacious sparkle of childhood, though she hadn't actually seen it in a very long time. She'd like to ask her why, but didn't know how. This was their only evening to spend together, and then she'd be gone again. Better they should enjoy the pizza, and keep things light.

"Aren't you having any?" she asked Lily, helping herself to another slice, just as a car pulled in the driveway. At least she'd get to say hello to Joe, after all. He was always so friendly and affectionate, and seemed to be genuinely interested whenever he asked about Gregorio and the family.

"I already ate, Iris," Lily said, stomping out her cigarette. "But thanks anyway."

Those few days back home had passed far too quickly, and now it was time to devote her undivided attention to the tasks at hand. The soft opening was slated for Monday, leaving just two weeks to gear up for the expected Easter crowds, and there simply were not enough hours in the day to accomplish everything that needed to be done. Iris still had to arrange staff meetings, conduct a final inspection of the guest rooms with the housekeeper, review the provisional menus and wine list with Paolo the chef and Alberto the maître d' who had followed her over from the Stella di Levante (Claudio had been more upset by the pair's resignation than by Iris's decision to end their affair, and vowed he would never forgive her for stealing them, though they had been the ones pleading to come with her), and attend to dozens of other things she had better not start thinking about if she wanted to remain sane.

"*No, non lì, Giovanni, là,*" Iris instructed the man in green overalls. "Over there!" Next time she had to prepare a CV she must remember to add "patience" under her qualifications.

After grumbling a remark in a typically Genoese *mugugno* (the dialect was particularly suitable for complaining, a pastime to which the locals were so notoriously devoted that they created a special word for it), the man disinterred the rosemary bush he had just planted, shuffled over to the spot Iris indicated, and began digging a new hole. Regardless of the little red flags Iris had stuck in the ground, each time she left the man alone to go tend to something else, she would return to find he had reverted to his haphazard methods. The result was a zigzag of empty holes that Giovanni would then have to fill again at the end of the day. The owner, Mirella Mangiagallo, the widow of an industrialist from Lombardy who had bought the derelict villa decades earlier with the dream of turning it into a hotel, in an initial meeting together with her son Sebastiano, and Alfio, his significant other, had informed Iris that thanks to the architect's grandiose schemes, overly optimistic cost estimates, and uncontrollable weakness for siphoning, the funds earmarked for additional embellishments no longer existed. All items deemed non-essential, which, in their opinion, included landscaping, would have to wait until next season. Iris could not bear the thought of opening any hotel with a barren garden, let alone one with such an exclusive target, and wished more than once that Claudio and his checkbook were around to support her initiatives. In the end, she had convinced the owners to allow her a shoestring budget, which she optimized by searching for inexpensive solutions at a local greenhouse, and appointing Giovanni, the maintenance man, to do the labor.

She had done extensive research on which types of plants would do well in different conditions of light and soil, back when the Leale family had purchased their villa. Iris had been sorry to give up the little seaside apartment she and Gregorio had shared as newlyweds in Santa Ida, but the idea of having a garden at the new villa had consoled her, as she recalled the childhood joys of walking barefoot in the grass, and harvesting homegrown vegetables. However, between her mother-in-law's conviction that plants belonged in pots, and Cinzia's insistence on dumping truckloads of pea gravel over the ground so the kids wouldn't dirty their clothes or track mud into the house when they played outdoors, Iris had succeeded in planting only one thing, a lilac bush, which stood just behind the wrought iron bars of the front gate. The lilac, like Iris, was not indigenous to this area, but they looked after each other: Iris tended to its few needs, and in return was comforted by the sight of the plant greeting her as she came and went. Its teardrop leaves seemed sympathetic when she felt nostalgic for her hometown, where the plants thrived so well it had been nicknamed the "Lilac City." She may only have one little bush in her garden now, but it was enough to remind her of springtime on Chestnut Crest, where the sweet fragrance of the blooming lilacs her mother had planted wafted in through the open windows for the entire month of May.

At least she was putting that research to use now, Iris thought, as she strolled along the flagstone walkway, her critical eye surveying the scene around her. Her simple Mediterranean garden was starting to take shape, and once the remaining rosemary and sage and lavender bushes were planted, the entrance path would not only look lovely, it would greet guests with flora that would convey to them with fragrant simplicity the essence of the Riviera and the philosophy of the Dimora. She followed the path to the terrace, which she envisioned filled with guests leisurely sipping their frothy cappuccinos and nibbling on flaky croissants so delicious they would revive the bored taste buds of the rich. Facing east, those sitting on the terrace would be kissed by the morning sun as it climbed over the promontory of Sestri Levante and illuminated the Gulf of Tigullio, gateway to the fishing villages of the Cinque Terre which lay beyond the craggy coastal mountains.

She imagined herself one of those fortunate guests as she gazed down at the shimmering waters of the cove just below the hotel, which reflected every hue of green glowing in the lush vegetation of the hillside: umbrella pines, olive trees, cypresses, a jumble of wild shrubs of broom and rosemary and heather. She closed her eyes and inhaled, thinking she would have known the plants were there, even if she could not see them, as she smelled their sweet aromas, coaxed out into the open by the early morning shower, followed by an afternoon of intense spring sun. She observed a group of laborers on the beach, busy sprucing up the red cabanas with a fresh coat of paint in preparation for the season. Were she a guest at this resort on a lovely summer morning, she would certainly surrender to the tempting water below, and enjoy an invigorating plunge before breakfast. She would fancy a glass of freshly squeezed orange juice or an espresso before heading down the short steep path for a swim, and made a mental note to instruct the breakfast crew that guests be allowed that option as part of their complimentary continental breakfast, without being charged extra.

"*Ciao, Direttrice!*"

Her musings were interrupted by an approaching voice and clatter of heels, both of which she instantly recognized as belonging to Beatrix. There would be plenty of clients like her, too, Iris thought. The type that wouldn't be caught dead, even at breakfast, sans their full regalia of makeup and jewelry and designer clothes.

"I've just spoken with the Mangiagallos," Beatrix said as she brushed each of Iris's cheeks with her own. "I know the hotel isn't even open yet, but I must say, they seem very happy with you. They like your style. *Brava!* Keep up the good work, and you can call this place home for as long as you want. I've known them for years, and I just knew they'd take to you."

"Thanks, Bea," Iris said, as soon her friend stopped for breath. "That's reassuring. Sometimes I feel like such a fake, though."

"What do you mean?" Beatrix asked.

"Well, you know, I never actually studied hotel management," Iris said. She ran her fingers through her hair and sighed. The longer she lived, the more she realized how much of her life required bluffing. She was tired of it, and wondered whether she was up to this test.

"Oh, nonsense. Do you have any idea how many fakes there are out there? How many incompetent nincompoops with puffed-up credentials who got where they are only because they knew how to sell themselves – or I knew how to sell them? But that's not your case, you are smart and dedicated, and you've been running the show at the Stella for years - without getting the recognition or salary for doing so, I might add. Now you'll finally be free to take charge and prove yourself to everyone, including yourself," Beatrix said. "It's time to kick some ass, dear Iris."

Beatrix always managed to make her smile, though she sometimes touched on subjects Iris would rather avoid. "Thanks for the pep talk. I just hope I can pull it off. There's still an awful lot to do. Did I tell you we're already booked solid for Easter weekend? Well, for Friday and Saturday anyway. Hopefully some guests will want to take advantage of the holiday on Monday and extend a night. If we don't screw up."

"Now stop that, Iris!" Whenever Beatrix raised her voice, it came out in a hoarse croak, produced by too many years of too many cigarettes and too many shouting matches, including those with her insolvent second ex-husband, who still relied on her for financial support. "Your insecurity simply exhausts me. Mind if I have a seat?" Beatrix asked, dropping her birdlike frame into a wrought iron patio chair, still wrapped in its packaging.

"Be my guest," Iris said, pulling up a chair for herself. Worn out from a long day on her feet, she landed heavily on the bubble-wrapped chair, setting off a round of pops.

Beatrix unzipped the Prada bag on her lap, extracted a silver Cartier cigarette case and offered Iris a Muratti before taking one herself. A matching lighter was produced, and the two women lit up.

"So, how's the rest of life? How are things up on the hill, at Villa Leale?" Beatrix asked, jutting her chin out and tilting it to the sky as she exhaled, her pose a combination of diva and Mussolini.

"Good, I guess," Iris replied. "Everyone's fine." She dangled her right leg over her left, kicking the air with her right foot. Of course, it hadn't been easy to give Gregorio the attention he deserved lately, and he had no qualms about pointing that out to her. She hoped things would improve once a routine was established, and things were running smoothly.

"How's that *stronza* of your sister-in-law?" Beatrix asked.

"Who, Cinzia? Come on, she's got her good points," Iris replied, her stubborn sense of loyalty compelling her to defend the woman who radiated more negativity than anyone Iris had ever met.

"Even though I never met the guy, I can't blame your brother-in-law - what was it, Franco? - for flying the coop when he did. You should do the same." Beatrix sucked on her cigarette, drawing the smoke deep into her lungs and holding it there. Iris half-expected to see it come out of her ears.

Iris's head was spinning after her first drag, even though she was smoking occasionally these days, mostly with Beatrix, and never at home. Even if Gregorio should give her permission, she did not want the house to reek of smoke, especially since Isabella, in order to allow Cinzia some free time after school, had developed the habit of bringing her grandchildren to study or watch afternoon television on the set Gregorio had bought Iris for Christmas (thinking it would help soothe a case of holiday homesickness, which of course it didn't; she had always found TV so bad in Italy she refused to watch it). Even though Iris did not like the idea of her apartment being invaded when she was not in the house (or ever, to be perfectly honest), she would feel selfish putting a stop to a practice Gregorio had encouraged. The family would certainly have something to say if the house smelled of cigarette smoke, even though they all seemed to enjoy Gregorio's pipe smoke. Probably because the smell was so masculine, and proved that at least one man had hung around.

"You mean Gregorio and I should move to a place of our own?" That would never happen, not now. She forced herself to take another puff.

"Well, that's not quite what I was thinking."

"What were you thinking then?"

"Well, I was thinking maybe you should leave, and forget to take Gregorio with you," Beatrix replied.

"What justification could I possibly have for doing something as outrageous as that?"

"Boredom," Beatrix said. Her expression was serious as she looked Iris in the eye.

"My life's not boring." She was tempted to tell Beatrix that she knew how to find some excitement on the side, if she wanted, but no thank you, ma'am, she had had enough of that. Something had held her back from revealing the secret of her affair with Claudio Olona; part of it was shame, part respect for Gregorio, part fear that the information might not be secure with someone as forthcoming as Bea. It was part of the past, anyway, and she felt better leaving it right there where it belonged.

"I have plenty to do here to keep me busy," she said instead. "Besides, Gregorio needs me. His family needs me. So what if I have to make a few sacrifices. That's part of life. 'The greater the love, the greater the sacrifice.' That's what my Auntie Rosa always says."

"No offence to your Auntie Rosa, Iris," Beatrix said, "but what I say is, 'the greater the sacrifice, the greater the sacrifice.'"

"And just what do you mean by that?" Iris asked. She stubbed her cigarette out on a scrap of slate she had retrieved from a pile of rubble to use as an ashtray, then reached her hands below the seat of her chair, to toy with the bubble wrap.

"What I mean is," Beatrix continued, "that it's bullshit. Sacrifice is not a virtue unto itself. Not unless you're a biblical lamb, brought into this world purposely to be slaughtered. You may have to sacrifice one thing in order to attain another, but all I'm seeing is you sacrificing everything, and other people benefiting from the trade-in. Where is your ROI?"

"My what?" Iris asked. *Pop. Pop.* Her attention started to drift as she punctured the bubbles; she had realized years ago that it was fairly easy for her to tune out things she did not want to hear, especially when others were speaking Italian, and especially if the Leales were involved in some way. Iris wondered whether her adeptness at blocking out uninteresting or unpleasant words had led to her growing tendency to block out inconvenient thoughts, but there were some things she would just rather not talk about. Not here with Beatrix, not with Gregorio when she lay in bed staring at the same paragraph of her novel, neither he nor she noticing that she never turned the page, not even with herself when she awoke at three o'clock in the morning, her heart racing around in circles for lack of anywhere else to go.

"Your ROI, your return on investment." Beatrix explained, rolling her eyes behind her Gucci sunglasses. Despite the rose-tinted lenses, Iris could see that the whites were shot through with blood. She had once told Iris she hadn't been able to sleep for more than four hours at a stretch in years. "In other words, what's in it for you?"

"I don't expect anything in return. That's how families work, in case you don't know. Besides, I get plenty out of it. I have a comfortable house to live in," Iris said. "And a husband who adores me and takes care of me. I could stop working tomorrow if I wanted to." She hoped it didn't sound like she was taking a jab at Beatrix's personal life; she had no family, and all her relationships had ended in disaster.

"A husband who adores *his version* of you," Beatrix said, as the last bit of cigarette ash dropped from the filter. "Look Iris, we've known each other for a while now, right?"

"Right," Iris said.

"And we've never once gone out together as girlfriends, just you and I, have we?" Beatrix said. "For a drink or a pizza or a movie? Have we?"

"I don't remember," Iris replied. "No, I don't think we have. And so?"

"And so. Would you like to?"

"Well, I guess. Sure. It would be nice," Iris said. She couldn't imagine what Gregorio would say if she announced she was going out for the evening without him; she had never tried.

"And I know you love to dance. When was the last time you went dancing, or to a party where anyone danced?"

275

"I can't really remember. It's been ages," Iris said. "Gregorio hates dancing."

"So you don't dance."

"Well, no. Only at home sometimes. When no one's around upstairs or downstairs and I can put on the music I like," Iris said. "Or when I go home. One Christmas Eve everyone brought guitars to my brother's place, and we had this amazing jam session. I even convinced Lily to sing. And my other sisters and I did backup. We improvised dance routines right on the spot. It was a blast!"

"And when was the last time you played the guitar?" Beatrix asked.

"The guitar is a thing of the past. I never was very good at it, despite all of Uncle Alfred's lessons. None of my friends play anymore."

"Have your friends changed, or have you changed friends?"

"Look, Bea, I'm exhausted. Let's call it a day here. How about we sneak a stop in Rapallo and have that aperitif? I'm already in the doghouse because of this job, and your friendship is driving me to drink. Let's have something strong. Like a nice Americano."

"Accidenti come piove!" Gregorio muttered through clenched teeth, flinging open the bedroom shutters. "I told you it would rain today." Cozily ensconced in the blanket, her loose hair doodling curlicues across her pillow, Iris instinctively drew her knees to her chest. With supreme effort, she hoisted her lids to half-mast, and focused her eyes on her first vision of the day: her fifty-something husband standing by the window in his striped pajamas, stomping his foot and shaking his fist like a capricious child who had just been told he could not go out to play.

Too relieved by Gregorio's weather report to feign chagrin, Iris yawned a silent prayer of gratitude to the pissing heavens, then rolled over to peer at the clock on the bedside table: 8:45. Reading the time on the digital display uplifted her spirits, not only because she had managed to sleep so late on her first day off in a fortnight, but because she did not need to grope around for her glasses before the numbers could be distinguished. Having obtained Gregorio's approval, subject to his review of a sufficient number of scientific publications and case histories to convince him of the procedure's safety and effectiveness, Iris had finally undergone laser surgery to rid herself of glasses and contact lenses once and for all.

With so much to do in this single day of repose, Iris was thankful for the inclement weather. She had absolutely no desire to assist Gregorio as he meticulously checked each piece of diving gear before loading it into the car, or accompany him to Santa Margherita, where she would be expected to pass the time with the annoying wife of Gregorio's diving buddy, who talked incessantly about her prodigious little boy, while their husbands sped off aboard the rubber dinghy. Each spring, Gregorio launched a campaign to persuade Iris to try diving again, and he had convinced himself (but not her) that this year would be the year, as her now perfect vision would certainly make her feel much more at ease. No matter how good her vision, no matter which arguments he used, the prospect of squeezing her body into a wetsuit, saddling herself with heavy gear, and throwing herself into the deep, dark abyss was simply not her idea of fun. Each time Iris begged off, Gregorio accused her of not wanting to spend time together, but that wasn't quite true; she simply wished to spend it differently. She would be happy to take a hike with him along the trails of Mount Portofino, for example, or a ride along the coast on her Vespa. Maybe she could even drive, and he could ride behind her; maybe he would allow her to act a bit like the teenager she had never had the opportunity to be, at least for half a day.

Her idea of fun would be to simply wander off, without a plan or cumbersome equipment, with nothing more than a hunk of cheese, some fruit, and a bottle of water in a backpack slung over her shoulder, with (or without) Gregorio. His fanatical approach to diving was one of those issues, like his relationship with Isabella, which stirred in Iris sentiments that oscillated between irritation and pity. His obsessive checking of airtight seals and gauges, the way he barked orders or snapped at her if he discovered she had not cleaned or stowed some piece of gear properly, reinforced her theory that a person's innate tendencies were just as evident in the leisure activities they cultivated, as in the careers they pursued. It was probably more comfortable for Gregorio to transfer the control and precision he relied upon in the operating room to an activity like scuba diving, than it would be for him to set off on a spur-of-the-moment hike. His carefree side, if he had one, had probably been sequestered by Isabella when he was still a boy, and expected to stand in the shoes of his absent and unfaithful father. It saddened her to think that the feel of the sun warming his shoulders as he walked the trails, or of the wind blowing on his face as he rode the scooter would cause Gregorio as much distress as scuba diving would cause Iris.

In any event, Gregorio had been right about the weather. The previous day had been a quintessential spring day in Liguria, with promises of many more to come dangling from the brilliant sun, floating on the sea of glass. Gregorio kept calling her at work, insisting that spring weather was fickle, and that if she was the boss now, she should make it known by delegating what needed to be done for the remainder of the day, and meet him at the marina. By his fourth call, her head was throbbing (compliments of the software technician's efforts to explain why a programming glitch kept causing the property management system to crash), it took Iris a great effort to reply in a calm manner. All she wanted was to be left alone to fulfill her responsibilities without the added pressure of Gregorio making her feel guilty for spoiling his Saturday and filling her with worries that he would force her to quit the new job he insisted she did not need.

"I guess we'll just have to make the best of it," Gregorio said. Unlike the grace of the Holy Spirit, known to descend upon the faithful with the gentle wings of a dove, to constantly hover over and guide them, anger swooped down on Gregorio with the rapidity of a hawk snatching a bunny, then just as swiftly flapped away. Iris did not react to his short-lived tantrum, having long since learned the best tactic was to simply wait it out. It was already over, in fact: Gregorio sighed, and lowered himself back onto the mattress. The bed springs groaned as he slipped under the sheet, and turned to embrace Iris from behind.

"A little extra time in bed can't hurt, can it?" he said. "After all, it is Sunday. We can always go to late Mass." He began rubbing the curves of her hip and thigh briskly, as if friction alone were enough to spark her desire, when the only urges Iris had at that moment were to go pee, then wrap her hands around a steaming mug of caffelatte. But it was apparent by the bulge pressing against her backside that her husband had something else on his mind, not to mention in his pajama pants.

Gregorio's intentions were further made clear by the delicate but firm pressure he applied to Iris's shoulder to make her lie flat on her back; within seconds, he was straddling her, his movements quickly falling into a perfectly syncopated rhythm. Her body had learned to submit to the patterns established by silent accord as the way Gregorio Leale and Iris Capotosti, two strangers born on different continents who had somehow ended up married, made love. She could predict, give or take a minute, exactly how long it would take for him to climax, and knew just when to roll out the reels of her illicit encounters with Claudio, featuring memories of her naked body sinking into the fluffy beds of Europe's most exquisite hotels, where her bare skin would be caressed by the finest of linens and Claudio's expert hands.

Until that moment, she would engage in the mental foreplay she had invented to distract herself during sex. In her fantasies, Iris was the lone contestant in a game show and Gregorio was a giant metronome. She was allowed ten seconds to come up with a song that would match the beat dictated by his pelvic motion. A Beatles tune was usually the first to pop into her head, something swingy, like "When I'm Sixty-Four" or "For the Benefit of Mr. Kite." This morning, Mick Jagger singing "Ruby Tuesday" kept interfering with the game. Lately, she had become obsessed with the song, but its beat was too slow, its words too penetrating as a soundtrack for sex with her husband on this rainy Palm Sunday morning, when the last thing she wanted to reflect on was the loss of dreams. And now the metronome was stepping up the tempo, and Iris knew she would be eliminated if she could not think of something faster to keep the pace, but still those same lyrics kept looping in her mind.

Gregorio pushed and panted purposefully on, leaving Iris lagging way behind, until she was saved by the memory of eating a sinfully rich chocolate hazelnut torte at an incredible restaurant in Lugano, and Claudio reaching under the table, nudging her legs apart, grazing his fingers over the soft skin above her stockings, and Gregorio thrust harder and faster, and Claudio slid one hand to the top of her thigh and with the other placed a snifter of cognac to her lips, as Gregorio grunted and shoved, and the velvety chocolate and the strong liquor collided in an explosion of flavor in her mouth, and Gregorio spent himself inside her and Claudio pushed aside her panties and flicked his fingers over her sweet spot and the current of pleasure surged through her and she arched her hips and ground her need into him, then fell still.

"Maybe we can still make the ten o'clock service after all," Gregorio said already on his feet.

"Still I'm gonna miss you," Iris whispered into her pillow.

"What are you talking about? Aren't you coming to Mass, too?"

"Of course," Iris said.

There were no Easter baskets with milk chocolate bunnies surrounded by brightly colored marshmallow chicks nesting in a bed of fake straw. There were no nickels to dole out to the lucky child who discovered the hiding place of the coveted Golden Egg. There was no Carlo Capotosti presiding over the Easter table with his plastic Our Lady of Lourdes bottle filled with the holy water siphoned off the font at church, which he would sprinkle over family and food with an Easter blessing. There was no Lily of the Valley twirling around in her "new" dress (the one Iris had reluctantly but inevitably grown out of), showing off the frilly but tattered pink bonnet which slipped from her head when she hopped up and down the driveway before Mass singing "Here Comes Peter Cottontail."

But on this Day of Resurrection, the fragrance of childhood Easters filled the house where Iris lived, and resuscitated her memories. There was a loaf of Easter bread fresh from the oven (though a luncheon commemorating a women's rights activist was not the best place to discuss baking, Iris had used the opportunity to access her mother's secret recipe). There was also an Easter table, prettily set for seven, with a potted lily in the center, and hand-painted hard-boiled eggs to mark the place of each person. She hadn't minded decorating the eggs all by herself; she had welcomed the opportunity to indulge in nostalgic thoughts of the messy egg-dyeing days of Holy Week.

"We're home!" Gregorio called from the entrance. Iris glanced at the table one last time and smiled. It would be childish to expect holidays to be like they used to, but Iris loved them just the same.

"Look what I have for my *Piccolina!*" Gregorio said as he entered the room, one arm linked with his mother's, the other holding up a large egg-shaped object wrapped in brightly colored foil. Italian Easter eggs were flashy and big, but it was all show. There wasn't much chocolate, because they were hollow, enabling a cheap plastic toy to be hidden inside. A blue ribbon dangling from the egg meant that the prize was meant for a boy. Cinzia followed with her three sons dressed in white shirts and black ties, looking like a funeral procession. Perhaps the priest hadn't made it clear that the agony and crucifixion were behind them, and today was a day to celebrate rebirth.

"How was church?" Iris asked everyone and no one in particular, as she greeted the family.

"The only way to know is to go," Isabella replied. "I don't suppose you could be bothered to fulfill your Easter Duty."

"Mamma, we've already gone over this," Gregorio said. "You know Iris had to go in early this morning to check things out at the hotel, so she would still have time to get things ready for us."

"I think God understands, Isabella," Iris said. She was glad for having had a valid excuse for skipping, and staying home to pray in her own private way.

"Maybe you could turn that music down, *Piccolina*?" Gregorio said. He spoke softly, with that subtle tone of condescension she recognized so well. His support of her and her ways could be counted on, but only up to a certain point.

"I'll just turn it off," she said, walking over to the CD player. "I've been listening and meditating on the Passion of Christ, right here on my own," she said. She neglected to tell them that she had done so by listening to and singing along with both discs of *Jesus Christ Superstar* from beginning to end and had been so moved, she had put it on again. She had found joy in the words Jesus preached, empathized with the confusion of Mary Magdalene, cringed at the betrayal of Judas, shared the Lord's solitary agony in the Garden of Gethsemane, wept with pain and rage during His crucifixion.

"How could you meditate, with all that noise?" Isabella said.

Iris flushed with the frustration of the misunderstood. She took a deep breath and attempted to explain, "That's 'Hosanna,' a beautiful piece from *Jesus Christ Superstar.* I still remember all the words to the album, from when I was a teenager. Lily and I used to act out the whole thing. You should have heard her sing 'I Don't Know how to Love Him.' It used to give me goosebumps."

Isabella looked at her as if she didn't know what she was talking about, which of course she didn't. She had met Lily once, years ago, and had even heard her sing at Iris's wedding, but she had probably removed the details of the event from her mind, and had certainly never listened to the rock opera. Rather than inquire about the music, about Lily, about anything, Isabella motioned for her son to escort her to his recliner chair, pausing as Gregorio shooed away Zenzero, who was curled up in a doughnut on the seat. After making a show of brushing away the cat hairs from the cushion, Isabella sat down.

"I'll just pop into the study a minute to make a call to the hospital. I'll be back in a jiffy," Gregorio said as Isabella made herself comfortable, opened the fresh copy of "*Settimana*

Enigmistica" Gregorio always picked up for her at the newsstand, and set about solving the first of the week's set of crossword puzzles and brainteasers.

"Can I help with anything, Iris?" Cinzia said. If she wasn't feeling the Easter Joy, she must really be into Easter Duty; she never offered to help with anything.

"No thanks, Cinzia," Iris answered, walking to the kitchen. "I love it in the kitchen, but as I told Gregorio, I wanted to keep things nice and simple today."

"Yes, I can see that." Cinzia had followed her anyway, and stood staring at the flameless burners of the vacant stove. "Maybe it's time you put the pot on, though. The boys are starving."

"We don't need a pot!" Iris said. "Everything's ready." After putting in a hectic twelve-hour day to guide the hotel and its staff through their first sold-out Saturday, she had come home and worked until late preparing food in advance. She was proud to gesture at the bounty on the countertop: a wicker basket filled with hard-boiled eggs, the homemade Easter bread, a fresh fruit salad, a ham and cheese quiche, and in concession to Ligurian tradition, a *torta pasqualina,* made with fresh artichokes.

"But we always have ravioli on Easter," Cinzia sniffed. "You know that."

"I thought it might be nice to change, and have a brunch instead. This way, you can all sample something of what my Easters used to taste like."

"What about the lamb? Don't tell me you didn't make the lamb?"

"The lamb was sort of what convinced me to do the brunch, Cinzia. I stood in that packed butcher's shop staring at those skinned pink cadavers for a good half hour, and by the time it was my turn to order, I just couldn't go through with it."

"You didn't have to do the roast, you could have gotten the ribs. Who ever gives a thought to where ribs come from?"

"It's not that. It's the whole idea of the sacrificial lamb thing. I thought of the thousands of innocent creatures being slaughtered so everyone can gorge themselves after performing their Easter

Duty. Even the symbolism seems out of kilter to me."

"What are you, suddenly? Some kind of vegetarian? My kids don't even have a father to celebrate Easter with anymore, and now you do this! You deprive them of their family traditions! You always have to be different, don't you? Can't you just try to blend in for once? Be like one of us? What is your problem? *Madonna che palle!*" Cinzia huffed out of the room; seconds later Iris heard her shrill voice competing with the blaring voices of the Sunday morning variety show someone had switched on, as she bore the sad tidings of Iris's kitchen to her mother and sons.

Iris looked again at the appetizing lineup of simple, wholesome dishes on the counter, wondering whether they felt as inadequate as she did. She opened the refrigerator and took out the bottle of Berlucchi rosé she had been chilling especially for the occasion. Her hands shook as she peeled the foil from around the neck, untwisted the wire cage, popped the cork. She poured a glass and gulped it down while it was still frothing, then poured a second. She raised the flute in the air and studied the *perlage* of tiny bubbles as they formed chains, floated to the surface and burst, like the tight tears of loneliness burning her eyes.

Iris had tasted passion, and knew all about penance, but she was beginning to have serious doubts about ever attaining redemption.

14. LILY

"Hello?" Lily said breathlessly into the receiver.

"Where have you been?" Joe demanded.

"I told you this morning - I had to go grocery shopping."

"That's all?"

"Yes," she replied. "That's all." Lily set one of the bags on the kitchen counter, then reached into her purse, pulled out a pack of cigarettes, and removed the cellophane wrapper with her teeth.

"That's the only place you went? The grocery store?"

"I said that's the only place." Lily set the second bag down on the floor, ignited the front burner on the stove, leaned over it, and lit her cigarette. She took a long drag. She would have to think about quitting. One of these days.

"What took you so long?"

"Joe, I was gone less than an hour-and-a-half. It takes thirty minutes just to drive back and forth." Lily exhaled as she spoke, smoke escaping through her nose and mouth in small puffs with each word, swirling itself about her head. "The only other place I went was to Seven-Eleven, to get cigarettes; they didn't have mine at the grocery store."

"So you didn't just go to the grocery store," said Joe. "Why do you have to hide things from me all the time?"

"I'm not hiding anything, Joe."

"Then why didn't you tell me you went to the Seven-Eleven

when I first asked you?"

"Because going to Seven-Eleven is part of doing the shopping."

"You didn't go anywhere else after that?"

"No, I didn't," said Lily. As if she had anywhere else to go.

"Are you sure, because if you did, I'll find out."

"I have to go, Joe - the ice cream is going melt all over the kitchen floor."

Joe's gambling had continued to escalate as time passed, culminating in crises that Lily learned to infer from their symptoms - a stern warning from the mortgage company, a suspicious hitch in Joe's gait, compliments no doubt of some angry bookie, or puffs of pent-up rage that seemed to pace nervously inside him, looking for any tiny opening through which they could erupt full force. It was an opportunity that Lily would inevitably, albeit unwittingly, provide. After one of his blow-ups, Joe always issued a tearful apology, telling Lily how much he loved her and how terrified he was that she would leave him. When he was at his most vulnerable, Lily tried to get him to agree to seek help, but he always unequivocally refused. His professions of remorse eventually became cliché, just one more way for him to mark Lily with the scent of pity, binding her to him through guilt, confusing her enough to keep her firmly in her place.

"I know I said I would go," Lily told Donna that evening. "But I don't feel like it at all. I just want to put my pajamas on and stay in tonight."

"You'll do nothin' of the kind," said Donna. She dumped a package of chocolate chips into a large orange bowl, and mixed them into the dough. "If it weren't for church on Sunday, I don't think you'd ever even leave that house. We hardly see you at PTW anymore. We pray for you when you don't come because we get so worried. It's not healthy to be holed up alone with nothing to talk to but that computer and those crazy exercise ladies you play on your TV."

"It's just so much easier that way, Donna. I'm so sick of the fighting and the questions."

"Well now, he doesn't give you a hard time when you go to church and such, does he?"

"No, that's the only time I go out without getting the third degree anymore," said Lily. "I think he's afraid of pissing God off. But I don't know - I just don't really feel like it. I'm tired."

"You've been saying you're tired a lot lately - have you gone to the doctor?"

"Yeah, I went for that stomach thing I had. They didn't find anything wrong with me."

"You look like you've lost more weight. How's your tummy been?"

"OK. It comes and it goes. It mostly only bothers me when I eat."

"Havin' a sick tummy is a sign that you need to do somethin' that feeds your soul. As you can tell," said Donna, gesturing to the bowl cradled in her arms, "I'm feedin' my soul just fine." Donna scraped a glob of cookie dough from the wooden spoon with her finger and ate it. "Lily, the choir is perfect for you. Besides," she added, "Nikki's been looking forward all day to havin' the boys over tonight. I do not want to put up with the fit she will throw if I tell her they're not gonna come." She wiped the spoon on her apron, and then slapped it against Lily's rear end. "Now git."

Lily drove to church slowly, relishing the solitude of the car. The only time she really ever got to be alone these days was when Pierce was in preschool and she had the house to herself for a few hours. But even then, Joe was there - his presence always either implied or actual. Like a crazed Santa Claus watching your every move to see if you're naughty or nice. Or like God, making His notes for judgment day.

The Christ Covenant Church choir was a hodgepodge of singers comprised of "volunteer junkies" who compulsively signed up for everything - lonely widows and retirees who sought to avoid going home where they would be relegated to watching reruns of *Law and Order*, frustrated former high school drama geeks who never made it out of Gates, and worn out housewives who desperately needed an evening away from the unrelenting

287

demands of their children. Lily cringed at the recognition that she was one of them.

Jeffrey Crane, the choir director, was a willowy man about Lily's age who wore purple coloring in his closely cropped Afro. His skin was the color of milk chocolate and whenever Lily saw him perform during Sunday service, she wondered if his skin was as creamy as it looked, and fantasized about asking him if she could touch it. At first she worried that this was a manifestation of the kind of attraction between Christian brothers and sisters that Bethany always warned against, but Lily was relatively certain that even if she were interested in Jeffrey that way, he would not be interested in her. She was surprised to see that he wore a gold band on the ring finger of his left hand, and wondered who it was he was trying to fool.

Jeffrey's voice was thick and rich, and Lily loved the way he held himself when he sang, his chest slightly puffed up, his arms held away from his body, his hands clasped at chest level. He looked like every drawing of every angel that Lily had ever seen. Except for the dark skin. None of the drawings in the books of Lily's childhood ever depicted angels with dark skin and purple hair. Lily wondered if Jeffrey's mother had access to books that did - ones where Adam and Eve and Moses and Jesus and the angels looked at least something like he did, or if Jeffrey grew up thinking that when God said, "Let us make man in our image," He wasn't talking about Jeffrey.

"OK, everyone, enough of the chit-chat," announced Jeffrey with a sharp clap-clap of his hands. "Let's get settled, shall we?" Jeffrey smiled and waved at Lily by putting his hand up next to his cheek and wriggling his fingers. Lily smiled and wriggled her fingers back at him.

"Now," said Jeffrey," When I come to you, you tell me whether you are a bass, tenor, contralto, or soprano, OK? Then we will sort ourselves out and do our warm-ups."

All of the women said they were sopranos, except for Lily and two others - Janise, a young African-American woman who attended the nearby Wesleyan college, and a woman about Lily's age whom everyone called "Scooter." Lily loved the deep rich tones of the alto line and contended that the only reason the soprano part was so lovely was because the alto line provided it depth and character.

Most sopranos Lily knew were prima donnas, but as she looked to her right, she saw Cora from PTW, another older woman of about eighty who was adjusting her hearing aid, and a few women in their forties who seemed to know each other, but whom Lily did not recognize. Lily wondered how Jeffrey would get a solid soprano line out of the lot of them.

"I know how much you all love running the scales!" Jeffrey threw his arms up into the air in mock enthusiasm, putting on a show, behaving exactly as they expected and hoped he would - a curiosity of androgyny at the very least and a fascination of anomaly at most.

Jeffrey sat at the piano and struck a chord at the left end of the keyboard. "Mi mi mi mi mi mi mi..." He moved his fingers up one-half step on the piano keys and struck a second chord. "Mi mi mi mi mi mi mi," they all sang. Key by key, Jeffrey's chords moved up through the lower registers where the bass singers were the only ones who could be heard, to the midrange notes where Lily, Janise, and Scooter hung out with the tenors, to the higher end of the scale where the self-ascribed soprano section screeched and wailed, much to Jeffrey's dismay, judging from the wince on his face. Lily couldn't be sure, but she suspected that Cora was only moving her lips.

"OK, OK," said Jeffrey. "Let's see now." He folded his hands as if in prayer, and bowed his head, the tips of his index fingers touching the end of his broad nose. He sat silently for a few seconds and then with a smack of his mouth he raised his head, opened his eyes and separated his hands with his fingers spread apart, palms facing the choir, bracing them to hear his next amazing idea, which had probably just been handed down to him by God, or the Holy Spirit, or Jesus, or maybe even the Angel Gabriel, since he himself was a bit of a musician.

"Let's try something fun, shall we?" Jeffrey clapped his hands together and scanned the choir. "Lily, why don't you," he said, pointing his finger first at her with great exaggeration, "try taking a seat over there." He traced an imaginary arch with his fingertip from where Lily sat to the soprano section.

"And you," he said, pointing to Cora, and tracing an arch in the air back to the alto section. "Move over there."

"But I'm a soprano," said Cora.

Lily looked to Jeffrey expectantly, hoping he would think better of upsetting the status quo that they had constructed only minutes earlier, but to which they were already firmly attached. Cora probably hated the relative obscurity of singing the alto part as much as Lily hated swinging for the high notes.

"Oh, it's just for fun!" said Jeffrey, placing his hands at his hips. "I've chosen pieces that don't go all that high anyway, Cora... we'll bring you in when they get more challenging. I'm just dying to hear what it sounds like if we mix it up a little, OK?"

Cora and Lily looked at each other, and then at Jeffrey. "Oh, humor me!" he said, with a dismissive flourish of his hands.

One painstaking section at a time, Jeffrey took the choir through several measures of one of the songs he was planning for Easter vigil, and then had them all sing together while he accompanied on the piano. Even though their timing was clumsy and a few people missed notes along the way, Lily had to admit that the soprano section sounded better with her in it, and Cora's lip-synching didn't matter as much in the alto section, which Janise and Scooter enthusiastically carried.

After a few more takes, the passage sounded noticeably smoother and fuller, as individual singers gained comfort with their lines, becoming emboldened to sing in full voice, including Lily. The final time they went through it, Lily felt inspiration and joy bubble up from her core, reminding her of the way she once felt, used to feel, in the days when Dolores had convinced her that she would one day be a famous singer. The dark burdens of the day seemed a shade or two lighter, and as difficult as it had been to come, Donna had been right - the singing soothed Lily's agitated soul. She was disappointed when Jeffrey announced that they were out of time.

Lily walked leisurely out to her car, enjoying the snap of early spring air against her face.

"Lily - wait up!"

Lily turned to see Jeffrey approaching.

"Hey, Jeffrey."

"Hey yourself, girlfriend," he replied. "Why have you been hiding your voice from me all this time?"

"I haven't been hiding," said Lily. "I just never seemed to have time for choir."

"I haven't been this excited in years," said Jeffrey. He placed his hand on Lily's shoulder, pausing to first look to his right, and then his left, and then he leaned in toward Lily, cupping his left hand around the edge of his mouth, though there wasn't a soul in sight. "You didn't hear this from me," he said, "But our choir - well, our choir sucks."

"I don't know how much of a difference one voice is going to make."

"I only need one really fine voice to do a piece for the Easter Vigil that I've been simply dying to do. It's sort of a responsorial song with a part that's perfect for you - it's technically a soprano part, but I don't have a soprano who can do it. That's why I had to move you." Jeffrey drew a piece of paper that was sticking out from the thick folder of sheet music he carried with him everywhere, and handed it to Lily. "You will make me the happiest unpaid choir director on God's green earth if you tell me that you can sing this for the vigil."

Lily looked at the music. " 'Lift Me Up'... hmmm... I've never heard of it. It doesn't look liturgical; are you sure they'll let you do it?"

"Oh, please," said Jeffrey, dismissing Lily's concerns with the wave of his hand. "Read those lyrics! How is that *not* an Easter song? It's like a conversation between the risen Jesus and his people. I still get choked up whenever I read them."

Lily scanned the first verse. "It is beautiful." She looked up at Jeffrey. "Did you write this?"

"I wish!" he laughed. "I can sing and play the piano but I cannot write to save my life, which is why God made me so pretty." Jeffrey traced the arch of his eyebrow with his middle finger, and then laughed. "It was written by my friend Jackson. And listen," Jeffrey punctuated every other word by shaking his index finger at Lily. "I work with that bunch of tone deaf misfits from Thanksgiving to Easter and I don't get paid a dime." He rested his hand on his hip. "I figure I'm entitled to do one song just for me. Anyway, I'm not about to ask first. My motto is that it's better to ask forgiveness than permission. What are they going to do, fire me?"

Lily continued to read from the paper. "These lyrics are really amazing. And the range looks OK - except for this bridge."

"Don't worry about the bridge - you were practically hitting those same notes during warm-ups. Do you have a piano or anything at home that you can use to practice?"

"My old guitar is stashed away somewhere. I can probably dig it up." Lily hadn't sung in front of an audience since Iris' wedding. "I just need to check with my husband to make sure we don't have plans." She knew they didn't, but these days, it was easier to leave the escape hatch slightly ajar, in case Joe decided that a particular activity to which Lily had committed herself was inappropriate, or would inconvenience him too greatly. Or in case Lily just got too scared and needed a way out. It was also a reminder to herself not to get excited. Not yet.

Jeffrey removed the cap of a blue Bic pen with his teeth, and rummaged through his shoulder bag, pulling out a scrap of paper. He scribbled and handed the paper to Lily. "Call me ASAP and let me know - I'm so excited that I probably won't even be able to sleep tonight!"

The next week, Lily syphoned off enough money from the grocery bill to buy a new set of strings for her guitar, which she transferred from the attic to the back of her bedroom closet, taking it out to practice only when the boys and Joe were away from the house.

"Why don't you just do it while he's home, darlin'?" said

Donna. She set a Tupperware container of peanut butter cookies down on the table in front of Lily. "It seems so silly to hide something like that from him. It doesn't hurt anyone for you to be playin' that guitar."

"I haven't told him about the solo yet." Lily filled their mugs with coffee.

"Well, why not, for Heaven's sake?"

"I'm afraid he'll put me through the third degree - or ask me to explain why I'm doing it. I don't know why I want to sing. I just do." Lily tucked a tuft of hair behind her ear. "And if I don't tell him, he can't stop me."

"You don't need a reason to use the gifts that the good Lord gave you, Lily. The Bible says that we should not hide our light under a barrel. You've got to own up to it at some point, darlin'," said Donna, patting Lily's hand. "I'll pray for you - that you have the courage to let your amazin' light shine." Donna popped a cookie into her mouth, "And I believe that Joe will not stand in the way of God's plan for you."

The following Sunday, Joe and the boys were nestled in the family room watching basketball while sauce for Sunday dinner simmered on the stove. Lily was overcome with the urge to sing, a phenomenon that had occurred with increased regularity over the past few weeks. Her hands tingled for her guitar, and she craved her song in a way that reminded her of the way she craved a cigarette with her morning coffee. She stealthily retrieved her guitar from the closet and sat down cross-legged on the living room floor, her back against the couch, the sheet music on the floor in front of her. She strummed the introduction to the song, and then began singing softly, careful not to be distracting, bracing herself for Joe's response.

By the time she reached the end of the first chorus, Pierce appeared at the top of the family room stairs. He walked over to Lily. "What are you doing, Mommy?"

"I'm practicing," she said.

"What are you pacticing for?"

"They've asked Mommy to sing in church on Easter, so I'm

practicing my song."

"Oh." Pierce bent down and strummed the guitar. A smile broke out over his face. He turned and ran back downstairs. "She's pacticing a song, Daddy," Lily heard him say.

"A song?" Joe asked. "What kind of a song?"

"It's a church song," said Pierce. "And I played the guitar!"

Lily held her breath, waiting for a burst of anger, or inquiry, or both.

"Hey - Barbra Streisand!" Joe shouted. "When's dinner?"

Lily rehearsed every free moment she could find, each time expecting Joe to challenge her or mock her, but he didn't. Perhaps since Lily had been a singer before they had met, Joe accepted it as part of the package. Or maybe he simply didn't take it seriously enough to care. She also considered that Joe knew he had to give in to her at least once in awhile, because permission to do this could be used as a sort of a currency in an argument against allowing her to do something else - something more objectionable - in the future. If he allowed this, she wouldn't be able to claim that he didn't let her do anything outside the house. She could almost hear him shouting, "What about that time I let you sing in the choir at church?"

Of course, there was also the possibility that Joe appreciated Lily's talent, or that he thought it was sacred that she was singing in the service of the Lord. That one was a long shot, and if she'd learned one thing over the years, it was that long shots sometimes did win, but more often, they did not. Whatever the reason for Joe's acquiescence, Lily took it as a gift, and as Easter grew closer, her excitement mounted.

"Hi there," Donna called over from the backyard. "Are you nervous about tonight?"

"I don't know what is freaking me out more - singing the solo, or doing it in front of Joe." Easter and Christmas were the only times Joe even considered going to church, but that was Catholic Mass - she never thought she'd see him set foot in Christ Covenant Church. Lily didn't want to tell Donna that she wasn't exactly thrilled. CCC was Lily's place, her refuge, something that was just hers. Except for Donna, none of her church friends had ever even met Joe; Lily preferred it that way.

Lily stood up from her weeding, brushed the dirt from her hands and walked over to the fence. "I still can't believe he's coming."

"Now why are you so surprised?" said Donna. "We've been prayin' for him, haven't we? You've been prayin', I've been prayin', PTW has been prayin'. And after all, it is the season of redemption. That's what Jesus' message is all about. No one is too far gone so as to be out of the reach of God's love."

"I guess," said Lily. "But I'll believe it when I see it."

"O ye of little faith!" Donna laughed. "'Blessed are they who have not seen and yet believe.' Hey - I have to set up the refreshments before service. C'mon over at six - we can ride together."

"Mommy, I want to go with you!" Pierce stomped his foot and stood in front of the door, attempting to block Lily's way.

"Sweetheart, Mommy and Donna have to go early. But Daddy and you and Joseph are going to come right away, and I'll see you there, OK?" Lily picked Pierce up and gave him a kiss on the cheek. "Will you come and listen to Mommy sing? Will you?"

Lily turned to Joe. "The service starts at seven o'clock, Joe, but you'll need to get there early if you want to get a parking space."

"Am I going to have trouble parking the car? You didn't tell me it was gonna be crowded."

"Joe - it's Easter vigil at a Christian church - of course it's going to be crowded." Lily set Pierce back down. "But you know, if you don't feel comfortable coming, you don't have to come."

"Why don't you want me there?" Joe asked.

"I didn't say I didn't want you there," said Lily. "I just said that if you don't want to deal with the parking and handling the boys and everything, I understand."

"Oh, I'm coming," said Joe. "Don't you worry about that."

As the congregation stood for the opening hymn - led in unison by the choir - Lily scanned the sea of faces from her place on the risers at the front of the sanctuary, looking for Joe and the boys. She noticed Bethany's hair, towering a few inches above her husband's head. The couple was flanked by their two children, Jacob and Ruth. Lily also spotted a few of the women from PTW, most of whom waved at her as though she were their daughter in the school play. She smiled and nodded, recalling Jeffrey's admonition that when they were in their blue and white choir robes, they were more like clergy than congregants, and were expected to conduct themselves as such. Just as the opening hymn ended and Pastor Halloway emerged from the room behind the altar and took his place at the pulpit, the doors at the far end of the room opened, and Joe and the boys tumbled in. An usher rushed over to greet them and to help them find a seat.

Pastor Halloway delivered an impassioned sermon as dusk seeped in through the windows, but Lily couldn't stay focused on the message. Her excitement had dwindled, leaving anxiety in its wake. What if she forgot the words to her solo? What if she missed her cue and didn't come in at the right time? What if she couldn't hit that high note in the bridge? What if she opened her throat to sing and all that came out was the fear and self-recrimination she was feeling? Was she crazy? Why had she agreed to do this?

After the sermon, Pastor invited everyone to sit down while the ushers passed out small white candles, each one fitted with a cardboard collar to catch melting wax. Lily had a clear view of Joe and the boys, who were wedged in between an old woman dressed in purple and a young family with a daughter about Joseph's age. She and Joseph were pressed up against each other, both of them looking annoyed, but neither one trying to move away.

After the candles were distributed, the head usher lit his from the altar candle, and then used his flame to light the candles of all the other ushers. They in turn went to the head of each pew and the lit the candle of the person sitting on the aisle. That person passed their flame to the person sitting next to them. Soon, the room began to glow and flicker, a soft warmth filling the church. Lily was touched at the metaphor of all light coming from one source, illuminating all. The faces of the congregants were calm and peaceful, as though the glow of candlelight cast a magic spell that revealed only their innocence and their beauty. Lily looked around at them and was filled with love and compassion - for Bethany and her overzealous but passionate dedication to the cause of the Christian wife, for Donna and her love of cakes and cookies, for Jeffrey and the way he took his place within the community even though the community chose not to recognize him for who he was, for Joe and the boys, for all the nameless faces that were - at least for this small space in time - sharing life with her. Her anxiety waned as she realized that these were her people, her family. They were not here to judge her, and she was not here to perform. She was here to help them pray.

Jeffrey sat at the piano and nodded to the choir. Lily stepped forward, placing herself at the microphone stand in front of the risers where her fellow singers stood. She looked over at Jeffrey, who winked and smiled at her. He placed his fingers on the piano keys, bowed his head and closed his eyes briefly, then began to play. After two measures of music the room seemed to fall away as the choir hummed in four part harmony.

Except for the candles, the only light in the room was a shaft of dimmed track lighting that fell directly on Lily, casting a glow over her head, falling on her shoulders like a stole of gold.

Lily drew in a breath and sang.

"When you looked for me, tell me,
What did you see?
Were you all surprised to find
That I'd left my old self behind?

"If you look inside your souls
Let go of all you think you know
You'll find that you're a lot like me
Just speak the word in love and be set free

"Although you may not have all that it takes
To reach your dreams alone
With open heart and open arms
You'll feel my strength
Become your own..."

Lily stepped away from the mic and deferred to the choir as it raised its collective voice in four-part harmony.

"Lift me up, take me higher
Feel the power, feed the fire
Lift me high above the clouds
Up to a place where love is true
Lift me high enough to touch
The sun the stars the moon..."

Lily stepped back up into the spotlight, and sang alone,

"You hold the power in your hands
To touch what most don't understand
Just trust your heart,
You'll know just what to do..."

The choir joined in and sang with Lily on the final line of the chorus.

"Lift me up, I'm reaching out for you."

Lily caught her breath and stepped back from the microphone as the choir again picked up their humming. She felt carried away by the power of their collective tones, and was no longer thinking about forgetting the words or missing her cues, or hitting the high note in the bridge. It was as though she had disappeared into the music; it filled her head and her heart. It ran through her veins; her lungs swelled with it. No matter where she looked, she saw, heard, and felt only the music. She was drowning in it, succumbing to it, surrendering as the weight of her fears, of her sorrow, of her life, pulled her more deeply into the song and its message. She imagined Jesus in the Garden of Gethsemane and saw herself there with Him, praying with such fervor that blood burst through the pores of His skin, as He struggled to understand how He could possibly find the strength to complete the task God had set before Him. *Thy will, not my will be done.*

Lily was no longer singing the words for Jesus, as Jeffrey had instructed her - or for herself, even. Though she didn't understand how, she felt as though she were now singing the words *as* Jesus, having slipped inside His skin, feeling His pain, understanding His sacrifice, knowing His love.

"With all my will and all my might
Got the mountaintop within my sight
I will reach the finish cross the line,
The memory forever etched in time..."

By the time Lily reached the end of the bridge, tears were rolling freely down her cheeks, and Jeffrey stood up, gently sliding the piano music out from under the choir and with a grand gesture he invited the congregation to join in the chorus. The choir swayed to and fro, slowly clapping to keep time. The entire congregation joined in, many of them with their arms stretched overhead, as if they were reaching beyond the clouds to that place they sang of - a place where love is true. They sang:

"You hold the power in your hands,
To touch what most don't understand.
So trust your heart you'll know just what to do..."

Instinctively, Lily knew to wait patiently, as the choir voices faded and Jeffrey resumed his place on the piano bench, slipping his accompaniment back in under Lily. She stepped up to the mic, and looked out over the congregation. People were rapt in prayer, some crying, some simply looking forward, their gazes fixed on her. She noticed the man near the back of the room, sitting at the sound board. His face was lit by a small desk lamp. All she could see were his eyes, looking straight through her, boring holes in her. She closed her eyes. She wanted nothing to distract her from this moment.

"Lift me up," she sang, slowing the cadence of her words. "I'm reaching out .... for.... you."

The room fell silent. Lily stood, reluctant to open her eyes, afraid of breaking the spell, refusing to fall from the wave of the Spirit upon which she had been riding. A hand on her shoulder caused her to turn and open her eyes. She felt confused, lost, not knowing exactly where she was or what she was doing there. Jeffrey led her quietly to the pew where the rest of the choir was already sitting, as Pastor Halloway cleared his throat to deliver the closing blessing.

Lily suddenly remembered Joe and the boys. She looked over her right shoulder to see Joseph's head bobbing up and down over the heads of the adults seated in front of him, and when he caught Lily's eye, he waved furiously and called, "Hi, Mommy! Good singing!"

Everyone burst into laughter. Lily blew Joseph a kiss, then turned back around and offered a silent prayer of thanks.

After service, Lily slipped out of the sanctuary and down the corridor to the choir rehearsal hall to hang her choir robe up so she could exit through the side door and meet Joe in the parking lot, as promised.

"That was pretty amazing," said a voice.

Lily turned to find a man standing in the doorway. "Oh! You scared me!"

The man chuckled. "I'm so sorry; I didn't mean to startle you. It's just that I had to come and tell you what an incredible job you did with that song."

"I know you," said Lily. "You're the guy from the sound table, right?" His hair had looked blond in the light of the desk lamp under which he worked, but here it looked darker. Sandy brown, that's what it was. But his eyes still looked the same. Blue, penetrating.

"That's me," he said. He extended his hand. "I'm Owen. Owen Bateman."

Lily shook his hand. He placed his free hand over their handshake, clasping it, all the while looking Lily in the eyes. After what seemed like an excessively long time to be touching someone she'd just met a few seconds earlier, Lily pulled her hand away.

"Nice to meet you, Owen." Lily looked out the window of the back door to see if Joe was waiting there, but more importantly, to make sure he would not be able to see her standing there talking to a man. An attractive man. With sandy brown hair and blue eyes and who thought she'd done an incredible job.

"You're not the guy who usually does that," said Lily.

"No - you're right, I'm not. I own the studio that leases the equipment and the sound guys, but this is Easter weekend - one of our busiest, so all hands on deck." Owen shoved his hands into his pockets. "Where did you get that song, if you don't mind my asking?"

"Um - you'd have to ask Jeffrey, really... a friend of his wrote it - Jack someone, I think he said."

"Beautiful tune."

Lily took her jacket from the closet and slipped her right hand in, shortly thereafter realizing she had slipped it into the left sleeve.

"Here, let me help you with that," said Owen. He flashed a smile as he helped her out of the coat.

"I am such an idiot," said Lily. She felt her face flush with embarrassment.

"You shouldn't talk like that about yourself." Owen repositioned the jacket as Lily slipped her arms into their proper holes, all the while continuing to watch out the window. "Or I won't invite you to come to my studio and record sometime."

A set of headlights appeared outside the window. "Shit!" said Lily.

"That's not a very gracious response," said Owen, tracing Lily's gaze out to the car.

"What?" said Lily. She flung her purse over her shoulder and closed the closet door. "I'm sorry - I gotta go."

"Tell me you'll think about it," said Owen. He pulled his wallet from the back pocket of his khakis and extracted a business card.

"Think about what?" A car horn sounded. "I really gotta go," said Lily.

Owen tucked the card into the pocket of Lily's purse as she opened the door and rushed out.

"Hey you guys!" said Lily to the boys as she buckled her seat belt.

"Yay for Mommy!" cheered Joseph.

"Yeah!" echoed Pierce. "Yay Mommy!"

"You boys were so good in church," Lily said. "I bet the Easter bunny is going to bring you lots and lots of candy in the morning."

"Yay!" they both cried.

Joe's silence as they drove made Lily uneasy. She would love it if he said she did a good job. She could understand it if he said she was awful. But she couldn't bear that he said nothing at all. At last they pulled into the driveway, and the boys scrambled out of their restraints and ran toward the house. Lily opened her car door and gathered her purse, her church program, and her vigil candle. Joe reached out and placed his hand on her shoulder, holding her from getting out of the car.

"Hey - Lil," he said.

"What?"

"You were pretty amazing," he said. "I was really impressed."

"Really?" said Lily. Something registered on his face. Lily couldn't quite place it, but he didn't look impressed; he didn't bear the expression of one who was amazed.

"Really." Joe looked at her and this time she recognized it - he had the look on his face that he had when he'd told her about the time his parents left him at the amusement park. A chill ran up her spine.

"Let's go inside," she said. "You can start a fire, I'll make some popcorn..."

"You go ahead," he told her. "I'm gonna go see if I can catch the last few races at OTB."

"Really, Joe? Tonight? It's been such a lovely family time. I know the boys would love to have a fire - it might be our last chance to have one now that spring is here."

"Goddammit, Lil," Joe pounded his hands against the steering wheel. "Why are you laying this guilt trip on me? I just spent two hours babysitting and sitting through a whole Mass and now I want a little time to myself. Is that so hard for you to understand?!"

Lily's throat burned as she choked back tears, watching her fantasy of an evening at home, basking in the warmth of the vigil and the magic it inspired in her, drive away into the night. She fell asleep waiting for Joe's return, her tears dampening the pillow sham.

Lily was awakened at sunrise by a familiar sound outside the window. It was coming from the back yard, and in her sleepy stupor, Lily struggled to place it. She stumbled downstairs in her flannel nightgown and discovered that Joe was furiously clipping back the branches of her tree.

She slid the patio doors open. "Joe, what are you doing?"

"Son of a bitch! No matter what I do to this tree, it keeps growing back," he said. "No matter what I do. Pisses me off."

Alarmed by his behavior, but still groggy from sleep, Lily attempted to reason with him. "I thought we agreed that I would take care of doing the pruning from now on - remember?"

"Well, you're not taking care of shit," said Joe. "It never grows higher, it just gets wilder."

"That's what trees do, Joe," said Lily. "Just leave it."

"What kind of tree is it, anyway?" he asked.

"I don't know, exactly," said Lily, folding her arms across her chest against the morning chill. "Some kind of a willow, I think. But that's how they are - you know - willowy. Free spirited. It's beautiful."

"It's a pain in my ass, that's what it is," said Joe.

Donna's back door opened and she peeked her head out.

"Joe, c'mon," Lily said. "It's Easter - the boys will be up soon. Let's just deal with this another time, OK?"

"Just give me five more minutes," said Joe.

Lily closed the door, unwilling to challenge him at such a delicate time of day, when an argument outside would surely draw the attention of the neighbors - more so than it had already. She switched on the coffee maker and placed a teaspoon of sugar into the bottoms of two mugs. Half an hour later, Joe came in from the backyard, his face red and sweaty, his demeanor one of exhilaration.

Lily peered outside to see huge mounds of branches lying under the tree, her bird feeders entangled in them. She reached back and pulled the elastic out of her ponytail, letting her hair fall down across her shoulders. *It will grow back*, she reminded herself as she fought tears.

"What - are you going to cry now?" Joe said. "It had to be done. Don't go getting all emotional; you'll ruin Easter for the boys." Joe took a gulp of coffee. "I'll have someone come out and clean up the mess tomorrow. I need a shower."

Two days later, a truck pulled into Lily's driveway and three men got out. They retrieved a chainsaw and some rope from the back of the truck. One of the men slung a coil of rope crosswise over his shoulder and climbed the tree.

Frantic, Lily punched in Joe's work number on the telephone.

"La Casa Bella, where your beautiful home is our business. This is Joe Diotallevi speaking."

"Joe - what's going on? There are two guys up in the tree."

"Oh, good - I was hoping they'd show up early. Yeah, they're going to start taking it down."

"What do you mean? Why?"

"Well, I was talking to the guys here at work and they said that a tree like that seeks water and having it close to the house is asking for trouble, so I decided to cut it down."

"But it's not causing any trouble. There's plenty of room for it to grow."

"I don't want it to keep growing. Anyways, I already paid those guys, Lil. I won't be able to get my money back now."

In the background, Lily heard the switchboard operator over the house speakers. "Joe - sales call on line two ... Joe - sales call on line two."

"Gotta go." Joe hung up, as the deafening grinding of metal against wood drowned out Lily's sobs.

Lily placed a carafe of fresh coffee and a set of mugs on a tray, and brought it out to the men. They stopped for five minutes to pour themselves a cup. One of them lit up a cigarette while the other one sat on the ground, leaning his back against the tree's trunk, wiping the sweat from his brow with a red and white bandana.

The men stacked the remains of the tree at the curb. Lily steeled herself as she looked out the kitchen window. All that was left of her tree was the stump. She slid the patio doors open, and stepped out into the fresh April air. At least it was a place to sit and recall the cardinals that came to feed there, and the mourning doves that groaned in the cool sunrise. All was not lost.

"Excuse me - I'm gonna need to get at that." Lily looked up to find a white-haired man toting a huge mechanical steel rod. Lily got up from the stump and backed away. The man positioned the rod at the base of the trunk. His body convulsed as he bored the machine into the dark soil, grinding the stump into mulch. When he was finished, he hoisted his pants, got in his truck, and drove away.

15. IRIS

"Perfetto! Now turn around and walk back toward me. Take it real slow this time, OK?"

Iris pivoted on her heels and reversed her course, concentrating on moving in slow motion without looking stiff. She had always been more of a sprinter than a stroller, and felt awkward walking at such a slow pace.

"Like this?" she asked, making an effort to control the impatient twitching in her long limbs as she walked across the hotel terrace in the soft light of the early evening.

"Shhh. Don't talk! Just walk, that's it, keep it fluid! Great. Got it!"

The man behind the camera stopped recording, stood up straight, one hand on the small of his back, and stretched. When he finished working the kinks out of his joints, he crossed his arms and stared point-blank at Iris. Seeing his eyes focused directly on her without the camera lens between them made feel her uncomfortable, as if her blouse had unbuttoned itself, her skirt unzipped itself, and both had fallen from her body, landing in a puddle of fabric at her feet. She was annoyed at the blush she could feel coloring her cheeks, especially since it apparently amused the man. He grinned at her and said, *"Signora* Capotosti, you're a natural."

"Really? Did I do all right?" Iris said, more flustered than flattered.

"Better than all right. Come and take a look." The man touched a command on his video camera and bent close to her, sharing a view of the playback on the display screen. He was several inches taller than Iris, and had to crouch to lower his head to the same level as hers. Leaning toward him, she noticed that his thick, shoulder-length hair smelled of the citrus shampoo she had selected for the hotel bathrooms. She could also detect a hint of musk, probably the remnants of a cologne he had splashed on his face after shaving early that morning before the sunrise shoot down at the marina in Portofino. Tufts of whiskers scattered randomly on his throat and jaw like cacti in the desert suggested he had performed the task hastily. By this hour, those subtle, fresh scents were challenged by the acrid aroma of a man who had been working under the sun all day. There was something both familiar and foreign in the odor, something overwhelmingly masculine, something that made her want to stay close enough long enough to decide whether it repulsed her or attracted her.

"See?" he said, enlarging the view of a miniature Iris moving across the display. "I caught it."

"Caught what?" Iris moved a few inches closer to look, to sniff.

"The contrast."

"What do you mean? What contrast?"

"I mean, when I looked through the lens at you, I was knocked flat on my ass by the insecure wild child I saw trapped under the *Direttrice*'s veneer of sophistication." He looked down as he spoke, his attention focused on the camera.

"You saw that?" Iris wanted him to look at her, to tell her more about what he saw, to replay the video and point out what gestures or expressions were still giving her away after so many years of practice. Despite her intimacy with Claudio Olona, she had never felt herself scrutinized with such intensity. Like most Italians, Claudio was a xenophile, and his interest in her background had been limited to the fact that she was American. In a way, she had been relieved at his lack of curiosity, as she would have felt uncomfortable talking about her upbringing in the chaotic Capotosti family to a man of such privileged provenance, and she certainly had never had any desire to talk to him about her marriage. And now, here was this guy who barely knew her, prying her open like a can of sweet corn.

"Shit, yeah," the man replied, finally looking up at her. His eyes were dark, the pupils barely distinguishable from the irises. "Like the contradiction I see in your face right now."

Iris waited for him to go on. He didn't.

"What contradiction?" she asked, at last, nervously. She was intrigued, though slightly perturbed by his disregard for the boundaries of their relationship. She had learned it was best for a woman in her position to keep her guard up at all times: cordiality was fine, as long as it remained professional. She constantly had to remind herself not to smile so much, not to act so interested in the people she met, not to get so personally involved in resolving their problems or satisfying their requests. Striking a balance was not an easy task when hospitality was your business, but it was absolutely necessary, especially when dealing with men, who were all too ready to mistake her kindness for an invitation to flirt, or worse. She had no intention of getting entangled in any banter that could open the floodgate to dangerous waters; once had been more than enough. All she wanted to know from this man was what he meant by his comment; she was curious, that was all.

"What do you mean?" she asked, again.

"I mean the smile. It doesn't match."

"Match what?" Iris asked.

"Maxie!" A short, bleached-blond woman in her twenties tottered over to them on stiletto heels, her well-padded hips jiggling as she wobbled along the irregular garden path. Iris wondered how this person, Rosina or Rosanna or something like that, who had been referred to in correspondence from RAI television as the "*assistente di produzione*," could assist anyone, with her movements so hindered by those vertiginous heels and the short leather skirt that sheathed her hips, binding her thighs together. At least while she was standing, anyway.

"We got a wrap, Maxie? Can I tell the guys to pack it up?"

Though Iris was irritated by the interruption, she was relieved to hear the words; she couldn't wait for the guys to pack it up. During the three days in which Massimiliano Vanesi had been filming at the Dimora Baia dell'Incanto, he had brought nothing but disruption to Iris and her hotel. Through some complex process of selection involving the Italian State Tourist Board, the State-owned, taxpayer-supported RAI Television, and a number of public and private sponsors, the Dimora was to be featured in one of a series of short videos promoting tourist destinations in each of Italy's twenty regions. When the RAI logistics office had called Iris from Rome to set up the Portofino film shoot, they said there would be a small crew, and assured her that discretion was their highest priority: they would in no way be invasive or compromise the guests' privacy. She had been hesitant to give her consent, but was convinced of the excellent marketing opportunity when she was told that in exchange for complimentary accommodations, the Dimora would be featured, at no cost to the hotel, in a video that would be seen by millions of viewers.

The hotel's opening had gone well, but she knew that was just the beginning: novelty wore off quickly, competition was stiff, tourists were fickle, and it took time to build up a solid base of faithful clientele. She hoped the initiative would pay off in the long-term, but in the short-term its effects had only been the source of trouble. What had started out as a three-man crew ballooned into a three-ring circus with astonishing rapidity, and as all circuses Iris had ever seen, their antics made her want to cry rather than laugh. Within hours, the camera man Vanesi, the sound man and the director were joined by four others who tumbled out of a white van with a blue RAI logo, smoking and shouting in crass Roman accents into the cell phones pressed against their ears. Shiny aluminum cases of equipment were unloaded, spotlights mounted on tripods, thick black cables snaked along the pavement of the terrace, dining room and lounge. The crew in the van had lodgings in Rapallo, but came and went at all hours of the day and night, enjoying long breaks at the bar, guzzling espressos and drinks without paying or specifying to whose account they should be billed. The blond assistant, who signed her tabs with Vanesi's name and room number, was an exception. According to the information Iris gleaned from the *voci di corridoio*, the reliable "corridor voices" of her staff, the young woman preferred to shed her skimpy garments in Vanesi's room, rather than in her accommodations in Rapallo.

Thank God it was over now. In those three days, Iris had been barraged with enough complaints from the hotel guests to last the rest of her career, which might well be short-lived, considering the incessant ranting of *Signora* Mangiagallo, who was as horrified at the behavior of such vulgar people, as if they had pulled down their pants and defecated on the cushions of the creamy white Alcantara sofas tastefully arranged in the lounge. In order to placate the owner, Iris had approached the director about letting her son and his boyfriend appear in a scene of the video. After nodding noncommittally, he answered his constantly ringing cell phone, and began ranting at whoever was on the other end of the line. Vanesi, overhearing the conversation, stepped in and told Iris he would take care of it, adding that the director was the last person she should talk to if she wanted to get anything done. Now, if only Romina or Rosita or whatever the heck her name was would get lost, Vanesi could finish what he had been saying to her about her smile, then leave.

"So, Maxie? Are we packing up?"

Vanesi eyed the blond, who had stepped between Iris and him and stood there with her arms crossed just below her bosom, artfully boosting her breasts up and out of her low-cut top with her clenched fists.

"What the fuck are you waiting for? We had a wrap an hour ago," he said. "I told you I was shooting this segment on my own. It's a personal thing, to thank the *Direttrice* here for her cooperation."

"*Va bene, va bene!*" she said, looking offended. "I get it, OK? Next time try saying what you mean. For once."

"Next time, try listening," Vanesi said. "For once."

The woman took a deep breath as if preparing to say something else, then apparently thought the better of it and employed the air in her lungs to thrust out her chest as she strutted away, hips jerking, heels clicking.

"*Cretina*," Vanesi muttered. He turned to Iris and smiled. "Excuse me, you were saying?"

"I wasn't saying anything. You were. Something about my smile? About it not matching?"

"Right," he answered. "Not matching your eyes."

"What do you mean?" she asked, a third time. Maybe the blond woman was right, maybe this man made a habit of not saying what he meant. "What about my eyes?"

"There's sadness trapped inside."

"How can you say that? You don't even know me."

"Right," he said. "Forget I ever said anything." He waved one of the guys over, gesturing for him to dismantle and pack away his equipment.

"Are you finished?" She could kick herself for letting him bait her.

"Yep, I'll be checking out early tomorrow morning," he said. "Mind if I ask you something?"

"By all means, *Signor* Vanesi," Iris said, hoping her formal tone would stave off any other gratuitous personal considerations.

"How about having a drink together, so we can talk about your eyes and smile some more?" he asked. Now it was his smile that did not match his eyes; the former was engaging and playful, the latter probing and lascivious.

"I'm afraid that won't be possible. It's late, and I have to take my sad eyes home," Iris said. "But it's been a pleasure having you at the Dimora." She extended her hand. Vanesi took it in his, and shook it slowly. His palm was warm and moist, his fingers long, though plump, more like those of a trumpet player than of a pianist. Iris turned and walked away.

She felt jittery as she backed her car out of its usual parking space, and kept looking in the rearview mirror to navigate clear of a palm tree she had effortlessly avoided for months. Each time she glimpsed the reflection of her eyes in the mirror, she looked away quickly, feeling like a peeping tom caught spying on herself. She threw the gearstick into first, headed for the exit and coasted down the hill to the Via Aurelia, where she made a sharp left turn, while tugging on her uncooperative seat belt which had mysteriously become too short to buckle. The little car swerved as she fumbled with a series of buttons to open the windows and sunroof with a whirring noise, letting in a rush of fresh evening air. She rummaged through her oversize handbag for the cigarettes she had bought the previous week just in case she should feel the need for an occasional smoke, which she did. She fished one out of the half-empty, crushed pack, pushed in the cigarette lighter, turned on the CD player, pulled out the lighter, touched the glowing metal to the end of the wrinkled cigarette dangling from her mouth, and drew on it. Wisps of smoke leaked from tears in the paper.

BeeeEEEEeeeep! An oncoming car blared its horn as it passed Iris in a blur of metal, shouted insults and furious gesticulations. She veered sharply to the right, returning her car to its proper lane just in time to avoid being sideswiped. Cigarette clenched between her lips, she grasped the wheel tightly to stop her hands from shaking, cursing herself for being in such a goddamn rush to leave the hotel and Vanesi behind her that she couldn't take a minute to compose herself and prepare for the ride home.

Iris always looked forward to her to drive to and from work, a brief quarter of an hour in which she could savor a slice of solitude, as she cruised up and down the hills, suspended between the duties of work and the obligations of home. She much preferred the sense of freedom and convenience of the scooter as opposed to the confinement and bulk of automobiles, but had grown tired of Gregorio repeating that she was no longer a teenager, and that women her age didn't drive Vespas in the dark or cold or rain. She had finally caved into his insistence and agreed to letting him buy her a car - as long as he didn't expect her to drive a white station wagon, ever again.

Between shifting the peppy five-speed four-cylinder Fiat

Seicento as she drove up and down the rolling coastal road, she used her right hand to free her hair from its ponytail, while her left managed the wheel and her cigarette. Her curly locks were sucked through the open top, and whipped madly about her face, its ends sticking to the gobs of lip gloss she had applied for the video Vanesi had shot of her. Embarrassment warmed her cheeks at the thought of such futile vanity.

There were advantages to driving a car, though, like it being slightly more difficult for a moment's distraction to get you killed, and the opportunity to have a smoke in peace while listening to some music, without worrying about the noise bothering anyone. Singing in the car soothed her jangled nerves and freed her cluttered mind, chasing away thoughts of work as she drove home, and of home as she drove to work. She fast-forwarded to "Ruby Tuesday" but had replayed the old Stones CD so many times, and there were so many bumps and potholes in the road as she bounced along in her little car with its rudimentary suspensions, that it kept skipping. She ejected the CD and continued singing on her own.

Her voice rose with the chorus, lowered with the verses, disappearing under the sounds of the wind and the traffic. Mouthing the words she knew so well, she glanced at her face in the rearview mirror, looked back down at the road, looked back up at the mirror. What had the man seen in her eyes, anyway? From the very first phone call he had made to Iris to inform her of his requirements, Vanesi's attitude had provoked conflicting reactions in her, and now that he was leaving, she still hadn't figured out why.

"*Che bella voce,*" he had commented during their first conversation. "I'm curious. Where does that accent come from?"

"It's American." Everyone always asked her the same question.

"But you speak perfect Italian."

"Thank you for saying so. I've been living here for a long time." That was the answer she gave everyone.

"How did you end up on this side of the Atlantic?"

More of the usual cross-examination. There was no need to

mention anything about a fairytale romance, or that a "long time" translated to a twenty-year-marriage, an unnecessary detail that would certainly lead the man to assume she was older and more boring than she would like to think. Not that there was any special reason for her to worry about what he thought, no more than she always worried about what anyone else thought.

"A series of reasons, I'd say," was her reply. "You could call it fate, I guess."

"Well, *complimenti*," he had said. "I look forward to meeting you next week."

"Thank you," Iris had said. "It will be a pleasure. *A presto.*"

After hanging up the phone, she had jotted down some notes for the receptionist to type up for the housekeeping and restaurant staff, instructing them to offer whatever assistance Massimiliano Vanesi would require. As she mentally reviewed their conversation, she could hear his voice outlining his plans, dictating his list of requirements, telling her that his instructions superseded any she may or may not have received from the director. The blunt way in which he asked for things, his language and phone manner slaloming between authoritative, flirtatious and manipulative, combined with the inflection of his voice with its not-quite-Roman accent, had her responding with accommodating expressions like *"nessun problema"* and *"assolutamente,"* though with all the work she had to do, a film shoot on the hotel premises was a complication she could live without.

Downshifting to second gear to climb the final few kilometers of the winding road home, she told herself she had every reason to be relieved that the shoot was over. Gone would be Massimiliano Vanesi and his crew. Gone would be the rude shouts shattering the silence of the refined atmosphere Iris had worked so hard to create, and with them the stinking cigarette butts that filled every available ashtray, and stood half-buried in the soil of the potted plants. Gone would be her struggles with bellhops and maids, receptionists and waiters, who instead of doing their jobs strutted about in the hope of being spotted and asked to appear in the film. Gone would be the thrill in her bones and the buzz in the air as she witnessed the spaces she inhabited daily being transformed into sets for a film that would be seen by millions of people, if she could believe what the people at RAI said.

"*Pronto,*" Iris said, punching a button to activate the speakerphone.

"How many?" cackled the raspy voice at the other end of the line. Iris was struck by the permutations of negativity the woman could compress into three syllables. *Signora* Mangiagallo could probably hold a chunk of Parmesan in her hand and watch the cheese flurry down to her plate of spaghetti, grated to perfection, by merely talking to it.

"*Buongiorno, Signora,*" Iris answered, determined to maintain a courteous attitude toward the owner. Beatrix had warned her that the woman had never had a pleasant character, and was sometimes downright ornery, but she was confident that Iris, being so even-tempered and diplomatic, would know exactly how to deal with it. Iris had been brought up to respect the elderly, and in fact had actually enjoyed being around her grandparents and other old people as a child, but now she wondered whether age alone was a quality worthy of respect. For what reason should a person who had been selfish and mean his or her whole life suddenly merit deferential treatment?

From the bedroom window of her villa located in the park above the hotel, *Signora* Mangiagallo could see Iris arrive, and invariably phoned her before she could settle in at her desk. She pressed Iris for information and statistics she did not know how to interpret, screamed complaints in her ear about the staff member she had targeted for persecution that day, and drilled her as to the whereabouts of her grown son, as if Iris were his nanny. Reaching for the stack of papers already awaiting her attention, Iris could picture the woman up in her villa being served breakfast in bed, a night's worth of spittle caked at the perennially downturned corners of her thin-lipped mouth. As Iris rifled through the papers, her attention was caught by the bold black handwriting sprawled across a sheet of hotel stationery. No doubt another complaint by a guest who had been disturbed by the crew, she thought, tossing the sheet aside to be dealt with later. First she had to get the *Signora* off her back; then, get a cup of coffee. She began sifting hurriedly through the stack, searching for the previous day's production statistics. The night auditor had standing instructions to leave the printout on her desk before going off duty, but for the second time that week, it was not there. She flipped the switch on her computer so she could retrieve the data directly from the property management system, then drummed her fingers impatiently on her desk as she waited for it to boot up.

Iris was in no mood for the shrew this morning; she had dozed only fitfully, her sleep having been interrupted by a series of disturbing dreams. She had awoken to the sound of the phone jangling, and the voice of Isabella reminding her that she was upstairs waiting for her injection of vitamin B12 as part of a "reconstitutional" remedy for the lethargy she had been experiencing of late. Isabella did not think it proper to bare her backside to her son, even if he was a doctor, and Cinzia had proven to be too heavy-handed for the job; using an orange for practice, Gregorio had taught Iris how to give the injection, leaving her with a new skill and a distasteful association between a fruit she loved and the shriveled buttocks of her mother-in-law.

Iris blinked her bleary eyes at the computer screen, logged in, selected the desired option from the main menu, then typed in the previous day's date.

"Twenty-five, *Signora*," Iris reported.

"Is that all? Twenty-five?" *Signora* Mangiagallo shrieked into the phone.

"That's quite good for a Thursday night," Iris replied, tapping into another function on the computer as she spoke.

"We have twenty-four double rooms, so if everyone is doing their job, in particular the manager, we should have forty-eight guests, correct?" *Signora* Mangiagallo said.

"But we had sixteen rooms occupied, and each was charged the full maximum rate for a suite. We are pulling in an excellent average daily rate." Iris was weary of trying to explain that obtaining the same production by having fewer beds occupied at a higher rate was actually preferable to having more beds occupied at a lower rate. "The week after Easter rush is always a little slow, *Signora*."

"Don't go trying to talk circles around me, Iris. You always want to have the last word." *Signora* Mangiagallo hung up without saying goodbye. Iris sighed, rubbed her throbbing temples, and reminded herself it was nothing personal, that she shouldn't allow her feelings to be hurt if the woman mistreated her; it was just a job. Still, she wished she were working for someone she could admire, or at least respect on a professional level, someone like Claudio, who had taught her everything she knew. Maybe she shouldn't have been so ambitious; the sense of accomplishment she had experienced at becoming the only female general manager in the Riviera was wearing off. So was the relief she had experienced when she had ended their affair before it could end her marriage, but by now, that was ancient history.

Iris stared at her desk, searching for enough motivation to begin the day's work. She would make the rounds first, inspect the premises, check on the staff, greet any guests she encountered. And get that cup of coffee. A nice *doppio espresso* should straighten her out. As she tidied up the papers scattered about her desk, her eyes wandered to the note she had set aside.

cara signora capotosti (can't I just call you iris you can't be much older than me) too bad you didn't stay for that drink last night you were very cruel leaving me on that terrace all by myself to stare at the moon i wanted to call you to tell you to look at how beautiful it was but the guy at the desk wouldn't give me your number. i also wanted to say the breeze reminded me of your breath on my neck when we were hunched over the camera. strange how it could feel so warm, but still make me shiver. was hoping to catch you for a cappuccino this morning but i have to hit the road. i'll send you

some stills when I get back to my studio.
pax, max
p.s. take care of those pretty eyes

Iris scanned the jumble of words a second time, knowing she should be indignant, yet was not quite convinced that the thought of him noticing the feel of her breath on his neck, and being affected by it, actually bothered her. She imagined Vanesi standing at the front desk in his cargo pants and multi-pocketed vest worn over a crumpled shirt with rolled-up sleeves, a gauze foulard looped around his neck (she had seen him use it more than once to wipe off a camera lens), his paraphernalia piled on the floor next to his sneaker-clad feet. He had probably borrowed the felt-tip pen he used to write the note from the receptionist, then he must have handed it over with his room key. The clod hadn't even been courteous enough to put the note in an envelope, or given a thought to the fact that anyone at the front desk could have read it. She could picture him as he left, slinging his backpack over his shoulder and striding out the door like an adventurer, waving aside the porter who trailed behind in hopes of a tip. He might have looked around one last time, as the guys finished loading the equipment into the RAI van and decided the light was too perfect to resist shooting one final scene. She could hear him cajoling the reluctant crew back out of the van and into action. She could see him waving to them when they finished, slamming the car door, starting the engine, pulling out and driving down the hill to the Via Aurelia, heading for his next assignment, who knew where, or for a weekend of fun in the exciting company of who knew who.

Tucking the note away in her drawer where it would be safe from indiscreet eyes, she selected another function on her computer, and typed:

VANESI (enter)

Three names appeared:

VANESI GLORIA

VANESI MASSIMILIANO

VANESI TOMMASO

She placed the cursor over the second name, hit "enter" again. Green letters pulsated against a black background, while her eyes darted over the registration record, pausing at the date of birth (he was almost three years younger than she), then the place of birth (Frosinone), then the place of residence (Rome), complete with address. The guy thought he knew so much about her; well, now she knew a few things about him, too. Possessing the power to retrieve his personal data by tapping a few commands on the keyboard made her feel in control, helped quell the sense of intrusion she had not been able to shake since the previous evening, when he had stared at her so intensely and made those inappropriate comments. Knowing when he had been born and where he lived made them even, in a way. If she wanted to, which of course she didn't, she could probably find out all other kinds of information about him on the Internet. He had said he worked as a freelance, so maybe he even had a website of his own. But why should she be interested? Hadn't she been disturbed by his probing eyes and comments, and relieved to say goodbye? What did it change if he recalled the feel of her breath on his neck, the way she recalled the peculiar scent of his nearness, and the odd way it had stirred her? There must be something seriously wrong with her if she was even thinking about him.

She opened her drawer, and extracted the note. The tactile sensation impressed upon her fingertips by the few grams of processed pulp was barely perceptible. She noted the childish script without reading the words again, then brought it to her nose and sniffed, but the only lingering scent was that of marker ink. She imagined Massimiliano Vanesi - "Max" as he had signed his note - sitting on the terrace after she had gone home. She wondered what he would drink. Probably a beer. Had she been there with him, she would have had an Americano; the barman made a fantastic one, with just the right balance of vermouth, bitters and soda water. She would have had the waiter bring them some sage focaccia, cut into little squares they could nibble on as they talked, and some chunks of Parmesan. And some olives, the little black ones from Imperia. She thought back to the previous evening, to what she had been doing when Vanesi would have been thinking of her as he sipped his beer.

She would have been driving home, her throat tightening so that she could not sing the final verse to "Ruby Tuesday." She would have been blinking back tears as she searched for another CD, her fingers fumbling to pry open the plastic case. While Max listened to the sea splashing against the rocks below, she would have been listening to the banjo of Béla Fleck leading the mandolin and fiddle and Dobro in poignant concert, as the strings of her aching heart were plucked and bent and strummed, her most private pain surging and swirling around her on the notes of "The Lights of Home." As Max contemplated the brightening moon in the darkening sky, she would have been pulling up the drive, switching off the engine, and finishing her second cigarette, wishing the song would never end. He may have been ordering a second drink just then, and she would have been hitting the replay button, and lighting a third cigarette off the butt of the previous one.

She couldn't remember exactly how long she had sat there, embracing her melancholy, while the ever-changing sky made each second seem shorter and more sharply defined than at any other time of the day. An ephemeral display of pinks and oranges and violets had glowed fiercely, then faded to nothingness, while Iris remained motionless, allowing a blanket of darkness to tuck itself around her. She had reclined her seatback, and looking through the open sunroof, had singled out one, then two, then a sprinkling of stars twinkling in the twilight, thinking how strange it was, knowing they were always out there somewhere, but could not be seen until the light of day faded. Then she had turned her head to regard the windows of the dark villa, wishing she could feel for this aesthetically pleasing conglomerate of stone and plaster even a fraction of the emotions Béla's music stirred in her.

It had grown late. She knew she couldn't sit in the car smoking all night, but the scenes she imagined on the other side of the windows pinned her to her seat. Bluish tones flickering from

Isabella's living room window suggested that Gregorio was upstairs dining with his mother; he had recently told Iris that if she couldn't be home by the eight o'clock news, which, as she well knew, he enjoyed watching during dinner, he wouldn't wait for her to eat. As she sat there, she pictured Gregorio and his mother, each balancing a tray on their knees, their jaws grinding to the dictates of proper mastication, their eyes and ears trained on the newsman who relayed the day's atrocities in his priest-like drone. They did not seem to mind the anchorman's swarthy complexion, his beady black eyes, the brown mole on his flaccid cheek, the jowls that jiggled as he spoke, his oily hair spread thin over a bumpy scalp. Iris had always thought the man looked like a crooked undertaker who relished his role, one who derived a morbid sort of pleasure in knowing that despite his respectable attire, his aspect instilled distrust in those who saw him, and despite its evenly modulated tone and a language of carefully chosen euphemisms, his voice conveyed more horror than reassurance.

As Iris had listened to the song one last time, a chorus of "if onlys" echoed in the deserted halls of her heart. If only on the other side of those windows she could pick out the shapely silhouette of a teenage girl pacing to and fro, her chin held high, her lips moving as she rehearsed a song, the way Lily used to. If only she could make out the images of a boisterous group of people jostling one another into place around a long table, suppressing giggles as their father led them in prayer. If only she could watch heads as lovely as those of Violet and Jasmine being tossed back in laughter, unleashing long, thick manes of hair. If only she could perceive through the shadows the insuppressible enthusiasm of Marguerite gesticulating animatedly, determined to make her point. If only she could steal a closer peek, and see a woman of ageless beauty silently drift into view, bearing a huge pot of steaming stew with dumplings and setting it on the table, her fair skin flushed from the heat of the kitchen. If only she could glimpse a squat, buxom woman wobbling over to the window, peering out into the darkness, and clapping her hands when she saw Iris arrive. If only she could switch off the wretched blue flickering and switch on the bright lights of home.

.

16. LILY

The Sunday after Easter, Lily noticed that Owen was operating the sound board; she hadn't realized how much she'd been hoping he would be. He was wearing a headset, adjusting levers and buttons, his glasses on the table next to a half drunk glass of water. Since the choir only performed on special occasions, Lily sat in a pew, wedged anonymously among families and old folks, having opted to allow the boys to stay home, under the unconscious guise that she would get more out of the service. Lily had to turn around in order to catch sight of Owen, and while she expressly told herself not to - reminding herself that it would be too obvious - she found that she couldn't help but glance over her shoulder several times throughout the service, and as if his stare were tapping her beseechingly on the shoulder, each time it eagerly waited to meet her.

"Do you have to rush off?" Owen asked after service. "Can't you stay for fellowship hour?"

Engaging in fellowship with Owen wasn't exactly what Lily had on her mind. It seemed almost sacrilegious to use church-sanctioned coffee as an excuse to stay. Like taking communion because you were hungry.

Ever since they'd met the week before, Lily found Owen creeping into her thoughts, her fantasies, even her dreams. It was ridiculous, really - they had only shared a few moments and exchanged a few words. Yet the stories she wove dismayed and thrilled her, each time leaving her feeling the way she had on the eve of Easter - warm with relief, high on inspiration, and afraid that the passion awakened from within would not so easily be tamed by her halfhearted demands that it furl itself back up inside her, knowing that it would leave her with only the taste of dead tree in her mouth. Today she imagined that they would skip the bad coffee and lard-laden pastries that had been laid out on a folding table in the church basement. Instead, they would slip out the back door, go past the playground, and head into the nature trails of the wildlife sanctuary behind the church property.

They would talk, although Lily didn't know about what. She would laugh, he would look at her, the spring sun glinting in his blue eyes, and he would smile. He would take her hand in his and lead her off the beaten path where they would sit together on an old fallen oak. He would raise his hand to her chin, tilt her face up toward his, and kiss her. His lips would be soft and warm, his breath gentle, his tongue sweet.

"Lily?" Owen repeated. "Can't you hang out for a bit? I've been wanting to have the chance to get to know you a little better."

"Oh, I just can't," Lily replied. "I have to get home."

"So, what is it that keeps you so busy on a Sunday morning?" Owen smiled. "Don't you get a day off? Even God got a day of rest."

Lily felt that he was looking right through her, those bright blue eyes jumping out from behind wire-rimmed glasses, peering into her mind, watching the scene of the two of them, kissing on a fallen oak in the woods.

"You don't believe me?" Lily asked. In her frustration she dropped her church bulletin and her Bible and when she bent over to get them, she farted. Not sure if Owen had heard it or not, but wildly embarrassed at the prospect, she struggled to recuperate as she stood back up. "I have a husband, and I have two little boys and there's a lot of stuff to be done, all the time, every day."

Owen knit his brow as his smile dropped away. "Lily - of course I believe you... I'm so sorry - I didn't mean to offend you."

"That's OK." Her voice cracked under the weight of humiliation. "I'm just having a bad day, I guess. I'm sorry." She dabbed at the inside corner of her eye with her index finger.

Owen reached into his pocket, and offered her a tissue.

"I'm sorry," Lily repeated, blowing her nose. "I really do have to go now."

"Sure, sure, no problem." Owen headed toward the door, both of them reaching for the knob at the same time, grazing hands before Lily yanked hers back with a gasp.

"Let me get that for you," Owen said softly, his voice dripping with tenderness. He opened the door and Lily darted out, like a bird that had accidentally fumbled its way into someone's house, and frantically found its way out again.

Lily played the scene over and again in her mind in the days that followed, each time feeling more foolish. Yet despite her efforts to stay as busy as possible (She could hear Bethany's voice singing, "Idle hands are the devil's workshop."), she couldn't get Owen off of her mind. The way he confidently sat in his chair at the sound table, the sadness in his eyes when he thought he'd hurt her feelings. The way the hairs on her arm stood up when she passed within inches of him to walk out the door. How could she ever face him again? How could she not?

The next evening while Pierce and Joseph were happily and drowsily settled in front of the television and Joe was at work, Lily booted up the computer and launched America Online. As she waited for the dial-up connection, her heart quickened. She extracted Owen's business card from the hidden pocket of her wallet.

She clicked the email icon and watched as a message window opened. She had no idea where he lived or what his life was like, but Lily was titillated to recognize that at that moment, Owen was just a few mouse clicks away. She didn't even have to leave the house to find him. This was her opportunity to clean up the embarrassment she'd created for herself, to smooth things over.

She would write something appropriate and intelligent and show Owen that she wasn't the basket case she appeared to be. She wrote message after message, but discarded them all. She intended to compose the perfect note and slip it into the crack between self-deprecation and whimsy; surely there was an ideal balance. After thirty minutes at the keyboard, she'd written:

Dear Owen,

I just wanted to apologize for getting so upset after service on Sunday. It certainly had nothing to do with anything you said or did. Just one of those days, I guess! I'm enjoying working on the music for the summer concert. Perhaps we'll run into each other again some time.

See you soon.

Mrs. Lily Diotallevi

PS: Thank you for the tissue; I'm having it cleaned before returning it to you. It will be ready next Tuesday.

In the subject line, she wrote, "So sorry!" Lily's heart pounded as the cursor hovered over the "Send" button, poised to make the commitment to jump, yet terrified of the fall.

"Mommy! Can we have some ice cream?!" Joseph shouted.

"Yea, Mommy - we want ice cream," added Pierce with a giggle, as both boys bounded up the stairs from the family room, Wishes following, vigorously wagging her behind in agreement.

Now or never, thought Lily. With a click of the mouse, her note flew off into cyberspace, leaving her trembling in its wake. Mechanically, she prepared ice cream sundaes for the boys, cleaned up the kitchen, set the table for Joe's dinner, and took out the garbage. Each time she passed by the computer, she signed in to AOL and checked for a response. When she heard Joe's car pull into the driveway, she quickly shut the computer down and busied herself at the stove.

Just after midnight, Lily woke with thoughts of Owen, her note to him, his potential response to her. Joe snored deeply. She slipped out of bed, tiptoed down to the living room, and turned on the computer. It whirred and wailed and made a concert of noises that she hardly noticed during the day. She hoped it wasn't loud enough to wake Joe up. What would she tell him if he came down and found her on the computer in the middle of the night? He had agreed to buy it because Joseph's school urged all families to have one, but if he thought that Lily was sneaking down in the middle of the night to do God-knows-what, she wouldn't put it past him to yank it from the wall and toss it out the window.

If he did catch her, she would say that she couldn't sleep, so she thought she would teach herself how to use the word processing software, to be able to help Joseph with his homework. The truth was that Joseph knew more about computers than Lily did, but that was one of the benefits of having a husband who wasn't around much - he was unfamiliar with the day-to-day operations of the house, so Lily was free to fill in the blanks for him as she saw fit. She had at least that much coming to her.

AOL opened, and the familiar male voice quietly announced, "Welcome!" followed by "You've got mail!" Lily could see from the header that it was from Owen; the subject read, "Re: No apology necessary."

mrs lily diotallevi - can't i just call you lily? please? (i'm married too) about sunday... don't give it a second thought... i completely understand about having bad days... it happens to all of us. i have forgotten all about it... well, not completely. i haven't forgotten about our painfully brief encounter, or about how lovely it was to have service enhanced by your beautiful face, and by the ever so fleeting glance into your eyes.
owen

A warmth surged through Lily's body. He had called her beautiful. "... how lovely it was to have service enhanced by your beautiful face... how lovely it was to have service enhanced by your beautiful face..." Lily read the words over and over again, the computer screen casting a blue-white glow on her face as she sat tucked into the corner of the dark living room. She felt silly having signed her note as Mrs. Lily Diotallevi. It was so old-fashioned. Her mother would have a fit if she knew. Hell, Grandma Whitacre would have a fit, too. She hit the reply button.

Dear Owen,
Thank you for your understanding, although I assure you that my eyes are green, not red as they were that day. Talk to you soon.
Lily

Lily clicked on the "send" button with less angst this time, and as she sat reading Owen's note yet once again, the familiar voice announced a new email. Owen was sitting at home writing to her at that exact same moment. The realization set her heart pounding. She opened the note.

hey... what are you doing up so late on a school night?
o
:)

Dear Owen,
I don't know - I just can't sleep. Got stuff on my mind, I guess. I was thinking of faking some sort of illness so I could stay home from school tomorrow. Do you know of one that will get me a day off, but that won't actually make me feel sick?
Lily
P.S. What is that little thing you put after your name?

id like to play hooky with you tomorrow
ps it's a smile, the colon is the eyes and the parenthesis is the mouth

Dear Owen:
I love your smile! I didn't realize what it was - how fun!!!!
:) :) :) :) :) :) :)

i love your smile too
wanna chat

Before Lily could write back and tell him that she didn't know how to chat - although she'd watched Joseph with his friends a couple times - a small window opened up in the upper right corner of her computer screen.

hey, not-sleeping beauty

Lily placed her cursor in the bottom portion of the window and typed. The conversation displayed on the screen.

Hey! Lily typed.
so whats got you up this lovely evening, wrote Owen.
I don't know. Stuff.
hmmm sounds important... just kidding
You're right - it's not important.
so is everyone else asleep at your house, wrote Owen.
Yes. Even the dog is snoring. Lily wondered why he never used uppercase letters, or even punctuation for that matter.
what kind of dog do you have
A Basenji, Lily replied.
i've never heard of that kind
It's a purebred. They don't bark.
they don't bark? what good is a dog that doesnt bark? what if someone breaks in?

Lily considered telling him that Joe practically bought the dog off the back of a truck, and that she was supposed to be a watchdog. She decided against it, mostly because she wanted to avoid the topics of husbands and wives altogether.

Well, she DOES bite!
lol
What is lol?, typed Lily.
laughing out loud
Oh! I'm still learning to use this computer. We just got it.
youre doing great so far

Thanks. Why don't you use any capital letters?
i like to break the rules when i can... its very freeing - so whats the dogs name
Wishes
what kind of a name is that for a dog
Ha ha - the kind that's chosen by a five-year-old.
i have my own wishes wanna hear
Lily hesitated.
Sure.
when we were talking after service the other day, i was wishing i could kiss you

The words pulsated on the screen. They seemed to reach out to Lily and brush themselves up against her. She stared at them for what seemed like hours.

are you still there
Yes. I'm here.
i probably shouldnt have told you that... damn. i have lots to do to set up for a morning session tomorrow so ill say goodnight now

Lily wanted to continue the conversation, but her fingers were frozen in place. She wanted to tell him she wished she could kiss him too, and that she wanted to run her fingers through his thick curly hair, bury her face into his neck and take in his scent, feel his skin against hers.

OK. Good night.

The system message displayed, "RecExec is no longer online."
For the next two days, Lily logged into AOL whenever she could grab a few minutes alone, and each time she looked for an email, or to see if Owen was online. She couldn't eat, and was having trouble concentrating. She replayed their chat repeatedly in her mind, each time conjuring up the delightful sense of danger and thrill it aroused in her. Her whole body seemed to be electric

with it lately, much to Joe's delight; she was more receptive to his advances than she'd been in all the years they'd been together. The sensation of wanting to have sex, of longing for it, craving it, was unfamiliar, and it frightened her. Surely Joe would notice. She wondered what he would do if he knew that each time, she'd been making love to another man in her imagination.

As the days passed, the memory of the chat faded, as did the tingling and the feverish distraction. The prospect of never feeling that way again was a terrifying relief. After three days, she found him.

I've been looking for you, Lily typed.
hey how are you
I'm OK. How are you?
i feel like an idiot, wrote Owen.
Why?
the other night... i am just very attracted to you and thought i sensed something from you too

Like gasoline on a smoldering fire, Owen's words set Lily's body ablaze

You did.
really
Yes. I wanted to kiss you too.
you said wanted... past tense
Want.
we should make that happen. soon
Absolutely.
you know i find it very interesting that your user name is LilCap
Why? That's just the first three letters of my first name and the first three letters of my maiden name.
well you know the story of little red riding hood?
Of course I do!
the modern fairy tale was based on an ancient story called little red cap and youre LilCap

So does that make you the Big Bad Wolf?
depends
On what?
on whats in that basket of yours

Their chat continued for three hours that night, and ended with their promise of returning the next. Every night, Lily lay in bed waiting for everyone else to fall asleep, and then she slipped down the stairs and turned on the computer. Lily and Owen spent hours swapping stories about growing up, sharing the dreams they'd both had of fame and fortune in the music business, their struggles with parenthood, and finally, of the loneliness they both felt in their marriages. The language was never explicit, but an eddy of innuendo churned beneath the surface of each exchange.

They chatted almost every night for a month, and Lily's life became marked with a lightness, an optimism even, and boundless energy. She often exercised twice in a day, skipping lunch in favor of doing lunges - regardless of her lack of sleep. And since she and Owen had only talked about kissing, and hadn't actually done anything, she reasoned that she was still faithful, and not doing any harm. He continued to operate the sound board at church on Sundays, and she continued to enjoy stealing glances from over her shoulder and coyly brushing up against him as the congregation squeezed itself out of the sanctuary at the end of service.

One night while hanging out online waiting for Owen to show up, Lily browsed through her account settings, and happened upon her online statement.

"Holy shit!" she said to herself. "This can't be right!" At two dollars and ninety-five cents per hour, Lily had racked up charges in excess of three hundred dollars chatting with Owen.

According to the statement, the bill had been sent via postal mail two days earlier. Tomorrow was Joe's day off. Her mind raced. What if Joe opened the bill before she could intercept it? She could tell him that it was a mistake, and that she would call the accounting department and give them hell, and demand that they straighten it out right away. And then she would have to come up with the money. Without Joe knowing.

The next day Lily watched in a panic, first as the mail truck pulled away, then as Joe retrieved the letters from the mailbox. He flipped through them as he entered the house.

"What's this?" he asked, holding up an envelope with the AOL logo on the return address.

"Oh, that's just junk mail," Lily said, extending her hand. "Here - give it to me."

"It's all trash anyway, unless it's a check," said Joe. He tossed the stack of letters into the garbage can.

Lily waited for Joe to leave the room, then fished the bill out of the garbage, wiped the wet coffee grounds from it, and shoved the envelope into her purse.

The next Sunday after service, Lily approached the sound table. "We need to talk," she told Owen.

"Sounds serious," said Owen, unbuttoning the cuffs of his shirt and rolling them up, revealing a hint at his slender but muscular runner's physique.

"It is," said Lily, in a near whisper. "I almost got busted."

"What do you mean?"

"Do you know how much we chatted this month? I had to intercept the bill so my husband wouldn't see it." Lily pulled the statement out of the envelope and showed it to Owen. "I don't even know what I would've told him - or how I am going to pay it."

"Can't you just tell him you've been online chatting with friends?" Owen glanced at the statement. "I know people who easily spend this much every month on AOL."

"You don't understand my situation, Owen." Lily shoved the statement back into the envelope. "This will cause World War III at my house. Joe cannot find out about it."

"What can I do?" Owen reached out to touch Lily's hands. She pulled away and then looked around to see if anyone was watching.

"Nothing. I don't know. Nothing. But we can't chat online

anymore."

"Let me give you the money for that."

"I can't," said Lily.

"Why not?" said Owen.

"Owen, that's a lot of money. I can't take that from you. It wouldn't be right. Plus, it would be kind of icky."

Owen looked at her and almost imperceptibly nodded in agreement. He scanned the ceiling of the sanctuary, as if he might find an answer there.

"How about if I pay that bill," he said. "And then you come and work at the studio in exchange?"

"Out of the question," said Lily. "What would I even do there? I don't know anything about recording."

"You don't have to. I still have a pile of Easter service recordings that need to be billed and shipped. I'm still editing them, but I have to get them in the can soon because new stuff has been coming in every week and I need to get to those."

Lily's heart raced at the prospect, at least for the second or two before reality set in.

"Joe would never let me," she said.

"Really?" Owen leaned in toward Lily as though he wanted to take her into his arms, but stopped himself. "Not even if you just said you were offered a temporary part-time job?"

"Not for you," said Lily.

"Why not me?"

"You're a man."

"What is this guy, a Neanderthal?"

Lily couldn't hide the shock and shame she felt.

"I'm sorry, Lily," Owen said. "That was uncalled for."

"No it wasn't, actually," she replied. "It's sad, but not uncalled for."

"Can't you tell him it's for church?" asked Owen.

"That's a lie," said Lily.

"Not really," said Owen. "You would be helping me with live church recordings. It really is kind of like helping to spread God's word when you look at it that way."

"But he would ask me for the money I make."

"So we'll make it a volunteer job," said Owen.

"But if it's a volunteer job, how will I pay the AOL bill?"

"It's not really a volunteer job, silly," Owen laughed.

"Oh, my God," said Lily. "I can't even keep my own lies straight. I can't do this."

"Sure you can. It's not that difficult. Just tell him it's a volunteer job for church, work for a few weeks, a few hours per week, and in the meantime I'll send the payment in. Just give me the envelope." Owen held his hand out for the bill.

Lily considered the idea. "No - he still won't go for it. He'll ask me about you, why you offered me the job, who else works there. It won't work." She glanced around the room to see Donna watching them. Lily smiled and waved. Owen followed suit. Donna waved back tentatively.

"Hey - I have an idea," said Owen. "We'll have Donna come, too."

"Donna?"

"Yes, you can tell your husband that I asked you and Donna to help me with a church project for a few weeks. Would he be OK with that? With you and Donna coming together?"

"Probably," said Lily. "But that means you have to hire her, too, doesn't it?"

"So?"

"So now you're paying my AOL bill, plus you have to hire Donna. That's crazy, Owen."

"It's not that crazy, Lily. Now that I think about it, I could actually use a little help with some things around the studio. I haven't cleaned or organized anything in ages. Yes, this is really a good idea, now that I think about it."

Lily's stomach filled with butterflies - partly at the prospect of working with Owen, but mostly at the realization that they were standing in the sanctuary, plotting their deception. There must be some kind of special punishment for an adulteress who conducts her business in church.

"We can't chat online anymore," said Lily.

"We won't have to, Lily. We can see each other, instead." Owen's warm smile melted Lily's resistance. She extended the envelope to Owen. Just as he reached for it, she yanked it away.

"I'm not making any promises. And you'll have to ask Donna yourself. It can't come from me."

"No problem," said Owen. "I'll tell Donna that I asked you to help out and that I needed someone else so you recommended her."

"Yes, that's good," said Lily. "It would also serve as an explanation to Donna why you and I are standing here speaking in whispers." Lily was surprised and pleased that she was catching on quickly.

They considered the conditions. Donna would take the job as long as the hours coincided with school and didn't interfere with the PTW meetings. And once Donna was committed, Lily was sure she could get Joe to go along - it's for church... it's only for a few weeks... Donna will be there, too. It really was the perfect plan. And it had the added benefit of getting Lily off the hook for finding a way to pay the AOL bill. She had to repeatedly remind herself that that was the whole purpose behind the scheme in the first place. That was all she wanted - a way to pay the bill.

"OK," said Lily, still distracted as her mind played out the scenario. She handed Owen the envelope. "OK."

Donna was thrilled to take the job. "It will give me a few extra bucks to save toward our family vacation to Disney World this summer," she said, clapping. "I've been hearing about this hotel called The Polynesian where they have a luau with authentic barbequed pork ribs - and then there's Epcot Center where they have restaurants that serve food from all over the world - all in one place!" She quickly added, "Oh, I'm sorry, Lily - was that bragging? I didn't mean to brag."

"No - don't worry about it. It's cool."

"What are you going to do with your pay?" Donna asked.

"I'll probably use it to help out with the bills, so just don't bring it up in front of Joe, OK? He'd be embarrassed."

"Of course not, darlin'."

"And maybe don't talk about what you're doing with your money in front of Joe or the kids, OK? Do you mind?" Lily would not be able to explain why Donna was getting a paycheck and she was not.

"Mum's the word!" Donna pantomimed locking her lips and throwing the key over her shoulder.

Over the next two days, Lily felt intermittently nagged by guilt for involving Donna in the plan that she and Owen had hatched, but she found consolation in convincing herself that if she had told Donna that she had racked up a huge AOL bill that she couldn't pay, that she was afraid to tell Joe, and that Owen had offered her a job that she couldn't take unless Donna worked there with her, Donna would most certainly have gone along. By not giving her more information than she needed to have, Lily was actually protecting her. Donna could not be condemned for being ignorantly complicit. Plus, she would be getting a nice rack of ribs out of the deal.

After an agonizing night of anticipation, the black sky turned gray, and an orange sun peeked out from behind the horizon. Lily busied herself in the kitchen, emptying the dishwasher and setting the table for breakfast. She caught herself humming and harshly reminded herself not to appear so chipper. If Joe suspected this was anything more than a boring volunteer job for church, if he sniffed it out and determined that today meant something to Lily, he would be sure to pull it out from under her.

Lily kissed Joseph and watched him climb up the stairs of the grimy yellow school bus. The smell of diesel fuel that it coughed out as it churned away transported Lily's thoughts back to Gates-Chili High School, the only school she had ever gone to that was far enough away from home as to warrant a bus ride. She'd often found herself running to catch the bus in the mornings for want of staying in bed just ten more minutes, and then spending homeroom obsessing about how she'd forgotten to take the ground beef for dinner out of the freezer, or wondering if she'd remembered to unplug the curling iron. Hard to believe that was so long ago. When had her worries become so much more grave?

"I might have someone stop over later to take a look at the toilet upstairs," said Joe.

Shit. Lily was hoping he wouldn't put her in the position of reminding him that today was the first day at the studio.

"I'll be here later on," she finally said, "But after I take Pierce to pre-school, I have that volunteer thing today, remember? With Donna?"

"What is that all about again?" Joe asked.

"Oh, I don't know," said Lily. "Helping this guy from church with some sermons he recorded."

"Who is this guy?"

"I don't really know him," said Lily. "I think he's gay."

"What, are all the guys at that church gay?"

"Pretty much."

"Why did they ask you again?"

Lily had the answers down pat. "Well, they asked Donna and she sort of volunteered me." She quickly added, "But don't say anything to her about it, OK? She would feel awful if she knew she was putting me on the spot."

"What time are you going?"

"Ten o'clock," said Lily. Dismissively, she added, "I think. Somewhere around there."

"What time is it now?" Joe asked, sliding his cuff up to view the face of his watch. "According to this," he said, tapping his index finger on the crystal, "I have half an hour before I have to leave for work." He winked at Lily and took her by the hand. "We have time to do it twice."

Joe had been particularly randy for the past couple of days, which could only mean he was winning. Normally Lily would begrudgingly accommodate him, and then poke around, ask questions, try to get her hands on some of the cash before it was gone again. But today she was grateful for his exuberance - both because it kept him appropriately distracted from her plans, and because it gave her an outlet for her fantasies of Owen, which had quickly become an addiction of their own.

"Coffee? Tea? Water?" Owen asked Lily and Donna. The three of them stood in the reception area of Star Recording Studio, which amounted to little more than a large foyer with a ragtag collection of furniture: a green velvet armchair whose nap was worn down to a thin film of fabric on the arms, a cane-back dining chair, a scratched glass display case filled with dust-covered CDs by local artists - who in all likelihood were parking their cars out in their driveways because their garages were filled with boxes of those same CDs, packed away with the dreams that had inspired them. Near the back of the room was a metal desk with a wood laminate top. Behind the desk sat two crooked black swivel office chairs. On top of the desk was a computer, a printer, assorted pen and pencil holders, a mail tray, and more dust. Beyond the desk was a wall with a bare window in the center of it that looked into Owen's office.

"I'd love a coffee," said Donna. "And," she added, pulling a large plastic zipper bag out of her even larger purse, "No cup of coffee is complete without cookies - I just pulled a batch of shortbread cookies out of the oven this morning, and they cooled just in time for me to dip 'em in chocolate!"

"I'm fine," said Lily. She smiled at Owen despite her nausea. She still couldn't believe they'd managed to pull this off - that she was standing here with Owen in a real recording studio.

Owen disappeared and returned a minute later with a green plastic tray that held two Styrofoam cups filled with coffee, a container of powdered non-dairy lightener, a white plastic bowl filled with clumped white sugar, two white plastic spoons and a white paper napkin.

"Here's where we are," he said, setting the tray down on the desk. "I have a bunch of techs helping me record, and then the files come back here for editing and a little post-production music. Between Palm Sunday, Easter Vigils, and Easter Sunday, we ended up with these fifty messages."

Owen held up a clipboard with a sheet that listed the title of each sermon and the name of the preacher.

"Each one is about an hour long. I've finished editing them, but I need you two to listen to make sure that there are no problems with the audio, and then I need your help in making labels, printing out the invoices, and preparing the finals for mailing. If each one of you can review three or four recordings each day, then in a few weeks I'll be all caught up. I really need to wrap these up before the end of the month."

"I can hardly believe that you are going to pay me to listen to the pastors of our community preachin' God's Word!" said Donna. She held a cookie between her long pink fingernails and bobbed it up and down in the cup of coffee. "I am truly blessed - thank you, Owen!"

"My pleasure," Owen replied. He and Lily exchanged a glance. Lily wasn't sure if she saw guilt or justification in his eyes.

By the end of the first day, Lily had listened to one message and Donna had listened to three, devouring them with the same gusto she devoted to sweets. Lily found herself rewinding her recording repeatedly, as her attention was continually drawn away from the Word of God to the Office of Owen, almost as frequently finding that he was staring out the window at her.

Lily's afternoons were filled with replays of the instances in which she had brushed up against Owen while passing him in the hallway, or of the snippets of conversation they'd shared, laced with double entendre that Donna either could not hear or did not discern. Emboldened by Donna's absorption in her task and by the attraction that grew between them, Owen and Lily became more relaxed, often forgetting that they were tending to a secret and should be scrutinizing every phrase they spoke to one another, rationing each glance they exchanged.

During their second week at the studio, Donna happily munched on Skittles while listening to Pastor Erickson of Blessed Hope Fellowship deliver a message that had been titled, "We Murdered Jesus." Lily turned around and looked through the window. Owen motioned with his head, inviting Lily to come in. She looked at Donna and then back at Owen, who dismissed her concern with a wave of his hand. Lily got up from the desk.

"Hey," she said, peeking her head into Owen's office.

"Hey yourself," said Owen.

Lily's face grew hot.

"It's driving me crazy, you know," he said. "Having you so close and not being able to kiss you, or hold you - or any of the other things I am dying to do to you."

"*Shhhh*," said Lily, stepping further into the room and leaning to look out the window at Donna.

"She's fine," said Owen. "She is so rapt in the Word that she wouldn't know if a bomb went off in here."

Lily walked closer to the desk and picked up a Rubik's Cube that sat there. "Did you ever solve this?" she asked.

"That was simple," said Owen, "compared to figuring out how in the world I can go even one more second without touching you. Please, give me your hand."

Lily looked out the window as Donna popped a handful of candy into her mouth. She extended her hand toward Owen. He took it in his own and stared into Lily's eyes. He brought her hand toward his mouth and gently placed it against his lips. He closed his eyes and groaned.

Lily sighed.

"It's all I can even think about anymore," said Owen.

"I know," said Lily. "Me too."

The sound of a door closing caused Lily to jerk her hand away from Owen's, and turn toward the window. Donna was no longer in the chair.

"Shit!" said Lily, as softly as her state of alarm would allow.

"She's probably just in the bathroom or something," said Owen.

"That means she saw us," said Lily. "Shit. Shit, shit, shit! I gotta get out of here."

Lily returned to her chair, put her headphones on, and pushed the play button on her deck. Donna returned, took her place in her chair, and placed her headphones over her ears without saying a word to Lily or even turning to look at her.

On the way home, Lily said to Donna, "So did you listen to any interesting messages today?"

"Not really," said Donna, taking a cookie from the baggie in her purse. She checked her rearview mirror. She popped the cookie into her mouth and reached for another. As she spoke, she sprayed herself with crumbs. "I mean they are all interesting because they're all about Jesus, but I don't really remember anything specific from today."

Good answer. What could Donna tell her, anyway? How could you share ideas about an Easter sermon without talking about sin and punishment, guilt and redemption? Donna must have known that she didn't have to say a word about it; Lily was sure that her guilt was oozing from every pore, that Donna could smell it on her. She was able at that moment to see how the situation must have looked from Donna's perspective, and she felt remorse at having used her only true friend to help her execute such a sinful scheme. She wished she had told Donna upfront about the whole plan, about the AOL bill - everything. After all, she still hadn't been unfaithful to Joe. But she had most definitely betrayed her best friend.

As Donna pulled the car into her driveway, she said, "Lily, I have to say something."

Lily closed her eyes and swallowed hard. *Here it comes*, she thought. Whatever Donna had to say, Lily knew deserved it.

"What is it?" asked Lily. She shifted her body in her seat, to face Donna, to at least take her punishment honestly.

Likewise, Donna shifted in her seat. "The thing is this -" Donna stopped to clear her throat.

Lily noticed a smudge of chocolate on Donna's face. "You've got a little something right there," said Lily, motioning to Donna's chin.

Donna wiped at her chin with her hand. "Did I get it?"

"No - here, let me," said Lily. She moistened the tip of her thumb with her saliva and then rubbed the chocolate from Donna's skin. "You were saying?"

Donna's gaze was at first fixed on Lily, then on the cookie in her hand, then on the hearty dusting of crumbs that had gathered on her lap. She put the cookie back into her purse.

"The thing is," said Donna. Her eyes darted about, as though she were trying to remember her thought. "The thing is that, well, I know I said I would drive this week, but can I just meet you at the studio instead? I have some things I need to take care of in the morning."

"Sure," said Lily. She smiled weakly. "We can do that." Lily imagined that perhaps Donna was going to tell someone what was going on - Pastor Halloway, or Bethany - to seek advice on how she should handle it. Or maybe she would try to go talk to Joe, to somehow let him know, warn him. Like a vise, fear clamped Lily's chest. She hoped that Donna knew better than to arouse Joe's jealousies, but she also knew that Donna was a good person, and not inclined to willingly participate in such unsavory goings on.

Lily had to put an end to it, before anyone else got hurt. She would just show up tomorrow, and tell Owen that she couldn't come anymore, and offer to pay whatever balance existed on the AOL bill - she would have to think of a way. Then she would beg Donna for forgiveness. And Jesus too.

"Where's Donna?" asked Owen the next morning. The look on his face was delight topped by a dusting of concern.

"She's coming," said Lily. "She had some stuff to do and said she would meet me here."

"Look, Lily - I'm so sorry about yesterday. Did she say anything about it?"

"No," said Lily. "But I wished she would have. At least then it would be out in the open. I feel like an idiot right now, and I'm sure she's hurt."

"It's - I just - I couldn't help it."

"I know," said Lily. "But we are playing with fire here." She felt tears come to her eyes. She wished she had played it smarter, had found a way to stay close enough to Owen to experience the passion between them, but not close enough to ruin it as she had. Too late now.

"Owen, we need to talk."

The phone rang and Owen ran into the back office. Lily heard him utter a few short phrases before he emerged again.

"That was Donna," he said. "She's not coming."

"What do you mean? What did she say?"

"She just said that something came up and she couldn't make it today."

"She said that?"

"She did."

"Oh my God," Lily said, covering her mouth, "She must be so angry with me."

"Or..." Said Owen, walking closer. "Maybe she understands."

"She could never understand this," said Lily.

"Sure she could, Lily. She's a Christian, not a saint. Or maybe she doesn't understand; maybe she just doesn't blame you." He took a few more steps. "I wish you could stop blaming yourself." Owen held his arms open to her. "I wish you could just come here, and let me hold you."

Owen walked right up to Lily and she leaned into him. He wrapped his arms around her as she bent her elbows and tucked her closed fists under her chin, her head resting in the crook of Owen's neck.

"There you go," he said.

Something inside Lily broke loose and flooded her body. She slipped her arms out and wrapped them around Owen.

"You go ahead and have a little cry," he said, rocking her back and forth in place as they stood in the middle of the room. "You have a cry now, and then dry your eyes, because I don't want any tears when I make love to you."

Lily stepped into Owen's office and he closed the door behind her with one hand while cupping his free hand around the nape of her neck, leaning in toward her, kissing her. The kiss began gently, the way first kisses should, followed unbroken by the second kiss, and the third one, waves of pent-up passion flowing between them, bringing them together deeper and more completely as they explored each other's tongues, ears, necks. Owen began unbuttoning Lily's blouse, when she broke away.

"Wait a second," she whispered breathlessly.

"I've waited so long already, Lily. Don't you want this to happen?"

"I do," said Lily, remembering the last time she said those words to a man.

Eyes closed, she sent her hands flowing over Owen's body, drinking in the feel of his unfamiliar skin, the novel curves of his shoulders, the contours of his buttocks, the smoothness of his hips as she nervously inched around to the front of his body. Despite Owen's admonitions against crying, the sting of tears collected in the corners of Lily's eyes. Owen kissed her with his whole body, as though his life depended on it, and Lily's body grew limp at the realization that someone could want her that much. In a flash, the past twenty years of her life played in her mind. She thought about the fights with Joe, the screaming, the accusations, the limitations, the rage, the nights she cried clinging to the edge of the bathroom sink, the sex endured with breath held and eyes clenched shut. Rather than becoming consumed with self-consciousness at her lack of experience, Lily's arousal was catapulted at Owen's desire for her, the way he softly groaned at her touch. She wanted him to devour her, slip her entire being inside of himself so she could be protected and warmed by his breath. Lily thought of the lies she told, the things she hid, the clandestine disloyalties and infidelities of her heart. She thought about the tree, the pile of severed limbs, hacked and bloodied, stacked in a huge mound by the curb. She became blinded by a mysterious craving for something she knew she'd never before tasted, having been stirred up from a place inside her that she had never known existed, like a secret room in the back of a closet, whose door was hidden behind musty old coats and boxes of outdated hats. As Owen peeled her blouse from her shoulders, Lily threw herself body and soul into the one act of betrayal that was not a fantasy, the one indiscretion that would all but guarantee that she could never return to the life she'd always known.

From: Iris Capotosti <iris.capotosti@gmail.com>
To: Lily Capotosti <lilycapotosti@gmail.com>
Sent: Thu, November 17, 2010 at 11:11 AM
Subject: Shocked

Dear Lily,

Now I'm the one who's shocked! What were you waiting for to tell me about your little fling with Owen?

Not that I don't understand how or why it happened. But what I don't get is how you could write me an email just weeks ago acting like poor little Lily who did no wrong, but took the fall for everything, while perfect little Iris could smash up her poor father's car and cheat on her wonderful husband and not get blamed for anything.

How could you let me go on talking about how ashamed I was, how wrong I was, and then just let the whole story slide?

I guess no matter what happens, you'll always see me as the lucky one, and yourself as the victim. I'm just really starting to wonder what we're getting into here. I'm not talking about what happened back then, but what you've been thinking about me all along.

Iris

Geez, Iris:

You're shocked? Really? My whole life people have been acting like I can't do anything right, and as though I can't be trusted to behave - so why are you surprised that I cheated? Surely you expected it - especially given that you say you "understand" why I did it. (Just because you read about my life doesn't mean you understand it.)

Anyway, I wasn't going to tell you about Owen. I had decided not to; I didn't think I needed the bad press. Didn't I have enough shit going on already in my life to adequately live up to my reputation? Why paint a picture for you that was so much more shameful than the one you already saw?

But then you told your story about Claudio and it made me brave. It made me want to be honest with you in return. Imagine my shock upon reading this most recent email and finding out that you also seem to corner the market on confession. So now you're a better Mary Magdalene than I am, too. I can't even screw up properly.

Maybe I will always see you as the lucky one and myself as the victim. Have you ever considered the possibility that I see it that way because that's how it was? I'm sorry if that makes you uncomfortable. Join the club.

I also wonder what we've gotten into here, but I hope you're not considering backing out of this now that my guts are lying all over the place.

Lily

347

Dear Lily,

I didn't expect you to have an affair, and I didn't expect you not to. I just didn't expect you let me go on feeling ashamed of myself for so long when you could have kept me company.

I understand a lot more than you imagine, Lily. I couldn't sleep last night because of it. But let's not get into that now.

Don't worry, I'm not backing out. I'll defer any conclusions until I have the whole story, and I think you should do the same.

Iris

17. IRIS

"*This* is what it's like," Iris said aloud, alone in her office. Snatches of conversations from her whirlwind trip home to Rochester before the hotel opening stood out in her memories like the boldface subject lines of the twenty-two unread emails on her computer screen. Just weeks ago, everyone had been so curious to hear about her glamorous new job. Now, the glamour and novelty were wearing thin, and all she was left with was a shitload of work. And this was what it was like, six days a week, Saturdays included. She glanced at her watch, and winced. It was late, again, but the emails were still coming in. She stared at her computer screen, trying to determine by the sender's address and subject line which messages would require immediate attention, which might be eliminated, and which she might leave for the following morning, when her phone shattered the silence with the piercing electronic ring she had started hearing in her sleep.

"*Signora* Iris, there's someone here to see you," a young lady's pleasantly modulated voice informed her. That morning, Iris had instructed the new receptionist to address her in this more informal manner, like the rest of the front office staff, instead of calling her "*Direttrice*." The title still embarrassed her, and she would hate to think she needed to rely upon its use in order to command respect.

"I didn't think I had anything else scheduled for today,

Marisa." Iris cradled the phone between her neck and shoulder as she flipped open her appointment book. "And I was just considering leaving. Who is it?"

"I don't know. He didn't give me his name. He seemed to know his way around, he said he'd be waiting on the terrace. I'm sorry, *Signora* Iris, maybe I should have insisted more, but he just walked away, and I didn't want to pester him. Should I go tell him you've already gone for the day?"

Iris sighed. "No, that's all right. I'll go myself and see what it's all about." Iris had learned back at the Stella di Levante to always give drop-ins a few minutes of her time, whenever possible, and her availability was often rewarded. In the few months since the Dimora had opened its doors to the public, her policy had resulted in an extremely lucrative booking by a wealthy guest, the owner of one of the major soccer teams, who had sent an assistant to inspect the accommodations and arrange the details of his stay directly with her. Another time, a travel writer from Chicago had stopped by unannounced to interview Iris for a piece slated for publication in a leading magazine. On yet another occasion, a glowing review of the Dimora had appeared in a German travel guide following the impromptu site inspection of the reviewer, to whom Iris had offered a tour of the premises and a drink on the terrace. You just never knew. Iris reached into her drawer for the mirror and lipstick she kept there, applied a fresh coat, and went to see who was going to be responsible for making her get home late this time.

"*Buonasera,*" Iris said, throwing back her shoulders as she walked across the terrace to the man slouched over the balustrade, his back toward her. She often wished someone had drilled into her the importance of standing up straight, back when she was a gangly adolescent embarrassed by her height, but no one had, and her quest for perfect posture was an ongoing effort. "How may I help you?" The man, who seemed to be enjoying the view, pivoted slowly to face her.

"*Ciao, bella Direttrice,*" he said. It took Iris a moment to recognize the deeply tanned face in the fading light.

"*Signor* Vanesi!" Surprise doused Iris like a cold shower, making her heart hop, her skin tingle. They shook hands in greeting; the feel of his soft, moist hand, with its long, meaty fingers was familiar, unexpected.

"I thought we agreed you would call me Max." Massimiliano Vanesi turned up the corners of his mouth in what could easily bloom into a smile, if he let it. "Or didn't you get that letter I wrote you? Did that jealous weasel of a guy at the front desk shred it to pieces instead of delivering it to you like I told him?"

Iris had never been good at training her body to downplay her emotions. Unlike the man's lips, if hers wanted to smile, like now, they did. "No. I mean, yes. I got the letter," she stammered, blushing furiously.

"And?" Vanesi faced her squarely, his backside resting against the balustrade. He ran the fingers of both hands through the thick black hair that hung from a jagged part down the middle of his scalp, then crossed his arms.

What did he expect her to say? It was not exactly the sort of letter you answered.

"Have you been thinking of me?" he asked. His bluntness caught her off guard. Was she supposed to tell him that not a day had gone by without her taking that letter out of her desk drawer and rereading it? Some days, several times. She especially liked the part where he said the feel of her breath on his neck had made him shiver.

"Well, you did say you would send me some pictures. I was sort of expecting to hear from you," Iris said.

"It's been a hell of a month. It takes those clowns at RAI TV forever to make a decision about anything, then they've got you running all over the place like shit in the sewer. When I left here, I went straight down to Elba, then Ponza, then on to Capri and Ischia," he said. "Have you ever been to any of those islands?"

"Only Ischia. I go every year in May. Oh, and once I took the ferry to Capri from there. Just for the day." She didn't even think about why she had automatically said "I" instead of "we." It had just come out that way.

351

"Ischia, huh?" Vanesi tilted his head slowly from left to right, ear to shoulder, like a scale being tipped by the positive and negative aspects of the island as they ran through his mind. "Not my favorite," he pronounced.

"It's actually very pleasant, if you find a quiet place to stay. The gardens are lovely at that time of year. And the thermal baths are rejuvenating." What kind of an answer was that? Something had prompted her to defend Gregorio's fixation with the island, but she cringed at the way her comments made her sound like a prim English spinster from the nineteenth century, who traveled to the Continent for its agreeable climate and salubrious baths. In fact, Ischia was over-developed, with way too many people and cars for her taste. But she wasn't about to tell *him* that.

"There are so many other beautiful islands. Why would you keep going to Ischia, once you've seen it?"

"Tradition, I guess." It was no business of his that Gregorio was the one who insisted on going there every May for the scuba diving. He had been livid when she told him she could not go this year; her presence at the hotel was crucial as the Dimora geared up for its first high season, and taking a week off was out of the question. Instead of going along without her, as she had insisted vehemently and hoped fervently he would, Gregorio had given up his vacation and spent the week complaining, relaying to her each evening over dinner the news he received from his diving companions about the ideal weather conditions and exceptional immersions they were enjoying. It still wasn't clear to Iris whether it had been the idea of going without her that Gregorio didn't like, or the thought of leaving her alone for a week.

"Tradition," Vanesi said, nodding his head slowly. "I never would have thought of that. Interesting."

Wincing from the man's blind stab at the private life about which he knew nothing, Iris quickly changed the subject. "So what brings you here, *Signor* Vanesi?"

"It's Max, remember?" He revealed the rest of the smile he had been dangling in front of her. It was even more captivating than she recalled. His teeth were stark white, in contrast to his dark skin, and so straight they almost slanted inward. Nice and even across, too, except for the canines, which came to a sharp point, well below the others.

"All right. You win. Max it is," Iris said. "What brings you here, Max?"

"I came to settle up." Max stood up straight, and crossed his arms over his slightly pudgy abdomen. She had forgotten how tall he was.

"Settle up what?"

"Like you said, I owe you some prints. Which I have come personally to deliver into your precious hands. As for you, I believe you owe me an aperitivo."

"I do?"

"Yes, you do. To make up for the one you skipped out on." His decisive tone of voice told Iris there was no way she could beg off this time without seeming rude or, worse still, scared.

"Then by all means, follow me." Iris crooked a finger at him and led him to her favorite table in the far corner, nodding and smiling at the guests she encountered along the way. The cocktail crowd had thinned out as dinnertime approached, and the waiter was busy tidying up. As soon as they were seated, he walked over.

"What would you like, Max? A beer? A glass of wine? A cocktail?" Iris asked.

"Champagne would be nice," Max said, without hesitation.

"Champagne?"

"I have a policy of never refusing free champagne. And this one is on you, remember?"

"Of course. Champagne it is then." Iris said to the waiter.

"Would you like a bottle, or two flutes, Signora Iris?" he asked.

"Two flutes will be fine, Giovanni." Iris said.

"To start with," Max added, grinning. He pushed his chair back, and crossed his legs. As he placed his right ankle over his left knee, his white linen trousers crept up his leg, revealing skin as tan as his face and arms. He reached into his backpack and pulled out an envelope. "Here you go, *Signora Direttrice*

Capotosti." He could not seem to resist teasing her in some way.

"If you're Max, I'm Iris," she said.

"I know. But I like Capotosti. Maybe you should just have people call you 'Capo' - that's a good nickname for a big boss lady like you.

"I don't think that would be appropriate," Iris said. She had never liked the term "boss" in English, and the same held true for its Italian equivalent "*capo*." After all, she wasn't the foreman on a construction site, she was the manager of a luxury hotel.

"Well, then *I'll* call you Capo." Iris wondered when exactly he planned on calling her that. Once they drank their glass of champagne, she would be on her way home, and he would head off to some other island hideaway, never to be seen or heard from again.

"Something tells me it would be pointless to argue with you," Iris said, feigning exasperation. "Go ahead and call me whatever you want. As long as no one else hears!"

Max laughed, then with a serious face and deliberate gesture, pushed the envelope across the table to her. Iris had a habit of imagining the dynamics behind the interactions she witnessed between people; it was a game she had begun playing more frequently ever since she had started working at hotels. She wondered what she would think of the two of them if she were an observer, watching from the outside. The complicit way in which Max was looking at her, combined with the obvious discomfort on her part, might lead one to suspect he was slipping her a payoff in the mysterious envelope. Or perhaps some compromising evidence that could be employed to blackmail someone.

"Aren't you going to look inside?" Max said. At that moment, the champagne was served, accompanied by a small silver tray bearing delectable tidbits to go along with it.

Iris waited for the waiter to leave, then opened the envelope. Inside, she found a series of eight-by-ten glossy photographs of herself, in various stages of movement, as she had walked across that same terrace a month earlier. She couldn't make out her facial expression that well because her features were purposely blurred,

354

but it was the sensation the photographs conveyed that appealed to her, the controlled way in which she carried herself, yet looked like she was poised to break loose, prepared to run fast and far. Fortunately, her posture wasn't half bad. "How did you do that?" she said, sitting tall in her chair as she examined the prints. "You were taping, weren't you?"

"Yes, these are stills I extrapolated from the tape. Do you like them?"

The light of that magical time of evening had been captured beautifully, and she had never seen an image of herself quite like any of these. The only person who ever took photographs of her was Gregorio, and she always looked so stiff. Not that it was his fault, of course. She just wasn't photogenic.

"They're very nice," she said. "Thank you so much for bringing them."

"Can you see what I was talking about?" he said. "About the wild girl beneath the sophisticated lady?"

Iris did, definitely. "Yes, I suppose I can."

"Look at the last one," Max said.

As instructed, Iris picked out the last photograph from the dozen or so in her hands. It was printed horizontally. She cocked her head, then rotated the photograph. She found herself staring at a pair of green eyes. Her eyes.

"Remember the other thing I said? That made you so pissed off, you left without having a drink with me?" Max said.

"Not really," Iris lied, her pulse accelerating. "You said lots of things."

"I said your eyes didn't match your smile. That they were sad."

"And so?" Iris hoped he wasn't going to start in on her again. She just wanted to drink her champagne in peace and go home.

"I just wanted you to see for yourself. That's all." Iris had seen for herself. That very same evening when she had gone home and stared at her face in the bathroom mirror and started to cry. And every day since, when she washed her face and put on her makeup. And any time she caught a glimpse of them in any mirror she passed. She looked down at the image of her eyes, which she held in her hand. He was right. They were sad. They hadn't always been like that, had they? Had her dreaminess changed to sadness, like Lily's sparkle had turned to glass?

Iris nodded, and swallowed, blinking back tears. She looked at Max.

"I'm going to tell you another little secret, Capo," Max said, leaning close. "Then we'll concentrate on drinking this champagne."

Not knowing what to say, Iris nodded again.

"When you walked over to me a few minutes ago and said '*buonasera*,' and I turned around, something important happened. Those eyes lit up, Capo. For a split second, the sadness vanished. I wouldn't be surprised if it actually had something to do with seeing me."

This man, this Max Vanesi! Why did he have to come here and start messing with her? She didn't need him to tell her what she felt. Yes, she had experienced a jolt of joy, a rush of excitement, a thrill of danger when she recognized him. She couldn't deny it, but that didn't mean she had to admit it. Least of all, to him.

"Let's just say I was moved by the beauty of the evening," she said, raising her flute.

"Let's." He touched his glass to hers, then downed the champagne in one thirsty gulp. "Such beauty deserves the rest of that bottle, don't you think?"

Beatrix splashed a second round of whiskey over the ice cubes melting in their tumblers. Gregorio and some colleagues from the Policlinico had been invited to dinner in Genoa by the area manager of a Swiss pharmaceutical company, leaving Iris free to slip next door to visit her friend. She had been dying to talk to her since Max's visit to the hotel a week earlier.

"So what happened next? Did he take a room at the hotel?" Beatrix said, offering Iris a cigarette, and lighting one for herself.

"No, of course not!" Iris said.

"Why not?" Beatrix asked.

"He suggested it, actually. I couldn't really tell if he was serious or joking, but he said I was the manager, or the 'Capo' as he started calling me, and I should be able to justify a free room for someone who worked for RAI television. Which I could, of course. I just didn't think it was right."

"Did you tell him that?"

"No. I said we were fully booked. I didn't want to get into some kind of moralistic discussion about my idea of right and wrong, you know? What would have been the point?"

"So you drank a whole bottle of champagne together, and then you sent him home?"

"Yes," Iris said. "Well, we talked, too."

"What did you talk about?" Beatrix said.

"Mostly about him. About his work as a freelance cameraman. Though he's really more a filmmaker than a cameraman, you know? Whenever he works on one of those projects for RAI, the director is off making phone calls, or having leisurely lunches on the production tab so it's Max who takes control and decides what to shoot. He says the only input he gets from the director is disruptive, at best, if not downright disastrous." Iris spoke with conviction, as if she had long been indignant at such a talented person enduring such injustice on the set. "I saw it myself, when they did the shoot at the hotel. Max was really the one in charge."

"And is that all you talked about?"

"Well, no." Iris smiled. "Every once in a while, he would just stop, mid-sentence. I'd ask him what was wrong, and he'd say nothing, he was just distracted by my lips, or by the way my tongue flicked when I pronounced certain words. He finally asked me to show it to him."

"What, your tongue?"

"Yes! He expected me to stick it out, right there, on the terrace. Can you imagine that?"

"And did you?"

"Just the tip. After I made sure no one was around," Iris said, laughing. "But I refrained from showing him how I can touch the tip of my nose with it."

"And how did that make you feel?" Beatrix said.

357

"A little embarrassed, at first," Iris said. She paused to take a sip of whiskey. "And a little amused, as if we were playing a game, like when I was a kid, and my sister Lily and I used to touch tongues to gross each other out."

"And is that all you felt?"

"No," Iris said, looking her friend in the eye as she took a drag on the Muratti. "I felt excited. Like I wanted him to ask for more."

"And did he?" Iris often thought Beatrix should have been a therapist, rather than a headhunter. She had a way a pulling the words out of Iris like magicians pull rabbits from a hat.

"No. Thank God, no."

Iris cleared some space on her desk, and spread open the first printed proof of the new, improved brochure of the Dimora Baia dell'Incanto. Although it had been printed on plain white paper and glued to flimsy cardboard backing, the draft was enough for her to see she had finally managed to get her ideas across. She approved of the layout, and had been able to scrape up enough decent photographs of the resort to make it work. She knew the results could have been better, but her hands were tied. Whenever possible, *Signora* Mangiagallo made it a point to engage the services of people she knew, often thwarting efforts already made by Iris to contact suppliers and compare estimates, then neglecting to advise Iris until it was time to sign off her final approval. In this case, the beneficiary was an old friend of the Mangiagallo family, a gentleman with a fairly large printing business in Turin, who was going through a period of financial hardship, having overextended himself to upgrade his equipment. Iris had nothing against the man, but a graphic designer he was not, nor was he a photographer. The first brochure had been a haphazard production featuring generic shots of Portofino and the coast, printed before Iris had been hired, and before there had been anything to photograph in the hotel's unfurnished guestrooms and barren garden. Fortunately, the hotel was located in a destination that sold itself on fame and beauty alone, and that had been enough to start with, but now it was time to get serious.

The only thing missing from the brochure at this point was the copy. Iris had been mulling over some ideas she wanted to develop and had taken it upon herself to put together the text. She had always enjoyed writing, even when it had been the technical prose crammed with maritime jargon back in her days at the Transoceanica office. She had made her first foray into writing more creative material at the Stella di Levante, where she was eventually relied upon to come up with all the copy for the hotel's first website, and for all the special offers promoted throughout the year, including print advertising and radio spots. For the Dimora's new brochure, all she needed were a few finely crafted sentences to convey the sensations she knew today's sophisticated travelers were seeking. Who in this age of Internet would be impressed that Guglielmo Marconi had conducted experiments with his telegraph invention in this very gulf? Who, on the cusp of the third millennium, really cared if two international treaties had been signed in nearby Rapallo in the 1920s? Those who wanted history could read a book. Her clients craved romance. They lusted after sensual pleasures. They yearned to live out a dream. She had to find a way to let them know they could have it all, right here.

"*Permesso, Signora* Iris?" The secretary knocked softly at the half-closed door which Iris rarely shut all the way, preferring to keep an eye and ear on what was going on, and to emphasize to her staff that it was literally always open to them.

"Yes, Rachel, come on in," Iris said, looking up and smiling. She considered herself fortunate to have hired this lovely young woman, who was half-Italian, half-French. Like all the front office staff, she spoke at least three foreign languages.

"I've brought you the correspondence. There is also an email for you. It was sent to the general email address. I printed it for you."

"Thank you, Rachel." The girl placed the stack of envelopes, letters, faxes, printouts and forms for Iris's review on her desk. When she failed to walk away, Iris looked at her with raised eyebrows. "Is there something else?"

"About that email, *Signora* Iris. I thought you might like to know, I eliminated it right away. I'm the only one who saw it."

"What email are you talking about?"

"It's in there," she said, indicating the stack of papers. "I just wanted to reassure you."

"Thank you, Rachel. I'll have a look."

The girl smiled, nodded, and walked away.

Iris turned back to the writing pad in front of her, on which she had jotted down then crossed out several phrases, salvaging only certain words that struck her fancy, which she had copied in a separate column at the right side of the page. The brief interruption had broken her concentration, and all that gibberish about an email was making it difficult for her to get it back. She might as well attend to the correspondence first, and come back to this later when she felt the inspiration. Iris found the email a couple of sheets down from the top. She picked it up and read.

Da: maxvan@postaweb.it
Data: lunedì 24 maggio 1999 23.47
A: info@dimorabaiaincanto.it
Oggetto: eyes and tongues and champagne
ciao capo!
how are your eyes doing these days? i can't seem to forget them i even printed another copy of the pic i gave you. i know what sad is that's why i recognize it so easy don't get me wrong there still beautiful like sad is beautiful but i got a charge seeing the way they sparked to life when you saw me out on that terrace and by the time we killed the whole bottle of champagne they were really starting to shine. the other thing i keep thinking about is your tongue it was so pink and pretty with that pointed tip and i bet it tasted like champagne. when are you going to decide to give me a taste we both know you want to.
pax,
max

How dare Max write such a message to her? How dare he

compromise her reputation by sending it by email for everyone to see? Was he really that stupid, or was he playing cat and mouse with her? She would have to set him straight immediately, before he created some serious trouble.

She logged in to her personal webmail account and sent off a reply:

From: iris.capotosti@liberomail.it
Date: martedì 25 maggio 1999 09.57
To: maxvan@postaweb.it
Subject: This is not funny!
Max,
An employee just handed me a copy of the message you sent to the hotel email! ARE YOU CRAZY? I would like to think it was unintentional and you may not be aware that the general email account info@dimorabaiaincanto.it is accessed by all the front office staff. PLEASE DO NOT, I repeat, DO NOT EVER WRITE TO THAT ADDRESS AGAIN!!!!
Iris

She certainly couldn't make herself any clearer than that. Even if he were incredibly stupid, there was no way he could misunderstand the message. She picked up his email again and reread it. If its content and method of delivery enraged her, the form irritated her. The increasingly common habit people had of using only lowercase characters annoyed her to no end, as did spelling errors. Max was guilty of both; he was even worse than young Peter Ponzio. And the sloppy way he had of letting his words tumble and fall where they may, without the benefit of structure or punctuation to warn the reader of where one thought ended and another began, was unnerving. She had already noticed the same thing in the handwritten note he had left her. He wrote exactly how he spoke, jumping hither and thither, blurting out whatever came to mind, ambushing her with disarming comments. He was uninhibited, you could say that for him, and spontaneous. A rarity these days, especially in fully grown men,

361

at least in the kind she knew.

Iris tapped some keys on her computer and accessed the hotel's email account on the server to eliminate the message permanently, just to be on the safe side. She glanced down at the printed copy of the note, to read it once more before destroying it. The man's impertinence was unbearable. *Impertinence?* Listen to her! She sounded like that old English spinster again. She poised her fingers at the edge of the page, but stopped them before they could tear the sheet. The truth was, she was flattered that he had looked closely enough and understood enough to read the sadness in her eyes. That he had been intrigued enough to notice the shape of her tongue. That he had been cocky enough to assume she wanted him to kiss her. She unlocked the top drawer of her desk and slipped the email inside the envelope containing the photographs and the handwritten note, then locked it again. Inspiration kindled within her, she turned her attention back to the brochure.

"*Piccolina*! Aren't you coming to bed?" Gregorio's voice traveled from the bedroom, down the hallway, and into the living room, where Iris sat at the walnut desk which had belonged to the father-in-law she had never met.

"I'll be there in five minutes, I promise! I'm just answering Violet's email," Iris called back.

She and Gregorio had gone out to dinner, nothing fancy, just a pizza Margherita and a Peroni; Iris preferred the simple fare of low-key, no-fuss restaurants when she was not working. After a busy day of meetings, it had been relaxing to let Gregorio do all the talking, and he had plenty to say, having been on the team handling a challenging surgical procedure that day. Everything had gone even better than expected, the prognosis for the patient was optimistic, and Gregorio was elated. Iris loved happy endings. She thought about how wonderful it must be to work at a job that really mattered. Her husband was literally out there saving people's lives, and she was proud of him. At the same time, she was slightly saddened to see how his responsibilities were starting to take a toll on him, thinning his hair, now more grey than sandy, and sucking the intensity from his watery blue eyes which now depended upon half-glasses to read the menu.

"All right, but don't keep me waiting!" Gregorio replied. Despite the tired look on his face, he had been on an adrenalin high all evening, and acting rather randy for a Thursday.

Love and miss you to death, Iris, she typed, then hit the "send" key. Just as she was exiting her email, she noticed a (1) next to the inbox header, indicating there was a new message. Maybe it was from Lily. She had written to her a week earlier, and still had not heard back. It would only take a second to check. With a click she accessed the inbox, where she saw the name "Massimiliano Vanesi" staring back at her. Over two weeks had gone by since she had received his email at the hotel, and there had not been a peep from him since her scolding. She had assumed he had gotten the gist of her message and would leave her alone. Her pulse quickening, she glanced quickly over her shoulder, then turned her eyes back to the screen and opened the message:

Da: maxvan@postaweb.it
Data: giovedì 03 giugno 1999 22.33
A: iris.capotosti@liberomail.it
Oggetto: are you still mad?
pantelleria. it's one of those nights that make me wish i knew something about stars. out of all those zillions i can only make out a dipper not sure if it is the big or small one but it doesn't really matter what matters is knowing there is someone like you out there who i wish was here gazing up at them with me. but you are so far away right now like over 1000 km i'd say you might as well be up there with the stars. wait, i think i might even see you winking at me. so maybe your not mad at me after all. i want to talk to you capo. send me your cell unless you want to find another email from me when you get to work. better yet come here i'm staying til next week.
pax,
max

Her heart slammed against her ribs, a mad monkey banging its head against the rails of its cage. She looked over her shoulder again, read the message again and, on an impulse, hit the "reply" key.

"*Piccolina!*" Gregorio called in a playful voice. "Are you playing hard to get?" The fine hairs on her forearms stood on end. Her skin tingled.

Da: iris.capotosti@liberomail.it
Data: giovedì 03 giugno 1999 23.01
A: maxvan@postaweb.it
Oggetto: are you still mad?
my cell is 353776292 but I can't talk so don't call!!!! And don't you dare write to me at the hotel again!!!!! EVER!!!!
Iris

She would write more tomorrow. She would point out that just because they had a chat or two didn't mean she was interested in anything more than a casual friendship. She would remind him that she was a married woman, though she doubted that would make much difference to a man like Max. And she would look up Pantelleria to see where exactly it was. Just for curiosity.

"I'm coming!" she said, shutting down the computer and switching off her cell phone. She went to her husband and the bed they shared, where thoughts of Max helped her through the next fifteen minutes, then kept her awake until the church bells sounded twice.

18. LILY

After her encounter with Owen, Lily spent her days struggling through a haze of confusion and fear. She couldn't eat; she couldn't make it through a workout. Her imagination conjured up a variety of chilling scenarios in which Joe discovered her secret. She imagined the violent outburst that would follow, the screaming, assorted items flying through the air, the boys cowered under the kitchen table, or up in their room, crying and clutching each other under their red, blue, and green bedspreads with the dinosaurs on them. For as many times as she'd recalled the utter ecstasy of being in Owen's arms - the way he grazed the skin of her back with his fingertips, how he swept her hair away from her eyes and urged her, "Open them... look at me," - for each time Lily relived the memory that sustained her during the interminable stretches between her mornings at the studio, she punished herself with the terrifying fantasy of getting caught. Yet the prospect was not enough to dissuade her. Just imagining Owen's face sent shocks of electricity through her body, awakening the numbness from years of indifference and neglect. In his arms, she'd found an oasis, and nothing - not even the prospect of poisoned water - could keep her from gulping it down.

She and Owen had made love two more times since that first day - both opportunities created when Donna called to say that she couldn't make it to the studio, due to last-minute tasks or delays.

"Uh-oh," said Owen. "There's that cloud coming over your face. What is it this time?"

"I'm just thinking," said Lily.

"You do way too much of that," said Owen with a chuckle.

"Let me ask you a question," said Lily. "Do you value loyalty?"

"Yes, sure I do."

"And yet here you are with me - making love with me - someone who is proven to be a person lacking in loyalty."

"Lily, loyalty is not an absolute. It has to be reciprocal. It's all relative anyway. What you might do in one situation - married to Joe, for instance - you might not necessarily do in another one."

"That seems really convenient," Lily replied. "You can justify just about any sin using that logic."

"Using your logic," said Owen, "You can justify just about any punishment."

They stood silently looking at each other.

Owen zipped up his fly and cinched his belt into place. "I also find it interesting that you didn't bring this up until after we made love," he said. "If you are so worried about the morality of this, why don't you ever bring it up before, while you still have the opportunity to choose?"

Lily felt a grinding in her gut, and the acrid taste of denial in her mouth as she struggled to hold down the truth of what he said.

"Because," she began, considering the thought for the first time. "Because it doesn't feel like a choice until after."

He took Lily into his arms and held her cheek against his chest. "Just for now," he said, "Just for this small space in time, try to be happy."

Lily tilted her face up toward his.

"Please," he said, looking down at her. "Just for now."

Owen kissed the tip of Lily's nose and her body swelled with renewed arousal, flushing out thoughts and feelings of self-incrimination. In his arms, she was drenched in passion; there was nothing else. She smiled.

"That's better," said Owen. "I have a surprise for you."

"Another one?" Lily giggled and nibbled on Owen's ear lobe.

Owen took her hand. "A different one," he said, laughing. "C'mere." He led her further down the hall away from his office. They entered a room with a long table that hosted endless rows of knobs and levers, a larger version of the sound board he operated in the back of the sanctuary at Christ Covenant Church. Just above the table was a picture window that looked into a separate room that was set with microphone stands, a piano, a few music stands and a complete drum kit.

Lily's eyes widened in fascination. "Is that the recording booth?"

"You got it," said Owen. "Wanna go in?"

"Really?" Lily could hardly contain her excitement and reached for the door before Owen could answer.

"Wow... it's so quiet in here," she said, stepping inside. "It's even quiet when I talk," said Lily. With a giggle she added, "I just realized how stupid that sounded."

"Not at all," said Owen. "You're right. See those panels on the walls? They absorb sound so even your voice doesn't reverberate like it does in everyday conversation. It gives the engineer more control over the tone and quality of the recording. Nothing you hear on the radio or on a CD sounds the way it did live. We apply all kinds of effects and enhancements. You'd be surprised what some famous singers would sound like singing in the shower."

"So it's all done with smoke and mirrors?"

"Pretty much," said Owen. "Just like anything in life."

Lily walked over to the corner and found a large crate filled with percussion instruments - maracas, a tambourine, a belt of sleigh bells, a triangle, a rain stick. They filled her with a sense of wonder. She wanted to reach in and pick them up, play with them the way she always had longed to play with the guitars, banjos, and ukuleles in Uncle Alfred's studio. Whenever she had dared, Uncle Alfred would inevitably happen along and mumble a few words that she could never quite discern but knew were intended to scold her. Then he would take out his can of Pledge furniture polish and a fresh dust cloth, and methodically set about scouring away the prints of Lily's bold curiosity, leaving her feeling unfulfilled and ashamed. Realizing that her self-control wasn't at its best these days, Lily thrust her hands into the back pockets of her jeans.

"Go ahead," said Owen, gesturing to the crate. "Dig in."

Delighted, Lily reached in and shook, knocked, and jiggled her way through the box until she found a pair of castanets, which she slipped onto her fingers, and performed a mock flamenco dance. She and Owen both laughed.

"Thanks for bringing me in here," said Lily. "What a great surprise."

"This is not your surprise, you silly goose," said Owen.

"It's not?"

"No - what kind of a surprise is that? You really need to learn to set higher expectations, Lily."

Owen rolled a mic stand by its base and placed it in front of Lily. He slipped a microphone into the sleeve at the top and positioned it directly in front of her mouth.

"What are you doing?" she asked.

"Patience, my sweet. Patience." Owen reached into a box under a table and pulled out a set of headphones. He plugged them into a small metal box with a knob on it, which sat on a stand. He placed the headphones on Lily, adjusting them so that each earpiece was properly positioned. Lily's stomach lurched with excitement with the recognition that she was standing in the vocal booth of a recording studio, wearing headphones - just the way she'd seen professional singers do on TV and in the movies.

Owen headed for the door.

"Where are you going?" she shouted, unable to detect the volume of her own voice.

Owen laughed and held his index finger up to his lips. "*Shhhh,*" he said. He pointed to the window and closed the door behind him. A few seconds later, he appeared in front of the mixing board on the other side of the glass and leaned in toward a microphone that was mounted on the table.

"Doing OK in there?" he asked.

Lily let out a yelp, startled to hear his voice come through the headphones.

She laughed. "Yes, yes - I'm fine."

"OK," said Owen. "Now just hold on one second."

He fiddled with a couple of the knobs and then sat in the chair. Music began to play through the headphones.

"Oh, my God!" Lily shouted, recognizing the introduction to the song she had sung at the Easter Vigil. "It's 'Lift Me Up' isn't it?"

Owen nodded and smiled. Lily closed her eyes and swayed back and forth to the music, holding onto the mic stand as though it were an anorexic dance partner. The music was just like they'd had at church - a simple accompaniment with Jeffrey on piano, but without any singing. The music stopped abruptly and Lily opened her eyes to see Owen lean toward his microphone. "Anytime," he said.

Did he want her to leave? "Oh! Sorry." She reached up to remove the headphones.

"You missed your cue," Owen said.

"My cue?"

"Yes, your cue - you know, that little introduction that tells you when it's time to start singing."

"You want me to sing?"

"You are a singer, aren't you?"

"Not really," said Lily. "I just -"

"You ARE a singer, aren't you?" said Owen, raising his brow.

Lily laughed. "Yes, OK - yes, I'm a singer."

"And you know this song, right?"

"Yes, I certainly do." It was burned in her memory. "This is the song that brought us together."

"And this is a recording studio, is it not?"

Lily replied playfully, "Why, yes - I believe it is."

"From the top, then."

The music began again, the beat of Lily's pulse racing ahead, out of time. She hoped that when she opened her mouth, something besides her heart would come out.

"When you looked for me..."

She sang timidly at first, taken aback by the way her voice fed in through the headphones, enabling her to hear every tremor, each breath sound, as though she were her own best friend, telling herself precious secrets.

"... tell me, what did you see?"

Owen reached over to adjust a knob. He gestured to Lily to keep going.

"Were you all surprised to find

That I'd left my old self behind?"

As Lily became accustomed to the way the music and her voice sounded through the headset, she began to relax, closing her eyes and letting her thoughts wander back to the Easter vigil and the power she had felt that night - was it just last month, or a hundred years ago? So much had happened since that night. So much seemed different now. She seemed different.

"Lift me up, I'm reaching out for you - ou..."

Lily recalled the way she had imagined Jesus saying those words to her, inviting her into His protective embrace, soothing her pain, easing her fears. The joy of that memory and the thrill of being in this moment, singing that beautiful song into a real microphone in an actual recording studio was tinged with the nagging idea that she tried to push into the wings of her mind but which kept re-emerging nonetheless: Jesus was faithfully in Heaven beckoning to her, and here she was, a cheat and a liar without even the decency to feel genuine remorse.

The song ended. Lily opened her eyes to find Owen sitting motionless in his chair, watching her. He leaned forward and spoke into the microphone.

"Don't move a muscle."

Owen got up and entered the recording booth, flinging the door open and striding directly toward Lily, taking her face between his hands and kissing her passionately, his hands gliding down her back and over her buttocks, around the curve of her hip and up under her blouse. Lily's desire erupted, banishing thoughts of Jesus and covering over the seeds of her guilt.

"You were made for this, Lily," he said, continuing to caress her breasts.

Lily's knees yielded willingly to Owen's invitation. They collapsed to the floor together, the headphones slipping from Lily's head and disappearing under a pile of clothing.

"That was the best surprise anyone has ever given me my whole life," said Lily, after they'd made love for the second time that morning. She stood at the studio entrance, fighting the tears that seemed to be her constant companion. Whether from happiness or sorrow, they always seemed to be lurking beneath the surface, ready to spring forth. "I will never forget this."

"It's not over," said Owen. "You are going to record that song. For real. I am going to make that happen."

"Owen, I-"

"Hush," said Owen, holding his index finger over her lips. "I am going to take care of everything. This is your time, Lily."

Lily drove home, savoring the flavors of passion and possibility as they lingered on her tongue, hoping it would be enough to sustain her for another day.

"Are you sure you know what you're doing?" Lily asked Donna.

Donna cracked an egg into a bowl containing a thick brown paste. Lily sat in a chair at Donna's kitchen sink, draped in a waterproof smock, with a tattered beach towel draped over her shoulders, its faded lettering hinting at some long forgotten family vacation.

"I'm sure," said Donna. "Don't you worry about it. This henna is a natural colorant and by putting this other stuff in there like eggs and honey, you are going to get a primo conditioning treatment, too."

"Or you could stick my head in the oven," quipped Lily. "Then all my problems would be solved and you would get a nice little cake."

"You bite your tongue!" said Donna, playfully slapping Lily's thigh with a dishtowel. "The real question of the day is, do you know what *you're* doing?"

"Absolutely not," Lily replied. She wondered if Donna was getting ready to finally confront her. She was a captive audience, sitting there with her head in Donna's kitchen sink.

"And by the way, if we stuck your head in the oven, it wouldn't solve my problems; I would miss you terribly." Donna drew the spray nozzle out of the panel of the sink and began to spray Lily's hair. "I love you."

Lily's throat burned and her tears mingled with the warm spray. "I love you, too, Donna. You're a good friend."

"Well now, I don't know about that." Donna replaced the spray nozzle and squeezed the excess water from Lily's hair. "Let's not forget that I am the one who insisted that you sign up for choir, and now look at the mess you've got yourself into."

Lily's face grew hot. Donna finally brought it out into the open. What should she say? What *could* she say?

"Yes," said Lily. "I guess I am in a bit of a mess." Tears came to her eyes. She was glad that she could not look Donna in the eye from where she sat. It would be much easier to take her lumps if she didn't have to actually face her.

"The Good Lord knows that I am a prisoner of my own brand of temptation, Lily. I know what it's like to feel powerless over carnal appetites - and as the Good Book says, 'How can you say to your brother, "Brother, let me take the speck out of your eye," when you yourself fail to see the plank in your own eye?' But then in Galatians, Paul tells us, 'Brothers, if anyone is caught in any transgression, you who are spiritual should restore him in a spirit of gentleness.' So I have been in constant angst over what to do to help you," said Donna. "Besides, I know what goes on over at your house, Lily; you don't even have to tell me half the time. I've got ears to hear and eyes to see. Our places are an arm's length apart and these walls are cheap. It breaks my heart what I know."

Donna pulled a pair of milky white latex gloves over her hands with a snap. She scooped up a handful of the paste and began working it into Lily's hair. "But sugar, I cannot in good conscience continue to look the other way with regards to Owen. Not when I know you are just storing up trouble for tomorrow."

If Lily's hands had not been trapped under the smock, she would have used them to try and shield her face, as though she might hide her shame from Donna. Yet at the same time, a wave of relief gushed forth; Lily was glad to finally have the issue out in the open. If she ever needed a friend, she needed one now.

"Joe would go ballistic if he found out," she said with a heavy sigh.

"Yes, he would, but that's not what I'm talkin' about. I care about your marriage, but I'm more concerned about your soul." Donna scooped more of the glop onto Lily's head.

"My soul," said Lily, "is dying anyway. But I can feel it come back to life when I'm with Owen, Donna. And this morning when he put those headphones on me and put me in that recording booth... and when the music started and it filled my head - filled my whole heart - it was like I was being replenished somehow." Lily slipped a hand out from under the smock and wiped the tears that had collected at the outside corners of her eyes. "How is that wrong? How can the survival of my soul not be a part of God's plan for my life, Donna? I can't understand a God who would place Owen in my path, tease me with passion and the opportunity to sing again - for what? To test me? To teach me? I've already passed all the tests I signed up for. And I'm sick of this lesson."

Donna scraped the last of the paste from the bowl, plopped it onto Lily's hair, which she then piled on top of her head and gently sat her upright. "I know you're hurtin'," she said. "But don't think for one second that it is God's will for you to have an illicit affair with another man. It's pretty clear in the Bible that He don't like that sort of thing - even wrote a whole commandment on it." Donna extracted a long measure of plastic wrap from the dispenser and began to wrap it around Lily's hair.

"I don't get it," said Lily. "And why are you wrapping my head in plastic wrap?"

"The plastic wrap keeps the heat in, which helps your hair

absorb the stain and the nutrients of all the yummy stuff I added in." Donna secured the plastic wrap in place and then added a layer of aluminum foil.

"Are we going to try and contact the Mother Ship?" Lily giggled.

"Hush now," said Donna. "You've been doing nuthin' but complaining about this since you sat down. We can't have you showing up for your recording session looking like an old lady with all that nasty gray hair, can we?"

"OK, well now I am thoroughly confused," said Lily, sitting down at the table and accepting a cup of coffee. "Out of one side of your mouth you're telling me that it's not God's will for me to be with Owen, and then out of the other side, you're dolling me up and sending me back there."

Donna placed a plate of peanut butter cookies on the table and sat down. "You are confused," said Donna. "Now I believe that God placed Owen in your life for a reason. But I also think that the two of you got the message all garbled up."

"But I have never been drawn to someone like that before," said Lily, taking a bite of a cookie. "I felt at home with him from the very beginning, and I wanted him with my whole being - more than I've ever wanted anything."

"And all this passion for a man you didn't even know," said Donna. "Don't you find that just a bit strange?"

"Love at first sight," said Lily.

"Sugar - I know that's what you believe, but I have to tell you that love does not go against itself. Love cannot sin, and when you say that love made you cross that line, I'm afraid you're gettin' into some mighty dangerous territory."

"How would you explain it, then?"

"I would say that the attraction you feel is for a part of yourself that you lost along the way. Owen promises to give that back to you, but he can't fix this for you, Lily. And you both are just makin' it worse." Donna reached across the table and took Lily's hand. "You fell in love with the man when you were supposed to fall in love with what he's pointing you toward. It's like driving

374

all the way to Arizona to sit and stare at a sign that says, 'Grand Canyon, 5 miles ahead'."

White hot heat radiated from Lily's chest, the same way it used to when William Nolan at Sacred Family grammar school made mocking cow sounds when she passed. She knew the sensation as shame, but then - as now - she had no response, could contrive no excuse for herself that would silence her accuser. She wished she could run away because she could not refute the accusation, nor was she willing to admit that such knowledge should induce her to stop. It was all Lily could to do pull her hand out from Donna's grasp in protest. What could she say? That she felt that her transgression was justified? That she didn't care if what she was doing was wrong? The only truthful response was that she knew it was wrong, and she cared, but she chose it anyway.

"It's the only happiness I have now." Lily said. "How can you ask me to give it up?"

"I didn't ask you to do anything, Lily," said Donna. "The Lord gave you free will and it is not my place to take that away from you. That's just your conscience speakin' to you. But that's not happiness, sweetie - not any more than dressing up in tights and a pink tutu on Halloween makes me a ballerina."

Lily laughed.

"Conjures up quite an image, don't it?"

"Don't make me laugh," said Lily. "This isn't funny."

"I know it's not, but do you get what I'm sayin'? You and Owen are not two lovers in love, even though that's what it looks like from the outside."

"Yeah, well, my life with Joe looks great from the outside, too."

"Only now, you've made Joe right; you've given him exactly what he wants - a reason to mistrust you."

"He didn't trust me anyway, so I figured, 'What the hell, I may as well.'"

"What do you think Joe will do when he finds out? He will find out, you know. They always do." Donna leaned in closer and looked directly into Lily's eyes. "And then," she said, "he can divorce you on the grounds of infidelity. Maybe even prove that you're an unfit mother. Take your kids away."

The look in Donna's eyes sent a chill down Lily's spine.

"He would never do that," said Lily tentatively.

"Are you sure?" said Donna. "Think about that and then ask yourself if your little rendezvous with Owen is still making you happy."

The two women sat sipping coffee from their mugs in silence. The burning in Lily's chest intensified as the realization sank in. She panicked as she thought about what Donna had said. Unfit mother. Take my kids away. Lily was seized with terror. What if Joe knew already? Or what if he had called when she was with Owen that morning? He could have driven by the studio and seen her car there. He could have peeked in the window and seen them passionately kissing good-bye. How could she have been so stupid? Seized by fear, she bolted over to the kitchen sink, and threw up.

"I'm so sorry, Donna," she said, turning on the faucet and rinsing regurgitated peanut butter cookies down the drain.

Donna appeared at her side, and gently rubbed her back in slow circular motions.

"If you didn't like the cookies, you didn't have to eat them. You know I would have happily taken your share."

Lily laughed weakly as a stream of tears ran down her cheeks.

Donna handed Lily a dampened paper towel.

"What have I done?" Lily asked her. "How can I fix this?"

"The first thing you need to do is break it off with Owen."

"I know," said Lily, blowing her nose on the towel. "I can't believe I have to give them both up."

"Both?"

"Owen, and my chance to sing again."

"Well now, who says you have to give up the singin'?"

"What am I supposed to do, tell Owen I can't see him anymore and then ask him to help me anyway?"

"His is not the only recording studio in town," said Donna. "If you ask me, his place is kinda dingy anyway. We'll find you a really nice place - something with class."

"But I don't know anything about how to do it - Owen was going to take care of coordinating everything."

"You are a master at setting up barriers for yourself, you know that?" said Donna. "Remember that you have help. You have God, and you have me. Between the three of us, I bet we can figure it out." She dampened another towel and dabbed at Lily's brow. "And if you ask me, givin' up Owen is the only way you can do that recording. No good song ever came out of a situation like that."

"I beg to differ," said Lily. "In fact, I think most of the best ones did. Anyway, what are we even talking about here, Donna? If I go to another studio, I'll have to tell Joe what I'm doing, and he will never let me record a demo. I can barely sing around the house without getting teased and criticized."

"You just never know," said Donna. "You're assuming that his heart is not capable of softening. I'd like to think that if you break it off with Owen, the Holy Spirit will honor you, be with you, and help you by opening up Joe's heart enough to let a little S-O-N shine in."

The long lost thrill of possibility that Donna's words aroused reminded Lily of the way she used to feel when Dolores was hatching one of her plans for stardom, a feeling that was soon soiled by disappointment and discouragement as Lily remembered Dolores' death and the end of her dreams. The room started to spin and Lily felt lightheaded as she tried to wrest the idea into the framework of her life.

"I don't see it," Lily said.

"That's why you have me," said Donna, returning to her place at the table. "I can see it clear as day." She took another cookie from the plate and dunked it in her coffee. "Let me ask you a question. I want you to think about it and reply as honestly as you can."

"Uh-oh," said Lily, joining her at the table. "I'm not sure I like the sound of that."

"Close your eyes for a second."

Lily complied.

"Now imagine… we've figured the whole thing out, and you've got this amazing recording of that amazing song – all with Joe's blessing. Can you see it?"

"You're going to have to give me a minute here. OK, I can barely see it, but you'd better hurry up because this is not going to last long."

"Now how do you feel about Owen?"

Lily pictured Owen's face and to her surprise, for the first time, it did not arouse her or make her nervous. Her eyes shot open. Donna raised her brow.

"You're confusing me," said Lily.

"Good," said Donna. "That means we're getting closer to the truth."

"Imagining it is all well and good, but in reality, I know Joe will not let it happen."

"You don't know that," said Donna. "All things are possible for those who love Christ."

The idea of even bringing the demo up with Joe gave Lily a stomachache. But maybe Donna was right; maybe Lily was reacting based on Joe's past behavior. Admittedly the evidence to mistrust him was compelling. Maybe it was Lily's recent recognition of her own capacity to act immorally, but she somehow now considered the distance between herself and Joe to be shorter, if only by a hair. She could see now as never before how one decision might lead to another and while none of them are significant enough to take you off course on their own, together they may get you lost. Joe certainly had spent the last several years lost; it wouldn't do anyone any good if Lily got lost too.

Life sure would be simpler if Joe would just come around, if he could be supportive. It was almost too much to hope for… the two of them working together, sharing dreams, being friends. If Donna was right, if the Holy Spirit would bless her if she ended the affair, and helped her put her marriage back together, she could be free both of the fear she felt when she was with Joe and the guilt she felt when she was with Owen. She could be free of the shame she felt whenever she looked at her sons. And then, maybe she could finally start to live her life the way she'd always dreamed of.

She knew what she had to do. She would miss Owen's touch, his adoration. Could she give that up? Wasn't that the whole point of being a Christian in the first place – to make sacrifices out of love... to do what's right even when it hurts? One thing was certain; she could never tell Joe about the affair. She would have to learn to live - and die - with the secret.

The next morning, Lily and Donna sat in the parking lot of Star Recording Studio.

"Ready?" Donna asked.

"No," said Lily. "But I doubt I ever will be." She wished there was a way to fast-forward her life and jump right to the part after telling Owen she couldn't see him anymore. "Give me fifteen minutes."

"I'll give you five."

"Five? That's not enough time, Donna."

"You are not going in there to have a discussion, Lily. This is you telling him it's over, and once that's been said, well, there just isn't anything left to say 'cept good-bye now, is there?"

"I guess you're right."

"I know I am," said Donna. "We don't want to leave enough time for him to cloud your thinking and change your mind. Remember what we talked about – no physical contact."

"Not even a good-bye kiss?"

"Not a good idea," said Donna. "What would be the point 'cept to rile both of you up unnecessarily?"

Lily placed her hand on the door handle.

"Repeat after me," said Donna. "'I can do all things through Christ which strengthens me.'"

"I can do all things through Christ which strengthens me," repeated Lily.

"You don't sound convinced."

"I'm not."

"Try not to think about it; just do it."

Lily took a deep breath, opened the car door, and went inside.

"There she is!" called Owen from his office. "My little star... I've been counting the minutes!" He strode out to greet Lily.

Lily held her hand up, palm facing him. "Stop right there, please," she said.

"What's going on?" Owen continued to approach her.

Lily looked into his eyes and backed up, continuing to hold her hand out, but with her elbow now bent, a weakened attempt at keeping him away.

"Please," she said. "I have something to say and I need you to stay right there while I say it."

"You're scaring me, Lily." Owen took another step toward her.

Lily took another step back. She swallowed hard, hoping to clear space for the words that were forming a burning lump in her throat.

"Just let me do this," said Lily.

"Oh, Lily – no... please don't." Owen's eye glistened with tears.

"I have to," said Lily. "I'm sorry, but I have to."

"Why?"

"A hundred reasons, Owen," Lily replied. "Because I'm married, because you're married, because it's a sin... because I can't live with the guilt."

Owen removed his glasses and wiped at his eyes with his fingers. "I thought we'd have more time."

"Me too," said Lily. "But it's not going to get any easier later on."

They stood separated by the pain and confusion between them.

"Shit!" Owen put his glasses back on and looked at Lily. "Boy, am I going to miss you," he said, with a crack in his voice.

Lily looked over her shoulder out the front window. If Donna had not been waiting there, watching, she would have run into Owen's arms, told him it was a joke, or a mistake, begged him to make love to her.

"I know," said Lily. "Me too."

"What about the recording?" asked Owen. "We can still do that. Can't we?"

Lily couldn't bring herself to tell him that she would be taking that dream with her when she left, and sharing it with Donna, and maybe with Joe.

"I don't know," she said. "But I was hoping you would send someone else to record at church on Sundays from now on. It would be better if we don't run into each other."

"If that's what you want," said Owen.

"None of this is what I want," said Lily. Tears ran down her face and dripped in through the corners of her mouth. They tasted sweeter than usual.

"Then don't do this," said Owen. "Let's just find a way to be together – for real." He took a step toward Lily and held his arms open.

"Don't!" she cried. "I can't."

Donna tooted the car horn.

"Thank you for everything, Owen. Good-bye" she said, turning and walking out the door. *I love you.*

Lily ran out to the car, and jumped into the front seat. "You'd better get me out of here before I change my mind." she said to Donna.

"I'm so proud of you, darlin'."

"Go!" Lily shouted through sobs.

That night after a dinner of Chicken *à la* King, Lily stood at the kitchen sink and steeled herself for the next stage of the plan.

"Joe, I want to talk to you about something."

"So talk," he said, scooping up the last pea on his plate with a biscuit.

"I've decided that I'd like to record a vocal demo." She reminded herself that Donna was "on call" next door, praying for God to guide her through this conversation, and would be waiting with tea and sympathy in the morning if Joe's heart remained hard.

"What's a vocal demo?" Joe placed his dirty dishes into the soapy water.

"It's a sample of my singing. So people can hear what I sound like." Lily scrubbed the white sauce from Joe's plate.

"Why?"

"Just in case I ever get the chance to audition for a play or something. Plus, you know, it would just be fun."

"So now you want to be a singer?" A grunt escaped from Joe's throat.

"I've always wanted to sing, Joe - you know that. And I can be a singer *and* a mother and a wife. People do it all the time."

"Where would you sing? You don't belong singing in a bar - you're a married woman."

Don't get sidetracked by the wrong argument, Lily told herself. *Give it to him in little bites.*

"I don't have anything particular in mind." Lily hoped her voice sounded appropriately casual; if he thought it was too important to her, he would resist. "Mostly, it's just something fun that I've always wanted to do. It won't take me away from you or the kids. And it won't cost that much." Lily had no idea how much it would cost. She would deflect that argument for another time.

"You have this beautiful home, you have me, the boys, your job of running the house. Aren't you ever satisfied? None of my brothers' wives ever get involved in that goofy shit."

"I'm not using them as a comparison. From what I've seen, they are not exactly happy."

"Oh, so now you're not happy?"

"I didn't say that, Joe. When did I say that?"

He didn't seem to hear the question. A shadow passed over his face. "Well, boo-hoo.... little Miss Lily isn't happy. Do you think *I'm* happy? Do you think I like working eighty hours a week and having nothing to show for it except bills, so you can have a nice house to live in? I hate that goddamn store, but I go in every day - and do you know why I do that?"

Joe was screaming at the top of his lungs, and had his finger pointed in Lily's face. She did not anticipate that he would react so vehemently. She struggled to get her bearings and gain control over the situation, but all she could think about was that if this is how he reacted to this, what would he do if he ever found out about Owen? Trembling, Lily kept one eye on Joe's hand and one on Pierce who had appeared around the corner and was hanging on their every word.

"Joe, please, calm down." She glanced at Pierce, hoping his presence would inspire Joe to reel in his rage.

"Don't tell me to calm down! Answer the fucking question: Do you know why I go to a job I hate, working for people I can't stand? Do you?"

"If you're not happy, maybe you can do something about that, you know? Maybe you can make some changes, find something you'd like to do, too. You have choices."

"I don't have any goddamn choices!" Joe pitched his dinner glass into the sink, splashing Lily with dirty water and suds. "I work because I have to take care of this family! And now you have the balls to tell me you're not fucking *happy*?!"

Pierce ran forward, and fearlessly positioned himself in an attempt to break up his screaming parents, his contorted face wedged in the space between the belly that had grown him and the one that bubbled and boiled with rage.

"Okay, okay! We'll get divorced!" screamed Pierce.

Lily and Joe both stopped shouting, mid-sentence. Lily raised her hands to cover her mouth, hoping to capture her cry of shame as it escaped.

"See?" said Joe, pointing down at Pierce. "Do you see what you've done? I hope you're happy now."

Lily stooped to pick Pierce up, as he reached his arms toward her.

"Oh no, you don't," shouted Joe, slapping her hands away. "You don't get to come in and rescue him, now that you've completely devastated him." Joe took Pierce into his arms.

"I want Mommy!" Pierce protested, his arms still outstretched toward Lily.

"Daddy's got you, Pierce," said Joe. "Mommy doesn't want to hold you. She'd rather go sing."

"Joe! Don't say that to him!" Lily cried. "Pierce, it's OK, baby.

Mommy loves you. Daddy and I are just having an argument, that's all."

But by then, Joe was carrying him away. Pierce was wailing, fat tears tumbling down his cheeks, forming a darkened splotch on his father's white cotton Oxford.

The following morning, Lily sat at the kitchen table sipping coffee and trying to read the paper, her eyelids swollen and tender from a sleepless night of crying and angst. Joseph and Pierce watched *Tom and Jerry* cartoons in the family room while she replayed the conversation with Joe in her mind, wondering what she could have done or said differently, trying to discern at which point she had ignited his anger. She must have been crazy to think he would agree. Now she had nothing. She choked back enraged tears, hoping to control herself until Joe left for work, trying to hang on until she could run over to Donna's – or until she got in the car and ran back into Owen's arms.

Joe's footfall beat down the stairs and approached the kitchen. He walked over to Lily and placed a business card on the table in front of her. It read "Black Rose Studio - A full service commercial and entertainment recording studio."

She looked up at him. "What's this?"

"That guy bought some office furniture from me a couple months ago. Maybe he can help you with your demo."

Lily looked at the card, and then looked up at Joe. "Really?" she said. "Thanks."

"That's it? 'Thanks'?"

"I guess I'm just so shocked. You were so angry last night. I don't really know what to say."

"I didn't mean what I said last night," he said. "You just made me so crazy. But I thought you would at least be a little happier that I'm letting you do it."

Every victory came at such a high price; Lily was exhausted from the battle. She forced herself up from her chair and walked over to Joe.

"I'm sorry," she said. "I am happy. Thank you." She kissed him on the cheek.

"That's all I get?"

Lily kissed him again, and he placed one hand on her buttocks as he slipped the other one up the front her pajama top and squeezed her breast. Still hurt, angry, and exhausted from the marathon argument, sex with Joe was not on her to-do list for the morning. But as he took her hand and led her up to the bedroom, she realized that if she wanted even a chance to fulfill her dream without any more fighting, she really didn't have a choice.

.

Dear Lily,

I don't know whether these last couple of chapters make me more sad, or angry. Of course, I've never been good at anger - I do frustration much better. I can still feel my throat constricting and my heart racing when I recall that sense of utter helplessness I lived with back then, trapped in a situation I didn't believe I had the power to change. How I longed for someone else to change it for me. Anyone, as long as it didn't have to be me. My fairy godmother, perhaps. Or God Himself. Or if they couldn't be bothered, maybe Claudio or Max would do.

Seeing the story from here, I am at a loss to figure out what was going on with us. Why were we so convinced we had to stick it out? Wouldn't it have been better for everyone if we had admitted that we had simply made a mistake getting married when we did, to the men we did? Maybe we had already invested too much love and time and work in our marriages. But it seems to me there should be a point at which you are allowed to reassess the investment and be free to cut your losses. Heck, even Mom gave up on Dad after 30 years and 12 kids.

In some ways I wished I had a husband a little more like Joe. Someone who would openly rant at me and threaten me. Someone who would provide a reason for the fear that gripped my heart, instead of someone who suffocated me with good intentions. Someone who would make me want to run away as fast as my legs could carry me, instead of paralyzing me with the spell of good sense and the call to duty.

Back in those days I used to have a recurring dream. I would be standing beneath a tall tree whose top branches were laden with fruit. I could see it dangling up there, well beyond my reach, so ripe and swelling with those "flavors of passion and possibility" you wrote about. I would keep looking around for someone to come by with a ladder. It never occurred to me that I could climb the tree myself and pluck the fruit I wanted. I would just stand there looking up at it, filled with longing as I watched the crows pick away at it, overwhelmed with a sense of loss as I watched it rot and wither.

The dream is easy to figure out. What I still can't figure out is why I was so afraid.

By the way, happy Thanksgiving, Lily.

Love,
Iris

From: Lily Caoptotsi <lilycapotosti@gmail.com>
To: Iris Capotosti <iris.capotosti@gmail.com>
Sent: Wed, November 24, 2010 11:41 PM
Subject: Re: Be careful what you wish for

Dear Iris:

When you are drowning and someone tosses you a lifesaver, is it a mistake to grab hold of it? I don't think I even considered who was on the other end of the tow rope. If we could have seen that, and if we could have known all of this already, and if we could have had a glimpse into what is yet to unfold in this little torture exercise of ours, what would we have done? Waved the lifeboat away, or climbed aboard anyway? I know too well that each choice has its own consequences.

I'm sorry you didn't get the kind of oppression you wanted. At least that's one thing I did better than you. Oddly enough, I also used to wish that Joe had been a little more obvious about it too, even with all that I endured. Where the hell was our threshold for pain? Seems like mine kept rising and rising and rising. No matter what happened, I kept thinking that if it got worse, well, then...

Yet no matter how bad it got, I kept adapting. It was the Capotosti way.

Love,
Lily

More from authors Angela and Julie Scipioni

The story continues…

What lies ahead for Iris and Lily as they struggle to make sense of the world in which they live? What difficulties are yet to be overcome? Do they have what it takes to survive?

For the complete story of *Iris & Lily*, read Book One and Book Three

Iris & Lily is also available ebook form.

Visit IrisandLilytheNovel.com

Made in the USA
San Bernardino, CA
30 August 2016